AT LAST

LISA RILEY

Genesis Press, Inc.

Indigo Love Stories

An imprint of Genesis Press, Inc.
Publishing Company

Genesis Press, Inc.
P.O. Box 101
Columbus, MS 39703

All rights reserved. Except for use in any review, the repro-
duction or utilization of this work in whole or in part in any
form by any electronic, mechanical, or other means, not
known or hereafter invented, including xerography, photo-
copying and recording, or in any information storage or
retrieval system, is forbidden without written permission of
the publisher, Genesis Press, Inc. For information write
Genesis Press, Inc., P.O. Box 101, Columbus, MS 39703.

All characters in this book have no existence outside the imagination of the author and have no relation whatsoever to
anyone bearing the same name or names. They are not even
distantly inspired by any individual known or unknown to the
author and all incidents are pure invention.

Copyright© 2003, 2008 by Lisa Riley. All rights reserved.

ISBN-13: 978-1-58571-276-2
ISBN-10: 1-58571-276-0

Manufactured in the United States of America

First Edition 2003
Second Edition 2008

Visit us at www.genesis-press.com or call at 1-888-Indigo-1

DEDICATION

Praise and thanks go to my mother, Ms. Gloria B. Riley, whom I will miss forever and love always. Thank you for everything, including your love, encouragement, support and patience. This book—and every one after—is for you.

I would also like to thank my sisters, Gloria, Kesha, Pam, Val, Tricia and Karen for being there and listening. Special thanks to Karen, Kesha and Gloria for edits, opinions, laughter and all the other things you did to keep me going. Thank you Grandma (Ms. Helen Mitchell) and Aunt Dean for worrying and encouraging.

To my friends, Anjuelle, Letena, Olivia, Tasha and Ms. Viola Anderson—thanks for being my sounding board and for your unwavering support.

Uncle Herbert, Aunt Marva, Uncle Rudy, and Jason, I love you guys.

PROLOGUE

Alexander Brickman looked at the Chicago skyline through his rain-drenched window. The city had really grown on him and he was glad of it. He'd had doubts about it when he'd first made that mad dash from Boston. Well, he'd had nothing to worry about and even if he had, he would have ignored it. He was a businessman and his kind of business—business that reduced people to their lowest forms—could be conducted anywhere. And it flourished everywhere.

"Everything is in place for the next implementation," he said to one of his underlings without turning around.

It wasn't a question, but Tom Mackenzie knew he'd better have an answer in the affirmative. And even though he did, he still swallowed nervously before answering. "Yes sir. The woman I've picked for the fifth venue of our downtown operation is from my old neighborhood and she'll do just fine. I'm ready to go when you give the word."

"Word," Brickman said softly and succinctly.

That was all that was needed and Tom walked from the room.

Ida Martinez waited anxiously for her visitor's arrival. She knew that selling drugs—especially in an office building—would be dangerous, but she so desperately needed the extra money. She paced the floor of her apartment with a worried frown.

When Tom Mackenzie had shown up at her door the week before, she'd just finished trying to stretch her checking account to pay off her bills. She hadn't been able to and had had to call her parents for a loan. They'd turned her down, so she was desperate and ripe for his proposition.

Her parents had refused to lend her the money because they, like the rest of her family, thought she had a gambling problem. Her sister Rose was the worst, going so far as to tell her that she had an addictive and an obsessive personality that could be traced back to their childhood when they'd been homeless for several months. Ida had been 12 when their dad had lost his job. Because the family had had no savings, they'd lost their rental home almost immediately and the children had watched as their things were put on the street. Rose had told her that because of that episode, she thought that Ida had a strong need to hold onto things and people that she saw as security.

She also told her that she thought the gambling was Ida's reckless way of trying to gain security. She'd begged her to contact "Gamblers Anonymous." Ida didn't agree and she hadn't called. She didn't believe she needed to, because she didn't believe she had a problem. It was her money and her business how she spent it. For her, gambling on one of the many riverboat casinos that dotted the Illinois and Indiana region was simply a form of entertainment.

So what if she often lost a whole month's salary at the tables. It was hers to lose. And besides, she often won that much—and more—as well. Ida listened to her furious thoughts and sighed as she sat down on the nearest piece of furniture. Maybe she did have a slight gambling problem, but all she needed was one big win and she'd never go back again.

She let out another sigh. Her financial troubles were just the tip of the iceberg. Never mind that she could barely pay rent each month or that she was living in an apartment that was little more than a hole in the wall. Her biggest problem was her romantic life. The love of her life was suddenly back in her life and she couldn't have been more thrilled. The problem was with him. He refused to admit that they were meant for each other. She knew that she'd blown it with Brian two years before. But she'd been unable to convince him of her regret and love and she hadn't seen him since.

After he'd first broken up with her, she'd tried everything to make him admit his love, but nothing had worked and she'd decided to give him time. Now she realized that she shouldn't have. Brian Keenan was her soul mate and she was madly in love with him. She'd known he felt the same about her, but like most men, was afraid of the concept and not ready to accept it. So she'd bided her time—knowing in her heart that since they were meant to be together that it would eventually happen.

Now fate was finally on her side. Her boss had left his job at the company and had started his own firm. He'd asked her to join him and she'd accepted. That Brian was a partner in the new integrated marketing firm and was not in a relationship were clear signs that they were meant to finally get on with their life together. He was still unwilling to admit anything, but that would change. It would have to because she couldn't feel so strongly for him if he didn't feel the same for her. Love was reciprocal.

—⁂—

Ida smiled as she rose to answer Mac's knock on the door. Her financial troubles would soon be over, and she and Brian would be together. Finally. She'd see to it.

BOOK ONE

CHAPTER I

Caroline Singleton slammed her car door, hurried across the parking garage and through the downtown Chicago early afternoon pedestrian traffic. Struggling to hold onto her large black portfolio as she juggled her purse, she sighed and tapped her foot as she waited impatiently for the light to turn green. If she were late for her job interview, she'd scream. She couldn't believe that she was cutting it so close, but as usual, it was all her fault. She'd had an idea for a painting when she'd awakened that morning, and she hadn't been able to tear herself away from her easel until it was almost too late.

As it was, she'd barely had enough time to jump in the shower, change her clothes and push, prod, and force her thick hair into the heavy bun currently resting at the back of her neck. Surprising for May in Chicago, it was incredibly hot. With her lightweight white suit sticking to her, she didn't feel like she'd only gotten out of the shower less than an hour ago. The little miniskirt of the suit showcased long, shapely brown legs resting atop slender ankles. Her 5'9" slender frame garnered looks to begin with, but to put that same frame atop three-inch heels and in a white suit that contrasted beautifully with her chocolate brown skin was akin to stopping traffic.

Caroline didn't notice the looks people gave her; she didn't care about them. She'd been told she was beautiful, but she knew that looks weren't important. As her mother had fondly told her practically every day of her life: at the end of the day, if you didn't have brains to go with them, the most good looks could get you was a free cup of coffee, and possibly a stale doughnut. Having brains and using them was what guaranteed one success in life.

Her wide, smooth brow creased into a frown as her snapping brown eyes peeked at her watch. Eleven lousy minutes; the light was taking far too long. When the light finally changed, her long strides ate up the distance of the street and she rushed through the lobby of the 48-story building where her interview was being held. While she waited for the elevator that would take her to the 18th floor, she tried to get into the right mindset for the meeting by consciously relaxing her face, closing her eyes to better clear her mind of annoyance, and smiling. Her eyes popped open as the bell signaling the car's arrival gave a discreet bing.

Smiling again, she moved to enter the car and was unceremoniously pushed back, causing her to lose her precarious hold on her portfolio and her purse.

"Excuse me," a deep voice rumbled while Caroline bent to pick up her things. "Allow me," the man said as he took her elbow to bring her to a standing position.

Caroline stood frowning impatiently and wondering why Murphy's Law seemed to be following her around that day. She looked down at the man's lavishly black hair as he bent to pick up her portfolio. "Oh damn, damn and double damn!" she said when she heard the elevator leave without her. Worrying her bottom lip with her teeth, she didn't look at the man as he stood. Absently thanking him when he handed her the case, she didn't take her eyes off the panel of numbers above the elevator. When the number 15 was highlighted, she turned away.

"How long do these things—" Shock made Caroline forget what she was going to ask. *Just breathe Caroline,* she silently told herself as she felt herself grow short of breath. The man standing in front of her was someone who invoked such strong feelings in her that they scared her. In self-defense, she took a step back. As she felt immediate awareness, *instant knowing,* course through her veins, Caroline stood there feeling like she'd felt when she was ten and had had the breath knocked out of her when she'd fallen out of the swing onto her back. The only message her stunned brain could communicate was "Run!" Pressing her fist to her chest as if she could still her galloping heart, she stared at the man in front of her from a face suddenly leached of its color.

Brian Keenan looked at the beautiful woman in amazement. He felt an almost irresistible need to take her in his arms and kiss her until the grinding ache in his stomach subsided. He wanted to take her home with him, he wanted to feel her slender body against his, he wanted…he wanted. God, he wanted. The message his brain communicated to him was, "I'm in trouble," and close on the heels of that, "MINE."

Taking her slender hand in his, he gently pulled her out of the flow of traffic. She docilely followed, never taking her eyes off his face. "What are you doing?" she asked dazedly and felt something shift inside of her while her eyes busily roamed his features. It wasn't a handsome face in the traditional sense. With the sculpted cheekbones, hard line of a mouth, cleft chin, dark gray eyes and slashing black eyebrows all against a tanned background, his face could only be described as rugged. Just as the more than 72 inches of frame showcased in a navy suit could only be described as rangy.

Brian studied her features as well, taking in the high cheekbones, the ridiculously long lashes, stubborn chin and full, luscious mouth. He bent his head, fully intent on having a taste of that tempting mouth.

Caroline read his intentions clearly and thought about meeting him half way. Common sense prevailed, however, and dropping her things again, she hastily raised her free hand and pushed it into his chest. "Wait," she said in a breathy whisper full of anticipation, regret and fear, "This is insane. Who are you? I don't even know you. I…I mean, for all I know you could be some sort of maniac! And here we are in a crowded lobby and you're trying to kiss me! And I haven't mentioned the fact that you're white!"

Brian looked down at her intently, staring into her candy-brown eyes. Releasing her hand, he smoothed her lined brow and made himself take a few steps away from her. "I'm Brian Keenan, and although I'm not a maniac, this is so crazy, I think I might be losing my mind. Though I do admit to being white, I don't think that's a crime in this state. And whereas up until two minutes ago I thought I was perfectly sane, I wouldn't blame anyone for questioning that fact now. And having said all that, I still feel it necessary to say that names hardly seem to matter, since I know you, and feel like I always have. I think you feel the same way about me."

"Really," Caroline said rigidly while she fought the urge to forget her inhibitions and take him up on his unspoken offer. She took a few cautious steps back. "Aah…I…uh…I'm confused. I can't say I'm a veteran of this sort of—thing," she said for lack of a better word, "and it feels weird, but normal in an odd sort of way." She took a deep breath. "I-I have to go, or I'll be late for my interview, and I really want this job."

"Interested in giving a white guy your phone number?"

Caroline hesitated. She'd never dated a white man before. How would that work? Deciding to find her courage, at least in this, Caroline rattled off her number in a nervous, unsure voice. "Call me tonight," she said as he handed her the portfolio and looped her purse over her arm.

Brian watched her walk away and laughed out loud as he realized she hadn't told him her name.

—⁓—

Caroline checked her face in the glass panel of the elevator, and was assured that nothing was out of place. In an effort to calm the rioting butterflies in her stomach that had nothing to do with her upcoming interview, she took several deep breaths and then pressed her hand there. God, what was she thinking? Was she crazy? All the man did was look at her and she felt disoriented, lost and breathless. She couldn't ignore the fact of his skin color and that it concerned her. But what bothered her more was her reaction to him. How could a perfect stranger make her lose all sense of reason and propriety?

Brian Keenan; the name sounded familiar. She'd heard it before, she just wasn't sure where. Was he a fellow artist? Had her brother Lee mentioned him? Had her friend Tracy? She was sure she knew the name. She let her mind worry with it a little longer, and then decided it would come to her when she didn't have so much on her mind.

It was her second interview with the new inte-grated marketing firm whose primary focus was the urban market, and she wanted to make a good impression. Two black men, a Hispanic woman and a white man owned the company. She reminded herself to thank Tracy again for telling her about the company's need for an art director.

She'd wanted to share her talents with a minority-owned company since she'd gotten out of grad school.

She didn't know how she was going to concentrate during the interview when something so frightening had just occurred. Could she actually get involved with someone who had the ability to take her breath away and almost make her forget herself in public? Still taking deep breaths, she decided that she'd wait to hear from him and take it—or not take it—from there. As the elevator doors opened, she smiled and walked over to greet the receptionist.

—∿—

Brian walked over to Potbelly Sandwich Works to pick up a sandwich for lunch. As the noisy crowd jockeyed for position around him, he mentally replayed his earlier encounter. Nothing like that had ever happened to him before, and it scared the hell out of him. However, he knew he would regret it—possibly for the rest of his life—if he didn't follow up with her and see where this odd ride would take them.

He looked at his watch, then lifted his gray eyes to impatiently stare at the line in front him. He had just enough time to grab his sandwich, eat it and hurry back to the office. His partners were interviewing a good prospect for the second time, and they'd asked him to poke his head in for five minutes to meet him. He didn't know why they needed him to do it, but he didn't mind. Just so long as they never asked him to interview anyone, he was fine. After all, he was the chief technology officer, and that was where his expertise lay. He knew absolutely nothing about interviewing people about other professions.

He sighed and let his eyes wander. He frowned again as he noticed Ida Martinez paying for her sandwich. He hoped he'd set her straight about the two of them. He'd had to have a long talk with her regarding her belief that they were going to get back together. He'd made it plain that he was not interested in picking up where they'd left off two years before. While she appeared to accept his decision, he didn't trust her and couldn't help but think she was up to something.

Ida approached Brian on her way out of the restaurant. She simply smiled in greeting and kept going. She knew he expected her to say something about their relationship or to flirt outrageously, so she did neither. She almost laughed out loud when he smiled cautiously back at her. *That's right lover,* she thought. *You can trust me.*

—⁂—

Maria Gonzales, a founder of the company and the President of Direct Marketing, smiled as she shook Caroline's hand. "I'm so glad to welcome you aboard Caroline," she said with a big smile. "This company needs more female blood; it was becoming too much of a boy's club," she said teasingly with a look at two of her co-founders.

"Well anything I can do to even things out…" Caroline said, and began to gather her things.

"Don't leave yet Caroline," Justin Hartley, a short, dark-skinned man with curly hair said. "We want you to meet our Chief Technology Officer, and fourth founder. He should be here any minute now."

Caroline smiled and said, "I'd be happy to. I was wondering if I'd ever get the opportunity to meet the technology wunderkind who single-handedly put this office together in less than three months. What is his name—" Caroline cut herself off as she suddenly remembered where she'd heard the name Brian Keenan before. Technically, he was her new boss.

"Are you okay, Caroline?" Maria asked in concern as she stared at her frozen face. Caroline was saved from answering by a brief knock on the door.

"There you are. It's about time you got here." Justin said teasingly.

"Brian, from the smile on your face, I can tell you've been to Potbelly's," Carl, the other founder, said. "Come meet Caroline Singleton, our new Art Director."

Caroline froze at the mention of Brian's name like a deer suddenly caught in headlights. She slowly turned her head towards the door, fearful and suspicious of who she was going to see. She never, ever dated coworkers, and, not that the occasion had ever arisen before, but dating your boss was strictly taboo.

She felt her heart drop to her feet when her head finally finished it's slow half-turn, and she saw those oh-so, familiar, gray eyes of Brian Keenan.

—◦—

"I can't believe you work at the company where I just accepted a job. And to make matters worse, you're a founder!" Caroline said in dismay. She hadn't forgotten about her earlier reservations and her impulse to just walk away was getting stronger. "This is completely unacceptable."

The rest of the meeting had gone well, but Brian had sensed that she was completely nonplussed by his presence. Talk about your rotten luck. He hadn't been able to believe it when he'd walked into the conference room and had seen her standing there. His first thought was that he must be the unluckiest bastard on the face of the earth.

There was an agreed-upon rule amongst the founders of the company that they weren't to fraternize with the employees. And even if there hadn't been the rule something had told him that Caroline would never date him as long as they worked together. To extricate them out of the sticky situation, he'd made some lame joke about thinking that she'd be a guy, and had offered to walk her out. She'd agreed, but just barely, and walked with him to the elevators. As they'd gone through the lobby, and outside the building, he had sensed that she was just barely holding on.

Never in his life had he been so affected by a woman—especially in so short a time. Normally a person who analyzed things until they switched position and were the total antithesis of what they'd originally been, Brian shied away from analyzing his current situation. He didn't want to overanalyze and talk himself out of going forward with her. The strange thing was, if asked why, he wouldn't be able to give anyone a coherent answer. He just knew he had to pursue the relationship.

He studied Caroline's tense frame as she paced back and forth in front of him. He'd brought her to the gangway side of the building where there was very little foot traffic. She'd unbuttoned her jacket and had her hands on her hips. The little pale, pink shell of a top left nothing to his imagination and the lace of the camisole he saw through the shell was driving him crazy. As he watched it fit itself to the contours of her small breasts as she moved in agitation, he cleared his throat, and said, "Caroline, have mercy on a poor, helpless Neanderthal like me, will you? You're driving me crazy."

Caroline stopped her pacing and looked at him in confusion. "What are you—" When she noticed the direction of his gaze, she looked down. Sighing and rolling her eyes, she dropped her hands from her hips to her sides so that the jacket fell into place.

"Men," she said in mock disgust, and began to walk slowly towards him with a teasing smile on her face. "I don't want to have to button this jacket

Brian," she said sternly, "but I warn you, I will. And suffocate martyr-like in this heat, if it'll get your mind on more important matters." Since this was the last time she planned to be alone with him, she threw caution to the wind and flirted outrageously.

"If you knew what I was thinking, there's no way you would have said that," he said when she was standing directly in front of him. Grabbing both sides of her jacket, he pulled her closer.

"Yeah?" She stared at his mouth and ignored the cautious part of her brain.

"Oh, yeah," he said and pulled her even closer. He bent his head to capture her mouth, but before he could, she once again stopped him with a hand to his chest.

"I mean it Brian, this is serious. Something like this just can't work."

"We'll figure something out," he said, reading the apprehension in her eyes.

She tensed. "What?! What can we possibly do?! I'm not going to give up this job, and you can't Possibly leave—you're a founder. Don't ask me to do this secretly, because I just can't. And we can't do it openly either. I won't have people thinking that I got the job because I'm sleeping with you, or that I'm keeping the job for that same reason."

Rubbing her back soothingly, he said, "We will think of something. I'm not willing to give up on this just because we work together." He whispered the last sentence as he bent his head to finally get a taste of her.

She jerked as far back in his arms as she could. "Don't Brian. Don't kiss me now," she said, her frustration and confusion making her voice soft and whispery. "It's best if we don't get anything started, if we're not going to be able to finish it." She bent her head away from him.

"Come on Caroline, we're not going to deny ourselves just because of some stupid little complication," he whispered as he pulled her completely in his arms to comfort her. She kept her head bent, but gave in and relaxed slightly. Leaning back so he could look into her eyes, he said, "Besides, we will hardly ever work together, unless there is something wrong with your computer, and even then, Larissa will probably handle it. We'll figure something out, even if I have to sell my interest in the company, fire myself or kill my partners! We'll figure it out. Now what do you say, Beautiful? Come on. Give us a kiss," he said in a cajoling voice.

Caroline lifted her head. How strange that it would feel so natural to be in his arms! He looked reckless and irresistible. Almost irresistible. She laughed on a breath and shook her head. "Oh no. I'm sorry but no kisses. I sense that we'd do it really well and that would only lead to trouble and a desire for more of the same. And quite frankly, I find that I'm not quite prepared to—"

"Not prepared or not willing?" Brian asked with a light squeeze of her arms. "I can tell you want to and I know I really want to. We're both adults and we won't be hurting anyone—or will we?" Brian's voice became less persuasive as he jerked his head up to look at her. "You're not involved with anyone are you?"

Caroline was indignant. "Of course not. If I were, I wouldn't be here with you now. Are you involved with anyone special?" She released a breath when he shook his head in the negative. "Well, that makes things less complicated, if not quite easier. Well, it doesn't matter anyway."

"If you say so," Brian said wryly with a crooked smile. He pulled her closer. "Just one kiss." He whispered softly behind her ear so that his breath stirred the delicate hair lying on the curve there. "One. Small. Kiss." He felt her involuntary shiver and closed his eyes. God, he wanted to put his hands on her.

Feeling that they were both too close to the edge, Caroline jerked her head back and away from him. "We can't do this Brian," she said breathlessly, "I don't even know your favorite color, your favorite movie, book or anything else. This is crazy!"

Brian tried to gather his senses and listen to what she was saying. Quite simply, she completely staggered him and he was caught up in his own attempted seduction. "Shh, shh," he said soothingly. "My God, this is scary," he said in a low voice to himself.

She lifted her head. "I didn't hear you."

He cleared his throat. He hadn't realized he'd spoken out loud. "I said it's going to be okay. We'll fix this. Do you believe me?" he asked.

She still didn't look at him. "I'd better go, and you'd better get back to work," she said as she stepped out of his arms. She picked up her things and jolted a bit as she thought she recognized one of the people from Inclusion walk pass the gangway. She hoped the woman hadn't seen anything.

Brian studied her as she rushed out of the gangway. When she got a few feet away from him, he called, "Caroline, the answers are not one in particular, *North by Northwest*, and *The Grapes of Wrath*." He watched her hurry across the street.

CHAPTER 2

It had been three weeks since Caroline had first met Brian, and though she knew they were in a no-win situation, she still thought of him constantly. She refused to see him outside of work, but he'd convinced her to talk to him on the phone so they could get to know one another. She knew that he had a quirky sense a humor, a keen intelligence and a strong moral core. The situation was so surreal. She didn't want to be drawn to him, but she was. The color of his skin and their work situation were of equal concern to her. She couldn't change his skin, but she could definitely control whom she chose to get involved with and she'd decided that she wouldn't see him. Getting involved with Brian would jeopardize her job and her reputation. In her short time there, she'd already made an enemy in the office femme fatale and she didn't know why, nor did she want to provide her with ammunition.

She'd met Ida, secretary to the founders, in a fairly inauspicious manner. Things had started off badly, and had been steadily going down hill ever since. It had been Caroline's first day on the job and she'd been told to ask for Ida when she arrived. Ida would be the one responsible for getting her situated in her office, getting her the supplies she needed, providing her with necessary paperwork, etc. In short, Ida was not only a secretary, she was office manager, human resources and almost anything else the fledgling company needed her to be while it got its feet off the ground.

Caroline sat back in her leather chair as she recalled that first awful meeting. She'd gotten off the elevator and said hello to Michelle the receptionist, who'd taken her to Ida's seating area. Caroline had been enthusiastic about starting a new job, but also a little nervous, since she knew it would also be the first day she'd be in close proximity to Brian. As a result, her smile had been a bit cautious when she'd first spotted Ida. Caroline's first response on seeing Ida was admiration. The Puerto Rican woman was petite with lovely black eyes, a wide, full, red mouth, small nose and copper-colored skin. The finely toned hourglass figure and generously thick bob-length black hair only added to her beauty.

The red v-neck sundress didn't hurt matters, either. In short, she was drop-dead gorgeous.

"Hi, I'm Caroline," Caroline said, and stuck her hand out. She watched as the other woman ignored her hand and came out from behind her desk. And in a move that could only be described as insulting, she made a point of looking Caroline over from head to toe.

Finally ending her scrutiny, Ida had said derisively, "Well! You're a tall, skinny giant of a girl, aren't you?"

Taken aback at first, Caroline recovered quickly. She recognized the all too familiar challenge and if the woman would rather not be on friendly terms, then she would oblige her. After all, she didn't have to like all of her coworkers to do a good job. "I suppose it may look that way to someone of your...shall we say...limited stature and voluptuous figure? But hey, we all have to make the best of our assets. And now that the preliminaries are out of the way, I understand you have some paperwork for me."

No more taken aback than Caroline had been, Ida only smiled snidely and said, "So, the kitten thinks she can handle the cat. That's the way it shall be, eh, chica?"

Giving a challenging smile and mentally picking up the gauntlet, Caroline said, "Of course. Did you think otherwise? Now, what about that paperwork?"

Ida smiled again and turned away. "Follow me."

"Caroline," Linda, a junior artist who worked on her team, poked her head in Caroline's office, snapping her out of her reverie. "I was asked to tell you that the founders want all of the department heads in the conference room. And that, boss lady, includes you."

Caroline smiled at the younger woman and got up from her chair. "I like that blouse. The color looks great on you."

Linda smiled and her light brown eyes danced. "I picked it up really cheap—I got it out of my older sister's closet. I figured I was doing her a favor, since the color does absolutely nothing for her skin tone," she said as she fingered the yellow silk.

Caroline laughed. She really liked the younger woman; the two of them had clicked almost immediately after meeting. They enjoyed each other's company and had already had lunch together several times. "Oh, you're so good for me Linda. You can always make me laugh."

Linda followed her from the office. "Well, I'm glad to hear I'm good for something around here. Thank God those four years of college won't go to waste."

Caroline stopped and looked at her. "Have I also mentioned that you're doing a great job in your real career as well? I couldn't have settled in so wonderfully these past two weeks without you here."

Linda beamed in appreciation, and her deep dimples appeared in the dark hollows of her cheeks. "Thanks. It's always good to hear when you're doing a good job. I mean, I'm pretty new at this, and sometimes I need encouragement so I know I didn't do anything more than break my parents' hearts when I decided not to go to med school."

"Well, I'm sure your parents won't appreciate my saying this, but you're a great artist. You have a wonderful, natural talent that people spend years in school trying to achieve. You'll go far, if you keep at it," Caroline said and turned to walk down the hall.

"You don't know how much your saying that means to me," Linda responded and touched Caroline's arm to halt her motion. "You see, I knew your work before I knew you. When I was in college, I used to study other people's work, even though design was not my major. I came across some of your work once in this book on graphic art. It was called *Great Graphics*, or something like that. Anyway, they used your piece from the ad for that non-profit children's network, and I was blown away. Since then, I've made a point of looking for your stuff. That's why I was so excited when I found out they were talking to you for the director position. I knew they wouldn't find a better person for the job, and that I would learn so much working for you."

Caroline was overwhelmed, and her face showed it. "Linda, I'm flattered. You'll never know how much it means to me to hear that I was some sort of inspiration for such a promising artist like yourself."

"I'm glad to hear you say that, because it makes what I have to ask you much easier," Linda said. "I already consider you a mentor, but I want to make it official. Would you mind being my mentor? You know, show me the ropes of the advertising world? I figured since you have so much experience with your freelancing and stuff, it would be a snap for you. Plus, I think we've hit it off really well."

Caroline smiled and studied the dark-skinned, slender girl with her beautifully twisted hair. "I'd be delighted. Now, I'd better go or I'll be late. We'll discuss your idea in detail later."

"Thanks Caroline."

Caroline hurried down the hall to the conference room in a much better mood and with a big smile on her face. "Hi everyone," she said happily to the other people in the room. Most of them were at one end of the room helping themselves to pastries and coffee. "I'm sorry I'm late. I hope I didn't hold things up."

"You didn't," Carl said. "We haven't started yet, we're still waiting for a couple of people. While we wait, why don't you look at the portfolio and annual report floating around the room? They're from Hodgkins, Inc. They've invited us to bid on advertising for one of their products, and before we make a decision to even put together a proposal, we wanted everyone's opinion."

"They're over here, Caroline," Brian said from the other side of the huge room.

Even though she hadn't actually seen him, she had known that he was in the room the moment she'd stepped inside. She'd been studiously avoiding looking at him. She could tell he knew that, because he smiled knowingly and waved the documents at her when she finally did look his way. When he made a point of laying the documents down in front of himself, she knew he had no intention of making things easy. *God, he could be perfect for me, but why is he white? Why do I have to work with him?*

Sighing, she narrowed her eyes at Brian in retaliation for his manipulation of the documents, and walked to the side of the room where he sat alone. Dressed casually in all black, he reminded her of a panther, his deceptively indolent pose hiding the fact that he could strike at any minute.

Brian's hooded gaze watched her lazily. The little multi-pastel skirt showcased Caroline's mile-long legs just the way he loved seeing them—out, in all their slender glory. The sleeveless, lilac, silk blouse showed off her slim arms to perfection and highlighted her skin. Her thick hair swung against her shoulders and framed her face.

Brian was rudely jerked out of his trance by a short slap to the side of his head. "Ow," he whispered with a smile on his face. "What'd you do that for?"

"You know why," Caroline whispered furiously after checking around to make sure no one was looking or listening. "Stop looking at me like that; you're all but licking your lips. You could have passed these to the other side of the room, instead of making sure I had to walk over here."

Still smiling, Brian said chidingly, "Now that wouldn't have done me any good, would it? It wouldn't have afforded me the opportunity to smell your beautiful scent or to watch you walk in that wonderfully languid way only you seem to have. Nor would it have given me the chance to smell your hair, or see how thick and lovely it is up close."

Though she wanted to wipe the smirk off his face, Caroline resisted the urge to hit him again. "Knock it off, you idiot," she said as she sat down in the chair on his right and began to look through the portfolio.

Brian looked at her bent head as she studied the information. "How have you been, sweetheart?" He asked.

"Don't call me that." She didn't bother to look up.

"See, I only ask because I have absolutely no way of knowing since you avoid me after work, and won't even spare me a glance here at the office. You see me coming and run the other way, as if I was planning to give you a disease or something," he paused meaningfully. "Well I plan to give you something all right, and I don't think you'll be running when I do."

Her tongue firmly in her cheek to keep from laughing, Caroline turned a page and still didn't look up when she said, "You know…some people might consider this sexual harassment."

"Well, I tell you what, sweetheart; I would too if I didn't know you were the woman I held in my arms exactly three weeks ago to the day. Hell, I couldn't keep you off me." Caroline's head jerked up and around in disbelief, but he continued as if she'd had no response. "You were all over me, and I know if given the opportunity you'd do the exact same thing again."

By this time, Caroline's mouth was wide open, belying her pure disbelief. A squeaky "You're, you're…" was all that came out when she was able to get her mouth in working order again.

"Yes?" Brian prompted solicitously with a straight face. "You were saying? I'm what? Perfectly right? Right on the money? Wrong and you don't need an opportunity to jump me, just half a chance? What?"

Caroline clamped her jaw tight to hold the laughter in, but she narrowed her eyes at him again in warning.

"Ah, sweetheart," he said, "I love it when you threaten me with those gorgeous eyes of yours. What say we meet at my place after work, so you can do it in private?"

"You're a clown," was all she said, before she turned away again.

"All right everyone," Carl said from the other side of the room. "Now that Anthony and Larissa are here, let's get this meeting started." He paused while people seated themselves. "As you all would have heard by now, Hodgkins has asked us to participate in the competition for the advertising of one of their products. What most of you don't know is the product is their new line of cigarettes they're calling Propulsion."

A murmur of dissent went around the room. Holding up his hands, Carl said, "Hold on, hold on. We haven't said we'd do it. Hodgkins is looking for an advertising agency that markets to the urban community. Specifically, they're looking for someone to successfully market Propulsion to that coveted bracket, the 18-24 year old."

Justin took over. "We've called this meeting to get your opinion. We're aware that some of you may have a problem marketing cigarettes, not only just to the Black and Hispanic communities, but also to youngsters as a whole. As we all know, whatever becomes cool amongst Black and Hispanic youth, will almost assuredly become cool amongst the rest of Generation

Y in this country. We have a decision to make here because we're a young company. What I'm asking is, do we have the moxie to turn down such a potentially lucrative account?"

—⁓—

Once the meeting had ended, Caroline hurriedly began stacking her things together, intent on escape. She knew just enough about Brian to know he'd try to delay her. She was just rising from her chair when the public relations director walked over.

"Hello Caroline. Brian. How have you been Caroline? It's been so crazy since you started, I feel like we haven't had a chance to talk."

Out of the corner of her eye, Caroline watched Brian make himself even more comfortable in his chair and smile. "Uh, I've been fine Anthony. Don't feel bad about not having time; I've been bogged down myself."

Brian finally stood, and in a move that Caroline knew full-well was intended to forestall Anthony and keep the conversation going, he said, "I'm glad we're not going to bid for the Propulsion account. Aren't you two?"

After watching the last person leave the conference room, Caroline turned and glared at Brian. Of course Anthony was glad they wouldn't be going for the account. Anyone who'd been in the room for the past fifty minutes knew that. The older man had gone on for more than ten minutes about his opposition to the account.

"Yes, of course. No one is sorry that we're going to turn it down," Caroline said, hoping to cut things short.

"Oh, I have to run," Anthony said, after looking at his watch. "I'm interviewing someone in ten minutes." He turned and rushed out.

Diligently avoiding looking at Brian, Caroline once again gathered her things. In her hurry, everything slipped out of her hands and onto the table again.

"I know what you're thinking, Caroline. You want to kiss me." Brian said, and held his arms wide open. "Well go right ahead, have me. I'm all yours."

Caroline balled her fist and punched him in his stomach; he grunted obligingly. "I could kill you," she said. "This is serious, and you're not playing fair."

"How's that saying go?" Brian asked as he walked around the table to stand in front of her. "'All's fair in love and war.' And if you think I haven't been playing fair up to now, you just wait. You're just lucky I was out of town that week you had off before you started here. If I hadn't been, I'd have been all over you." He finished and sat on the edge of the table and took her things from her.

Caroline looked over her shoulder. "Brian," she whispered firmly, "not here, not now. Someone could see us." She used his chest as leverage and tried to push away.

Brian pulled her closer and said, "I believe it was the great Jesse Jackson who said, 'if not now, then when? If not here, then where?'"

Caroline tried not to laugh at his credible imitation. "You're such an idiot. I don't think he said all of that. And even if he did, I'm sure he didn't mean for it to be applied to this kind of situation," she finished and pushed again.

Catching her unaware, Brian quickly kissed her smiling mouth, making her gasp and jerk back in his arms. Caroline wanted desperately to give in and take the kiss further, but she remembered their situation and where they were and resisted.

She folded her arms against his chest and pushed harder until he released her. "You take far too many risks. And liberties."

Sighing in heavy defeat as he released her, Brian gave her her things. "And I don't think you take enough of them," he mumbled lowly.

Stopping at the threshold of the room, she looked at him over her shoulder, "Even if you hadn't been out of town, I'd already accepted the job," she reminded him, and then frustrating him completely, she said, "I don't think any of this is a good idea." With one final look, she rushed away.

CHAPTER 3

From his fifth floor window with tinted glass, Alexander Brickman watched the attractive Hispanic woman suddenly get in her car and speed away as if the hounds of hell were on her tail. He often had that affect on people. She hadn't been able to see him, but he'd bet his Lamborghini that she'd felt his stare and had had an inexplicable, self-preservationist urge to get away from danger that she could only sense, but not see.

It had been the second time in a week that she'd shown up in front of the non-descript building where he conducted his business. He'd only taken notice that first Friday because she had gotten out of her car and stared at the building as if she were trying to see through it to the inside. He had yet to meet her, but he already knew her name, her address, her telephone number and where she worked. He could even find out her favorite color if he so chose.

Since she appeared each time after Mac brought in his weekly cash haul from the downtown business, Brickman had easily surmised that the woman was one of his office soldiers. In fact, all of the information he had, he'd gotten from that idiot Mac. Mac had even told him that she was his most profitable soldier, consistently selling out the product each week. Yes, he knew who she was, he just didn't know what she wanted, but he'd find out soon enough.

Ida's tires screeched in protest as they were forced to burn precious rubber when she pulled out of her parking space. The need to get away from the building had been sudden and urgent. She couldn't explain it, she just knew she had to get away and quickly. She shuddered as a chill traveled from the nape of her neck to the end of her spine. She drove faster and didn't feel comfortable in slowing down until she was at least a mile away.

She'd known when she'd gotten in her car that she shouldn't follow Mac. But she'd wanted to find out who she was working for and she also wanted a larger cut of the profits for gambling, which was almost out of control. She knew Mac couldn't approve the cut. She needed to meet the man in charge. Added to that, her emotions were in such turmoil after what she'd seen in the conference room that afternoon that she was feeling more reckless than usual. How could Brian have done that to her? The hurt and betrayal she'd felt at seeing him and Caroline together had been overwhelming. The scene had only confirmed what she hadn't wanted to believe she'd seen as she'd walked past the building's gangway the day Caroline had accepted the job offer.

They weren't doing anything when she'd caught a glimpse of them in the gangway that day, but their body language and the mere fact that they were in the gangway alone had made her think that there was something between the two of them. Ida had successfully convinced herself otherwise, however, and this false confidence had caused her to waste valuable time in her quest to get Brian back. But now, she'd put all of her effort into getting him back. They were meant for one another.

So if that skinny, wanna-be artist thought that she would be allowed to interfere with destiny, she'd better think again, Ida fumed silently. She'd hooked up with Mac on this cocaine deal because she needed the extra money for gambling, but now it would also come in handy to buy expensive clothes to grab Brian's attention away from Caroline. Which was another reason why she needed a bigger cut; she needed every available weapon to compete with a trust fund baby's wardrobe.

—∽—

Brian worried about that last statement Caroline had made in the conference room as he let himself into his loft. Carrying his case through the large living area, he bypassed the dining room, kitchen and bathroom and walked up the stairs to his bedroom. It was bad enough that he seemed to be in this perpetual state of desire since he'd met her, but for her to throw confusion into the mix was more than infuriating, he thought as he threw his briefcase on the bed and took off his shoes.

Besides, he thought, as he walked down the stairs and into the kitchen to grab himself a bottle of beer, he'd thought they had come to an understanding during the telephone conversation they'd had the first day they'd met. He still recalled the sound of her sexily husky voice as she awakened from an apparent catnap.

"'*Lo?*"

He'd recognized her voice instantly. "Hello, sleepy-head, it's the man of your dreams. I guess we do need to take some time to get to know one another better. I wouldn't have guessed you'd be in bed by seven on a Friday night."

She chuckled huskily and he closed his eyes in supplication as the sexy sound rolled over him. "Hi Brian. I wasn't down for the night; I was simply taking a nap because I didn't sleep well last night. But my hours can be erratic. I'm usually up by 5:30 every morning and I can fall asleep anywhere between nine at night and one in the morning. What about you?"

"Your wish is my command. What would you prefer?"

She laughed again. "I can't control the times you sleep."

"You'd be surprised," he mumbled low, still recovering from her sexy sound and his own imagination. "Listen," he said, deciding it was time to change the subject, "tell me about yourself. Don't leave anything out. I want details."

"All right. Let's see, I'm 30, no children, never been married, and I suddenly find that I can't stop thinking about a certain tall, white guy with beautiful, gray eyes."

"Is my being white really going to be a problem for you?"

"Well, not really a problem, but more of an issue. I've never gone out with a white man before and I'm worried about what a relationship with you could bring."

"Well, I can't pretend that I don't know what you're talking about. I've thought about it as well. But I still want to spend time with you and get to know you. And after our interlude outside the building today, I'm guessing you feel the same. Am I wrong?"

"No, but only because this sort of thing has never, ever happened to me before. I promise you, if you were just a white guy who I was only attracted to, I'd ignore the attraction and go the other way."

"Hmm." Brian said contemplatively. "Why?"

"Because you're white and I'm not and I'm black and you're not."

"Are you afraid of what people will think? What they will say?"

"No. I believe that who a person dates is her business. I've just never thought about dating anyone who isn't black. I was taught to have pride in the black race and to be proud and feel lucky that I am black. But since I met you this afternoon and you knocked the breath out of me—literally and figuratively—I find myself reversing a position I didn't even know I held."

"I won't try to make light of the situation because I'm a realist and I know a relationship won't be easy, but it certainly won't be impossible. And being proud to be black and dating a white man aren't mutually exclusive things," Brian said.

"I just don't know what we could have in common. I'm sure our realities are completely different simply because you are a white man and I'm a black woman. I'm just not so sure a relationship would work."

"How will we know if we don't try? There are always going to be differences, Caroline. We shouldn't ignore them, but should we let them stop us altogether? I'm well aware that the world is a different place for a white man than it is for a black woman, and for practically everyone else for that matter But my question to you is this: Is that one fact worth you and I ignoring this wonderfully rare, breath-stealing, soul-stirring relationship we were lucky enough to stumble upon?"

Caroline sighed. "I don't know and I wouldn't call this a relationship. I just want us to be honest with each other if we do decide to 'damn the torpedoes and full speed ahead,' it's going to have to be all or nothing."

Brian closed his eyes gratefully. Though she hadn't said it, it sounded like she was going to give him a chance. "Agreed. Shall we talk about something else?"

She sighed again. "Yes, but we haven't really solved anything."

"We're on the right track. I'm 35, I've never been married and I have no children." He was determined to change the subject. And after they'd talked about all the practical things like family and backgrounds, he turned the conversation again.

"Listen sweetheart, since you're not going to let me see you tonight, how about giving me something to work with until I do see you again? Paint me a picture of what you're wearing."

If Caroline was surprised by his request, she didn't say it. Delicately clearing her throat, she said, "I don't think that's a good idea. We barely know each other."

"Come on, please. Just tell me." In his most persuasive voice, he said, "Even if you decide not to give a relationship a go, I'll at least have this phone conversation."

He didn't expect capitulation, but he got it when she said nervously, "You should know that I don't usually do this sort of thing." She cleared her throat again and said, "In deference to the heat, I'm wearing a satin T-shirt—"

"What color is it?"

"White with blue trim."

Brian closed his eyes, having no problem seeing her. "With your creamy, brown skin and dark hair, you look good in white. Is your hair up or down?"

"Up," Caroline answered, and continuing the game, she said, "The shirt is sleeveless, with lace around the neck and arms…"

"Uh-huh, go on."

"It's not long; it stops at my navel," she said in a low voice.

"Is it v-neck or regular?"

"V," she whispered softly and nervously cleared her throat. "Underneath I'm wearing matching bikinis. They have a blue butterfly fanning the front of them…"

Imagining her long, smooth legs and thighs bare made Brian groan aloud and picturing her small, tight butt hugged in white satin made him want to beg. "Enough, Caroline. I can't take anymore," he pleaded. "You sure catch on fast."

She chuckled weakly. "You started it. I was just doing what was requested."

"I wish I was that lucky butterfly," he said, making her laughter stop abruptly.

She whispered, "Brian."

"Yeah?"

"This whole situation is crazy. I've never done anything like this before and it bothers me that something about you inspires me to do the unusual."

"It definitely doesn't bother me. Take my phone numbers down, and if you change your mind about seeing me this weekend, call me. Anytime—day or night." He heard rustling and after a moment, asked, "Ready?" After receiving affirmation, he recited both his home and his cell phone numbers.

"All right, Brian. Good night."

"Good night, though I'm sure it will be impossible for me to sleep now after the conversation we just had."

She hadn't called him, and he'd gone a little mad that weekend thinking about her and her decision. Everything was so up in the air. The description of her sleepwear was all he'd been able to think about. He didn't even want to think about his dreams.

Taking his beer with him, Brian walked into the living area and plopped down on the black, leather couch. The situation was almost untenable, he thought. He wanted her more than anyone he'd ever wanted in his life, but it was more than that. He already felt a bond with her that went beyond sex. He felt an intimacy that he'd never felt with any other woman, even the ones he'd slept with.

He wanted to do things with her; go to the movies, the park, out to dinner. He wanted to watch her brush her hair. He wanted to see her in one of his shirts after they made love. He wanted to just hold her and talk to her in the dark. He wanted to do all those things that signified an intimate relationship.

He picked up the phone and punched in the required seven digits. "Listen," he said, when the other end was picked up. "I got a problem. A big one."

"What?" Justin asked.

"It's Caroline. Caroline Singleton."

"What about her? You got a problem with her work? She came highly recommended, and you've seen her stuff. It's excellent."

"It's not that. It has nothing to do with her work."

"That's good, because I'd hate to have to let someone with her kind of talent walk out the door. Did you know that she's also a painter, sculptor and an heiress to an ice cream fortune?"

"No, I didn't," Brian was taken aback. Heiress? "How did you?"

"Caroline and I have a mutual friend, her name is Tracy. You've met her once. She and Caroline have been friends since they were kids, and I know Tracy from college. She used to keep some of Caroline's paintings in her dorm room. She even had a couple of her sculptures in her apartment." Justin paused. "Hey, if you didn't call me to complain about her work, what did you call for? You said you had a problem."

"I do. I'm very strongly attracted to her, and if my feelings are anything to go by right now, I'll probably end up spending the rest of my life with her," Brian finished.

There was complete silence on the other end of the line, then, "Excuse me?"

Sensing tension, Brian straightened. "Is there a problem?"

"Yeah. She's black and you're white."

"And?" Brian said in frustration, because Justin was echoing Caroline.

"And? And you shouldn't date her. I mean we're friends and all, but there are very few things that bother me more than seeing a white man with a black woman."

Curious now, Brian said, "I never knew that. But given the fact that you've dated white women before, don't you think that that's a double standard?"

"Perhaps it is. But the last thing I'm going to be concerned about is being fair to the white man when it comes to dating our women, because he's already got more advantages than can be considered decent by any fair-minded person."

"So even though we're friends, you don't think that I should be allowed to date Caroline—or any other black woman for that matter—because of the advantages I have just by virtue of being white?"

"You're almost right. You're a great guy Brian and nobody knows that better than I do. I'm not saying that you shouldn't be allowed to date black women, because after all, if that's what the two of you want, then who am I to say no? What I am saying is as a black man it would bother me to see it."

Barely pausing for breath, Justin continued, "I'm fully aware that if you said the same thing to me about my dating white women, you'd be called a racist and it would probably be true. I say that because you could have no other reason for saying it, whereas, other black men and I have a multitude of reasons. Chief among them is that black people have traditionally been under siege in this country and that has largely been at the hands of white men.

"So yes, my knee jerk reaction to seeing a black woman with a white man is dismay. I find it difficult to applaud, yet again, another advantage in the white man's favor. It's nothing to do with you personally, but everything to do with white men generally."

"So what you're saying is that white men have too much power as it is and it's wrong that we should have access to black women as well," Brian stated in complete disgust.

"I'm not saying it's wrong, I'm saying I don't like seeing it. Who am I to say if it's right or wrong? As you pointed out, I have dated white women. I'm not one of those people who lays blame at a couple's door—I don't blame the woman for her attraction and I don't blame the man for his. I simply don't like it. And because you're my friend, and from what you've said about Caroline, that may be something I have to work on."

"Thanks." Brian said sarcastically.

"I'm serious, Brian, and in light of the friendship we've had, I know the things I've said bother you. Nonetheless, they're true. I actually think you're a great guy and any women would be lucky to have you. I know it's difficult to separate that from the other things I've said, but I really mean it."

"You're right, it is difficult, but the strange thing is, I understand what you're saying. However, I'm not going to let it get in the way of what I feel for Caroline. There's nothing I can do to change the color of my skin and I wouldn't anyway."

"No one's asking you to Bri. I can see Caroline means a lot to you. So now what? Are you sure the two of you have just met? I mean, this seems awfully fast."

"I never saw her before the day she came in for her second interview, and this did happen fast. Real fast. I bumped into her right before she met with you guys, and I tell you, something in me just went haywire and I haven't stopped thinking about her since."

"How does she feel about it? Does she even know?"

Brian was surprised he could still laugh about the situation. "Of course she knows. What do you think I am? Some kind of a stalker?"

"Well, how does she feel?"

"As far as being attracted to each other, she feels the same way, that's why I have a problem. Since we work together—"

"Yeah, I know. You guys haven't done anything have you?"

"No, we haven't, but I tell you it's damned hard. She refuses to see me, and of course there's the agreement among the founders—"

"Say no more," Justin said in understanding. "I see your dilemma."

"Good. What do you suggest?"

"I can't tell you what to do here. All I can say is we'd probably have to let her go if the two of you started something up. I mean, there can't be any hint of special treatment to any employee from any one of us. Not that I'm saying you'd ever do that—hell, the two of you will probably never even work together. I am saying that some people don't need much to get something started. If you want me to say a name, I can."

"Ida," Brian surmised.

"Exactly. Ida's the kind of person to find a small thread and pull on it until everything unravels. And I should tell you, I think she already has it in for your girl."

"For Caroline? Why?"

"Let's just say Caroline is too attractive for some people's peace of mind. It's nothing big. I've just heard Ida make comments here and there." Justin said.

"Well, it had better not go any further than that." Brian said in warning. "I think Caroline could handle herself quite well if a situation ever presented itself."

"I'm sure you're right."

"I wouldn't worry about Caroline and Ida if I were you. What you need to worry about is how you're going to handle this whole situation. I mean, you not only have to worry about work, but you need to be thinking about society as well."

Brian grunted. "I'm not concerned about society."

"Well, you should be, because if you and Caroline ever get together, there are going to be some brothers who aren't like me and they are going to want to whoop your ass."

"I can handle myself; I'm not worried about getting my ass kicked—"

"*Whooped*. I didn't say kicked, I said whooped. There's a world of difference. There are plenty of brothers out there who can't stand to see a sister dating outside the race, but like me, they mind their own business and let it go. But Caroline is the cream of the crop, man—beauty, brains and talent. It's because of that combination that you are going to run into some brothers who will not only be willing to mind your business, but will feel that your relationship is their business."

Still unconcerned, Brian said, "Well if and when that happens, there won't be much I can do but take care of it. Back to the work situation…"

"Like I said Brian, there's not much I can tell you, except one of you would have to leave. And since you're a founder, I'm assuming it would have to be her."

Brian sighed heavily, "The point is moot anyway, because as I told you, she isn't willing to budge an inch. Do me a favor and keep this conversation to yourself, okay?"

"Won't tell a soul."

Brian hung up and sighed. He knew that if he and Caroline ever began a relationship that there would be some people who would have a problem with their being different races. He was willing and ready to deal with them. After all, he also believed that it was nobody's business who he chose to date. But the fact that Caroline herself had reservations worried him.

The fact that she was an heiress also concerned him. He was a simple man who came from a simple background. His dad had been a cop and his mom, a homemaker. They hadn't been poor, but they'd been far enough away from rich for him to notice the difference. Sure, he was more than comfortable now, but at heart, he was still an uncomplicated man with simple tastes. He wondered if that would be enough for Caroline and if he'd be able to keep up with her.

CHAPTER 4

Caroline tossed and turned in bed, kicked the light blanket off and wrestled with her pillow. Finally deciding to give up the idea of falling back to sleep, she turned flat on her back and stared up at the ceiling. This just won't do, she thought. It was the third night in a row that she hadn't been able to sleep through the night, and she was sick and tired of it. Turning her head, she peered at the illuminated alarm clock on her bedside table. She may as well get out of bed; she had less than two hours before she'd normally wake up anyway. Sitting up and swinging her legs to the floor, she turned on the light. "Thank God it's Saturday," she said aloud to the empty room, "at least I can take a nap whenever the need hits me," she said around a yawn.

The phone rang, startling her. "Hello?"

"Caroline? It's me, Tracy. I'm sorry if I woke you."

"Tracy!" Caroline said with a rush of true pleasure on hearing her best friend's voice. "It's so good to hear from you! What's it been—about six weeks since I last talked to you? What is it—about two in the morning in Vancouver? What are you doing up so late?"

"Slow down, Caroline," Tracy said around a laugh. "Now in order: it's good to hear your voice too. Yes, it's been about six weeks since we last talked, yes it's almost two in the morning, and I'm up so late because I couldn't sleep. I'm too wired. What about you, what are you doing up so late—or should I say early?"

"Same reason as you; I can't sleep. But anyway, tell me about Vancouver. How is the new office coming?"

Tracy worked as a CPA for a medium-sized accounting firm based in Chicago. In her seven years with the company, business had steadily increased, and Tracy's responsibilities had paralleled the firm's growth. Several months before, she and three other people had been sent to Vancouver to open the company's first Canadian office. "Everything's going well," she said now. "In fact, it's going much better than any of us expected it to."

"I'm glad to hear it. Does that mean you'll be coming home soon? I miss you."

"Oh, if I had to guess, I'd say we'll have things wrapped up here in another month or more. Tell me, how did things go with Justin and those guys over at Inclusion Integrated? Are you going to freelance with them?"

"Actually, they offered me this great deal to come on full-time, and I decided it was too good to pass up. I started about a month ago."

"Oh? What about your art? I mean, I thought you were going to try to get a show at one of the galleries." Tracy said.

"I'll still paint and sculpt, but I just won't have as much time to devote to it. And my agent is still working to try to get me a show at one of the galleries."

"Well, with all the freelance jobs you get, I know you don't need the money. And I know you don't like to talk about it, but you do have a boatload of family money. So why exactly did you take a full-time job?"

"It was the atmosphere and the people. I mean, the place has a certain energy and excitement about it, and I know it's going to be successful. I just thought it would be cool to be on the ground floor of something that is a definite can't miss." Caroline said.

"You said you've been there about a month. Is it all you thought it would be?"

"Yes, it's been all that and more," Caroline said in a soft voice.

Sensing something in her friend's voice, Tracy said, "And?"

"And…I've met someone. Maybe."

"You've met someone? Where? At work?"

"Yeah. Oh God, Tracy, this is going to sound weird, but I think I've met the man who's perfect for me or at least the one man who I can't get off my mind—"

"Whoa, slow down," Tracy said in shocked confusion. "You think you've met the man of your dreams, and you've only known him a month? That doesn't sound like you."

Closing her eyes, Caroline sighed. "I know. Crazy, huh? But when I first met Brian, Tracy, something…something in me just gave way, and left me completely helpless and confused. But it's more than that. When I met him, there was this instant knowing, you know? Like he was a part of me, even though that was the first time I'd ever laid eyes on him. I felt this urgency, this need, to not let him walk away. I felt if I did, I would regret it. Even though all of this took place inside of me in a span of about 60 seconds, I felt like if I ignored that one instant, I'd spend a lifetime mourning a missed opportunity."

"Wow," was all Tracy was able to say.

Caroline laughed humorlessly. "Tell me about it."

"Well, if he's the one for you, why don't you sound happy? Does the intensity of it scare you?"

"Sort of, yes. I mean, I was shocked that it could happen so fast, and to me of all people. You know I've never talked about love at first sight, but I've never not believed in it either I don't know if that's what this is, but I've certainly never felt this way before about anyone else. I mean, Brian just invokes all sorts of strong feelings in me."

"So, what's the problem then?" Tracy asked.

"Did I mention that Brian is white and that he's one of the founders?" Caroline asked wryly.

"White? A founder?" Tracy asked. "Surely you don't mean Brian Keenan?"

"That would be him," Caroline said solemnly. "Do you know him?"

"I met him once briefly at one of Justin's parties about a year ago. He was on his way in as I was on my way out, so we didn't get to say much to one another.

If I recall though, he's got that indefinable something about him that catches a woman's eye," she said reflectively. Then, "Do you have a problem with the fact that he's white?"

"Not a problem, exactly. A concern. I've never dated a white guy before."

"I'm aware of that, but so what. Make him your first. And from what you're saying, he could be the last guy you date. Ever. I think it's worth your taking a chance."

"I'm surprised to hear that coming from you, considering how you feel about white men," Caroline said.

"I don't have anything against them, you know that," Tracy said. "I just can't see myself dating one. But that's me. Let's talk about you."

"We can't really do anything because we work together."

"Have you talked to him about how you feel?"

"Yes, and before you ask, it was the same for him. Instantaneous."

"Well, I know you probably won't like hearing this, but why don't you just quit? I mean, like I said earlier, it's not like you need the money."

"I know, but I can't. I really like this job, and I have to face the fact that I may never be successful in the art world with my paintings or my sculptures. If that proves to be true, I'll have to stick with commercial art, and having the title art director on my resume can only help me. Also, I made a commitment before I knew who he was."

"I guess," Tracy said, unconvinced of the possibility that Caroline wouldn't be a success. "I think there's more to it than that, and knowing you, you're worried that he's only interested in you because of your family's money, aren't you?"

"It has happened before."

Tracy expelled a breath. "Sweetie, you can't go on doing this—turning guys away because you think they may be after your money. What makes you think Brian is?"

"I don't," Caroline said hastily, "he's done nothing to make me think that. It's just that I don't want to get hurt again, like I have before. And I'm afraid that because my feelings for Brian are already so strong, I could be devastated."

"Have you told him about your family's money? Does he even know?"

"I haven't told him anything about it."

"Well how can he possibly know? It's not as if you broadcast it anywhere. And a good, clear picture of you hasn't been in the society pages in years. Every since that incident in college, you avoid the press as best you can. I think you should tell him and see where it gets you." Tracy said.

"That may be unnecessary—"

Tracy interrupted her. "Caroline, are you planning on staying single for the rest of your life?" When she got nothing but silence from the other end of the line,

Tracy continued, "I didn't think so. You have to trust at some point. What better time than now—when a guy has knocked you off your feet? Come on! Take a chance. Besides, since you work together, you should be able to take things slowly and get to know each other. You can't do anything and it will be difficult to know what you're missing."

Delicately clearing her throat, Caroline mumbled, "That's the problem. I do sort of know what I'm missing."

Tracy gasped and in mock censure said, "Why Caroline Singleton, you harlot, you! I'm surprised at you—sleeping with someone you've only known a month. I didn't know you could be such a slut," she finished teasingly.

"We haven't done that. In fact, we haven't done much of anything, really."

"Just how much of anything have you done?" Tracy asked.

"Well, we've almost kissed. Twice."

"What kind of kisses? The chaste kind, the getting-to-know-you kind or the hot-wild-I-can't-wait-to-get-you-in-bed kind?"

"Probably the last one, both times," Caroline said, feeling like they were still in high school and were talking about a first date.

"Um-hmm," Tracy said, knowing there was more. "What else?"

Clearing her throat again, Caroline whispered, "Phone."

"Phone? What do you mean, phone?"

"We talk on the phone all the time, but there was this one time...well things just got out of hand and we had phone sex. Maybe it was just phone foreplay, I don't know."

Tracy burst out laughing. "You've had phone sex with the guy? Oh my God, you poor babies—things must be desperate."

"They kind of are, and Brian isn't happy about it."

"I'll bet," Tracy said knowingly. "How do you handle seeing him at work?"

"I avoid him as much as possible, which should be easy, since we never work together. He doesn't see things my way though, and won't really let me avoid him."

"Good for him!" Tracy said.

"Tracy!"

"What? I hope he goes for it. I mean if this is truly it for the both of you, then he probably feels he can't afford to waste any time, job or no. It's your scruples that are holding things up."

"Not exactly," Caroline said and told Tracy about the founders' rule. Closing her eyes in frustration and sighing heavily, she said, "Brian tries to obey it, but he won't let me avoid him completely."

"I say it again: good for him," Tracy said implacably.

Caroline wanted to scream. "You're no help. I figured avoiding him was the best thing, then I wouldn't be tempted. It's hard enough to be in the same building with him!"

"I'm sorry, Caro. I wish I could tell you what to do, but it sounds like you're in a no-win situation—for the time being anyway."

"I know."

Trying to make her feel better, Tracy said, "Why don't you treat yourself this weekend? Go to the spa, get the works."

"I can't today. I've got too many errands to run."

"Well, tomorrow then."

"Can't. I've got to go into the office. I have some things that I'd like to get done by Monday."

"Well, I guess you'll have to try to use work to keep your mind off Brian."

"I would, if he'd let me."

—⁂—

For the third time in ten minutes Caroline stifled a yawn and watched the words on the paper in front of her blur into a mass of black and white. Stretching her arms over her head, she swiveled her chair around so that she was looking out her office window at Lake Michigan and the Chicago skyline. She really needed to do something about her lack of sleep. Lately, she hadn't been able to manage any more than three to four hours a night. And here she was at work on a Sunday unable to accomplish much of anything because she was too sleepy. She may as well go home.

Swiveling back around, she laid her head on her folded arms. Thinking she'd be safe in taking a quick nap since she was alone, she closed her eyes and finally began to sink into sleep.

Brian stood on the threshold of Caroline's office and stared at her as she slept. Like most people, sleep made her look oddly peaceful and took about five years off her face. Despite her reservations and his, he couldn't help himself and he smiled in anticipation, walked into the office and shut the door behind him, just in case someone else arrived unexpectedly.

Moving around the desk, he studied her attire. Because it was Sunday, she was dressed a lot more casually than usual. The red tailored shorts stopped mid-thigh, and were a perfect match for the red and white stripes of her sleeveless tank. Allowing his eyes to travel down the long length of her legs, he smiled when he saw the pristine white tennis shoes with the thick soles. Even when she was casual, Caroline was a true clotheshorse. He was sure she could make a gunny sack look like the most expensively priced gown.

He smiled again, this time with satisfaction. They were completely alone. Bending over, he ran his hand over the thick hair she'd left hanging, and putting his mouth to her ear, he whispered her name. Dreaming of him, Caroline stretched under the caress, whispered his name and smiled, but remained blissfully asleep.

Brian sucked in his breath at her soft whisper and bent his head and pressed his mouth to her smiling one. She was warm and soft, and he simply lost control. Caroline swam to semi-consciousness with his mouth pressed to hers. Oh God, she felt the heat to the core of her. Still thinking she was dreaming, she whispered his name again and began participating in the kiss. "Mmm," she murmured, raising her hand to the side of his face.

As the kiss became more heated, her eyelids fluttered for a few seconds, and finally lifted fully. "Brian?" she tried to say, but as he began to explore the caverns of her mouth with his tongue, she could only close her eyes again and kiss him back. Before she was aware of what he was doing, she found herself lifted and then placed sideways on his lap as he replaced her in the chair, all without taking his mouth from hers.

Putting her arms around his neck, she gave herself up to him, and took a few moments of scorching pleasure before reality intruded. Brian released her mouth to press kisses to her face and neck. She kept her eyes tightly closed and let her head fall back to allow him better access. As he placed open-mouthed, lingering kisses on her neck, she felt heat travel from her stomach to pool between her legs, and knew if she didn't call a halt to things, it would soon be too late to stop at all. Tunneling her fingers through his hair, she opened her eyes and lifted his head from her neck.

Brian placed one last kiss on her mouth and smiled wolfishly, "Hi. You were right—we are good at this. Very, very good."

Caroline smiled back. "Hi, yourself," she whispered, still caught up in the intimacy they'd just shared. Then she remembered where she was and jumped from his lap. She looked at him and blurted, "Oh God, this is bad. Really, really bad. And I'm in trouble. I can feel it." Flustered, she covered her mouth with her hand and paced away from him.

Brian watched her stop and straighten her shoulders. When she turned back around she looked determined. *Well, that was fun while it lasted,* he thought.

Caroline walked back to the desk. "What are you doing here? You know my feelings on this and that we shouldn't be doing it—especially in the office! Get out of my chair!"

Brian studied her as he stood and he smiled. "How hard was it to pull yourself back? I hope you're not going to pretend that it was easy. It wasn't for me."

"I'm not pretending anything." Caroline said stubbornly. "You never should have kissed me that way. Nothing about this 'relationship,' or whatever you want to call it, has been settled."

"I know that, but I'm not sorry. In fact, I'd do it again if I had the opportunity."

She sighed and said, "Well, you're not going to get another one. Now what are you doing here?" She asked again and moved around him to take her seat.

Brian sat on the edge of her desk. "I had some work to finish up. What about you? What are you doing here?"

"I wanted to put the finishing touches on the Castles piece. My team and I have been working double duty on that account."

"I'm sure it will be great and Justin and those guys will love it. Is that it? Can I take a look at it?"

Caroline snatched up her work, opened a drawer and put the sketches in it. "No, you'll have to wait and see it when everyone else does."

Brian raised his brow in surprise, but only toyed with the ends of her hair that trailed halfway down her back. "You know, you have beautiful hair. It's so thick."

Recognizing the hooded look in his eyes, Caroline removed his hand from her hair and tried to shove him off her desk. He didn't budge. "Hey," she said, determined to get their minds on other things, "since we're both here unexpectedly and we are alone, why don't we finish our telephone conversations? You can tell me everything personal I ever wanted to know about you, and I'll do the same."

"All right," Brian agreed. "Where should we start?"

"First, get off my desk." She said and pushed him again. When he stood up, she pointed to the two chairs she kept in front of her desk for visitors. As he sat down she said, "There, now this will make things less tempting. Tell me about your education. Where did you go to college?"

Brian smiled knowing the desk wouldn't stop him from touching her, but he obliged her "I went to Circle campus for undergrad," he said referring to the Chicago campus of the Illinois public college system, "and I went to Northwestern for law school." He finished, watching the surprise on her face.

"You're a lawyer? Why aren't you practicing?"

"I did for about a year, and decided it wasn't for me. I used to be a police officer too, but that wasn't for me either."

"You were a cop? For how long?"

"Oh, I was one of Chicago's finest for about five years before I decided to quit. I took law school classes whenever possible while I was still a cop."

"What kind of cop were you, and why'd you quit?"

"I was vice, and no, nothing really traumatic happened to make me quit. I just knew it wasn't what I wanted to do."

"Interesting. I had no idea."

"I'm surprised Linda didn't tell you I used to be a cop. Her dad was my captain."

"Linda? Cute, witty Linda Thompson who works on my team? That Linda?"

"Yeah, that Linda. I've known her since she was a kid. When I joined the force, her dad took one look at my ineptitude and me and decided to take me under his wing. I still go over to their house for the occasional Sunday dinner or barbecue. Gloria Thompson is the best cook I know, bar none, including my own mother."

"Interesting. I wonder why Linda didn't mention it."

"I don't know, though I am surprised. For as long as I've known her, the kid could out-chatter a magpie," Brian said with a fond smile.

Smiling at his apt description of her junior team member, Caroline said, "Yeah, she does talk a lot, doesn't she?"

"That's putting it mildly, I'd say." He shrugged his shoulders. "Anyway, that's enough about me. Tell me about you, Miss Artiste. Tell me more about your painting and sculpting."

Caroline frowned. "It's strange that we didn't get into this stuff on the phone."

"Maybe." Brian thought about it. Their conversations were usually more about likes and dislikes, politics and family. "So, why aren't you out selling your paintings to a gallery or giving exhibitions, instead of this? Isn't using your talent in the commercial world considered to be selling out?"

Caroline smirked. "I'm not one to suffer for my art," she said wryly. "Besides, I like doing this type of work."

"Where did you go to college? Did you study art?"

"God no, you couldn't be further away from the truth. I think my dad would have had a heart attack if I'd majored in art. I went to Spelman, and I was a math major I did take some art courses, though." Caroline said.

"Spelman. Isn't that the all girl African American college in Atlanta?"

"Yes. After that, I got a graduate degree in business from University of Chicago."

"You have an MBA from U of C, and you're working here as an art director? Did your parents want to kill you?"

"You have a law degree from Northwestern, and you're a technology specialist." She said, shrugging her shoulders. "Did your parents want to kill you?"

"It's not the same—"

"Course it is; we both started out intending to do wildly different things than what we ended up doing. I'm happy where I am. It's the same for you, right?"

"You're being evasive. I thought the purpose of this was to get to know each other," he said.

Caroline studied him as she remembered her conversation with Tracy. She looked down at her desk. "You're right. My parents paid for everything and no, they weren't happy when I decided not to pursue a career in business. Actually, it was just my dad. He had other ideas for me. My family owns Grandmother's Ice Cream." She looked up at him to see his reaction. His gaze was completely impassive and she looked away again.

"Anyway, my dad had dreams of me joining the company, but I just couldn't. I was in my last year of grad school before I decided to just do what I wanted. I finished the program, but as soon as I did, I started working on my art portfolio. I got my first job with a children's foundation and the rest is history."

Brian studied her bent head for a moment and then asked, "Why did you have such a hard time telling me that? Specifically, why did you have such a hard time telling me the part about your family owning Grandmother's?"

Caroline hunched her shoulders in discomfort. "Because men typically do one of two things whey they find out my family has money. They run the other way because they're afraid they won't measure up or they pretend feelings they don't actually have to get close to me and try to take advantage."

Brian resisted the urge to squirm. A small part of him still took a step back at the thought of her being an heiress, but his desire for her and to get to know her won out. "Caroline, Justin told me you were an heiress shortly after you and I met and I'm still here and interested. And as I knew nothing about you before I bumped into you, you can rest assured that I don't want your money. I have my own."

She looked at him again. "I know you're not like that, but I've had situations where I didn't know if men were interested in me because of me or because of my family's money."

"Caroline you shouldn't ever doubt that men can be attracted to you without wanting your money. You're a beautiful woman." He watched her grimace in disgust and smiled. "I know that there's a lot more to recommend you besides your looks and I'm thrilled, but I'd be lying if I said I didn't love the look of you."

"That's not what's important. Wanting to be with someone because of how he or she looks is just as bad as wanting to be with someone because he or she may be wealthy. I mean, the initial attraction is expected, but staying with someone because of looks is just wrong."

Brian became exasperated. "You know as well as I do that that is not the case for either one of us. Come on Caroline."

"I didn't say that it was. Why don't we finish with the questions?"

"All right. Have you ever had a showing of your work?"

"Not yet, but I'm working on it. Art being a completely subjective thing, it's not easy."

"If you were able to get a showing and make a living from your paintings and sculptures, would you be working here?" Brian asked.

"No, I'd have to concentrate on my art then."

"Well then sweetheart," Brian said with meaning, as he looked her in the eye, "will you hurry up and dazzle somebody so I can get my hands on you without feeling like I'll be arrested?"

Caroline laughed at him. "I'll do my best, but as I said, it's not easy. You'll just have to wait until I can finesse it."

Brian studied her; marveling at their easy banter and the heat that always seemed to generate between them whenever they were within two feet of each other. He didn't know about other people, but he had never experienced this kind of phenomenon before. Surely "love at first sight" was a rare occurrence. "How long have you been painting and sculpting?"

"I wasn't a child prodigy or anything like you read about so often nowadays. I guess I started drawing really early on—I think I was about four. But I didn't start painting until I was about thirteen. Sculpting came much later; I'd say I was about twenty."

"Other interests?"

"I'm a big photography buff. I love just taking my camera on the weekends and exploring the city, especially the parks and the lakefront."

"Will you take me with you one weekend?"

"Yes," she said hesitantly. "I'd love to spend a weekend with you," this was said with perfect candor as she looked at him.

"Any other hidden talents I should know about?"

For some reason, that question marked an end to practical conversation and Caroline couldn't believe this newly discovered side of herself that compelled her to let go of her inhibitions and do and say things with Brian that she normally would not do on such a short acquaintance.

"Well…" she said as she caught her bottom lip between her teeth and sent him a look from beneath her lashes. "There is this one thing I know how to do, but considering where we are, I don't know if I should tell you. Your reaction could…get out of hand, so to speak. I'd never show it to anyone else though, only you."

Brian's relaxed posture became alert and he narrowed his eyes. "Really?"

A slow nod of the head, a quick glimpse of a pink tongue as it licked her lip. "Really."

"Tell me." A quiet demand.

"Can't." A breathless, teasing refusal.

He stood up with the grace of a large, jungle cat, walked slowly over to her and pulled her to her feet. "Tell me," he said again quietly when he had her in his arms. The anticipation was like a slow-acting drug, and he softly placed leisurely, open-mouthed kisses on her temples, her eyelids, her cheeks and finally the corners of her mouth.

Wetting her lips again, she crooked her finger, wordlessly telling him to bend down. Closing her eyes, she put her mouth on his ear and softly, teasingly whispered her secret talent.

Brian's hands tightened on her waist as he got the gist of her sensual promise, and eyes that had closed the moment he felt her lips on his ear suddenly opened in amazed speculation. Have mercy. "Can you do that?" he asked hoarsely. "Is that possible?"

Caroline wrapped her arms around his waist, rested her head on his chest, closed her eyes and just enjoyed the feel of her body pressed to his. This roaring need for him was going to be her downfall. "Entirely."

CHAPTER 5

"Hi, baby."

"Mom!" Caroline said gladly into the phone When did you get back in town?"

"Your father and I got in last night at about 11. And before you ask, the trip to Montreal went well. Your father and I believe it's just a matter of time before we'll have the Grandmother's stores open there."

"That's great, Mom! I know you've been working hard to get this to happen for a long time." Caroline's father and uncle had started Grandmother's thirty-five years before, using recipes for strawberry and banana ice cream their grandmother had created.

"Anyway, baby, your father has taken himself off somewhere with one of his golfing buddies, and since I so rarely have a Saturday off to do what I want, I thought I'd call and see if you'd want to spend it with me. We could have lunch and go shopping and you can fill me in on what's going on in your life."

Caroline had a million things to do that day; her condo was a mess, she needed to do laundry, go grocery shopping and there were a host of other things that needed to be done. But she gave them up without regret and said "yes" to her mother's idea.

"That's wonderful, dear." Mrs. Singleton said. "How about we meet at Field's in about an hour?"

"Sounds great, Mom." Caroline said, never questioning that her mother meant the ritzy, flagship Marshall Fields department store on State Street. "See you there."

—⁓—

"Mom!" Caroline shouted as she spotted her mother through the summer crowd. Waving, she began walking towards her.

Patricia Singleton's eyes lit up as she watched her daughter's long, lazy saunter as it cut through the throngs of people on the sidewalk. She shook her head and smiled in admiration at Caroline's clothing. The girl had never in her life gone anywhere without looking like she'd just stepped off a Paris runway. The silk, peach blouse that tied in front at her midriff complimented the long, tangerine-orange, floral, sarong-styled skirt perfectly. She'd topped the outfit off with a large tangerine leather bag, a wide-brimmed straw hat with a tangerine scarf tied around it and strappy orange sandals.

"Hi, Mom." Caroline said when she reached her, and Patricia closed her eyes and let Caroline's light scent surround her as she was enveloped in her daughter's warm embrace. Pressing her cheek to her daughter's before she released her, Patricia studied her closely and said, "Hi, baby. You look good. Now, what has put that special smile on your face, and that hint of trouble in your eyes? Or should I be asking who?" Patricia said as she held her at arm's length and looked in her eyes.

Caroline laughed softly, and leaned in for another hug, "I swear Mama," she said falling back on the name she'd used in childhood. "Sometimes I think you must be able to read minds. Either that, or you must be omniscient."

"I can and I am—but only where my children are concerned." Patricia said only in half-amusement. She'd felt the slight desperation in that last hug her daughter had given her.

Caroline stepped back from her mother's arms and smiled. "Do you mind if we eat first and then go shopping? I didn't have breakfast, and I'm starving."

"Of course I don't, baby. Where would you like to go?" She asked as she put her arm through Caroline's and guided her down the street.

"It doesn't matter, you pick."

"All right then. We'll go to that little Italian restaurant right around the corner."

Caroline studied her mother as she sat across the table from her. The thick salt and pepper hair only added to the almost flawlessly smooth, brown skin. The deep brown eyes added a certain mystery to the beautiful face. It had never been a question as to whom she'd gotten her looks from. She had her mother's eyes, hair, skin and frame. She only hoped that she would age as well as her mother had. At fifty-five, Patricia was often thought to be in her early forties.

"Okay," Patricia said once their orders had been taken, "tell me who put that look on my baby's face and I'll have your big brother beat him up."

"Oh, Mom," Caroline said around a laugh and looked down as she fiddled with her silverware. "It's not like that, and besides, if Lee ever touched him, I'd never speak to him again," she said, not really teasing.

"Ah," Patricia said thoughtfully. "It's like that, is it? Who is he, how do you know him, and why haven't I heard about him before now?"

Caroline finally looked up at her mother and there were tears in her eyes. "Oh Mama, I think I'm in love," she whispered. "And there's nothing I can do about it."

Slightly alarmed, Patricia reached across the table and covered her daughter's hand. "What do you mean there's nothing you can do about it?"

"I'm sorry." Caroline said as she used her napkin to wipe away the tears that had begun to spill down her cheeks. "It's just that this has been going on for more than six weeks now, and it's killing me to have to hold everything in. It's so hard to pretend that there's nothing there when there's so much that sometimes I feel like I'll explode if things don't change soon."

"Don't apologize for crying Caroline, especially not to me. Now drink some water and explain what's going on." Patricia watched her daughter in concern as she drank the water She wondered what in the hell was going on. Six weeks?

Caroline drained the water and sat the glass down. Taking a deep, fortifying breath, she said, "That does feel better, thanks." Cutting to the chase, she said, "His name is Brian Keenan and I think I'm in love with him. I'm sorry I didn't tell you right away, but it hit me so hard, and then you were gone and…and…"

"And you wanted to savor your feelings alone for a while, I understand. But sweetheart, what I don't understand is why you say there's nothing you can do about it."

Caroline hedged. "Well…we work together and I'm not comfortable with having a relationship with someone I work with. In fact, he's my boss in a round-about way. He's the founder of the company." Caroline finished and watched as her mother's eyes briefly flared in surprise.

"Oh, I see. That is a sticky situation, isn't it?" Patricia said in complete understanding.

"Right, but Mom, it's so hard to deny myself. I mean, I want to do the normal things people do when they first start a relationship—hang out together, movies, dinner, long walks—whatever. I just want to be able to do something—anything—with him!"

"Well, honey, if you haven't done those things with him, how do you know you might be in love with him? I mean, it doesn't even sound like you two have even had a conversation."

Caroline squirmed uncomfortably in her chair for a moment, and then looked at her mother "Actually, we speak on the phone all the time. But…don't think this is weird Mom, but I just know, and I've known almost from the moment I laid eyes on him. It's hard to explain," she said when her mother looked at her in surprise. "It's just that it was instantaneous, and it was more than lust, although he is pretty sexy. I just knew, right away, that he was meant for me, and vice versa, of course. I knew him when I saw him, if you take my meaning. There was instant recognition when I first saw him, and I knew I would be miserable for the rest of my life if I didn't get to spend time with him."

Patricia studied her daughter quietly. She'd never talked like this before, not even as a teenager when most people are prone to believe in love at first sight. Caroline had always been practical and grounded in reality, and Patricia had been waiting for this day— this day when her daughter would come to her because love had hit her right between the eyes.

Now that the day had finally arrived, Patricia wanted to laugh from sheer delight. She didn't doubt that Caroline was in love, because at 30, her daughter had never once said that word about any man besides her father and brother before; she'd always been practical concerning matters of the heart, almost too practical. So if Caroline said she was in love, then Patricia knew it was the real thing.

"Well, baby, how does he feel?"

"I think he feels the same way I do. I mean, I haven't told him that I could be in love with him or anything, and he's never said it to me. But, he's as miserable as I am, and he felt it immediately as well. It was so weird Mama. As soon as we saw each other we wanted privacy to get to know one another better. I met him when I was going in for my second interview at Inclusion, of course I didn't know then that he's one of the founders. Anyway, he bumped into me in the lobby of the building, and when he stopped to help me pick up my things and our eyes met, it was like something you'd read in a romance novel, or hear in a love song. The world became still all of a sudden, as did everything inside of me. I know it sounds corny and sophomoric, but…internally, I just shook when I saw him that first time."

"It doesn't sound corny at all, baby. It sounds lovely," Patricia said, and felt her own eyes fill. Her baby was in love. "I'm so I'm happy for you, darling," she said and sniffed the tears back. "Now tell me all about him," Patricia said with a big, watery-edged smile as they were served their meals.

"Oh Mama, he's wonderful!" Caroline said as she sprinkled her pasta with Parmesan cheese. "That's the best way to describe him. He's smart, witty outgoing, personable, kind and funny—everyone at work loves him. But he's also the kind of guy not to be trifled with. And," she said holding up her hand in great drama. "This is the best part. He doesn't act crazy over this face of mine and the money thing doesn't matter.

Umm, what else can I tell you?" She said contempla-tively. "He's a technology whiz who used to be a cop."

"Your Brian used to be a police officer?"

"Yeah. He also used to be a lawyer. He says he left both professions because he realized he wasn't suited for them. Now he's the Chief Technology Officer at our firm."

"Well, at least you know he's intelligent—how could he not be, and be successful in the career he's chosen?"

"Right," Caroline said, and stalling took a sip of her lemonade. Deciding she couldn't put it off any longer, she said, "There's something else you should know Mom. Brian is also white."

"I see," Patricia finally said, after a long pause, and put her fork down. Seeing the crestfallen look on Caroline's face, she hurriedly said, "Well, I'm not going to lie and say that when I pictured you with the man of your dreams that he wasn't a black man, because he was." She put her hand over her daughter's once again. "However, darling, if he's a good man and treats you the way you deserve to be treated, then I don't care if he's black, white, orange, red or blue."

Caroline released the breath she didn't know she'd been holding. "I'm glad you said that. I have misgiv-ings myself. I'm still trying to work through them. I didn't know how you'd react, since it's not a subject that's come up before. How do you think Dad will take it?"

"Well your father's a different matter. I can't say he'll be happy about his daughter planning on dating a white man, but I think he'll come around. I'll get started on him, then maybe by the time he finally meets your Brian, he'll be able to be civil. And Caroline, I do expect to meet him. Soon."

"I know Mom, but with the situation being what it is, I don't see that happening in the near future."

"Well, if you're determined to be with this man, you'll work something out. You'll have to." Patricia said with finality, and took a bite of her chicken.

—∿—

Ida slapped money into Mac's large, wide palm. "That's $8,000 dollars Mac. I bet no one else has ever made that much money for you. And I bet no one makes it as fast. I want a larger cut."

Mac looked up from counting the money. "I can't authorize that Ida. I'll have to talk to the boss, but since you're already getting 10 percent, I doubt he'll give you more."

Ida scowled. "Then let me talk to him. I'm the one risking my job and my neck by selling his cocaine. I deserve more money."

"You know I can't take you to meet him Ida. Like I told you before, he doesn't like too much company. Just let me talk to him for you."

Ida studied Mac. He was fat with ruddy skin and dull brown hair. He looked like an ox. He was also about as stubborn as one. She knew she had no chance of changing his mind, but she had a contingency plan. "Okay then." She said with a false smile and watched in scorn as he breathed a sigh of relief— he was also as dumb as an ox. "It was worth a shot." She took her cut of the money and the fresh load of drugs from him and walked him to the door. "Since I'm doing so well for your boss, Mac, do you think he'd be willing to do something for me?"

Mac had reached out to put his hand on the knob and now he turned back towards her. "Like what? What are you asking?" He wondered if he could get her to admit to following him. Brickman wasn't happy about it, but he was waiting her out.

Ida was nonchalant. "Oh, you know like scare someone enough to make them go away."

"Yeah. Of course he could do that. The question is why would he want to?"

Ida thought about Caroline and how happy she'd be without her around. She ignored his question. "Thanks Mac. I'll call you when this batch runs out."

"You do that Ida." Mac said and let himself out.

Ida snatched up her keys and ran out behind him. She watched as he got on the elevator at the end of the hail and then ran to the stairwell. She ran down the three flights of stairs to the first floor and made it out the door and to her car just as Mac ambled through the front door of the building.

She watched as Mac pulled out onto the street and let two cars pass before she followed. She would just see for herself what Mr. Brickman had to say about a raise. She knew it was Alex Brickman because that idiot Mac had let it slip one time. This time she wouldn't chicken out and drive away. She was determined to meet the big Kahuna at last. She needed the extra money and his help with Caroline.

Mac watched as Ida pulled into traffic and smiled. He'd known she'd follow him again. Brickman was going to be happy about this. He was finally going to meet Ida.

—~~~—

By July the Inclusion office was so busy, they had to hire three more people just to keep up with the demand. Caroline was no exception to the rule, and had been burning the candle at both ends for almost two weeks. She'd hired someone else to work in the department, bringing their total to four, but she knew that she would need to hire someone else soon, at least on a part-time basis.

Caroline leaned back in her chair, closed her eyes and rubbed her temples in an effort to relieve the tension there. She knew she wouldn't be able to keep up the frenetic pace much longer: she was exhausted, her diet was suffering, her temper was frazzled and she hadn't had a free weekend since she'd had lunch with her mother. To make matters worse, Ida was turning out to be to be a bigger problem than Caroline had originally thought she'd be.

For some reason, the other woman disliked Caroline and had set about making her job harder than necessary. It wasn't just the snide comments—though those were bad enough—it was her making it almost impossible for Caroline to get needed supplies or having to wait an entire week for the air conditioning in her office to be fixed. Caroline had finally had to speak to Carl, something she'd hated doing. However, she didn't feel like she'd had a choice, as the temperature had been hovering around the 90-degree mark since May, and it was unreasonable for her to have to suffer.

She'd tried everything to get Ida to get the air conditioning fixed; she'd even told her to give her the phone number and she'd call herself. Ida had made some nasty comment about Caroline being far too important for such a menial chore and had refused to give her the number. The final straw for Caroline was when she'd learned that Justin's air conditioner had stopped working three days after hers had, but his had gotten fixed the next day. In further frustration, she'd learned that the repairman had come while she was at lunch and Ida hadn't told him to fix hers while he was there.

When Caroline had confronted Ida about this latest slight, Ida had sniffed and said Caroline should have been present while the repairman had been in the office, as Ida wouldn't dare dream of entering her office when she wasn't there. Instead of screaming, as she had wanted, Caroline had marched past Ida, and after a brief knock, straight into Carl's office. She'd felt like a child tattling, as she'd told him that her air conditioning had been out for a week and had yet to be repaired. When Carl asked why Ida hadn't arranged it, Caroline had simply said that she'd asked her to have it fixed, but as yet, Ida seemed incapable of doing it, or perhaps she was just too busy. She'd gone on to say, in confusion of course, that she understood the repairman had been in to fix Justin's just the day before, but he hadn't fixed hers and she didn't understand why.

Carl had promised to make sure it was fixed by the end of day, and as Caroline had left their area, she'd heard Carl call Ida into his office. She didn't know what was said between the two of them, she only knew that her air was back on by day's end as Carl had promised, and that was all she cared about. Of course now Ida's dislike had reached vitriolic levels, and the malice that poured from her now like a geyser, threatened to poison Caroline in its ferocity.

Caroline opened one eye in surprise at the knock at her door She'd thought she was the only one still in the office. "Come in," she called without moving from her comfortable position. It was after eight, so she could be a little lax. Whoever was at the door would understand. She even closed her eyes again.

"It figures," Ida said mockingly. "I knew you were lazy, and it was just a matter of time before I was proven correct."

Caroline sighed, but still didn't open her eyes. The headache that had begun to fade, now came back full force. "What do you want Ida?"

Ida looked at Caroline for the hundredth time that day and for the hundredth time, she angrily suppressed an envious sigh. The tramp always wore the most expensive clothing. *My day will come, though,* she thought. *The deal I have with Brickman through Mac should start to pay off soon and I'll be rolling in it,* she told herself smugly.

She stalked over to Caroline's desk. Leaning over, she said furiously, "You think because your parents are rich and you wear expensive clothes that you're better than everyone else, but I've got news for you, you're no better than the rest of us!"

Caroline became alarmed at how close Ida was and warily opened her eyes. The pure anger and dislike in the other woman's voice propelled her to her feet. "I repeat Ida, what do you want?"

Ida's eyes narrowed as she said in a voice so full of anger that it only came out as a whisper. "You're such a phony, but I figure everyone will find out soon enough what I've known all along." She took a deep breath and stepped back. Dropping papers on the desk so they scattered everywhere, she said, "These came in for you, your highness."

Completely confused and taken aback by so much dislike, Caroline looked down at the papers. "How long have you had these?" she asked when she saw that they were design approvals from a client. "I've been looking for these for two days! I haven't been able to take the necessary next steps because of you!"

Thrilled that she'd been able to get a rise out of her, Ida said calmly and with a smirk on her face, "I have no idea what you're talking about. I just found those lying around. Can I help it if my desk gets loaded down with work, and it takes me two days to get to stuff sometimes?"

"What were they doing on your desk anyway? They clearly have my name on them!" Caroline was enraged as she came from behind her desk to confront the other woman.

"As I said, I have no idea what you're talking about. Maybe your papers wouldn't end up on other people's desks if you deigned to check the fax machine once in a while. But you're too good for that. Aren't you Miss High and Mighty? You probably think that it's too menial a chore for you!" Ida said.

"I don't know what you're talking about, and frankly I don't care. All I'm concerned about is how these papers got on your desk and why you waited two days to give them to me."

"Well you should be concerned," Ida said, her voice becoming louder. "Or else more of your things may come up missing. What do you think of that, chica? Suppose one of your precious designs came up missing next time? I bet you'll be concerned then, won't you?"

"All right, Ida, that's it! I'm sick of you and your antics! So far, I haven't reported your behavior to the founders because I wanted to be sure that it wasn't my imagination, but you've crossed the line this time! I'll be reporting you tomorrow."

Ida only smirked again. "Go ahead. It will be your word against mine."

Caroline thought about what a big headache that could be—with her accusing and Ida denying and heaved a sigh. They could both potentially look like petty women in a catfight. The was the last thing she wanted, but she said anyway, "It doesn't matter. I may not be able to prove anything, but you give me little choice but to report you. And the next time you attempt to sabotage my work, there'll be a record of your having tried it the first time."

"Fine, whatever. Do what you want; you'll be the one left looking stupid." Ida was defiant.

Exasperated, Caroline said, "God, what is your problem Ida!"

"My problem? You think I've got a problem, puta? No, you're the one with the problem. And it'll get even bigger if I ever told everyone what I know about you!"

"What are you talking about?" The question came out as a strangled scream.

"I saw you, you slut. I saw you outside with Brian. You didn't think anyone saw you, did you?" Ida asked disgustedly when she saw the surprise on Caroline's face. "For God's sake, you were right outside the building and in the conference room! And when the other founders find out, you'll be out on your ass so fast, you'll leave skidmarks!"

Marshaling her defenses, Caroline became ramrod straight, looked Ida in the eye and said, "So what. You saw me outside the building and in the conference room with Brian. It doesn't mean anything. Besides, why on God's green earth should you care?" She figured if Ida had actually seen the kiss, she'd have reported it long ago.

The smirk left Ida's face for a moment and then she said, "Oh I care, but not for the reasons you may think. I care because your sleeping with Brian gives you an unfair advantage over the rest of us. No one should be getting any special favors—we should be rewarded based on merit, not on how we perform on our backs."

Although her heart was racing a mile a minute, Caroline fixed her face in bland lines and said, "God, you're crude, but that's neither here nor there. I want you to get out of my office, Ida. Get out. I have nothing to say to you or about your petty, little insults."

"Pretend all you want, puta, but I know the truth." Ida said before she turned and stalked out.

Caroline slumped down in her chair, and put her face in her hands. She knew that Ida couldn't do anything, but it still bothered her that the woman had seen Brian and her together. Ida could never prove that Brian had given her any special favors, because there hadn't been any. She and Brian never even worked together and they rarely saw one another, unless it was at their weekly company meetings. But of all the people to see them, why did it have to be the one person who hated her? Caroline sighed and tried not to let this new knowledge taint her pleasurable memories of those meetings.

She straightened in her chair. There was nothing she could do about Ida knowing about Brian's and her attraction. She took solace in the fact that Ida had not seen anything, because if she had she would have told by now. She flipped through the drawings on her desk and wondered how Ida had gotten the black eye that she was trying unsuccessfully to cover with makeup.

Sitting at her desk, Ida took deep, calming breaths and studied her eye critically in her mirror. She knew Caroline had noticed the bruise, but she couldn't regret it as she applied more makeup. Brickman hadn't been happy when she'd shown up behind Mac that day, but at least now she was in and close to getting rid of Caroline. That poaching bitch would learn to stay away from what rightfully belonged to others.

CHAPTER 6

Caroline stood at the entrance of her building and craned her neck to see if Brian was coming. When she saw no sign of him, she looked at her watch, and saw that she was a few minutes early. She smiled to herself as she remembered how she'd frantically showered and dressed in preparation for his visit. It appeared that she'd been wrong when she'd assumed all of her gussying up had taken up too much time and would make her late. She was on time, with five minutes to spare. She looked down at herself to make sure everything was in place. She'd chosen the sleeveless sundress with its slightly flared miniskirt to keep cool, yes, but she'd also chosen it because she knew the pale yellow cotton flattered her coloring. Because it was so hot, she'd taken her hair and pulled it into a loose ponytail at the nape of her neck.

When Brian did arrive, his eyes flared when he first caught sight of her. She ignored the fluttering in her stomach, as he looked her over in undisguised need. "Hi—"

Her words were cut off as he grabbed her hand and pulled her with him around the building and into the parking garage. "What are you doing?"

"How about a kiss, beautiful?" He backed into the wall and pulled her close.

Caroline decided to stop fighting her attraction and stood on her toes to fit her body more comfortably to his. She'd wanted this for a long time and she was feeling reckless after her confrontation with Ida.

Brian bent his head and covered her mouth, tantalizing her with brief, open-mouthed kisses. Now that he was finally getting a taste of her again, he didn't want to rush it. Her light, breezy scent was making him heady, and he deeply inhaled it as he moved from her mouth to her chin and then finally her neck.

Caroline tired of waiting and ducked her head to force a full kiss by gently capturing his bottom lip between her teeth. He groaned and she softly…slowly licked the small wound.

Still groaning, Brian maneuvered her so that her back was against the wall and ravenously explored her mouth in a kiss that was so openly carnal that Caroline felt her breath catch and her knees turn to water. Wrapping her arms tightly around his neck, she welcomed his tongue by drawing it in and delicately sucking. Liquid heat rushed to her stomach, and she broke the kiss off to catch her breath and gather her thoughts. She rested her head on his chest. "Oh God." She whispered almost despairingly.

Brian kissed the top of her head in commiseration. "I know." And in a move that shouldn't have been familiar or comfortable, but was both completely, he palmed her bottom, and let his hand rest there. "Are you all right? After your call about Ida—"

She shivered and nodded as she stepped out of his arms to walk out of the garage. She really didn't want to talk about Ida and she kept walking without saying anything.

Brian stopped her with a hand to her arm. "Caroline. Talk to me. Less than an hour ago, you were practically in tears on the phone and it was all about Ida. Now you act as if nothing is wrong."

Caroline remembered her frantic call to Brian all too clearly and wanted to squirm in embarrassment as the conversation played through her mind.

"Listen Brian," she said. "We've got to be more careful of how we act at the office. I've just found out that Ida saw us in the gangway that day and she's threatening to tell the other—"

"That's ridiculous; she's got nothing to tell!" he yelled into the receiver. "I barely see or talk to you as it is at the office and now you're telling me to scale it back. Hell, there's nothing to scale back!"

Feeling her own anger and frustration rise to the surface, Caroline said, "Don't yell at me! I'm only trying to tell you that Ida saw us, that's all, so we need to be extra careful!"

"I'm already as careful as I'm going to get! I'm sick of this; it makes no sense! I wish—"

"What?! You wish what?!"

"I wish this wasn't happening, that's what. I wish things weren't so up in the air!"

"That's not fair, and you know it. Even if I were willing to get our relationship started while we worked together, you would still have to follow company policy and not see me. I refuse to ignore my feelings about our different ethnicities, so don't ask me to." Her frustration and anger made her perilously close to tears, and she hated herself for it.

Brian had heard them in her voice and sighed. "Are you crying?"

"No," she said through her clogged throat, and sniffled loudly.

"You are. Come on baby. I'm sorry, don't cry. I'm frustrated, and I'm taking it out on you. It's just that I want so much for us to be together. I want to do the things that couples do, you know? I want to be able to hold your hand in public and not care who sees it. I want to take you to dinner. Hell, I'd even settle for being able to have a cup of coffee with you."

The longing his words invoked in her made Caroline catch her breath and the hated tears spill down her cheeks. "Now look what you've done. I hate to cry; it's silly and it accomplishes nothing except to make me feel stupid."

"If we had a different relationship, I could come over and comfort you. I'd take you in my arms and just hold you. What if I came over now? I promise, we'll both feel better."

Tempted beyond belief, Caroline remained silent for a few moments. Finally, taking a deep breath and biting her lip, she said softly, "God, Brian, I really want you to. You don't know how much—"

"That's the point Caroline; I do know how much, because I want to just as much. You're not alone in this, you know. Let me come over and we'll talk."

On the verge of capitulation, in a small voice she asked, "Just talk?"

"I'll promise, if you will."

"I don't think I can," she said in an even smaller voice than before.

He said quietly, "Whatever you want to do Caroline, I'll do it. Believe me, it won't be a hardship as long as it involves seeing you."

"You can come over, but you'll take me to dinner. I'll meet you outside my building. I don't think it would be a good idea for us to be alone anywhere."

"If dinner's what you want, then I'll take you to dinner."

"What time will you get here?" She asked.

"I can be there in 45 minutes."

"Okay. I'll be ready."

"Caroline?" Brian lightly shook her arm and jolted her out of her memory. "Are you going to finish telling me about Ida?"

"There's not much more to tell. I had a little confrontation with her this evening and I let her worry me, that's all. I'm fine now, I promise."

Brian didn't look convinced. "We'll pick this up at the restaurant." He steered her towards the street.

Caroline felt her hair brush her shoulders and said, "I'm sure I look a mess with my hair down like this. What got into you?"

"You in that dress got into me. I do not have the resistance of a saint. Hell, I don't want it." He keyed open the passenger door and helped her into the car.

Caroline located her compact. "Okay, whatever." She said distractedly and flipped open the compact. "Look at me! My hair looks like it's been through a tornado! And in this humidity, it's liable to expand to twice its normal size."

Brian smiled unrepentantly as he put on his seat belt. "I think it's beautiful. You're beautiful."

Caroline held out her hand and said flatly, "This is no time for games. Give it."

Brian tried to look innocent. "Give what?"

"You know what—my ponytail holder"

Choosing to skip the preliminaries, Caroline surprised him and dove across her seat and began checking his pockets. He laughed as he found himself trapped by his seat belt. She straddled his lap. "Okay," she said as she trapped his hands on either side of his head, "now you're in for it. Now I'm going to have to get down and dirty."

He laughed up into her face. "Do what you have to do. I can take it."

Caroline leaned down so that her breath feathered across his lips. "Brian?"

Staring at her mouth, he mumbled, "Hmm?"

Feathering his mouth and chin with clinging kisses that teased in their lingering, she said, "I really need my ponytail holder. If I have to go to a restaurant looking like this," she continued as she spaced each word with a kiss, "you'll regret it."

"Mm hmm," Brian said as he tried to capture her mouth with his.

"I mean it," she whispered, releasing his hands to continue her search. Keeping her mouth tantalizingly out of reach, she hit pay dirt when she checked his back pocket. "Brian," she whispered again and watched as his eyes slowly opened.

"Hmm?"

"Thanks!" she said, and moved off of his lap before the excitement killed her.

Brian watched as she fixed her hair. "You really do play dirty."

The teasing abruptly stopped once they sat down in the restaurant and began discussing Ida. She explained to Brian what had happened and he became furious, calling Ida a vindictive little bitch. Trying to reassure him, she told him that she was fine and had handled Ida.

Refusing to be placated, he threatened to have Ida written up for unprofessional behavior for what she'd done with the fax and for her threats to do damage to Caroline's art work. "This should go in her file; it's completely unacceptable behavior."

"That's the very last thing you should do. It would give credence to what she said about you giving me special favors. I know how to handle Ida." Caroline said.

"Listen Caroline, I know Ida and doing nothing about the situation won't stop her from doing something worse next time."

"I didn't say I wasn't going to do anything. And how do you know how she'll react?"

"I dated her and I know how she operates."

"You dated her?" Caroline was stunned.

"Yes. It was a few years ago. In fact, I'm indirectly responsible for her working at Inclusion. When we were dating, I asked Justin to ask Carl about any available positions at his firm. There was one and she started working with Carl. He liked her work so much, that when he left to form Inclusion, he asked Ida to come along." Brian finished and noticed that she was just staring at him. "Are you okay?"

"I'm fine, just surprised. How long did the two of you date?"

"Six months."

"What was the cause of the break-up?" She asked, still surprised.

"She's too damned possessive. I couldn't take it anymore, and I told her it was over."

"Wow. I never would have guessed it. You and Ida. No wonder she was acting so intense about seeing us those times. I *thought* her reaction was completely irrational—considering what she was reacting to. Maybe she wants you back."

"She does, but there's no chance that will ever happen. I've already told her that. Even before I met you, there was no chance I'd have gotten back together with her. Our relationship has been over for more than two years now, and I never even saw her again until she started working at Inclusion. So if she still has that idea in her head, I've done nothing to encourage it."

Caroline remained quiet for a while and he asked, "Does it bother you that I dated Ida?"

"No, that's in the past," she said. "I understand why you started dating her; she's beautiful. I guess I don't understand how you could have stayed as long as you did."

"Well, she wasn't possessive at first. It wasn't until we'd been dating for a few months that I saw that side of her."

"I can imagine she made things difficult for you when you broke up with her."

"At first she did, yeah. But then I guess she realized that things weren't going to go back to the way they were and she stopped calling me."

"Hmm. So now what?" Caroline asked.

"What do you mean?"

"I mean I can tell from the look on your face that you're planning something, and I want to know what it is. I don't want you saying anything at all to Ida about that fax."

"There's nothing for you to worry about." Brian said.

"Brian, don't do anything! I told you I handled her."

"As a founder, I have a perfect right—in fact, I have a responsibility—to reprimand an employee when she has deliberately sabotaged the work of another employee."

"Brian," she began furiously and urgently, "If you say anything—anything at all—to Ida about what happened today, I'll never forgive you."

"Listen, Caroline," he began patiently, "Ida has broken several rules, chief among them was keeping your fax and delaying the project. She has to be dealt with."

"Yes, but not by you."

"I'll handle it, Caroline," he said with a finality that suggested she stop discussing the topic.

Caroline snorted. Whatever, she thought. "If you do, she might tell everyone what she thinks she saw. I don't want to become the subject of rumor and innuendo."

"It won't happen like that, because she didn't see anything. All she can say is that she *thinks* there's something between us."

"That will be enough to give me a bad reputation. I don't need you to protect me. I can take care of Ida."

"How will you take care of her? Look how long it took before your air conditioning was fixed. If you'd come to me with it, you wouldn't have had to suffer."

"Let's get this straight, Brian. For as long as you and I are working together at the same company, I will never come to you to fix any problems I may have. It would be like a teenager running to her boyfriend and ratting out a bully."

"So? What's wrong with that?" Brian shrugged unconcernedly. "I am—for lack of a better term—your boyfriend. I'm supposed to take care of you."

Sighing heavily and eyeing him with narrowed, irritated eyes, she said, "You're not my boyfriend—"

Brian's laid-back slouch suddenly became alert. "It appears that I'm not the only one who needs to get something straight here. You belong to me, and you have ever since we bumped into each other in May. Just because we haven't been able to have a traditional relationship, don't mistake the matter—I have only been delayed, not dissuaded. You're mine in every sense but the physical one."

Flabbergasted and insulted both at the same time, she said, "Now wait just a damn minute!"

"No, you wait a minute," Brian said calmly, but still with the same implacability. "You and I belong together, and there's no sense in pretending otherwise simply because we've had to delay the process. When I say you belong to me, I'm not trying to be chauvinistic. I'm saying that you belong to me, I belong to you and we belong to each other."

"I disagree completely." She said furiously. "Nobody belongs to anybody. I'm not a thing to be owned."

Brian studied her. "That's not at all what I'm saying. Let's just say that I don't like it when people are treated unfairly and when I have the power to do something about it, I do."

"Um hmm. Translation: You're going to go Neanderthal on me and talk to Ida."

Brian only smiled.

"God, you're infuriating!"

"So I've been told." He said around a self-satisfied grin. "But seriously Caroline, I know why you hesitate to have a relationship, but don't you think things would be less complicated if we weren't working together? I can't take much more of this. I can't see you when I want, can't talk to you when I want. It's really ridiculous."

"Wait a minute. Slow down. Even if this were a traditional relationship; I'd have to say that things are moving too fast."

"Do you really think so? Everything feels so right to me. I mean, there are no set parameters on what speed a relationship should progress at. Everyone's situation is different. And speaking for myself, I have never felt this way about anyone so quickly before and I'm compelled to go forward."

"That may be true, but I feel our pace has been too fast."

"Fine, we can slow it down. That still doesn't take care of the work situation."

"I'm not quitting. That's out of the question." Caroline said.

"I'm not asking you to quit. I've got some thinking of my own to do."

"What do you mean? I won't let you give up the—"

"Well now, it looks like what I give up will be my decision, as it's mine to give up, isn't it?" he said, unconsciously sounding like his Irish mother.

"Brian," she said anxiously, drawing the word out to its fullest extent in desperation. "Don't do anything you'll regret."

"I know what I'm doing."

Caroline went to bed with a heavy heart that night as she thought about their predicament. Brian would be leaving town the next week for a technology conference. He'd be gone for more than a week. Things should be considerably less stressful at the office without him there.

CHAPTER 7

When she heard the doorbell ring, Caroline froze in the act of putting lotion on her legs. Making sure the belt to her short, summer robe was tied securely, she checked herself in her bedroom mirror. Seeing a worried face with big, nervous eyes, she pressed her hand to her stomach. God, part of her had been anxiously waiting for this moment for almost three months, and now that it had finally arrived, she was scared to death.

She knew who was at her door. Even though she hadn't spoken to him in more than a week, she knew Brian was at her door. She knew he'd come over when he found out, but she didn't think it would be so soon. Which explained why her hair was still wet and up in a towel, and she'd only had time to put on her panties before she slipped her robe on over her freshly showered and scented body.

When the doorbell rang again and she imagined she could feel his impatience shimmering through its musical peal, she gave her face one last look and left her room. "Coming," she called softly, but knew he heard her. She stood frozen in front of the door. It was one thing to want someone and not know when you'd be able to consummate things, but it was another thing to have the consummation right upon you and know that you had to deny yourself and your would-be lover.

"Caroline," Brian said and the rough urgency in his voice sent a delicious shiver down her spine. "Let me in, baby."

The obvious sexual tension in his voice worried her and she decided to go get dressed. The bell rang again and Caroline indecisively stepped closer to the door. "I'll only let you in to talk."

Taking a deep breath, she pulled the door open. God, he looked good. He stood there in his jeans and a black T-shirt with his arms spanning the width of her doorway and looked down at her with hot, ready, determined eyes.

"Uh, hi…" Nervously, she wet her lips, and like a predator who's sighted his prey, his eyes lasered in on the small movement. Making a harsh sound in his throat, he placed his hands under her arms, picked her up and stepped in, pushing the door closed with his foot. Caroline braced her hands on his shoulders and looked down at him. "Open your legs," he said roughly, and she did, wrapping them around his waist and crossing her ankles. She forgot all about the talk that she'd planned to have with him.

Twin groans of relief and ecstasy escaped their throats as she settled upon the hard bulge in his jeans. It was like coming home, and her mind wiped clean of all thoughts, Caroline clutched his shoulders and began to rock forward. Brian moaned and turned so that her back was against the door. Removing the towel from her head, he buried his hands in her hair. "I've been dying to get my hands in this for weeks," he said huskily. He pulled it gently so that her head fell back and her neck arched. The pure, clean, brown line of it made him clench his teeth and he bent his head to feast and devour. Using his teeth and his tongue, he traveled the length of it, making her cry out.

Nuzzling the cotton of her robe aside, he sucked her collarbone and soothed it with gentle laps of his tongue. When he reached her breasts, he sucked in a breath at their beautiful, smooth roundness. Pushing the sides of her robe even further apart, he buried his face in the small globes and inhaled her scent. Caroline let out a little, feminine squeak of desire and held the back of his head. Brian pushed the robe off her shoulders, freeing her breasts completely. Seeing that her dark brown nipples were hard and distended, he gave them his mouth's attention. She felt her breathing sharply cut off. "Oh, God Brian," she said as she felt the pulling of his mouth all the way in her stomach.

Tangling her hands in his hair, she began tugging frantically. "Kiss me Brian. You…haven't…aahh…kissed me yet."

He ignored her plea at first, making sure he gave both nipples equal attention and making her squirm restlessly in the process. Lifting his head, he watched her intently as he methodically rocked his hips against her. It wasn't until she closed her eyes in aching pleasure that he captured her mouth with his, using his tongue to lap up what he had come to think of as his own personal ambrosia.

Caroline accepted his tongue hungrily, turning her head sideways and bringing her hands up on either side of his head to hold him in place so she could better partake of her own feast. Brian tore his mouth from hers and touched his forehead to hers. "I need a bed. Where is the bed, Caroline?"

Caught up in their intimacy, Caroline didn't hear him. Brian caught her securely under her buttocks and slowly lifted her so that she was straddling his stomach. Making a soft sound of protest, Caroline opened her eyes and looked at him. "Brian, please," she whispered plaintively.

Unable to resist her heavy-eyed sexiness, Brian bent his head. "The bed, sweetheart. Where is it?" He asked with his mouth against her and kissed her.

Caroline fought the sensual fog. "Hmm? What?"

Brian smiled. "I said tell me where the bed is, unless you want our first time together to be against your front door."

Caroline became instantly alert. She hadn't meant for things to go so far. Pushing against his shoulders, she pulled the sides of her robe together, and tried to unwrap her legs from around his waist. 'Put me down.'

"What?" Brian asked, holding her in place.

"We can't do this right now, Brian. I meant for us to talk—not have …not do…uh, do this." She said while still struggling to get down.

Brian merely tightened his grip under her thighs. "Talk?" he said looking at her. "What do you mean—talk? Baby, the last thing I want to do right now is *talk.*"

Caroline avoided his eyes. "I'm sorry I let things go so far, but we do need to talk." The situation couldn't have been more embarrassing for her.

Brian sighed heavily and fought back his frustration. Taking his eyes from her, he saw that they were at the end of a long hallway. He began walking while still holding her. He figured there would be some place where he could sit down.

Coming to a large living area, he spotted a long, cream-colored sofa and carried her to it. "Now," he said once he was seated with her ensconced in his lap. "Explain."

Caroline bit her lip and gave him a sidelong glance. She started to remove herself from his lap and found that she couldn't budge. "Brian, will you let me up, please?"

"No," Brian tightened his grip on each thigh as they straddled him. "At least not until you explain," he said. "I mean two minutes ago, I was all but inside of you, and now you're sitting here with swollen lips and seductive eyes and saying we need to talk. I'm asking you to please explain."

She felt her face heat and avoided his eyes again as she looked down and fiddled with a loose thread on his shirt. She couldn't believe she was having this conversation.

Brian looked up at the ceiling as if asking for divine intervention. "Caroline," he said as he slid his hands beneath the ends of her robe to stroke her thighs. "Whatever it is, it can't be that bad. Just tell me."

She took a deep breath and swallowed her consternation. "We can't do anything," she said, looking at him with determination, "because I don't have any protection."

Brian laughed in relief. "Is that all? You don't have to worry about that. I brought condoms."

"No, that's not all. We still can't Brian, because I want my own protection. I would just feel safer that way."

Seeing the stubborn set to her mouth, he sighed in resignation. "This may seem like a silly question, but why don't you have protection?"

"I have an appointment with my gynecologist on Monday."

"Monday? Today is Friday; that's a whole three days."

"I'm aware of that, but I couldn't get an appointment sooner."

"The soonest appointment you could get was for next Monday? It takes that long?"

Caroline shrugged her shoulders and began to pull at the thread again. "I only just made it last Friday."

"Last Friday? But when I got to the office and Justin said you'd only given a few days' notice before quitting, I thought for sure that meant you were ready for a relationship with me." His frustration was clear.

Frustrated herself, tired of being embarrassed and taking exception to his attitude, Caroline moved from his lap, and this time he let her. Standing over him, all dignity, despite having the look of someone who has just been debauched, she said, "Well you assume too much! Besides, I wouldn't know the usual procedure for getting birth control, as I have no experience with this sort of thing! You stupid...baboon!" Turning on her heel, she stalked away.

Baffled by her sudden anger and her words, Brian could only watch her slim back as it disappeared around a corner. "What does she mean, 'no experience'," he mumbled to himself. "No experience?" he said again, and when it dawned on him that there was only one thing she could possibly mean, he shot off the couch. "Caroline!"

He found her in the kitchen, with her back to him and looking out the window. "Caroline...baby," he said softly and started toward her. She whipped her head around and the dangerous glint in her eyes told him not to try to touch her. He ignored it, and gently grasped her shoulders to turn her to face him. "Sweetheart, why didn't you tell me?" He asked simply.

His soft question melted her anger, and once again she shrugged her shoulders. "It just never came up. We've barely even spent any time together. What was I supposed to do—just blurt it out? When I spent time with you, the fact that I'm a virgin never even entered my mind."

"Caroline, you overwhelm me," Brian said softly and meant it. "I couldn't be more surprised. You don't kiss like you're inexperienced, and you sure as hell don't tease like you are. Hell, your kisses turn me on faster than the time it takes to switch on a light."

She smiled. "Well, I'm not a complete neophyte. I had boyfriends before I met you. I'm a virgin, but I'm not naïve or ignorant about sex."

"Why were they so unlucky?"

"I just never wanted to with any of them. None of them were worth going on the pill for. I don't even know if you're worth it."

"What are you getting at?" Brian asked.

Caroline laughed at the suspicious look on his face. "I mean that I may not go on the pill because I don't like the idea of putting foreign objects in my body. I've heard some horror stories about the pill, and I want to be careful, that's all. That's why I'm going to my gynecologist on Monday. There are alternatives to the pill, you know."

Brian pulled her fully into his arms and hugged her close. Breathing in the scent of her hair, he closed his eyes. Words couldn't express how thrilled he was to be the first, and he was thinking the only, man to possess her. Maybe his feelings made him a chauvinist, but he didn't care. "I wish Monday would hurry up and get here."

Caroline stepped out of his arms. "That's part of what I wanted to talk to you about," she said and sat down at the table.

Brian followed and sat down as well. "What?"

"Whatever birth control I get on Monday, I still think we should wait before we make love."

After what he'd just learned from her, he wasn't surprised. "Okay," he said simply.

"You're not surprised? I mean, I don't mean to be a tease, but it seems that every time I'm near you my actions completely contradict my words. I never intend to get physical with you, but that's the way it always ends up. So I wouldn't be surprised if you thought I was ready for things to become more intimate between us." Caroline said.

"I admit that it makes me crazy when things like what happened today happen, but I'm the one who initiates it. However, you always respond arid that reassures me that you are interested. But to answer your question, I'm not surprised that you want to wait. The fact that you're still a virgin at 30 tells me that you need to trust before you sleep with someone."

"I don't mistrust you Brian. I just don't know if I trust us as a couple. I don't even know if I'll be able to handle it. But," she paused and took a fortifying breath. "I am willing to see what dating you would be like. I realized that I should at least give it a try. So, I want us to date first, you know? I want to see what that's like before I make a decision to go any further. These last few months have been a roller coaster ride, and we've barely had time to catch our breaths. Nothing has been normal with us from the beginning, and I want us to have normalcy. Well, actually, I want to see if we can have a normal relationship, given the circumstances."

"I don't think the fact that you're black and I'm white will make things that difficult, Caroline. I'm not expecting things to be easy, but I don't expect things to be exceptionally hard either."

"We'll see."

"That's all I'm asking for."

"Good, I'm glad you understand. Now let me fix my hair, and we'll have lunch."

He trailed her from the kitchen. "What are you going to do to your hair?" He asked with interest.

"Oh, I'm going to wet it and put some moisturizer in it so it doesn't dry out."

"Get the stuff, and show me how. I'll do it."

Caroline stopped, turned and looked at him. She considered him for a moment before asking, "What is your fascination with my hair?"

"It's not fascination. I'm in love with it." He said simply as he studied it.

Startled, Caroline laughed. "You can't be in love with hair, Brian."

"I am with yours," he said. "I love its thickness, its fullness and how alive it is. I love to see you wear it down, which you rarely do," he finished accusingly. "Why not?"

"Because it's been too hot outside. I never wear it down when it's this hot, and the humidity is high. It's too much of a burden."

"Hmm," he said noncommittally. "Are you going to let me put the moisturizer in it for you?"

"Sure," she said with a shrug. "I love it when people play in my hair. It'll be just like going to the hair-dresser's."

Later, Brian sat on the couch and squirted a thin, coconut-smelling lotion onto a piece of saran wrap that he'd flattened on the table, as Caroline had instructed. Still following her instructions, he dipped his fingertips into the moisturizer. "Now what?" He asked Caroline as she sat on the floor between his spread knees.

"Just take your fingertips and massage my scalp. That will get the moisturizer in really good." Caroline said. "Do it all over." She'd washed again and had gotten dressed in a blue and white striped T-shirt and white Capri pants.

Brian plunged his hands into her hair, and watched as the soft mass completely covered his hands. Like vines, it clung to his wrists and hands like it was alive. There seemed to be masses and masses of the thick stuff and he reveled in it. He learned the shape of her skull as he ran his fingers over her scalp, not missing an inch.

At his knees, Caroline closed her eyes and softly groaned at the intimacy of him doing her hair. Taking the saran wrap, Brian flattened it on his palm so that he could take up the rest of the moisturizer. He rubbed his palms together and then put his hands in her hair again, this time concentrating on the hair itself. "Make sure you get the ends of my hair, Brian. They dry out the quickest." Caroline said.

"I'm at your service," Brian said softly and leaned down to gently kiss the vulnerable curve behind her ear.

Caroline shivered, and said in soft warning as she closed her eyes, "We can't finish what you're about to start."

"I know," Brian said and smoothed his hands over her hair. "But we can have fun just getting there." Picking up the brush she'd given him, he brushed her hair in a backward motion until he was satisfied he was finished.

Caroline handed him a black barrette over her shoulder and winced as he roughly tried to gather all of her hair in one hand. Brian struggled some more and looked at the barrette and then at the hair he was barely able to hold in his wide fist. The task struck him as impossible and he said, "Sorry, babe, it can't be done."

Caroline reached over her shoulder, palm out and waited until he placed the barrette in her hand. Taking the brush, she ran it through her hair a couple of times, gathered her hair in her hand and then efficiently snapped the barrette into place at the nape of her neck.

Brian looked at the neat, fluffy ponytail as it bounced between her shoulder blades when she stood.

Minutes before it had looked so defiant and uncontrollable. "How?"

Caroline turned to him and smiled. "Trust me, it took years of practice. Years. I was fourteen before I would let my mother stop wrestling with my hair I was too lazy to deal with it, and only shame made me finally take it on. All of my friends had been doing their own hair since they were twelve. Come on, I'll show you where the bathroom is so you can wash your hands."

Brian followed her, finally paying attention to her decor. Black and white photographs peppered one wall, while colorful paintings decorated another. He recognized two as being from the Impressionist period and as being the real deal. In addition to the long, cream sofa, she had a mahogany bench covered with cobalt and emerald green pillows and two expensive-looking matching arm chairs on either side of the fireplace that graced one side of the room. On the other side of the large, airy room, she kept a mahogany entertainment center. Near the bay window, she had two mahogany bookcases. The hardwood floors were polished to a gleam, with a Persian rug covering the length of the hall leading into the living area.

"I like your home," he said, uncomfortable with the quiet wealth surrounding him.

"Thank you," she said with a quick smile over her shoulder. "It took me six months to decorate it. My dad thought I should hire a decorator, but I insisted on doing it myself."

A decorator? Brian thought, but said aloud, "Well you did a good job. It fits your personality. It's warm, deep, sensual and comforting at the same time."

They were standing at the sink, and Caroline bumped him playfully with her hip. "Flattery will get you nowhere."

"Hey, I see an opportunity and I go for it," he said, forcibly pushing his concerns about her wealth out of his head. He turned to dry his hands on a rich red towel. "Which reminds me, why didn't you tell me about your opportunity? Why did I have to hear about it from someone else and a week after everyone else?"

"I wanted to surprise you, and I wanted everything to be taken care of by the time you got back into town." Caroline said as she left the room and went back into the kitchen. "That's why I asked Justin and those guys not to tell you over the phone, but to wait until you got back. I'm sure they thought it was a weird request, but no one really asked any questions."

"You knew how I would react when I found out. When Justin told me, I dropped everything, and rushed over here. I couldn't wait to get my hands on you."

"Well, I expected you to at least wait until after work to come over. I didn't expect you to show up in the middle of the day." She said as she checked her refrigerator to see if she had anything to eat. Finding nothing, she closed the door, turned around and found herself trapped between Brian and the refrigerator.

Smiling down at her, Brian said, "It sure made me happy to hear that you'd left the firm."

"Thanks," Caroline said wryly.

"You know what I mean," he said, familiarly sliding his hands under her T-shirt and smoothing them over her torso. "When Justin told me that you'd resigned and left the firm all within a week's time, I was ecstatic. It was a happy surprise."

"That's why I did it," Caroline said. "I wanted to call and tell you about the Rutledge Gallery offering me a January showing, but I figured it would be better for you to find out once you were back in Chicago. That way, you wouldn't be in Seattle wishing you were here instead." She finished.

"Never mind about me; tell me more about the show."

"Oh Brian, this is like a dream come true for me. I can't believe it! The Rutledge Gallery is one of the most prestigious in the country—in the world, for that matter, and they want to feature my work. At first I couldn't take it all in, you know? I mean, it seems I've been working towards this for most of my life, and suddenly, here it is."

Brian smiled at her excitement. "What all do you have to do?"

Unable to keep still, Caroline left his arms to pace the kitchen. "God, there's so much! I have to decide which of my pieces are usable and from there I'll know how much more to create. Not that *that* will be easy, considering I've never created on demand before, I mean, I just painted or sculpted when I couldn't do anything else, you know? Well, if you consider my work in advertising, I have created on demand before, but that was always from a concept already formed by someone else. This will be different because I first have to have an idea before I can paint or sculpt anything. And speaking of sculpting, I don't even know if I have anything that's good enough for a showing. I wonder if they would…" Caroline trailed off and smiled sheepishly when she saw how Brian was looking at her. "Sorry, I get carried away sometimes when it comes to my art."

"Don't apologize. I think this is great, and I'm dying to see your work. Where is it?"

"Oh, I don't keep it here. I have studio space a few blocks away. I do keep a few things here in case inspiration strikes, but the bulk of everything is in my studio."

"Well, when can we go? Here you are on the verge of becoming this famous artist, and I've yet to see anything but the stuff you've created at the office. Which, is very good, by the way."

Caroline smiled. "Thanks, but wait until you see the real deal. The stuff I do for work is not even on a par with it. Why don't we go to my studio after you've taken me to lunch? I'm starved."

"Sounds good to me."

CHAPTER 8

"Thanks for meeting me for lunch Caroline," Linda said as she and Caroline settled with their sandwiches at their table at Potbelly. "I know you're busy with your big show coming up and all." She said and took a bite of her turkey sandwich.

Caroline broke her sub apart along the cut-line and watched as steam escaped. "It's okay," she said with a smile. "I've been working pretty steadily since I left Inclusion, so I have the time." Taking a bite of the veggie sub, she grinned in happiness as the brown mustard and other spices flavored her tongue. "Potbelly is another thing I'll miss about not working at Inclusion. They have the best subs in town."

Linda grinned as Caroline licked sauce from her fingers. "I agree, they are the best. Taking a deep breath, she said, "So how are things going?"

Detecting a hint of nervousness in the younger woman's voice, Caroline said, "Fine. As I said, I've been working steadily in the weeks since I left Inclusion. Why don't you tell me what's on your mind?"

Uncomfortable, Linda avoided her eyes. Trust Caroline to get right to the point, she thought. "I don't know how to say this, except straight out. Ida's telling everyone that you left Inclusion because she found out you were sleeping with Brian and she was going to tell the rest of the founders. She says you quit before they could fire you. I know it isn't true, but I wanted to hear the real story from you—if you don't mind telling me, of course."

Caroline knew she shouldn't have been surprised that Ida would spread rumors about her, but she was. "No, I don't mind telling you. It's true that Brian and I are seeing each other, but I wasn't sleeping with him when I left Inclusion. And I didn't leave Inclusion so I could sleep with him, either. I left for the reason given at the time; I need to prepare for my show at the Rutledge Gallery."

"I knew Ida was lying!" Linda said.

"Believe me, I would have never left Inclusion just so I could sleep with someone. And I would never, ever have left unless I had something else lined up first."

"I'm so glad to hear that." Linda's eyes sparkled with interest as she asked, "When did you start seeing Brian?"

Caroline laughed. "I'm only telling you this, because I you're my friend. I met Brian the day I came into Inclusion for my second interview. However, I didn't know who he really was until after he showed up at the end of the interview. Once I found out who he was, I decided we shouldn't see each other."

"Why?"

"One of the reasons was because we worked together. So when I resigned from the company, that's when we started our relationship. End of story."

"Why didn't you tell me? I mean, I know we haven't known each other for very long, but I thought we had a good rapport." Linda looked hurt.

"We did and we do. I didn't tell you because it was supposed to be a secret and I didn't know if I wanted to take a chance on a relationship with him. And besides that, you talk too much. You tell everything you've ever known!" Caroline said.

Linda joined her in laughing. "Okay, that might be true, but I would have never told this. So how's it going? I mean, I can't believe you're dating babe-a-licious Brian of all people. You know he's like family to me, right?"

"Babe-a-licious Brian?" Caroline choked on her last bite of sandwich. "He told me about his relationship with your family, but I had no idea that that was the family's nickname for him."

"It's not." Linda said with a mischievous smile. "It was my sister's and my name for him. My sister slipped and called him it once. I thought he would die. We started calling him that when we were 12 and 13, and had discovered that the opposite sex could be attractive, and that Brian was the most attractive of them all. It was a riot. Whenever he came over, my sister and I would just stare at him and then fight with each other over who was going to hang up his coat or pass him the salt, or something equally silly."

Picturing how uncomfortable it would have been for Brian to have two young girls mooning over him and following him around, Caroline smiled. "It sounds so sweet." She said, eager to learn as much as she could about the man who so enthralled her.

Linda snorted. "Please. Don't kid yourself; this was a bloodthirsty, ruthless war between my sister and I, and to the victor went the spoils. It was just Brian's bad luck that we considered him the spoils. I bet he didn't tell you what I did to him when I was fifteen, did he?"

Fascinated, Caroline shook her head, "I can't say that he has, no."

"Well, it was Thanksgiving and Brian was coming over for dinner because he wasn't able to make it to his mom's house in Detroit. Anyway, I had decided that Brian Keenan was going to be my first. And I do mean first EVERYTHING. Not only was he going to give me my first real kiss, but he was also going to be my first lover. I pulled out all the stops. I borrowed this siren-red dress from a friend of mine, because my parents would never have allowed me to have anything like it in my closet. It had a straight, tight skirt on the bottom and the bodice kind of flared at the waist and scooped at the neck. The sleeves were 3/4 in length and were also tight fitting.

"My parents didn't allow my sister and me to really wear makeup until we were sixteen, but when I turned fifteen, my mom took me shopping for lipstick. I say all this so you'll know that I had no idea how to apply makeup or even what looked right on me, but I sure put it on that day! I put on eyeliner, lip liner, mascara and anything else I thought would make me look older. My face was one mass of colors; blood red lipstick, blue mascara, beige face powder—oh I was a mess. But I thought I was the bomb!

"To top off the ensemble, I went to my mother's closet and borrowed some four-inch heels that I had no idea how to walk in. Knowing my parents would make me take everything off if they saw me, I hid upstairs until Brian came. When the doorbell rang, I told myself that we truly were meant to be together because even my body knew instinctively that it was him at the door. I conveniently ignored the fact that we weren't going to have one, single, solitary guest other than him.

"So the doorbell rings, I go racing out of my room and tripping—not trippingly, mind you, but *tripping*—down the stairs, those four-inch heels almost making me break my neck—"

"Stop it, Linda," Caroline said with a weak wave of her hand. By this time, she was laughing so hard that her sides were hurting and other diners were starting to look at them.

"To continue," Linda said in bland tones, once Caroline had stopped laughing. "I made it to the door with just a slight limp, after calling out that I'd get it. I opened the door and just stared at him. I don't remember what he was wearing, but I do remember thinking that the sharp way he dressed was just another sign that the two of us should be together.

After all, I was always dressed to perfection myself. Anyway, the man didn't even notice what I was wearing as he stepped into the house.

"'Good afternoon, Brian,' I said in my most grown-up voice. He didn't even notice as he took his coat off and said 'Hey Lynn. Do an old man a favor and hang this up for me, will ya?'

"'You're not old,' I said. 'You're just mature.' 'Okay, kid.' He said. 'Whatever you say.' I held his coat in my arms like it was a precious first-born child, and then I tossed it on the stairway banister.I didn't have time for niceties; I needed to talk to him before my family started looking for him. I grabbed his arm and I dragged him into the den, which is in the opposite direction of the kitchen where my family was.

" 'I need to talk to you. It's very important,' I said. And before he knows it, he's got this skinny fifteen-year-old bundle of bones in his arms, pressing her lips to his and hanging on him like a barnacle. Despite all my joy and excitement, I finally realized he wasn't pressing his lips to mine in return, and I opened my eyes to find him looking down at me with all the panic of a fish on a hook.

"I finally released him and stepped back. I just knew he was going to tell my parents, or worse, not take me seriously. So I turned my back on him and waited. To my surprise he took my shoulders and turned me to face him. And do you know what he said Caroline?"

Absorbed in the story, Caroline could only shake her head no.

"He said that I was so beautiful that he didn't know why I would want to waste myself on him, but if I were sure that he was the one, then I should come back when I was 25 and let him know. Isn't that sweet? He saved my ego and my pride all at the same time. He knew if he'd said anything else, I would have balked. But as it was, he even convinced me to change my clothes and take off my makeup before he was through."

"What happened after that? Did your family find out?"

"No, I never told them, and it wasn't until I was about 18 that I figured out what he had done. I called him on it."

"No you didn't." Caroline said.

"Yes I did," Linda said matter-of-factly. "I only did it to tease him and see what his reaction would be. Predictably, he tried to pretend like he had no idea what I was talking about, and it became a game between us. Every year on my birthday I call him and tell him how many years I have left before I turn 25 and he always says he'll be waiting for me."

"I think that's lovely." Caroline said softly.

"Uh huh." Linda said. Pretending to study her nails, she said jokingly, "I only have three years left until I'm 25 Caroline."

Now it was Caroline's turn to snort. "Dreaming's good for you." She smiled as the other woman laughed in delight.

Linda settled down. "To be serious, I wasn't kidding when I said that Brian is like family. I'm here to gather information and report back to base, so to speak."

Caroline smiled again. "Do I pass muster?"

Linda grinned impishly. "With flying colors!"

———

Brian sat behind his desk and looked at the other three people sitting in his office. "I want to thank all of you guys for meeting with me. I won't take long."

"What's this about Brian?" Maria asked. She looked at Carl and Justin to see if they were as clueless as she was.

"Immediately after we complete this meeting, I'm going to be meeting with Ida. She's done several things in the past few weeks that should not be tolerated in a professional environment. I'm meeting with her to let her know that they will not be tolerated at Inclusion. I called this meeting with the three of you because I wanted you to know before I did anything." Brian looked at Carl and Maria to get their reactions. He'd already told Justin of his plans the night before.

"I don't understand. What are you talking about?" Carl asked.

"First, you guys should know that I'm dating Caroline Singleton, and have been since she left the company." He watched as Maria's brow rose in surprise and Carl's eyes narrowed in speculation.

"What's that got to do with this meeting?" Maria finally asked.

"It isn't just that I've been dating Caroline since she left. We've been attracted to each other since her second interview, but we didn't act on that attraction because…well it's obvious why not. At any rate, Ida figured out that there was an attraction and harassed Caroline about it." Caroline would kill him if she knew what he was doing.

"I repeat: what's that got to do with this meeting? I mean, Caroline no longer works here, so the point is moot." Maria said.

"Yes, but while Caroline was working here, Ida tried to sabotage her work. An example is a fax that Caroline looked for over a period of two days. They were design approvals from a client, and Ida had them hidden on her desk, knowing full well that Caroline was looking for them. Caroline reported it to Carl at the time."

"Yes she did," Carl began. "But there was nothing I could do since she had no proof and Ida flat-out denied doing it."

"Yes, I know that." Brian said. "But I also know Ida—we all know Ida—and it would not stretch the imagination at all to believe that she would do the things Caroline accused her of doing."

"As Maria said, though, Caroline no longer works here. So…I mean, we all know you used to date Ida, so we can probably assume that Ida reacted to Caroline that way out of jealousy because she suspected, for some reason, that you were interested in Caroline. She probably won't do anything else." Carl said with a shrug.

"Hey." Maria said in protest. "We can't just assume that this is female jealousy at work here. As far as I'm concerned, there's never a good reason to sabotage someone else's work, but let's not be stereotypical Carl."

"Her reasons for doing what she did don't matter." Justin finally joined the discussion. "Her conduct was, and is, unacceptable. I don't know about the rest of you, but I've heard the rumors she's been spreading around about Caroline. As we all know, the world of integrated marketing is a small one, and she could ruin Caroline's professional reputation. Besides that, we all agreed before Caroline left that if she had the time, and we needed her, she would do some freelance work for us. How can we expect her to work in an environment where her talent would be put into question?"

Maria sighed heavily. "What are you planning to do to Ida Brian? Surely you don't mean to fire her?"

"No. Though I would like to fire her, we simply don't have the proof that she did anything. What we have is another employee's accusation—an employee I'm currently dating who knows that I used to date Ida. Can any of you imagine what fodder that would be for a sexual harassment lawsuit? No, I can't fire her, not yet.

"But the stunt she pulled with Caroline could have cost us a client and it warrants some kind of action from us. It's true that time was on our side with that particular project, but Ida didn't know that. It could have been a case where Caroline needed the approval urgently because she was already behind schedule. As a new firm, we can't afford to take on a lawsuit that Ida would bring against us—and we all know she would sue—nor can we afford the publicity. So for now, we warn her in writing and we watch her." Brian finished.

As the others began to leave his office, Brian asked, "Are you okay with this Maria? Do you see any other alternative?"

"No, I understand what you're all saying. It's just that I can't believe Ida would do something so potentially self-destructive. Also, I'm thinking about what you said about a lawsuit. Seeing as how you've dated Ida—"

"I haven't dated Ida for two years, and if she tries to say that I gave Caroline special privileges, she'd have a hard time proving that, as it never happened. Caroline barely even spoke to me in the halls while she worked here. She stayed away from me."

"I think the question is: did you stay away from her?"

Brian smiled wolfishly. "I did my best."

Maria laughed. "Well, I'm glad she doesn't work here anymore. That smile on your face makes me think she wouldn't have been able to resist you for much longer."

Ida studied Brian across the conference table as he walked into the room and shut the door. The indigo shirt hugging his wide shoulders so beautifully enhanced his gray eyes and contrasted wonderfully with his black hair, while the white T-shirt just peeking out of his collar gave the shirt some flair. His belted black slacks showed off his slim hips and long legs. He always did wear his clothes well, she thought with a mental shake of her head. The way he filled out a nice pair of slacks and a tailored shirt was only one of the many things she missed about him.

"Hello Brian," she said with a sly smile and an assessing look as he seated himself across the table from her She'd get him back, she thought. If she could just get him alone away from the office, he'd be begging her to take him back.

"Hello, Ida," Brian said unsmilingly. "I called this meeting with you to discuss the unprofessional behavior you've recently displayed—"

"Unprofessional behavior? Excuse me, but you "Hello, Ida," Brian said unsmilingly. "I called this

"No, I don't," Brian said with a shake of his head. "The other founders and I know all about the fax—"

"What did your whore tell you?! It's a lie! You can't trust her Brian!"

Brian's jaw clenched as he silently counted to ten. Trying to maintain his calm, he pulled out a sheet of paper from the file he'd been carrying. "This is a state-ment listing the things you've done that we won't condone here at Inclusion and we've also put down the things we expect from you in the future."

Ida reached across the table and snatched the paper Glancing over it quickly, she raised furious and disbelieving eyes to his. "You dare to tell me how to behave in a work environment? Let me tell you something Mr. Brian Keenan, your little slut could use some pointers on how to behave professionally! And so could you! I saw the two of you together and I—" Ida stopped herself after noticing the fury in Brian's eyes.

Giving him a smile that didn't reach her eyes, she walked around the table and sat in a chair next to him. "Listen Brian, I would never do these things that you're accusing me of in this statement. You know me better than that. Now I don't know why she's doing it, but Caroline—"

"Enough!" Brian said, and stood up. "If you call her another name Ida, you'll regret it. This meeting is about you and your behavior. Read over the statement and sign it. Otherwise, you can look for another job. Those are the terms. Take them or leave them." He said and left the room, shutting the door with a loud click behind him.

Fuming, Ida snatched up the statement and signed it. *I miscalculated,* she thought. *But I'll get him back, and when I do, I'll leave that cow to eat my dust.* She thought about her alliance with Brickman and a crafty. self-satisfied smile spread across her face.

CHAPTER 9

Seated behind his large desk, Alex Brickman studied the two men standing in front of it. He could smell their fear. They were right to be afraid. He held their lives in the grip of his hands, and they knew it was a very precarious grip indeed. Lowering his eyes and making them sweat more, he picked up the jewel encrusted letter opener and began to slowly clean his already meticulous fingernails. He wanted them to wait and be terrified.

Frozen with fear, Pete Kovlovsky tried not to move a muscle as he watched the blond-haired man behind the large desk. Brickman was a small man, no taller than 5'4" and as slim as a wand. He was certainly no physical match for Pete's big, husky frame. But Pete feared him nonetheless. He feared him because Pete feared power, and Brickman was power, the kind of power that could eliminate a life with one phone call. Pete knew that normal people would look at Brickman and see a harmless, unassuming man. Their mistake would be in failing to take notice of his eyes.

Only two kinds of people could immediately tell that Brickman was evil by glancing at his eyes: the truly innocent and those who'd learned from experience how to recognize pure amorality. Babies and small children usually cried when they saw him and people like Pete and law enforcement either tried to curry favor with him or take him down. Everyday people just smiled and kept going; never realizing that they'd just had a brush with madness. Brickman had the cold, emotionless eyes of a madman. They were a pale, glacial blue and every time he looked in them, Pete knew he was looking into the eyes of a man who had everything and nothing to lose. Therefore, it meant everything and nothing to Brickman to kill anyone whom he thought was necessary. Or unnecessary.

Breathing slowly so as to not show any movement and catch Brickman's notice, Pete struggled not to blurt out an apology or to say anything at all. His first instinct was to talk and try to explain it all away, but that would be a mistake. When dealing with Brickman, especially when you've screwed up, you had to keep your counsel until he gave the signal, which could be anything from a lifted eyebrow to a flick of his eye. Pete looked out the corner of his eye at Stan, his partner for this latest job. Stan was a good, smart guy, but Pete couldn't help but notice while working with him that Stan had some nervousness in him. Some days Stan acted as jumpy as a child on a diet of candy and pop.

Pete saw Stan's eyes open and close at least twenty times in rapid succession. A sure sign that he was nervous and was going to do something stupid, like open his mouth. Pete turned his eyes forward, resigned to the fact that Stan was a dead man.

"Listen, Mr. Brickman," Stan began nervously, as he held up his hands, palms outward, in appeal. "We'll find the girl, that black photographer. All we need is a little more time—"

Pete didn't blink—didn't flinch—as the letter opener flew from Brickman's hand to land dead center in Stan's heart, killing him instantly.

Brickman pressed a button on his phone. "Send someone in to dispose of the human rubbish on my floor," he said and lifted his eyes to Pete. "Now then. I dislike incompetence Mr. Kovlovsky," he said in a voice that was all the more menacing for its softness. "And nervous incompetence," he said with a flick of disdain at the body on the floor, "makes me…nervous. What are your plans to remedy this situation?"

Pete said, "Well, sir, as you know the photographer gave her cards to several people. We had no luck with the lady who had the toddler in the park that day. Stan followed her and took her purse, but when he opened it, the photographer's card was not in there. I followed those two old people who were playing chess, so I know where they live. I figure I'll go back there and watch and wait for them to leave. There are a lot of nosy neighbors in their building, so I haven't had a chance to get in the apartment yet."

"Why didn't you just kill them and get it over with?"

This time it took everything in Pete not to flinch. Kill two harmless, old people? "Well sir, I know you want to keep this as quiet as possible. It was broad daylight and everywhere I followed them, it was crowded, so I had no chance to do that. Uh, have Charlie and Joe had any luck with any of them other people she took pictures of that day?" He sidled quietly out of the way of the two men who removed Stan's body.

"If they had, you wouldn't be here now. This situation is quickly becoming ungovernable. Don't let it reach that level Mr. Kovlovsky.

"When you find the girl, I don't want you to harm her; I want you to bring her to me. Her and her film, or as the case may be, her pictures. Do you understand?"

"Yes sir." Pete said, feeling quite sorry for the beautiful woman and thinking that she didn't deserve Brickman's attention. It was just her rotten luck that she had drawn it.

"Keep me abreast of your progress." Brickman turned his back in dismissal.

He'd been born with all the advantages in life: a wealthy family, servants, expensive homes and cars. But somehow, none of it had been enough for him. Being one of the landed rich hadn't been a challenge for him. So he'd decided to make his own challenges. He'd started with petty larceny while still in prep school. From there, he'd gone on to be the go-to man for drugs on his Ivy League college campus. It was only natural that he'd become the chief of a large drug cartel after that. It had all been too easy and his arrogance from knowing that had made him a little careless three years before and he'd almost gotten caught. But he'd faked his death in a boat explosion and he'd been able to give the feds and the Boston police the slip and remain on the top. He didn't mind having had to relocate.

And now, simply because he'd wanted to partake of the fresh air and an iced coffee with his current bed partner one hot Sunday morning, he was in danger of losing everything. One of God's little ironies, he thought. If he hadn't stopped to look at the beautiful woman taking pictures, then he wouldn't have been snapped as part of the background in one of her photos. He was sure the woman had no idea that she was taking a picture of a man that two different national governments would love to get their hands on, if they knew he was alive.

He'd have gone after her to get the film that very day, if he hadn't recognized that the man she was with was a police officer. He didn't recognize the man himself; he'd just recognized the essence of COP. So, he'd had to send his 'security force' after the people she'd given her cards to that day. He'd only had four of them with him, so he hadn't been able to trail all of the people of whom she'd taken photos.

He knew that Ida, the greedy bitch, knew something about the photographer and wasn't telling him. She'd been standing right next to him and there had been something in her eyes when he'd told his men about the woman taking pictures. She'd looked at the woman and for one second, Brickman could have sworn he'd seen recognition in her eyes. But he'd take care of Ida. He'd let her play whatever game she was playing for a little while and in the meantime, he'd keep enjoying her prowess in bed.

He hadn't trusted Ida from the moment she'd approached him after following that idiot Mackenzie, but she'd intrigued him with her brash attitude, false bravado and sexy beauty. She was also his fastest moneymaking soldier. So, he'd only punished her slightly for her rash decision to track him down—an insult that would have normally been punishable by death. No he hadn't killed her; he'd just given Mackenzie her true punishment. Ida, he'd put a few bruises on, kept around and given a promotion of sorts and a raise. Until now, he hadn't been unhappy with her, but she was only human after all and as such, she was prone to mistakes.

He'd find the photographer, either with the work of his men or through Ida. He'd find her and when he did, he'd get his picture from her. And in the process, he'd get her as well. He'd always had an obsession for beautiful things. Had felt, in fact, that he was entitled to them and that they were his for the taking. So, he'd get that photographer. And when he was finished with her…well, even as a small child, he'd enjoyed destroying pretty things that he'd previously obsessed over. After all, who could gainsay him?

Ida realized that Brickman knew that she recognized Caroline and Brian in the park that day. But she just couldn't tell him who Caroline was; she didn't want Brian to get hurt. And by all indications, he would be caught right in the middle. Ida had been able to tell by looking at Caroline and Brian that they had finally moved their relationship forward. And if that weren't enough, that Chatty Cathy at work, Linda, talked of nothing else but how perfect Caroline and Brian were for each other.

She knew that if she told Brickman who Caroline was that he'd find out where she lived and Brian would get hurt or killed trying to save her She wanted to tell him, she really did, because there was nothing she would like more than to have Caroline away from Brian. In addition, she actually liked Brickman. His money and power made him a strong aphrodisiac for her and sometimes, she could barely keep her hands off him. But, Brian was the love of her life and she would die before she let him get hurt. No, she couldn't tell Brickman who Caroline was, but maybe she could get her to give him what he wanted and get what she wanted at the same time, she thought with a malicious smile.

—⁓—

The heat wave the city had been experiencing since the spring didn't abate as the summer continued. If anything, the temperature increased. The hot weather didn't prevent Caroline from running though, as she'd been doing almost every day since the age of fourteen. Her mother had convinced her that running would be a good way to add muscle to the skinniness that had plagued her since she'd been a toddler.

Throughout all of her school years, she'd been teased about how skinny she was. Though she was still skinny; thanks to the running, there were toned muscles beneath the skin so she didn't look so emaciated anymore. Caroline slowly stopped running to work out a sudden muscle cramp she had in her right calf. As she stretched her leg in front of her, she looked around. She loved her neighborhood. She felt it was one of the prettiest and safest sections of the city. Lincoln Park, with its many trees, zoo, lagoon, conservatory and playgrounds, was right outside her door and Lake Michigan was just two blocks away. Lincoln Park Zoo and the park itself were two of her favorite places for her runs. She also liked to run along the lakefront.

The summer is going by so quickly, she thought as she ran down her usual path in the park. The night air was heavy with people's laughter as they enjoyed the waning days of summer. She smiled as she passed a teenage couple making out against a large, oak tree. The moon shined from behind the oak tree, peeking through the fat leaves and bathing the couple in multiple rays of broken light. Committing the image to memory, she determined to sketch it out as soon as she got home. She'd capture the slenderness of the girl's bare arms as they rose to embrace her boyfriend's neck and the boy's head was at just the right angle to be caught in one of the moon's rays. Perhaps she'd blend all three, the girl, the boy and the tree, so that they looked as if they were all one. She'd call it *In Love and Nature.*

Her fingers itched for a sketchpad and pencil as she thought it through and she absentmindedly patted her pockets in search of the items. "Damn it," she said aloud to the dark sky, "I hope I can remember this." She looked at her watch and picked up her pace. It was past 10 and she needed to hurry home. She hadn't even thought of the time when she'd changed into the running gear that she always kept at the studio. She kept it there because she often needed to get out and clear her head, and running helped her to do that.

Her painting and her sculpting were both going well, but she'd gotten sick of being cooped up inside. She estimated that she'd be finished preparing for her show by late October or early November. She didn't know what she'd do to keep herself busy after that. Perhaps she'd freelance some more, or maybe she'd take a quick vacation. Hawaii would be perfect right about then. She wondered if she could drag Brian away from his busy schedule to accompany her.

She smiled. Their relationship was better than she'd hoped it would be. He was clever, generous, patient, understanding and he could make her laugh. He could also be aggravating when it came to her health and sometimes his cop instincts made him act a little too protective, but all and all, he wasn't a bad bargain, she thought. She hadn't really considered marriage, and wondered if he had. Marriage seemed to be the next step. Naturally. They were already spending the night with each other. Never mind that it was in two different places and there was no consummation of their attraction for one another. She had stuff at his place and he had stuff at hers, and it was more than just the essentials.

Still, they had only known each other for a few months, although it seemed she'd known him forever She didn't know if she wanted marriage, but she did know she didn't want to spend her life with anyone else but Brian. She shook her head with a laugh. How contrary, as her mother would say. She shrugged her shoulders, I don't want to get married now, but I guess I will eventually, and it will be to Brian.

"Excuse me miss," Caroline jumped at the deep voice that seemed to sound from nowhere. She stopped and found herself staring up into the colorless eyes of a large man.

"Yes?" She asked.

"I'm looking for Zamboni's Bar. Can you tell me where it is?"

Smiling over her jumpiness, she said, "I'm sorry, what did you say?"

"Zamboni's. Do you know which way I should go to get to Zamboni's?"

"Oh, yeah sure. Just go to the end of this path, make a right and cross the street at the light. After you cross the street, make another right and Zamboni's is at the end of the block." She finished cautiously, wishing she hadn't stopped to help. Although the man was being very polite, she felt a shiver go down her spine. He kept his eyes on her face the entire time, but she felt as if she was being very thoroughly checked out and measured. It's his eyes, she thought, he wants them to look kind, but they're not, they're just…empty. Suddenly Caroline was scared, and she wanted to be far away.

Pete couldn't believe his luck. After sitting in his car for 15 hours, he'd realized that the old people were probably not going to leave their apartment that day. He'd driven away thinking that Brickman did not need to hear that he'd had no luck. As he'd driven through the park, he'd noticed the tall, slim black woman running in bright, blue, calf-length, running pants and a matching sleeveless, half-shirt. Scared to even blink for fear he would lose sight of her, he'd pulled over and had gotten out to follow her. She was even more beautiful up close, the poor girl.

"Thank you." Pete said, still looking at her. He could tell she was impatient to leave and trying to stall her, he pasted a smile on his face and asked, "So, uh, you live around here?" He saw immediately that he'd made a mistake. She was spooked.

The false joviality of the smile made Caroline stiffen and back away from the man. Why, oh why, did she have to wait so late to take her run? She didn't want to leave for fear he'd follow her home and what if he caught her when she tried to run? But all of her instincts were screaming for her to get away. From the corner of her eye she saw a couple coming across the grass towards them and turned to wave frantically. "Hi!"

Pete knew when to back off. "Thanks for your help."

Caroline didn't acknowledge him as she continued to wave. From the corner of her eye, she watched him walk away. The couple she'd been waving to shot her odd looks as they came abreast of her and then walked past. She smiled nervously and fell in step behind them. God, it's so dark, she thought as she looked around and hurried on.

She bit back a scream as a squirrel rustled some bushes and came scurrying out. Taking deep breaths, she told herself that she was overreacting, that the strange man had really only wanted directions and nothing else. She'd halfway convinced herself that she'd blown the matter out of proportion when her shoulder was grabbed from behind. She screamed and turned, with her balled fist at the end of her upraised arm.

"Hey." Brian said in surprised concern as he caught her arm. "What's going on?"

Caroline threw herself in his arms, burrowing her head in his chest and wrapping her arms around his waist.

"What's wrong?" Brian asked. "You're shaking. Tell me what happened." He demanded and tightened his grip protectively as she only shook harder.

Caroline could only shake her head as she fought back terror. Telling herself to calm down, she held on tighter and burrowed deeper.

Brian stroked her hair, alarmed. Gently taking her shoulders, he tried to hold her away from him so he could see her face. She held on tighter. Despite the warm night, her skin was surprisingly cold and he became even more alarmed. "Caroline," he demanded urgently. "Tell me what's wrong."

"Th-there was a m-man. Eyes." was all she got out before just the thought of the stranger made her mind shut down. She was so cold and so scared, and she couldn't stop the terrible shaking.

Brian stiffened. "A man? What man?"

Caroline tried again. "A man stopped me and asked for directions, but it felt like he really wanted something else. And he asked me if I lived around here and his smile and his eyes...they made me panic."

"What did he look like?"

"Big, white, stocky...I don't know, I can't think. Why?" She asked feeling safer as time passed.

"I'm going to go look for him. You stay here." Brian said and tried to loose her arms again.

Just the thought of him leaving made Caroline panic and she tightened her arms again, she would have crawled inside him if she'd been able to. "Don't leave. Stay here with me. It was probably nothing, anyway. Maybe it was just my imagination. Let's just go, okay? I just want to go home." She said desperately.

Brian gave up. The man was probably long gone anyway. He held her closer, kissed the top of her head and rubbed her back soothingly. "It's okay. Whoever he was, he's gone now," he said as he turned his head from side to side, knowing it was useless to try and spot the man. "Come on, let's go." He said, finally breaking her hold and putting his arm around her waist.

Safe behind a wide, fat tree a few feet away, Pete watched them as they left the park. Brickman was right; the man oozed cop from almost every pore. He'd ducked behind the tree earlier, thinking he'd wait until the other couple left and just follow her home. But things didn't work out the way he'd planned. He may have followed her with that cop around under ordinary circumstances. But the cop's radar was up, and there was no way in hell he'd follow her now.

When he felt it safe, Pete stepped from behind the tree, thinking that this was another incident that he would be better off keeping to himself.

"God Brian," Caroline said after they'd gotten out of the park and she felt she'd gained a semblance of control. "I've never been so scared in my life. I know it's weird, but he really just creeped me out. And then when you came and touched me from behind, I...I just lost it, I guess," she finished, inhaling his scent as she rubbed her face in his shirt. "What are you doing here, anyway?"

"That's a good question." Brian said. "I was just going to ask you the same one." He stopped and looked at her. "When you weren't at your condo or in your studio, I decided to look for you here."

Caroline moved her shoulders restlessly. He'd asked her several times to stop running so late at night. "I was just taking a run, like I always do."

"Yes, and look what happened. When I think of what actually *could* have happened, I want to shake you for your stubbornness!"

Caroline knew she really had no defense, but she tried anyway. "I always run through the park and nothing has ever happened. There are always people out and about. Especially in the summer."

"And how many people would have been able to help you if that guy had tried something Caroline? There aren't that many people out this late precisely because it is so late. Do you know how I found you? I know your route. You run the exact same route, almost every day. Someone could be watching you. Did you ever think of that?"

"I'm sorry. I just needed a little exercise."

"With all the trees and bushes in this park, you make yourself an easy target," Brian said, pressing his point home. "The guy could have had you behind a tree in seconds and no one would have even noticed."

She knew he was justified in being angry and said, "I won't run so late again.

"I'd feel better if you said you wouldn't run in the dark anymore."

Caroline moved into his arms again. "I won't run in the dark anymore," she said.

"And you won't run the same route all the time anymore either," Brian said as he lifted her chin. "It's good to switch."

"I won't run the same route anymore," she promised. "It's good to switch."

"I mean it, Caroline. This is serious."

"So do I. Now, can we please go home?"

CHAPTER 10

Brian stood in front of the Ferris wheel at Navy Pier and waited for Caroline. They'd agreed to meet for a lake cruise and he was early. He looked around at the scenery. Navy Pier was one of his favorite spots in the city. The most popular destination for tourists, the pier was planted on the east coast of the city and stretched nearly a mile into Lake Michigan and offered everything from a Shakespearean theater to museums, a skating rink, a movie theater, restaurants and carnival attractions. Chicagoans loved their lakefront and Navy Pier was the premier attraction in winter and summer.

He'd invited Caroline to come on one of the lake cruises with him. Though there were several different kinds of cruises, including architectural and skyline, Brian preferred the one given by Sea Dog Cruises. The boats were some of the fastest speedboats in the country, and the entire lakefront tour, cruising at 20-25 knots, took about 30 minutes. Brian loved the speed and the excitement.

He looked at his watch. It was still a little early. He was anxious for her to arrive and he knew why. They'd been out together several times since the episode in her condominium and each time he felt as if she were pulling away from him. He'd wanted to pick her up for their date today, but she'd insisted on them meeting. She was creating distance between them and he intended to find out why.

"Hi." Caroline said as she walked up to him. She stood on her toes for a peck.

He pressed his lips slowly to hers and made the kiss last a little longer. "Hi." He said and passed his hand over her hair. He felt her pull back a bit and watched as she looked nervously around. "What's wrong, Caroline?"

"What do you mean?"

"I mean I can feel you pulling away from me and I want to know why. If you don't want to see me anymore, just tell me."

"It's not that!" She hastened to say. She sighed and looked around again. "Look, can we find some place to sit down? I need to talk to you."

"Let's go over here." Brian said and led her to a seating area a few feet away.

Caroline folded her hands on top of the table and took a deep breath. "Okay, look. You know I love the time we spend together, I love that you know me almost as well as I know myself and vice versa. I love your sense of humor, your intelligence—everything. Sometimes it scares me to think about how much I enjoy being with you, but I do like being with you."

"Then what is it? Why do you keep pulling back?" He asked again.

"I'm just nervous. Have you noticed that every time we're out together people stare at us? It's unnerving. People are even doing it now and I don't like it."

"Yes, I notice the stares Caroline, but I can't believe you would let them bother you so much that you would put distance between us."

"I didn't realize I was doing that. As I said, being under constant scrutiny unnerves me. I can't stand for people to stare at me." She paused and thought for a moment before making up her mind. "Look, there's something I haven't told you. It happened a long time ago, but it's like it was yesterday and I never talk about it."

"What is it?" Brian asked.

"When I was a freshman in college, my parents gave a large donation to a children's charity to help them build a library. Pictures of my family had been in the papers—mostly the society page—before that, but after my parents gave the money for the library, the press coverage became intense and intrusive. I was home from college for spring break at the time and for a few days after the donation was made, it seemed that every time I turned around, there was a camera in my face.

"Anyway, I was only 18 and I was totally freaked out. I thought going back to school would help me escape. It didn't. One photographer even followed me back down to Atlanta. He took a picture and sold it to a wire service. The caption not only said who I was, but it also mentioned the donation and where I went to school."

"That must have been extremely difficult. Knowing you, I'm sure no one down there knew that your family is one of the most successful ice cream producers in the country. It must have been quite a shock when everyone on campus found out."

"Yes, that was difficult. People started looking at me differently, but I had a couple of good friends whom I'd already told and those people were very supportive after the picture ran. There were others who I knew I couldn't trust. As I said, that was hard, but that wasn't the most difficult thing I had to deal with. I was almost kidnapped about two weeks after that picture ran."

"You what?!" Brian said incredulously. "You're not serious!"

"I wish I weren't. It was one of the worst experiences in my life. I'm surprised you didn't hear about it; it was in all the papers here and on television."

Brian thought about it. "It sounds familiar, but it's hazy. Tell me what happened."

"I was walking back from class by myself one evening—it wasn't quite dark yet. Since the press seemed to have had enough of me, I was finally comfortable again. For about a week after that picture ran, I'd looked over my shoulder every time I went out of my dormitory. The stares from the other students were pretty bad that week as well, but things soon cooled down and I went on with life as usual.

"Anyway, I was going to my dormitory, when two guys jumped out of nowhere and grabbed me. One put his hand over my mouth and the other one held my arms.

I struggled, but I couldn't break free. The next thing I knew, my hands were tied behind my back and I was being lifted from behind. One of them whispered for me to stop struggling or they would hurt me. I continued to struggle, of course, and he then said he didn't know what my problem was, that they just wanted a little bit of money from my 'rich daddy.'" Caroline shut her eyes as she remembered each terrifying moment.

Saying nothing, Brian reached out, covered her clinched hands and squeezed them in comfort.

Caroline turned her hand over and gripped his gratefully. "Two professors turned the corner of a building, saw the three of us and ran over to see what was going on. The men heard them coming and they let me go and ran away. I gave a description to the police and my parents were called. They flew down to get me and I spent the rest of the school year at home. The police caught the men, who said they'd seen my picture in the paper and just thought they could make a quick buck.

"The plan wasn't well conceived at all. They were a couple of unemployed cousins who saw what they viewed as an opportunity and they took it. They didn't think it was a big deal, but what they did had a huge affect on me. It was weeks before I felt safe enough to even leave my parents' home and I needed therapy before I could even think of going back to school. I had to learn how to trust the basic kindness of people again and to take care of, and defend myself. My parents wanted to hire a bodyguard, but I refused and insisted on self-defense lessons instead. I was back at Spelman that fall."

"Well, I'm impressed. Not many people would have been able to do that. Some would still be in therapy."

"It's not that big of a deal, I mean it's been more than 12 years. I knew I had to eventually get on with my life. And I was lucky, a lot of people don't have access to therapy and my parents were able to get me one of the best psychologists in the city. Besides, eventually, it became a matter of letting the kidnappers win or letting myself win by managing my own life. I wanted my own life.

"At any rate, I'm telling you all of this so you will understand why I've been acting the way I have been lately. Ever since we started seeing each other, people just stare at us. It's like we're a part of a freak show or something and it takes me back to that time when I was 18 and it bothers me. So, I guess in my effort to protect myself, I subconsciously pulled away. I'm sorry. I didn't mean to do it."

"I'm glad it wasn't intentional, but I'm concerned that it bothers you so much. Did the guy in the park remind you of being kidnapped?" When she shook her head no, he continued. "What do you propose we do? We can't stay in all the time, that would be hiding. Do you want me to beat them up for you? I will." Brian joked.

Caroline laughed and squeezed his hand. "No, that won't do. As I said, I didn't know I was doing it, but I'll make a conscious effort to stop. I'll just have to learn how to ignore the stares and not let them bother me."

"People like you get stared at all the time. You're tall and pretty and you dress like a runway model, so I'm sure you turn heads constantly."

"That's not true. It only happens occasionally because of my height—it's not a constant thing. Anyway, the stares we get are different—some of them are hostile."

"I know, but I should tell you, I wasn't willing to give up so easily. When I first met you, I thought I was probably in love with you. But after spending time with you, I know it's true." He held up his hand when she tried to speak. "You don't have to say anything right now. I know I'm probably moving too fast for you. However, I can't be less than honest, not with you and especially not with myself."

Caroline was quiet for a moment. "I think I feel the same way about you and it scares me. I've never felt anything close to what I'm feeling for you for anyone else. It's all happened so quickly and I still feel that we barely know one another."

"No, we haven't known each other all that long, but I have to tell you that these past weeks with you have been the best weeks of my life. Like I said, I know this is an uncomfortable pace for you, but I can't keep my feelings to myself any longer." He paused for a moment and then continued. "I never told you much about my father, but we had a really good relationship. I told you he died when I was 15. He had lung cancer and he suffered with it for a long time. The last month of his life was spent in the hospital and it was a miserable time for him.

"I was visiting him the day he died and he had so many regrets, the biggest one being that he had actually wanted to be a doctor and not a police officer. Until that day, I'd had no idea that police work, in his mind, was his only option. He had no money for college, so he just trained to be a cop, something that paid him enough money to support his family. He didn't dislike being a police officer, but it wasn't his first choice for a career and even when he was dying, he was still talking about wanting to become a doctor. That had a profound affect on me and it taught me a lesson."

"Aren't going to tell me what it is?" Caroline asked when he remained quiet.

"Don't be so impatient." Brian said with a smile. "I just learned to go for what I want. I didn't want to be dying or reach an age where it was impossible to change my life and have to say, 'God, I wish I had tried this, or done that.' I want to be able to say that I have no regrets and even if I don't get what I want, at least I can say I tried. I admit, I didn't heed the lesson at first, but I eventually did. I became a cop because I was convinced that that was what I wanted, but it was really because my dad had been one."

"And the stint as a lawyer?"

"Oh, that was my escape hatch from police work. At that point, I didn't really know what it was I wanted to do. I discovered quickly that it wasn't lawyering. Then I found that I had an affinity for computers and technology and the way they work and the rest is history. Now, getting back to you. When I saw you, I was blown away and I knew I couldn't miss an opportunity to know you. If I did, I knew it would turn out to be a major regret—possibly the most major one—of my life. So if I am moving too fast for you, I'm sorry, but I learned from my dad's situation that I have to go after my desires."

"Brian. I don't know what to say." She stopped and took another breath. "No, that's not true. I do know what to say. I couldn't be more pleased that you have such feelings for me. It thrills me because of the feelings I have for you. I'm so glad I decided to go forward and get to know you, because I was afraid of what would happen if I didn't. So like you, I didn't want to regret not trying."

Brian smiled and lifted her hand to his lips for a kiss. "What do you say we take that lake cruise?"

"Sounds good." They rose and Caroline made a point of taking his hand as they began walking.

—⁓—

Traditionally, Chicago could not be considered a port city, but its inhabitants practically lived on the water during the summer months. Lake Michigan stretched for miles along the city's eastern border and the various leaders of the city over the years had always made sure to use that geographical fact to its greatest advantage.

The lakefront held several beaches, recreational sites and even a museum campus. The campus allowed visitors to walk from one famous museum—the Field Museum, Shedd Aquarium and the Adler Planetarium—to the other, all while keeping the magnificent view of the lake in their sights.

Brian had originally thought it would be fun to take a water taxi from the pier to the museum campus, but had decided against it when he thought of the Sea Dog cruises. "Isn't this great?" He shouted to Caroline over the noise from the engine of the boat.

She turned to smile at him. "Yeah, I love it! Everything is going by so fast, I can hardly catch my breath." She turned back to look at the city as it sped by. She'd traveled many places, but in her opinion, Chicago had the best skyline in the world. "This is a great cruise. I'm glad you suggested it. Thanks." She kissed him on the cheek.

"I'm glad you're having a good time." He said, just as the boat began to dock. "This is my third time taking it and I always enjoy it. My mom and stepdad always want to take this cruise when they come to town."

"I can't blame them." She said as they stepped from the boat onto dry land.

Brian took her hand. "I know you're hungry. How about Riva Ristorante for lunch? I remember you saying that it's one of your favorite restaurants."

"Oh, I love Riva. But actually, I'm in the mood for something else right now. Would you mind something a little less formal than Riva? They have great sandwiches at the Häagen-Dazs café—not to mention the terrific ice cream."

"Sure, I could go for a good sandwich." They started walking towards the café, passing an entrance to the Chicago Children's Museum and the merry-go-round on the way. "Aren't you afraid you'll hurt the family business if you heap compliments on the competition?" He asked teasingly.

Caroline laughed. "Of course not. Häagen-Dazs has *terrific* ice cream, but Grandmother's is the best. Please take note of the difference." She said in mock censure.

"Oh, I stand corrected." Brian said.

"Besides, we don't have service here at the pier. My parents are working on it, but it's slow going. I love this place." She said once they arrived at the café. "It reminds me of the one on the Champs-Elysees in Paris."

Her French was flawless, as was her Spanish. Brian had found that out at a Spanish tapas restaurant two weeks before. He wondered what other languages she spoke. "So, how many times have you been to Paris?"

"I don't know, about eight or nine times, maybe." She said and placed her order..

Brian gave his order "Who goes to Paris almost 10 times by the time they're 30?"

"I guess I did. I was 10 the first time I went. It was a family vacation." The smile left her face when she noticed the way he was looking at her. "What's the matter?"

"I've just never dated anyone who was so wealthy before. I mean I have friends who come from wealth, but that's different."

"Does it bother you?" Caroline asked with a frown.

"No, bother is not the right word. *Worry* is a better one."

"Worry? Why should you be worried?"

"First, let me make it clear that this is my insecurity and it has nothing to do with you personally. When I first heard that your family owned Grandmother's Ice Cream, I was taken aback. I didn't know if I could compete with the way of life you must be used to. But now that I've gotten to know you, I realize that you're really no different than I am, just wealthier and more used to wealth. My insecurities only show themselves when you mention certain things, like going to Paris ten times or hiring a decorator."

"Wait, let me finish," he said when she looked ready to interrupt. "I feel insecure because I didn't have those things growing up and I don't do those sorts of things now. I'm used to a very simple life and I worried that you weren't."

"Aren't you going to say anything?" Brian asked when she only looked at him.

"Only that you don't live any cheaper than I do. You own a two-level loft in one of the most expensive neighborhoods in the city, you own two expensive cars and you go to a tailor to be fitted for your suits. You could go to Paris if you wanted—ten times in ten months, if the notion struck you.

"The average person on a moderate income doesn't do those kinds of things Brian. People who have money do. It's nothing to be ashamed of—if you have the money to do it and it makes you happy, then do it. I'm not ashamed of my background and I don't think you should be ashamed of yours either."

"I'm not." Brian found that he couldn't defend himself. "But when you put things that way, I feel ridiculous. You're right. Okay, then. You'll work on your worries about people staring and I'll work on my insecurity about all the money you have. And then maybe we can get this relationship on the road."

CHAPTER 11

Caroline ripped her latest sketch from the easel and put it up to the light. This is horrible, she thought to herself. How am I supposed to have a show if I can't even produce work that doesn't even show a modicum of talent? Balling the paper up in her hands, she tossed it across the room so that it landed in a pile with other discarded work.

She looked at the huge pile and made a sound of disgust. For two days she'd been trying to produce, and had nothing to show for it. For two days, she'd holed up in her studio and made herself sit at her easel and still there was nothing. She had a million ideas in her head, but for some odd reason, she hadn't been able to transfer those ideas to the canvas. It had been the same with the clay. Her studio was littered with lumps of unfinished pieces.

"Damn." She said aloud to the empty room, and the word came out as a sigh. She was filled with a restlessness that she was unable to explain, even to herself. The restlessness had been building for a while now, and had only taken hold in the past two days. "This just isn't working." She said, and unbidden, an image of a shirtless Brian popped into her head. "God, he has a sexy chest," she whispered, and this time she wasn't even aware she was speaking aloud.

Her brow cleared and her lips pursed in thought as she realized why she was so restless. It wasn't restlessness at all; it was nothing but pure, old-fashioned sexual frustration. She and Brian had been circling each other sexually for weeks. They'd done almost everything but the act of intercourse itself. She was the one insisting that they wait, and she didn't know why she insisted upon torturing herself and him.

They'd been dating out in the open for several weeks and had been able to do all the normal things that couples do. She'd also decided on a method of birth control. He was a great guy and everything she could hope for in a partner. More importantly, she loved him and wanted to be with him. So why the wait?

She sighed in disgust when she realized she was holding back simply for form's sake. There was nothing she could do about the color of his skin and waiting around wasn't going to change that fact. He was a wonderful man who made her heart flutter and her mind race with possibilities. She needed to take a leap or climb back down the mountain, as her grandmother would say. What she was doing —waffling, pushing him away one moment and pulling him close the next—was not fair to either of them.

She knew if he was half as frustrated as she was, he was in trouble. Walking around in a constant state of low-level desire played hell on the nerves. She'd wondered why he was sleeping less and less at her condo. Now she knew why. It was too hard. "Aw, poor baby," she whispered with a smile. An idea flashed in her head, and feeling freer and happier than she had in days, Caroline whistled as she began gathering her things to leave. She had a lot to do.

—ɯ—

Caroline heard Brian's key in the lock and she nervously wiped her hand down the front of her shirt. She ran into his room, closing the door behind her. She made herself as comfortable as she could and waited. She'd planned everything carefully, down to the last minute, and her excitement bubbled hotly just beneath the surface. She'd gone home and showered. Her body was scrubbed, loofahed, shaved and slick with jasmine oil. Her hair was freshly washed and dried and was hanging down the middle of her back, the way he liked it. His white Oxford shirt was a last minute addition, as she'd felt ridiculous waiting around in the nude.

When she heard his foot hit the first stair, nerves made her lick her lips. But the nerves disappeared when he opened the door to his bedroom and saw what she'd done to his room. The expression on his face when he looked at her gave her all the confidence she needed. He had the look of someone who'd been hit in the stomach with a hard-as-granite fist. She'd put in a small dining table and covered it with a linen tablecloth. There were lit white, tapered candles on the table and ones of different shapes and sizes throughout the room. The table was set for one and had a large serving platter in the middle of it. *She was sitting on the platter.*

"Hello Brian," she said as he stepped into the room and dropped his briefcase. "I thought you'd be hungry and want to eat. I'm the main course."

Brian looked at her and was surprised the top of his head remained on. Praying his knees would remain steady, he walked over to the table and kept his eyes on her the entire time. He saw from the confidence and hint of laughter in her eyes and the curve of her lips that she was fully aware of the effect she had on him. Stopping in front of the table, he grabbed her folded knees and pulled her to the edge. "Am I allowed seconds?"

She chuckled huskily and twined her arms around his neck. "As long as you have room for them."

"What are you wearing under this thing?" He asked as he proceeded to find out for himself by sliding his hands underneath the ends of the shirt.

Caroline tilted her head to the side and pretended to think. "Umm, let's see. That would be skin and...flesh and...oh yeah, that's right...I believe that would be more skin." She said before she closed her eyes and enjoyed the feel of his hands kneading and caressing her thighs.

Brian bent his head and took her mouth with his. Quickly and voraciously. When she responded by sucking his tongue into her mouth, he knew he'd soon be lost and broke off the kiss before all of his concentration was gone. He rested his forehead on hers. "Listen, Caroline, I want you more than I've ever wanted anyone or anything before in my life. You have to know that. But before we make love, you need to be sure that you're absolutely ready for this. Be sure, because there'll be no going back after this."

Caroline squeezed his neck in appreciation for his asking and pressed a soft kiss to his mouth. "Darling, I'm ready. I realized today that I've been ready for weeks, but scared to take a chance. It's time to take that chance. I can't afford not to." She said softly and fanned her hands inside his opened collar to caress his chest.

"You'll never know how hard it was for me to ask that question. I don't know what I would have done if you'd changed your mind."

"Brian."

"Hmm?" He asked between kisses.

"Shut up and take me to bed."

"Yes ma'am." Brian said and carried her to the other side of the room where he deposited her by the side of the bed. Stepping back, he let his eyes take her in: the rich lashes framing glowing brown eyes, the legs that seemed to stretch for miles and miles, the slender ankles, delicate feet and long toes. Letting his eyes trace the same route up, he stopped when he saw that her nipples were distended and were pushing against his shirt with every breath she took. He extended his open palm. "My shirt, if you please."

He watched her eyes widen with humor as she shrugged her shoulders. "If you must have it, then I guess I have to give it back." Slowly, starting at the pulse in her neck, she began slipping each button through its eye, one by one. When she reached the swell of her chest, he watched her fingers as they brushed her skin. He was sure sweat was dripping out of every pore of his body as he watched her unbutton the shirt, all without ever taking her eyes off his face.

When she'd loosed the last button, she shimmied her shoulders so that the shirt slowly slid off her and fell to the floor. "Have mercy," Brian breathed reverently when he saw her.

Caroline smiled and took the step necessary to bring them closer. "Now we just have to get you undressed."

As she stood in front of him, naked as the day she was born and unbuttoning his shirt, Brian wondered why he hadn't exploded yet. With every brush of the backs of her hands against his skin, he felt his temperature rise another notch. She lifted her mouth for a kiss and he obliged, kissing her hard and long. Reaching around her, he placed his hot hands on her cool buttocks and moaned low in his throat when she shivered and pressed her body against his. He felt his eyes nearly cross as her hardened nipples nestled into his chest. Grabbing her shoulders, he gently put her away from him.

"Sweetheart, I need you to get in the bed or else this will be over with before it has even begun."

Caroline only smiled again and climbed into the bed. Her eyes never left him as he hurriedly undressed. She let her eyes trail from his muscular chest with its sparse sprinkling of hair to his flat as a washboard stomach. Her eyes widened when he lowered his pants and boxers. Swallowing convulsively, she licked her suddenly dry lips, and unconsciously pressed her knees together. When Brian climbed into bed, he could tell that she was nervous and he set about arousing her again. Turning on his side, he pressed one bent arm into the bed and leaned over her. "Rest your head on my arm." He told her and when she did, he bent his head and kissed her again, his tongue repetitively thrusting until her hands were helplessly clinging to his forearm as she arched upward into the kiss and her legs moved restlessly against his.

Caroline closed her eyes at the riotous sensations his hand was causing as it trailed from her collarbone to her breasts. Brian slowly traced each nipple in turn and watched her closely as she bit her lip and arched her chest closer to his hand. Adjusting his position so that his weight rested on his legs as he straddled her hips, he ground her nipples with his opened palms, causing her to suck in her breath. "You like that, don't you?"

"Hmm." She agreed and reached down to put her hands on his thighs.

Brian slid his hands under her back and lifted her so that her back arched and his mouth could have better access. Laving a nipple with his tongue, he drew it into his mouth and pulled, sucked and then raked his teeth over it. It wasn't until she moaned his name that he turned his head and gave the other nipple the same treatment. His actions caused tingles of electricity to explode in her stomach and she cried out. "Stop…can't…"

Brian lifted his head and laid her back against the pillows. As she looked at him with slumberous eyes, he reached down between their bodies to test her readiness. "God, you're so wet," he moaned.

Caroline jerked at his touch and felt hot sensations begin to build as he delicately separated her folds and began to rhythmically rub and caress her. As the sensations began to take over and swamp her, her eyes closed helplessly. "Brian," she said in shocked surprise, "you're supposed to be with me. You're supposed to…be in…side me." She finally got out as she concentrated on what he was making her feel.

Brian caught his breath as he watched her start to succumb. The pleasure and ecstasy on her face made her even more beautiful and he hurried to grab a condom so that he could join her as she went over the precipice. Sliding his hands under her thighs, he lifted each leg and placed them over his as he assumed a kneeling position.

He pressed his hips forward and slowly sank into her. Feeling her internal resistance and her nails digging into his biceps, he strained to stop and looked down at her. The tears sliding out the corners of her eyes made him stop completely. "God, baby. I'm sorry. Do you want me to stop?"

Caroline frantically shook her head no. Her pleasure had somewhat dissipated at his slow invasion, and she was sorry for it. "It hurts a little bit, that's all. I think if you just don't go so slow, it won't hurt so much."

Brian reached down and found her again and began to fondle her. When her hips began to arch up frantically, he began to move again. He sheathed himself to the hilt, thrusting faster and faster, each thrust taking him deeper. Caroline matched his rhythm and screamed as she felt herself come apart and fly into pieces.

Brian looked at her and the look of pure ecstasy on her face, sent him forcefully, violently over the edge and he hoarsely yelled out her name as he found his own pleasure. Resting his forehead against hers and keeping his weight on his arms, he waited to catch his breath. He lifted his head and saw her involuntarily flinch as he slowly began to leave her body.

She tightened her arms around his neck and said, without opening her eyes, "Don't. Not yet."

"Sweetheart," he said and leaned down to kiss the lid of each closed eye. "If I don't, you'll be more tender than you have to be. As it is, I know you're already going to be quite sore. And besides that, after the workout you just gave me, my arms are fast losing the ability to hold me up. I'm going to be crushing you in a minute. You can lay on top of me."

Caroline smiled, as pleased as a cat with a belly full of cream. She looked at him through slitted eyes. "It was wonderful, wasn't it?"

Brian laughed, withdrew from her body and lay on his back. Taking him at his word, she climbed aboard and stretched out on top of him. He put his arms around her and gave her a squeeze. "Well, if your screams were any indication, I'd say it was more than wonderful. It was downright *orgasmic!*" He said teasingly.

Caroline shyly buried her face in his chest and smiled in embarrassment. "I didn't mean to be so loud; it just happened."

He rubbed his hands down her supple back. "Well all I can say is thank God for sound-proof walls."

She twisted his chest hair between her fingers. "Stop teasing. I wouldn't exactly call you silent. At least I can claim inexperience. What's your excuse?" She asked tartly.

Rubbing his chest where she'd pinched him, he said quietly and seriously. "You are. I'd always heard that making love with someone you're in love with was unlike anything else in the world. But until tonight, I never knew how true those words were. I do love you Caroline. You absolutely stagger me."

"God, Brian," she said as she lifted her head to look down at him. She smiled as he wiped the tears from her face; she hadn't even known that she was crying. "I feel the same way. I love you so much that it scares me sometimes. I've never wanted to give so much of myself to anyone before."

"Don't be scared. I feel the same about you," he said and shifted to look at her. "Are you ready for me "Are you ready for me to meet your parents? I know you were concerned about that. I definitely want you to meet my parents. My mom is going to love you."

"I want that as well." She took a deep breath and thought to herself, *leap or climb down, Caroline.* "I want them to see how wonderful you are and how happy I am. We usually have a barbecue at our cottage for Labor Day. Would you like to come?"

Brian looked at her in appreciation. "Of course I would." He said and brought her head down for a kiss.

Caroline began to squirm. "I need to wash Brian, and I'm a little sore."

Brian slid from under her and got out of bed. "Don't you move. I'll take care of everything."

Caroline smiled and let herself drift. *Life is wonderful,* she thought as she drifted off to sleep. She awakened to find Brian sitting on the side of the bed and holding a wet cloth between her legs. He smiled down at her. "This should help you. It should keep you from getting too sore."

As she felt the coldness of the cloth seep through and soothe her delicate tissues, Caroline reached up and hooked her hand behind his neck. Pulling his head down, she kissed the corner of his mouth. "I really do love you." She dropped back on the pillows and closed her eyes again.

Brian held the towel until he was sure she was fully asleep, and after putting the towel back in the bathroom, he returned to bed, gathered her in his arms and joined her in sleep.

Three hours later, Brian was roused from sleep by movement on the bed. "What?" he said uncomprehendingly, and rubbed his hand down his face.

"Hey. Where are you going?" He asked playfully and grabbed Caroline's arm when he noticed her climbing from the bed.

She smiled and kissed him. "Sorry. I didn't mean to wake you. I'm hungry and I was going to sneak down and grab a quick bite to eat."

Brian looked at the illuminated dial of his watch. He sighed and looked at her again. "Caroline, it's 9:30 at night. Can it wait until morning?"

"No. I haven't had anything to eat since this morning, and I'm starved."

Brian turned on the light and eyed her suspiciously. "What time this morning?"

Knowing what was coming, Caroline rolled her eyes in exasperation. "Don't start that again Brian. I told you that *sometimes* when I'm working, I lose track of time and don't eat. I eat when I'm hungry that's all."

"What time this morning?" Brian asked again.

Caroline snatched her arm away. "Why does it make a difference? All you need to know is that I'm hungry now."

"It makes a difference because I worry about you not eating at regular intervals. And then when you finally do eat something, it's usually junk food. You're already underweight. What time this morning?"

"It's not *usually* junk food," she said, mimicking him. "You exaggerate. Just because you saw me eat at a fast food restaurant a couple of times, you condemn me as a junk food junkie. I can't eat disgustingly healthy all the time like you do. And before you ask again, the last time I ate was at 10 this morning. And I'm not underweight, I'm just thin."

"What did—"

"I'm not going to stand here and let you treat me like a child. It doesn't matter what I ate this morning. The point—a very salient point, I might add—is that I'm hungry now!"

Brian smiled lecherously and said, "After what happened a few hours ago, I would hardly call you a child."

Caroline scoffed. "This is serious Brian. I hate it when you try to handle me. I'm not a child to be taken care of."

"You're not going to stop me from worrying about you when you're in your studio and don't eat anything, so there's no point in trying."

"Fine. You do that. And while you're worrying; I'm going to go get something to eat," she said as she bent and snatched his shirt from the floor. She made it as far as the door before he grabbed her from behind and swung her around.

"You're right and I'm sorry. I can't help it; it's how my dad treated my mom and I learned at his knee." He said as he nuzzled her neck, ignoring how she stiffened. "I'll get us something to eat. It's the least I can do. After all, you've already served me a fantastic main course, and you'll need to keep up your strength because I do plan to cash in on those seconds you promised me." He released her and was out the door before she could react.

—⁓—

"Caroline." Brian said later that night. She had her arm flung across his chest, her head on his shoulder and was fast on her way to going back to sleep. The second round of lovemaking he'd awakened her for had exhausted her.

"Hmm?"

"After what you did tonight, I don't think I'll ever be able to look at a serving platter the same way again."

Caroline sleepily punched him. "Shut up."

"I'm serious. I don't think I'll ever wash the one you used, and I *know* I'll keep it forever. Do you think I could find a place to get it framed?"

"Go to sleep, you pervert," she said sleepily.

"Caroline?"

"*What?*"

"Have you given any thought to the limitless possibilities of a gravy boat?"

She muffled a laugh. "Idiot."

"Brian," Caroline whispered urgently as she gently bit his ear.

"Hmm." Brian murmured, not fully awake.

"Brian," She said again and licked a trail from his ear to his neck.

Brian burrowed down into the pillows and made himself more comfortable.

Frustrated now, Caroline straddled him and set about raining openmouthed kisses on his face and chest. "Brian," she said again and this time he responded to the urgency in her voice.

He woke up with narrowed eyes and a smile on his face. He placed his hands on her hips. "What is it, babe? Or should I ask what it is you want?"

Caroline smiled slyly and reaching down, she found him and held fast, making his eyes pop open and his hands clench on her hips. "I want to try it on top this time, that's what I want. I just need a little help," she said with a purely feline smile.

"Have mercy," Brian said. "Your wish is my command." And so saying, he proceeded to show her exactly what to do.

CHAPTER 12

"Yes, Mom," Brian said into the phone. "I promise I'll come up and see you and Frank soon. As soon as I can manage it, I swear. Work's been kind of crazy lately, and I haven't had a lot of free time."

"Yes, well, you find some free time and come and see your family." Fiona Applegate said, her Irish accent shining through, despite the fact she'd lived in the U.S. for most of her 57 years. "We were expecting you for the July 4th holiday, and when I didn't see you, I was sorely disappointed. After all, the least a boy can do is take time out to see his mother on the Day of Independence."

Brian rolled his eyes and tried to shake off the sword of guilt his mother wielded so expertly. "You're right, Mom. How about I make a date for mid-September to see you and Frank? And I'll even throw in Thanksgiving to sweeten the deal. How's that?"

In Detroit, Fiona could only be thankful for the inadvertent blindness of distance. She was certain if Brian had been able to see the look of unholy satisfaction on her face; he'd be onto her and her tricks. Trying to keep the sound of it out of her voice, she said, "That's just fine then. As I said, a boy should always make time for his mother, no matter how busy he is. Now, tell your mother how your love life is going. I'm certain your computer chips can't keep you cozy at night."

Brian laughed out loud. His mother had always been this way, even before his dad had died and she'd had to rear a teenage boy alone. She'd been the one to talk to him about sex and condoms and anything else he may have been curious about. Telling him that his looks could get him into trouble, the kind of trouble a young boy was ill-equipped to handle, she'd told him everything by the time he'd turned 12. It turns out she'd been right to do so, as he'd had his first sexual experience at the tender age of 16.

"I have been seeing someone, Mom. She's a wonderful woman. I know you'll love her."

Fiona hesitated, her sharp ears catching the 'you'll'. As an adult, Brian had yet to bring one of his girl-friends to Detroit to meet her. Trying hard to sound casual, she asked, "Does that mean you'll be bringing her to Detroit, then?"

"Yes it does. I'll see if she can join us in September, if she can't, then I'll ask her to come with me for Thanksgiving."

"What's she like, Brian? Is she pretty?"

"She's gorgeous, Mom. She's got this smooth brown skin that looks like—"

"Oh, is she African-American, then? Is it that lovely Kendra Phelps you dated so long ago?"

"Kendra Phelps?" Brian murmured, trying to remember. When an image of a pixie face with pigtails came to mind, he laughed. "God Mom, we were 10 years old then and we didn't date. The only thing I did was steal a kiss. And if you'll recall, I came home with a black eye for my troubles. It was worth it though; she was the cutest girl in the fourth grade."

Fiona sniffed. "Hmmph, I'm glad it isn't her. A nasty, little snot of a girl she was, and unattractive with it."

Brian chuckled. "Mom, you just finished saying how lovely she was."

"Well, I've changed my mind. Anyway, tell me about your lady. What is her name?"

"Her name is Caroline Singleton, and she's an artist. You should see her work. You'd love the way she blends color and form to come up with things that an ordinary mind wouldn't even think of. She sculpts as well."

Fiona closed her eyes and silently thanked her maker for the quiet joy she heard in her boy's voice when he mentioned his lady friend. She figured she was due a grandchild, finally. "Well, me boy, what of her parents? Her family?"

"Her family lives here in Chicago, I haven't had the opportunity to meet them yet. But, I know you've heard of them. You know that Grandmother's Ice Cream you're so fond of?"

"Know it? It's the only kind I buy."

"Well, that's the Singletons. Her family owns the company. Her father and uncle started the company with a recipe from a great-grandmother, I believe. Her mother, brother and a couple of cousins work at the company as well."

"Well now, that's as it should be, isn't it? Keep the family business in the family. I like that. I like that a lot. Well, what are you waiting for? When will you be presenting yourself to Mr. and Mrs. Singleton?"

"I'll be meeting them Labor Day, which is why I can't come to see you then."

"Don't you worry about me; there's no hurry. You just take yourself up to meet the Singletons. I'm sure they'll love ya."

"Thanks for understanding Mom." Brian said dryly. "Listen, Mom, you don't mind that Caroline is black?"

"Mind? Why should I mind? Did I mind when you dated the Chinese girl or the Jewish one? Now, I did mind when you dated that Jenny O'Brien. Nothing but a tramp, that one was! And her family— nothing but crooks and thieves, the lot of 'em. But you were only 17 then. I trust your judgment has improved since."

Laughing, Brian said, "Don't ever change, Mom; there's not another person like you in this world. I gotta go. I love you. Tell Frank hello for me."

In Detroit, Frank Applegate walked into the living room to find his wife sitting on the sofa, with her hand still on the receiver and her gray eyes staring vacantly into space.

"What is it Fi?" He asked as took hold of her arms and pulled her up.

"Oh, Frankie," Fiona said as she came out of her daze. "Our Brian is getting married." She finished and leaned back in his arms with tears in her eyes and a happy smile on her face.

"Married? Brian? Since when?" Frankie asked, surprised. He was a medium-sized man, only a few inches taller than his wife's 5'5" frame. He was stocky with a thick, bull neck and arms roped with muscle. He scratched his hand through his salt and pepper hair as he looked down at his wife with questioning green eyes.

"I just got off the telephone with him. She sounds like a nice girl, his lady friend. He'll be bringing her to meet us in September or at the Thanksgiving holiday." She said, moving out of his arms and walking into the kitchen.

Frank watched his wife's trim figure as it walked away from him. Something didn't sound right. "When are they getting married?" He asked following her into the kitchen.

"Well, he didn't exactly say." Fiona said as she pulled out bread for sandwiches. "But I know they'll be getting married soon."

Frank smiled at his wife's back. "He didn't even mention marriage did he?"

"No," Fiona said as she turned to him with a sheepish smile. "But I could tell from his voice that this girl, this Caroline Singleton, is the one. I've never heard this kind of happiness in Brian's voice before."

Frank shook his head. "Don't jump the gun on this, Fi. He may not be ready to settle down. He's young yet, he's got time."

"Trust me," Fiona said, her smile still in place. "This girl is the one who will make him want to settle down."

"If you say so, honey." Frank said as he walked over to run his hand over her black hair. "If you say so."

———∾∾∾∾———

"I'm so glad you're back in town, Tracy," Caroline said as she settled down on her sofa with a big bowl of popcorn.

"Me too." Tracy said digging into the bowl for a big handful. "Thanks for letting me sleep over. I just didn't feel like facing my dusty, food-less house tonight. And the unpacking," she said with an exaggerated roll of her eyes, "girl the unpacking would make you weep." Tracy had gotten back in Chicago earlier that Friday afternoon and had called Caroline almost as soon as she'd gotten in the door. Caroline had suggested that she sleep over and wait to take care of her unpacking and the rest of her Chicago life the next day. Tracy had happily agreed and the two of them were now cozily dressed in pajamas enjoying a good conversation and junk food like they'd done on a regular basis during their years growing up together.

They'd been best friends since pre-school and had been inseparable ever since Brandon Robinson had put glue in three-year-old Caroline's hair and Tracy had come to her rescue with a punch in his nose. Caroline had repaid the favor two years later when she'd helped Tracy settle a stolen hair ribbon score with the Paxton sisters. She was sure the twin girls still had nightmares about the worms in their macaroni and cheese.

"So," Caroline said, looking at her friend. "Tell me about Vancouver."

Tracy's black eyes grew pensive as she thought about her time in the Canadian city. With a light complexion, short, curly hair and medium height, she was almost an exact opposite of Caroline. Her full mouth, Patrician nose and delicately formed face and frame always garnered second looks wherever she went. Sighing through that full mouth, she said, "It was okay. It will mean a great deal towards a promotion for me. I'll probably be traveling quite a bit between here and there in the next year or so."

Looking at Tracy's solemn face, Caroline said, "Isn't that supposed to be happy news?"

Tracy frowned. "Ordinarily, it would be. But lately, I just don't know what's wrong with me. The thought of a promotion doesn't make me as thrilled as it would have a year ago." She shrugged her shoulders, "Or even six months ago."

"Well what is it that's bothering you?"

"I don't know. You know how much I've always loved numbers and math and figuring them out, right? I mean, to me, numbers were the most fascinating things in the world. Now, though, they don't excite me like they used to. Work doesn't even excite me anymore—not even the thought of the vice presidency that the CEO's been hinting about for the past few months. I don't know what the problem is; I've just felt so restless lately. I've felt like I should be doing something else. I just don't know what."

"Maybe you've been pushing yourself too hard. After all, you're only 30 and here you are in line for a vice presidency at one of the top accounting firms in the region. Maybe you need to slow down and take things easy for a while. You've always pushed yourself hard. I can remember your being that way in elementary school, even. It's time you stopped."

"With surgeons as parents, it was only natural that I would push." Tracy said with honesty. "Anyway, I *have* been thinking about taking a vacation. Maybe a week off would do me some good."

"Are you kidding me? A week? Tracy, you need a month at least. Surely, they'd let you do that, after all the time you've put in."

"You're right." Tracy said with a smile, after a moment of quiet. "Why not? They owe me at least that much. Hell, I could probably take two months and not get any guff about it. I've only taken one vacation since I've been with the company and that was only for four days five years ago."

"Good for you! Take two months. Where will you go?"

"I don't know. The possibilities are endless, aren't they?" Tracy asked, feeling excited about something for the first time in months.

Caroline nodded in agreement. "Will you be taking anyone with you?" She asked.

"If you're talking about Andrew, the answer is hell. no." Tracy said the last two words succinctly with a hiss through her teeth for emphasis.

Caroline looked at her in amusement. "Not just no, but hell no, huh?"

"That's right. The jerk is out of my life. He didn't come to see me once while I was in Vancouver, not once."

"I thought you guys were just casual anyway. That's what you told me."

"True, we were." She said. "But he could have at least asked me if he could come for a visit."

"Well why would he, when you told him the same thing you told me? Maybe he didn't want to seem like he was crowding you."

"I know, I know." Tracy said impatiently. "After all, I'm the one who suggested that we take things slow, aren't I? But the brother never even tried to get me in bed. Not once in the five months I knew him! What's up with that?"

Caroline burst out laughing and hearing how contradictory she sounded, Tracy laughed as well. Winding down and wiping tears from her eyes, she said, "Well how about that? I'm a tease and I didn't even know it!"

Chuckling now, Caroline shook her head. "You are so crazy. No wonder I missed you so much while you were gone. I can't remember the last time I laughed so hard."

"I can't remember the last time I did either. I guess there hasn't been much for me to laugh about lately."

"How could there be, when you've been working so much?" Caroline put the empty bowl on the floor, and folded her legs. "So, what about Brazil for your trip?"

Tracy didn't miss a beat at the quick switch in topics. "No," she said with a shake of her head. "Not there. And I don't want to do Africa again yet. I mean, I know that trip we took to western Africa the summer after our senior year was a long time ago, but I want to go some place different. I'm thinking maybe Europe: France, Germany, Great Britain, Switzerland. I hear that Switzerland is a great place to meet single men. Maybe I'll hook myself a white guy," she said with a smile that said 'tell me everything', "like you did."

Caroline laughed. "Yeah, right. That will be the day—you dating a white guy. Anyway, I didn't 'hook myself a white guy', as you so delicately put it. It just happened, like I told you."

"Yeah, yeah, whatever. I know that part; tell me what's happened since you first met."

Caroline smiled. "Well—"

"You slept with him, didn't you?! You slut!" Tracy said gleefully. "Tell me all about it!"

Caroline straightened indignantly. "I will not!"

"Not all the sexy details!" Tracy said with an impatient wave of her hand. "Just gloss over it. You know, tell me without telling me, so to speak."

"Well, I seduced him." Caroline said simply with her tongue between her teeth, and proceeded to tell Tracy exactly how she'd gone about it, watching as her friend's eyes first widened with surprise and then narrowed in speculation.

"I bet his eyes popped out of his head when he saw you. He probably didn't even know what hit him."

'The man was practically drooling by the time he took it all in."

"Wow, I'll bet he was. I knew when you finally decided that you'd found the right man, you'd fall hard. I've been told that there's nothing like intimacy with the man you love. Nothing compares."

"Exactly." Caroline said with a secret smile.

Tracy studied her friend as Caroline lost herself in reverie. The soft smile playing around her mouth and the dreamy eyes could only mean that she was thinking of Brian. Tracy smiled in happiness for her. Whether Caroline knew it or not, she'd been waiting a long time for Brian to come along, and now that he had, Caroline was happier than Tracy had ever seen her.

"So, tell me," Tracy said. "When do I get to meet this sex god of yours? Again, for the second time, that is."

"He's coming over in the morning, so you'll see him then. He says he sort of remembers meeting you last year at Justin's."

"What? You mean, I've finally found the one man who wasn't bedazzled by my stunning beauty?"

"'Fraid so. Besides, after me, any beautiful woman he's ever seen has been wiped from his mind."

Laughing, Tracy poured herself more wine. "I like that in you. Has he met your parents? What about your brother?"

"No, not yet. He'll meet my parents, Lee and the rest of the family Labor Day weekend at the cottage. You'll come too, won't you?"

"Of course. I never miss Labor Day at the Singletons. How's Lee?"

"He's fine, I guess. He and Catherine have been in Spain since early June, so I haven't heard much from him. They've been having problems, and I think this is his last ditch effort to save the marriage."

"That's too bad. I hope things work out for them."

"Yeah, me too. Things were bad before she had the miscarriage, but they've just gotten worse since then. The baby has been spending her time between my parents' and Catherine's parents' houses."

"Baby?" Tracy asked in amazement. "What baby? If you mean that three-year-old terrorist you call a niece, I hate to inform you, but that's not a baby, that's a 50-year-old despot masquerading as child!"

Caroline laughed. "I admit, Genevieve is a handful, but she's a charming one. Besides, children sense when their parents aren't getting along and it's been hard on her."

"Yeah, you're right, the poor kid. Will they be back in the states before Labor Day?"

"Yes. They're supposed to be back next week."

"I guess Lee and Cat don't know about your show at Rutledge, huh?" Tracy continued once Caroline shook her head, "They'll be so happy for you when they hear about it. Tell me about it. How's the preparation going?"

"Wonderfully. It's like I have all of these ideas and energy; it's unbelievable! Lately, I have at least nine or ten productive hours a day. It's amazing."

"Why is that amazing? You've always been prolific in your work."

"Well…" Caroline drew the word out between her teeth and cleared her throat. "At one point, I'd hit a rough spot. Brian helped me get through it."

"How?"

"Let's just say that the night of inspiration I had on the platter stemmed from a few days of non-inspiration in the studio."

"I'm not mad at you."

"Didn't think you would be. Neither was he."

"You're more wicked than I knew, Caroline. That's good." Tracy said with a definitive nod. "Very good."

"Glad you approve. Anyway, my work is looking great, if I do say so myself."

"Are you going to let me see it?"

"You know I don't let anyone see my work until it's completely finished."

"Yes, but I'm sure you have at least a couple finished. Why can't I see those?"

"Because everything is part of everything this time. When I'm finished it will be a complete work. Every piece is part of the whole."

"I'll bet you let Brian see them."

"Wrong. Not even him."

"Oh, well then I guess I lose this argument." Tracy said with a sigh. "What time is he coming over tomorrow? You guys have anything planned?"

"He should be here at about nine. And no, we have nothing planned. We're just gonna hang out, maybe catch a movie. Wanna come?"

"Sorry, can't. I have to go out to my parents tomorrow. They're already upset that I didn't come over tonight."

"I guess they would be." Caroline said around a yawn. "I'm tired. I'm going to bed." She stood up and started walking towards her bedroom. "I put clean sheets on the bed in the guest room. Good night."

"Good night. See you in the morning."

—⁓—

Across town, Brickman angrily stalked away from the window. His efforts to find the photographer had all failed and he was fast losing patience. He wanted the girl and he wanted her immediately. Barely restraining himself from destroying it, he picked up the phone and punched in a number. "Meet me in my home office. You have 30 minutes." He said and slammed down the receiver.

There was going to be hell to pay if he didn't get what he wanted soon.

CHAPTER 13

"So, what's this your mother's been telling me about you dating a white boy?"

Caroline rubbed her hand over her face and reached over for her bedside clock. Squinting her blurry eyes at the face she sighed and flopped back on her pillows. "God Dad, it's 5:00 on a Saturday morning and I was working until one. Call me later," she said grumpily.

"Caroline Louise Singleton, don't you dare hang up on me!" her father demanded in his notoriously loud, booming voice. "I want to talk to you."

Knowing it was useless to fight it, Caroline adjusted her pillows, sat up to clear the cobwebs from her mind. "What do you want Dad?"

"Wake up baby, and talk to me. I asked you if you're dating a white boy."

Aw, man, Caroline thought. reverting back to the phrase she'd habitually used as a teenager to express, dismay, disappointment, and frustration all at once, *This is all I need after a long night of unrest.* "Leave me alone Dad. Where's Mom? Does she know you're pestering your only daughter so early on a Saturday morning?"

"Your mother is still sleeping. She's got a slight cold. Which reminds me, you need to get your little, narrow behind over to the house to visit more often. Your mother and I miss you. But don't try to change the subject. Are you or are you not dating a white boy? I've been out of town so much lately that I haven't had a chance to give the matter the attention it deserves. But I've got time now, so speak to me."

Caroline sighed again, and fixed the sheet around her "He's not a boy Dad, he's a man," she said, just to be perverse.

"So you really are dating a white boy. I never thought I'd see the day."

"Why not? It's not like we ever talked about it. The subject of dating outside the race was never even discussed at home. I never once heard you or Mom say anything negative about interracial couples."

"That's because I never thought what other people did was any of my business."

"That's a good philosophy Dad. So why don't you stick to it, and don't badger me about this?"

"Because, as you were so quick to point out only seconds ago, you're my daughter. And that makes you my business."

"My personal life is—"

"I love you Caroline." He said softly, cutting her off and weakening her frustration. "You're my baby girl and I don't want to see you get hurt."

"I know Dad, but Brian is a good guy. You'll like him a lot, I promise you. He would never hurt me—"

"I wasn't talking about him. I was talking about society. Despite the fact that we're starting a new millennium, there are people out there who will hate seeing you two together, and they will do everything they can to hurt you."

"I'm not naïve Dad, but I can't let society dictate how I live my life. Brian is the man I love and I want to spend the rest of my life with him. Why should I let what people think or do ruin that for me? I'm not going to give anyone that kind of power over me." She said quietly.

Her father was quiet for a few moments and she could picture him sitting behind his big cherry wood desk smoking from his forbidden pipe. Patricia would read him the riot act if she knew about it. His tall, football player frame would be covered by his favorite robe, while his large, dark face would be wrinkled in a frown. Everything about Charles Singleton was big: his body, his face, his personality and most importantly, his heart. It was what she loved about him most, his generous spirit. Clearing his throat, he said, "Just be sure, baby. It's a tough world out there, and good people like you tend to get roughed up a bit if they aren't careful."

"I'm sure Dad. He's the one."

"Couldn't you have found yourself a good black man?"

"Yes, I suppose I could have. But I didn't. I found Brian."

He heard the ring of conviction in her voice and closed his eyes. It was about time she settled down, he thought. He knew she would disagree with him, but he firmly believed that a person should be settled down by the time they were 30. Hell, he'd married her mother when he was only 22, and it was the smartest decision he'd made to date. He would rather that she married a black man, but…well, he'd just reserve his judgment until he met this Brian who had the ability to make his little girl's voice go all soft and dreamy when she mentioned his name. "Well, you bring this Brian to me. I want to meet him."

Caroline laughed at him. "Quit trying to sound like some sort of feudal lord, Dad. You forget, I know the real marshmallow."

"Mind the sass, minx. I want to meet this Brian. You'll bring him to the cottage Labor Day weekend."

"I don't know Dad. I'll see if he wants to come." Caroline said, tongue in cheek.

"He will. You just bring him to me. Now tell me about him. Your mother says he's some sort of technology wizard."

"He is. When he had his own consulting firm, he developed IT systems for some of the large advertising agencies downtown."

"Good, good. Our system at the office could use some updating. Perhaps your Brian could come in and take a look—"

"No way, Dad." Caroline said serenely. "I'm not going to let you use Brian for free technological help.

Stop being such a cheapskate and hire someone. Besides, Brian doesn't do consulting anymore; he's a partner in Inclusion, but I know Mom has already told you this."

"Cheapskate! No man's ever called me that to my face and—"

"Lived to tell about it." Caroline said blandly, cutting through his bluster. "Yes, yes I know Dad. But I'm not a man; I'm your loving daughter, so I can tell you these things without fearing for my life. I can ask Brian to recommend someone for you."

Charles chuckled softly to himself. His little girl always saw right through him. Sometimes it made him swell with pride and other times it made him wish for progeny who was less astute. He laughed out loud. "You do that. Have this Brian recommend someone." Hearing movement upstairs, he frantically looked around for a place to stash his pipe. "I've got to go baby," he said hurriedly. "There's something I need to do and I'm running out of time. I love you."

Caroline laughed. "I love you too, Dad. Don't forget to open the windows." She said and hung up.

Just as I said, Charles thought to himself as he hurried to open the window, the girl was just too smart sometimes.

—⁓—

Brian watched Caroline lick ketchup off her fingers, thinking she looked like a kid with her blue jean cut-offs and the thick braid she wore. It was

Sunday afternoon and they were having lunch after spending the morning in the park where Caroline had taken pictures. He'd enjoyed watching her work. This had been his second photography excursion with her and it had been an experience seeing how fiercely she concentrated when she had a goal in mind.

He'd watched her charm smiles out of everyone from a gaggle of seven year old girls playing jump rope to a group of teenagers fiercely competing in soccer. They'd all succumbed to her smiles and playful attitude and had allowed her to snap their picture. She'd handed out her personal card, promising to send photos to anyone who wanted them. And all the while, he'd watched and wanted to take her home to bed.

Caroline noticed him staring at her mouth and slowly and lasciviously ran her tongue around her lips. Laughing teasingly when he met her eyes, she picked up one of her fries and reached across the table to feed it to him. "Concentrate on this, Brian. Because what you're thinking about is not going to happen for at least a couple of days."

Knowing her feelings on the subject, Brian didn't mention that they could still enjoy each other while she was menstruating. He chose to bite into the fry instead, finishing it off in two bites as he held her gaze. He watched her bite her lip as he licked the last of the salt and ketchup off her finger. Pulling her finger into his mouth, he sucked gently and watched as her lashes fluttered.

Snatching her finger away, Caroline balled her hand into a fist on her lap. "You're not being fair Brian."

"I'm just giving you a taste of things to come." He said as he picked up his pop and took a long swig.

Taking a nervous look around to make sure no one else in the little grease spoon had witnessed his teasing, Caroline finished off her burger and decided it was time to change the subject. "How are things at work? Did you guys get the Riddle account?"

Eyeing her knowingly, Brian shrugged his shoulders. "We don't know yet. We won't have an answer until next Thursday."

"That's a huge account. If you guys get this one, you'll be in league with the big boys. How does it feel?"

"It will be good for us. After all, it's what we've wanted all along. We'll see what happens with Riddle. If we don't get them, someone else will come along."

"How's Ida?" She tried to sound casual.

Brian wasn't fooled. "Why would you ask about Ida? She hates you."

Caroline shrugged. "I don't like her either, but the last time I saw her she had bruises and nobody deserves that."

"She came into work recently with a black eye and a bruise on her cheek. Maria, Justin and Carl all offered their help, but she brushed them off and said that she'd been in a fender bender over the weekend. I don't feel comfortable saying anything to her at all anymore, for fear she'll take it as a sign that I still want a relationship."

"She's obviously being abused. What are you guys going to do?" Caroline asked out of curiosity.

"Maria brought in a counselor to talk to everyone about abuse. You know, how to recognize the signs if you're being abused or if you're doing the abusing. Ida sat there the whole time, not saying anything. Hopefully she was listening and will think about what the counselor said. Who knows?" Brian said with a shrug. "In the end, it's really none of our business. I think we've done all we can."

Caroline sighed. "I guess you have." She changed the subject. "How is everything working out in the art department? You guys check out any of those names I gave you?"

"Everything is fine. Perry stepped right into your shoes; he hasn't missed a beat. I think one more person added to the team, someone mid-level, should make them complete. I think they've narrowed it down to two people from your list."

"I knew Perry would be a good director. I went to school with his sister, so I sort of knew him before we started working together." Caroline said.

"Well, he can't say enough good things about you. Every time I bump into him, it seems he telling someone else how talented you are."

"Really? Oh, that's sweet." Caroline said with a smile.

"Sweet, my ass." Brian said in disgust. "Anyone with two eyes in his head can tell he admires more than your talent."

"Brian," Caroline whispered in pretended shock. "I'm surprised at you. Perry is perfectly harmless. He only has a slight crush."

Brian looked at her twitching lips and nodded his head knowingly. "A crush is fine, so long as it doesn't go any further than that."

"Okay, macho man." She cooed teasingly. "I promise." She said in a helpless, little voice, giving him a sexy pout and a delicate shimmy of her shoulders.

Brian watched as her small breasts jiggled slightly behind her loose, white T-shirt and narrowed his eyes. Lifting his gaze, he looked straight into her knowing, teasing eyes. "Now who's not playing fair?" He asked dryly.

Caroline winked licentiously and said, "My mother always taught me that turn-about is fair play, what's good for the goose is good for the gander and any other phrase you can think of that fits this situation."

"How about 'just wait; you'll get yours'?" Brian asked meaningfully.

Caroline laughed and covered his hand with hers. "That too, and no one is looking forward to you to giving it to me more than I."

A young man walked by, bumping her chair. "Excuse me, sister." He moved on.

"That's okay." Caroline looked up with a smile, but he was already past her. Brian narrowed his eyes at the man's back, but didn't say anything. It seemed to him that the man could have easily avoided bumping into her chair.

Caroline patted his hand and stood up. "I'm going to the bathroom. You'll keep an eye on my equipment, won't you?

"You've had me lugging it around all day; I'm not going to lose sight of it now."

She leaned over the table for a kiss. "But you're so good at lugging heavy stuff around." She whispered against his mouth. "Who else would I ask, macho man?"

Caroline dried her hands and checked her hair in the mirror. Swinging through the door, she was brought up short when a man stepped in front of her. "Oh, excuse me." She said and moved to walk around him in the small alcove.

When the man moved in her same direction and blocked her path again, she looked up. She had a long way to go; he was at least 6'4". It was the same man who'd bumped her chair. Looking at him with his folded arms and purposeful eyes, she realized that both actions had been deliberate. Squaring her shoulders, she said, "Is there something I can do for you?"

The man looked surprised at first, but then said slowly, "Lousy, stinkin' sell-out."

Caroline raised her brow. She was taken aback, but not for long. "Presumptuous, close-minded idiot." She said succinctly.

This time, the man couldn't get beyond his surprise. "Presumptuous? What do you mean, I'm presumptuous?"

Caroline put her hands on her hips. "What do you mean I'm a sellout?"

"I mean you're selling out. Dating that white man, when there are plenty of brothers who would love to have a sister like you."

"Well, let me tell you something." Caroline said as she poked him in the chest. "How dare you presume to treat me like I'm something to be owned and am therefore anyone's for the choosing? How dare you presume to decide whom I can date? How dare you presume that blacks should date only blacks? How dare you presume to judge me? Who are you? Do you know me? You know nothing about me!"

Completely outdone now, the young man could only stare at her.

"And another thing—" Caroline began, still poking him in his chest.

"Is there a problem here?" Brian demanded. He'd decided to look for Caroline after remembering how deliberate the bump into her chair seemed to be. He wasn't happy to find the man responsible for it standing there in confrontation with her. When no answer was forthcoming from Caroline or the man, Brian stepped forward in front of Caroline, blocking her view. "I asked if there was a problem." He said to the man.

The man took his time before answering. "No." he said slowly. "No problem."

"Let's keep it that way." Brian said and turning away, he looked at Caroline. "Are you all right?"

"I'm fine," she said as he took her hand.

"Ooh, that kind of stuff just makes me so mad!" She said as they walked outside.

Brian pulled her into the shadow of the building, maneuvered her against the wall and stood in front of her "Why didn't you call me when that guy started harassing you? I would have taken care of it."

"What?" Caroline asked in a baffled tone. Her mind was still on her argument.

"I said you should have called me when that guy started bothering you."

Caroline looked at him and realized he was mad because she hadn't asked for his help. Shrugging her shoulders, she said, "I didn't think I needed any help."

Brian was more than mad; he was furious. When he thought about the man stopping her and what had almost happened in the park, he became livid. "He could have done more than just talk to you Caroline. What if he'd wanted to hurt you? What then?"

Caroline studied him closely. "I don't know. I was just so mad, I didn't see him as a threat. I know you're thinking about that guy from the park, but this wasn't like that, Brian. This guy wasn't a threat, he was just an idiot."

"Sometimes idiots are the ones you have to worry about the most. It's not something that can always be recognized right away."

Caroline nodded. "Okay." She said agreeably. "I do know how to ask for help Brian, but I only ask for it when I feel I really need it."

"I understand that, but I need you to understand that I'm not going to stand by and watch while someone threatens you, harasses you or anything else. Call it macho or whatever you like, but that's how I am and that's how it's going to be."

Caroline eyed him from under her lashes and said demurely, "Yes, but you will agree that I can handle myself verbally, won't you? I don't need the big, strong man stepping in for that."

"It's not funny, Caroline."

"Yes, it is. In fact, it's pretty ridiculous. I will admit that there might be-and that's a huge might—times when I'll need you to take care of things for me, and I'm sure I'll probably even want you to. But let's face it Brian, unless I suddenly become president or the next Whitney Houston, I don't need a bodyguard."

Satisfied, despite her sarcastic response, that she saw his point of view, he kissed her resistant mouth. "Smart ass." He took her hand again and they began to walk towards her condo. "You haven't seen that guy from the park again, have you?"

Caroline rolled her eyes. "No, Brian. I told you I would tell you if I did. Besides, I think it was just a fluke and I got spooked. I'd like to talk about something else now. This is the first time someone has actually confronted us about our dating. How does it feel?"

Brian shrugged his shoulders. "It probably won't be the last time. We can't let it bother us."

"You know, I guess I've been waiting for something like this to happen. But to be called a sell-out as if…as if…everyone else but me has a right to choose who I date. He acted as if my body and mind belong to the black race and I have to get approval."

"I know it seems that way, but it's like you said, the kid doesn't know you. Probably most of the people who will confront us, won't know us. They won't have any idea what they're talking about, and no one can tell you whom you should be with. It's stupid for them to try." Brian said.

"It still bothers me. Almost everywhere we go, there's someone who stares at us or cuts his or her eyes at us. Who are they to judge?"

"That's just it; they have no right to judge us, and if they had any sense, they'd realize there's nothing to judge. We're not doing anything wrong. If you just keep that in mind, it won't bother you so much."

"I guess you're right." Caroline said and leaned her head on his shoulder. "But he seemed so young to be thinking that way. He couldn't have been more than 20."

Brian thought about the stunned look on the kid's face as she'd poked him in the chest and laughed and stopped walking. Positioning her in front of him, he looped his arms around her waist. "I think you may have scared the kid into a little critical thinking." He said and kissed her in the middle of the pedestrian-clogged sidewalk.

BOOK TWO

CHAPTER 14

"Hey man, what's up with you?" Justin asked Brian as he slapped him on the back and settled down next to him at the conference table. It was four p.m. and the company was having its usual Friday happy hour. Justin had noticed Brian sitting alone drinking a beer. He'd decided to come over and see what the problem was.

Brian took a long swallow from his beer and shook his head. He'd been thinking about Caroline.

"It's not Ida, is it?" Justin asked. "I hope she's not giving you any trouble. She seems to have mended her ways. She came to me and apologized and told me that I could expect nothing but professionalism from her from now on."

Brian glanced over at Ida who was standing in the corner with one of the junior level PR people. He hadn't even thought of her since he'd had that meeting with her. "No, it's not her. I barely even see her anymore. But I'd advise you to watch her carefully. As you know, Ida doesn't like to lose."

"I know, which is why I'm telling you to take your own advice and use it personally." Justin said around a mouthful of peanuts. "We don't have to worry about her screwing up at Inclusion," he explained patiently when Brian looked at him in question. "Caroline is no longer here. Ida's not mad at us; she's mad at her. And since her target no longer works here, we don't have to worry. It's you two who need to worry."

Brian twisted his mouth. "There's not a whole lot she can do. I'm not worried."

"You'd be surprised. I'm just telling you to watch your back, that's all. Don't think Ida wouldn't hurt you if she could."

"I didn't say I *don't* think she'd do anything. I said there's not much she *can* and I'm not worried. There's a difference."

"Well, if it's not Ida that's got you over here practically courting that one beer, what is it?"

Brian debated with himself for a moment. "Caroline was running in the park a couple of weeks ago and got approached by this guy. Something about him spooked her and she was terrified when I caught up to her."

"What exactly happened?" Justin asked.

Brian told him and then said, "The problem is Caroline has convinced herself that it was nothing, that she went overboard, but I think it was more than that. I think the guy was up to something."

"Well I guess as a former cop, you'd have more of an instinct for that sort of thing."

"That's sort of what Caroline said, but she's putting a different spin on it. She keeps telling me that I'm letting my cop's imagination run away with me. I don't agree. If the guy were going to mug her, why would he stop her first and talk to her? Why not just grab whatever he wanted and run? Same thing for rape. Why talk to her first? Why didn't he just grab her?"

"It looks to me that you may have just won Caroline's argument for her. I mean, maybe his only motive was to get directions."

Brian was shaking his head before Justin finished. "I don't buy that. I would if I didn't know Caroline as well as I do. She's not the kind of woman to get hysterical over someone just looking at her and giving her a phony smile. She's too practical for that. You know her. Does she strike you as someone who would get hysterical because a man has weird eyes?"

"No." Justin said immediately.

"But you should have seen her that night, J. She was shaking so hard; I wouldn't have been surprised if I'd heard bones knocking together. No," he said definitively. "If the guy spooked her that badly, then he was up to something. I just feel it.

"She's also been getting these phone calls lately. She gets at least two or three a week. The person doesn't say anything, but he holds the phone for a little while and just breathes really hard. I just found out about them yesterday, when she and I accidentally answered separate phones in her condo at the same time. They apparently have been coming during the day when I'm not there. She's been blowing them off because the calls have been sporadic."

"So what are you going to do about it?"

Brian rubbed the back of his neck. "There's not a whole lot I can do, but I did call in a few favors down at my old precinct. She wasn't happy about it, but I had Caroline draw a sketch of the guy and I took it down to the precinct. His face didn't ring any bells with anyone down there, so one of the guys is going to pass it around to other precincts and see if anything develops."

Justin studied him for a moment. "I've never seen you act this way over a woman before. I know you said that you thought she might be the one you'll spend the rest of your life with, but that was months ago. How do you feel now?"

"The same, except now I'm more confident that it's going to happen." Brian said and laughed at Justin's look of surprise.

"I'm happy for you, Bri." Justin said, once he was able to gather his thoughts. "So, what makes her it? You know, the one and only for you?"

Brian didn't have to think about it. "She fits me. We communicate on a level that I've never achieved with anyone before. And I know that when I'm with her, nothing else matters. Nothing. She's my peace." He took a sip of his beer, embarrassed to have said so much. From the corner of his eye, he watched Justin do the same thing and avert his eyes. He hadn't even known what he was going to say when Justin had asked him the question, but he'd just opened his mouth and the words seemed to flow out naturally, as if they'd only been waiting for his cue.

Trying to help them both recover their dignity, Justin said flippantly, "So I'm the best man, right?"

Brian laughed. "We haven't discussed marriage yet, but I know we will be getting married. There's no rush."

Justin turned serious. "Have you told her what you've just told me? I mean about how nothing else matters and everything?"

"Not in so many words, no. But I have told her that I love her. I tell her that all the time."

"I guess she feels the same, because if she didn't, you wouldn't feel the way you do, right?"

"Yes. Yes, I would. Of course her feelings matter, but I can't cut mine off like you would a faucet. If she didn't feel the way I do, it would be hard for me, but my feelings for her probably would never really change. If they did, it would probably take a lifetime for them to do so."

"I guess you two are lucky to have found each other."

"Yes," Brian said and finished his beer. Standing up from the table, he said, "I guess we are. I'll see you later. I'm going home."

Ida watched Brian leave the party early and ground her teeth. She had wanted to speak to him, maybe flirt a little, and had thought that the informal gathering of coworkers would be the perfect place. She was sure he was leaving early to be with Caroline and became angry with herself for dragging her feet on her scare campaign. She was off to a slow start, but she'd pick things up.

—∞—

"I'm glad you came over Lee." Caroline said as she and her brother sat down on the sofa.

"Me too. I missed you Cee Cee."

Caroline grimaced at the nickname he'd given her when they were children. He had been, and still was, the only one to call her that. "So tell me how things went in Spain. Are you and Cat going to be okay?"

Lee sat back, stretching his long legs in front of him. "Spain was wonderful. Madrid was gorgeous, and Cathy and I really enjoyed ourselves in the beginning. But as time went on, things just seemed to get worse."

"Oh Lee," Caroline said, taking his hand in hers and giving it a squeeze. "I'm so sorry. I know how much you were counting on this trip to help you guys work out your difficulties. How are you doing?"

"I'm fine. I've grown used to the fact that Cathy and I just aren't meant to be with one another. It was nothing either one of us did; we just seemed to slowly grow apart."

Caroline studied her brother quietly. He had always been handsome, too handsome, their mother would always say. He was tall and muscularly built with a head he'd kept bald since his early twenties. His eyes were black and piercing like their father's and his strong, aquiline nose set off high cheekbones, a full mouth and a cleft chin. Caroline patted his thigh. "How is Cat doing?"

"About the same. We both became resigned to the fact that it wasn't going to work about the third week we were there. It's weird, you know, but it was something so normal that made me realize that we didn't have what it takes to stay together."

"What was it?"

"Well, one morning I woke up in bed with her. Cathy was sleeping heavily, like the dead, like she usually does after a night out. We'd gone out dancing the night before and had a great time. Everything was fine, but then when I woke up, I looked over at her as she slept on her back. And I looked at the curve of her neck. It was still the same; dark as the darkest chocolate, delicate and vulnerable looking.

"But that particular morning, I looked at it and knew that I would never be able to find the enjoyment in touching it that I had before and that I didn't even want to touch it anymore." He said with a shrug. "And that was it. Cathy woke up soon after I did, and she looked at me and I looked at her and we both knew. We just knew it was over."

Caroline cried for him, for both of them. "Oh Lee," she said, going into his arms for a hug, "that's so sad and beautiful."

Lee chuckled as he stroked her hair. "You always were a soft touch Cee Cee." Laying his head atop hers, he closed his eyes and took solace in her comfort.

Caroline wiped her face on his shirt and said, "At least the two of you can be friends. That will be good for Genevieve."

"Yeah." Lee said with a fond smile as he thought of his child. "Cathy and I are going to do everything we can to make this as smooth a transition as possible for my little angel." He patted her back a couple of times. "Enough about me. Mom and Dad tell me you're seeing someone. He's white?"

Caroline moved out of his arms. "Yes I am and yes he is." She looked at him suspiciously. "Why?"

"Are you sure this is something you want to do?"

"Everyone keeps asking me that, and the answer is always the same. Yes. Yes, I'm sure I want to be with Brian." She sighed. "Look Lee, I know you're worried about how society will treat us—"

"No I'm not. Well, I am, but that's not my biggest concern. He's my biggest concern. This Brian guy."

"What about him? You don't even know him."

"For starters, he's white. And white men have a history of treating black women like chattel, like something to be owned. History has shown that they don't even think of black women as human; just something to be raped or taken and then thrown away"

"What are you talking about?!"

Lee sighed. "Caroline, when I was in college, the white boys had a saying: date a whore, marry a virgin. I don't think that they ever elevate black women up to marriage status. To most white men, a black woman can never be anything but a whore."

Caroline was so stunned that she could only look at him quietly for a moment. Gathering her thoughts, she took her hand and cuffed him in the back of the head, watching as his head sprang forward. "That's the dumbest thing I've ever heard!" She said and stood up with her hands on her hips.

Lee chuckled, rubbed the back of his head and stood up as well. "You did that when were kids too." He said knowingly.

Caroline wanted to slap the superior smirk right off his face. "What?!"

"Resorted to hitting and name-calling when you knew you were in an argument you couldn't possibly win."

"I only did that to you and only when you said stupid, irrational things, things don't have any merit."

"Just listen to reason Caroline—" he began.

"I'm perfectly willing to," Caroline said angrily. "When you start saying something reasonable!"

"I'm serious," he said as he sat down, and grabbed her wrist to pull her down beside him.

"I know you are, which is what bothers me." She said in frustration and passed her hand over her face in a bid for patience. "Listen Lee, have you ever known a white guy who has treated black women like you just described?"

"Yes I have. I've met a couple."

Caroline nodded. "And have you ever known black men who have treated black women that way?"

"Yes, but it's not the same—"

"Of course it is, Lee. I'm not saying it doesn't matter who it is who's treating someone badly, because it does. But what matters the most to that someone is that she is being treated badly, and she wants it to stop. What I'm saying is that the abuser doesn't matter as much the abuse itself. Abuse is abuse no matter who doles it out."

"And I'm saying I'd rather not see the abuse at all, but it happens. And it doesn't make it better for me to see a black man doling out abuse to a black woman, but it makes it worse to see a white man doing it."

"But when you see a black woman with a white man, that doesn't mean that he thinks of her as a whore or just some object to be used for sex. I'd say that that would be more of an aberration than it would be the norm."

"Maybe. I don't know. However, I do think white men are more likely to treat black women that way than black men are."

"Really? What about your friend Roger? And how about Marco? Would they treat me that way?" Caroline asked in challenge.

"No, of course not. But I wouldn't want you dating them, either." Lee said.

Caroline folded her arms. "Have you seen any black rap videos lately? In the majority of those videos, it's like 'look at me, I'm successful I've got all these *things:* cars, homes, jewelry and oh yeah, women, too.' In most of those videos, the women are nothing but objects, sex objects. Do you think the black woman is elevated to more than anything than a whore in their minds? I mean, as long as we're going to generalize…"

"I see your point." Lee said after staring at her for a minute. "And I don't like seeing those videos either. But like I said, I don't like seeing white men with black women because the history of how sisters were treated by them really bothers me."

"That's crazy Lee; you can not judge Brian by what you've seen others do or by what's been done in the past. It's just not fair."

Lee sighed. "I know that Caroline. I knew that before I came over, but it will still be hard for me to see you with him. I'd rather see you date anyone but a white guy."

"Well, I'm sorry for it," Caroline said with a shrug of her shoulders, "but it's not about what's hard for you, it's about what's good for me. And Brian is that, he's very good for me."

Lee studied her. He tugged a wayward curl. "I know it's not how I feel that matters Cee Cee, and I'll work on changing so it won't be so hard."

"You'd better." She said and punched him in the arm. "Here's your chance to start working on it now." She said as she heard Brian's key in the lock. She rose and went into the hallway.

Meeting him as he opened the door, she swallowed a sound of surprise as he took her in his arms and hungrily possessed her mouth. Wrapping her arms around his neck, she met his passion with her own, moaning softly as he nipped her bottom lip with his teeth. When he started to lift her to straddle his waist, she broke off the kiss. "We can't Bri." She whispered, placing her fingers on his mouth. "My brother's here."

Brian lifted his head and looked down the hallway to see Lee standing against the wall with his arms folded and his narrowed eyes on him. "I see," Brian said, taking the other man's measure. *Don't want me touching your sister, do you pal?* he guessed. Defiantly, he bent his head and pressed another hard kiss to Caroline's mouth.

Lee frowned in mild annoyance. Cocky bastard, he thought. If he didn't know what a good judge of character Caroline was and if he didn't trust her instincts, Brian would be flat on his face right now. He waited as Brian started walking towards him.

"Brian." Brian said and held out his hand challengingly.

Lee took his hand. "I know. I'm Lee and I'm staying for dinner." He decided right then and there.

"Glad to have you." Brian said so dryly that Lee had no doubt that he was lying and he had to struggle to keep himself from pushing back in some way. The man had fight in him. He'd give him that much.

"Okay, now that you two alpha idiots have so maturely let each other know where you each stand,"

Caroline said in disgust. "Why don't we decide what we're going to do for dinner? Your choices are Brian cooks, Lee cooks or Mr. Wong at Wong's Takeout cooks." She finished and walked away from them.

Lee turned and watched her go and then turned back to Brian. "You sure you're up for this?"

Brian's eyes never wavered. "Positive."

Over a light dinner that they'd all contributed to, Lee observed their relationship and the way they interacted. Mostly, he watched to see how Brian treated his sister and was pleased to find that he treated her as an equal in all instances and like a pampered queen, which was something that Caroline seemed to demand without saying a word. As he watched Caroline lean over to whisper something in Brian's ear and Brian smile and softly cup her cheek, it hit him. The man's in love, he thought and just then, Brian turned his head and looked at him. Brian nodded as if in affirmation of his thoughts.

Lee inclined his head and lifted his glass.

CHAPTER 15

"Well, you're lucky I own a tux. I never would have been able to rent one on such short notice," Brian said in disgruntlement as he looked in the mirror to adjust the tie.

On the other side of the room Caroline finished putting on her lipstick and turned to look at him. While the crisp black tuxedo and pure white shirt gave him the look of a gentleman, the contrast of his almost-too-long black hair and sinful gray eyes made him look a little dangerous, and she sucked in a breath at the heat curling in her stomach. Turning back to her vanity mirror she tsk-tsked in commiseration and said, "I know, darling, and I am so proud of you for being so resourceful in our time of desperation." Turning her head, she blew him a kiss. "And you look gorgeous, too."

Brian walked over and wrapped his arms around her waist. Meeting her eyes in the mirror, he said, "Don't be such a wise-ass. I think you knew how much I hate big, swanky parties, and that's why you waited until the last minute to tell me about this one tonight."

Caroline widened her eyes and tried to look blameless. "Don't be silly, darling. How would I have

known? The subject has never even come up before."
In truth she had known. She'd just had a feeling that
he wouldn't be the type to like 'swanky' parties, as he
called them. She didn't think she knew a single man
who did. And he was right; she had waited until the
last minute to tell him, precisely because she didn't
want to give him a chance to come up with an excuse
not to go.

Brian kissed her shoulder, bared by the little, black
sheath she called a dress. Optimistically, he thought
now as he studied it. It was strapless and had a deep vee
in the back. Stopping at her knees, it was form-fitting
and made of satin. The strappy, black Manolo
Blahnick heels almost put her eyes level with his and
he met her gaze in the mirror again. "Don't try that
innocent act with me. I know you too well."

She placed her hands on his and leaned back to rest
her head on his shoulder. "It's for a good cause," she
said appealingly. "It's the annual Black and White Ball
for Chicago's Children First and since I'm on the
board, I need to be there. Besides, I'll make it up to
you when we get home." She finished with eyes full of
promise as she angled her head to give his lips better
access to her neck.

"What does the foundation do again?" He asked,
brushing her heavy hair aside with his chin to playfully
bite the side of her neck.

"Almost anything that we can for underprivileged
children—tutoring, mentoring, test preparation,
emergency shelter recommendations, playground

equipment, after-school programs—you name it, we try to do it," she said as she released his hands and stepped out of his arms. "Should we take my car or yours?"

"Let's take mine. Your viper makes me feel like I'm in a sardine can."

"Can I drive?" She asked as she picked up her matching satin shawl.

"Sure, once you learn how to drive like the hounds of hell aren't chasing you." He said as he shut and locked her condo door.

"Where's your adventurous spirit, Brian? Speed is a wonderful thing." She preceded him onto the elevator.

"I agree. Driving somewhat above the speed limit can be fun. I would even say driving at warp speed can be entertaining. But driving at the speed of light, like you do, well, that's just not my idea of amusement. Suicide maybe, but not amusement."

Caroline linked her fingers with his. "Chicken." She said softly.

"Precisely. Which is why you'll never get behind the wheel of my car." He proclaimed and pulled her from the elevator "Never."

—⁂—

"Remind me to trust my instincts and not give in the next time you flash me those pearly whites and bat those big, brown eyes at me," Brian said, taking her elbow as he joined her at the entrance of the hotel.

"I did neither of those things." She said and then gave him a guilty smile. "But I am sorry about going so fast. I just couldn't help it. I've never driven anything with so much power before. I couldn't resist seeing how fast she would go. Just the feel of all those horses under me made me go crazy."

"Save it for the next time I'm under you." Brian said in a low voice as they stepped into the ballroom.

Caroline was saved from answering when Tracy appeared out of the crowd, but she discreetly gave him a retaliatory elbow to the ribs. "Behave." She said from the corner of her mouth just as they met Tracy halfway into the ballroom.

"Hi you two!" She said and gave each of them a hug.

"Hi Trace. You look fabulous." Caroline said with a smile.

"You like?" Tracy asked, twirling around to show off her white ankle-length, sleeveless satin creation. "I found it in a shop on Oak Street just today. I'd almost forgotten about the ball—can you believe it?"

"Well, that's understandable," Caroline said. "Considering you were out of town during much of the preparation."

"True. The place looks fabulous, don't you think?"

"It always does." Caroline agreed, taking in everything from the black and white photos of children lining the walls to the black and white streamers falling from the ceiling.

"So Brian," Tracy said with a smile. "We've got most of Chicago's black elite here—mostly, their progeny—but anyway, what do you think?"

Brian studied the roomful of expensively clad people who were mostly in their twenties and thirties and shrugged his shoulders. "They look just like anyone else at a fancy shindig—hopeful that the main course won't be a rubbery, chicken dish."

Tracy laughed and then turned serious. "I actually came over here to warn you guys. I heard a couple of people whispering when you came in. Brian," she said, looking at him, "are you ready to be stared at, questioned and in general, just plain disliked?"

Brian took in the room with narrowed eyes, returned a few stares, and then shrugged his shoulders again. "I'm game."

Caroline smiled and took his hand. "Don't pay any attention to Tracy; she's just borrowing trouble. I've known most of these people for at least fifteen years or more. You'll be fine."

Brian squeezed her hand. "I'm not worried. Ladies," he said, offering his other arm to Tracy. "Shall we?"

"Wait a minute, Brian," Caroline said, her face filling with pleasure as she watched a tall woman dressed stunningly in a white, silk dinner suit approach them. The slim, tapered pants and short-waisted jacket showed off a fabulous figure.

"Karen Kesha Patrickson!" Caroline said in a rush of pleasure as she embraced the woman in an enthusiastic hug. "I haven't seen you since we had lunch in June!"

The woman made a face as she turned to greet Tracy in the same ardent manner. "I've told you time and again not to call me that Caroline. It's K.K." She said as she stepped back from Tracy to give Brian an interested once-over. "Who's this?"

Brian studied the woman who was as tall as Caroline, but a bit more voluptuous. Her dark-complected face was an interesting one with its hollow cheeks and Patrician nose. The honey-colored hair and eyes threw him off a bit, but it was the devil-may-care look in those eyes that made him smile. "Brian Keenan. Nice to meet you."

"K.K.," she said slowly, firmly shaking his hand while still giving him an assessing look. "Shall I take a guess and say you're here with Caroline?"

"That's right."

She turned to Caroline. "So he's what the room's all abuzz about. You always did like to take chances. That's what I've always liked about you."

Caroline studied her friend's everywhere and anywhere corkscrew curls and fantastically made up face. "Yes, well you know what they call me, Caroline the daredevil." She said dryly. "It's so good to see you K.K. I have to admit that when I sent you an invitation, I didn't know whether you'd come or not. I'd hoped that you would."

"I'm surprised you're here too." Tracy said. "You've never made a secret of how much you hate these society parties. What did you used to call them? Gatherings of the Rich and Aimless, I think it was."

"I still do and they still are. Of course, I don't think of you two in such terms, which is why I'm here. I wanted to see you and Caroline's carefully worded demand could not be ignored. And of course, I think it's a great organization."

"Well no matter your reason, I'm glad you're here." Caroline said, taking K.K.'s hands in hers. "As usual, you look fabulous. I see you stopped straightening your hair."

"Yeah, I finally decided to be happy with the color and texture God gave me."

"Where's your date? I'm interested to see the man who would brave that tongue of yours." Tracy said.

"I've never been known as a cruel woman, Tracy. When I suffer, I suffer alone. I didn't bring anyone."

"Well, you'll sit with us at dinner, then." Caroline said. "If you're not already seated at our table, I'll make arrangements so you will be."

"Sounds good. Well, now that you're here, I can take a breather. I don't mind being the subject of titillating gossip, but when I'm the topic of speculation for the unimaginative…well, it just becomes so…tedious." She said with a slow, lazy wave of her hand and bored eyes. "It's your turn now." She finished and looked at Brian.

"Bring it on." Brian said rubbing his hands together in mock anticipation.

K.K.'s lip top curled up in slight amusement. "Well," she said, looking at Caroline and Tracy. "I'll see you later."

"Bye, K.K."

"K.K. Patrickson." Brian spoke under his breath. "Is that K.K. Patrickson, the newspaper columnist and cartoonist?"

"The one and only." Caroline said, as she watched K.K. walk towards the exit.

"She's also one of three heirs to the Roberts Publishing fortune, and hating every minute of it." Tracy added. "See that obsessively skinny woman in the white dress whose eyes are following K.K.'s every movement?" She asked Brian.

Brian followed her gaze to see a pencil-thin, light-skinned woman with the same color hair and eyes as K.K. staring at her as she left the ballroom. "Yeah, I see her."

"That's her cousin Tiffany. She hates the idea of K.K. being an heir as well."

"They both hate it?" Brian asked. "Why? I can understand Tiffany not liking it out of greed, but why doesn't K.K. want to be an heir?"

"It's a long story. Let's just say K.K. knows how to hold a grudge."

Brian looked at Caroline. "Did you guys grow up with them too?"

Caroline nodded her head. "Sort of. We've had the misfortune of knowing Tiffany since preschool. But we didn't meet K.K. until the 7th grade, and we didn't actually become friends until sometime in high school. Right, Trace?"

"That sounds about right." Tracy agreed.

"Now if we're finished gossiping, I'd like to walk around and mingle a bit." Caroline said and took Brian's hand again.

—◆◆◆—

"Are you having a good time yet?" Tracy asked Brian as she sat down next to him. The gala had been going strong for two hours and thirty minutes. They'd sat through a number of speeches and the requisite rubbery chicken dinner. The party had been moved into another ballroom for dancing. Brian felt like he deserved to relax for a moment, so he was sitting down in one of the chairs lining the walls while Caroline took a turn around the dance floor with yet another donor who wanted some of her time.

Brian let his mouth quirk as he considered Tracy's question. He turned and smiled at her. "Good enough, despite the fact that half the people in this room have stared at me all night and the other half have been asking me questions."

Tracy chuckled and patted his shoulder. "You can handle it. I've been watching you. You're no slouch when it comes to handling the rude and the ignorant."

"It hasn't been that bad. I think the biggest problem has been the single men. They all seem to know you guys and they all seem to resent me being the one here with Caroline tonight."

"That's putting it mildly. They want to kill you. You could be orange and they'd still want to. They're jealous. Caroline and I have been best friends since pre-school and we've known most of the idiots in this room since at least junior high. Being an ice cream heiress was not a big deal in our neck of the woods— it wasn't a big deal, but it wasn't typical, either. And Caroline didn't make matters easier on herself by growing up to look like her mother, who was one of the first black models in New York. Just about all the guys wanted to date her. Are you following me, so far?"

Brian looked at her "I'm following, but it's a winding road. What are you getting at?"

"I'm saying that Caroline has not trusted easily. She learned that growing up; she never knew if guys wanted to date her for her parents' money, for her looks or for herself. She'd never really been in a serious relationship before she met you and I worried about that at first. I've always worried about her and looked out for her because she's Caroline, and I couldn't do anything else."

"You're a good friend Tracy. Now I just have one question. Who looked out for you and your interests? You're beautiful and Justin tells me that both your parents are surgeons, so I know there's money involved."

"Ah, but not the kind of money that an ice cream empire commands. And besides," she said noncha-lantly, "I didn't need as much looking out for as Caroline did. She just has this soft edge to her that makes opportunists think they've struck gold when they meet her. Don't get me wrong, Caroline is no pushover. She was there for me, just like I was for her, but she still has a naïve side to her."

"I know she's not a pushover, but you're not as hard-edged as you'd like me to believe. If you were, we wouldn't be having this conversation." Brian said.

"Never claimed to be hard-edged; just jaded. Don't confuse the two."

Brian laughed. "I'll remember that."

"I like you Brian. You're good for her. That's why I'm going to stop talking in circles and get back to your original supposition. You were right about some of these guys resenting you. Most of them have been trying to get with Caroline since high school. She just wouldn't have them. And now it seems that you got her with no effort at all. And that, my friend, pisses them off."

"They'll live." Brian said.

Tracy laughed out loud. "You wear your arrogance well."

Brian shook his head. "It's not arrogance. Caroline is mine and anyone who doesn't like it, will just have to deal with it. It's as simple as that."

"Well." Tracy said and was quiet for a moment before she cleared her throat. "I don't suppose you've told her that, have you? Because if you did, I'm surprised you're still able to walk around. In fact, your statement makes me want to ask you to stand up and take a turn around the room just so I can make sure that your knuckles don't actually scrape the ground."

Brian looked at the glint in Tracy's eyes and sighed. "Now I see why the two of you are such good friends. Your reaction is much the same as hers was. And being that I do know how to walk upright, and have known how for a long time, I'll amend my statement for you like I did for her. I don't mean that I own Caroline, I mean that she and I belong together. I belong with her, she belongs with me. It works both ways."

"Uh huh." Tracy said skeptically. "I guess if she bought that, then I will too."

"Good."

Deliberately changing the subject, she said, "So tell me what you think about the incident in the park."

"She told you about that?"

"Yes. She tried to convince me that she'd overreacted, but it doesn't sound like it to me. What do you think?"

"I think that I'm glad you're her friend." Brian said, studying her. "I didn't think she'd told anyone. She doesn't want to tell her family, because she says they'll worry needlessly."

"The only reason she told me is she thought I'd think the way she is about the whole situation, but now she knows I don't. Again, what do you think?"

"I think that the guy was up to something and was probably going to hurt her."

"So you think he may have tried to kidnap her and ransom her to her parents?"

"That had occurred to me. But the only thing is that she doesn't make a habit of telling people her family owns Grandmother's."

"So, what are you doing about it?"

"She drew a sketch of the guy and it's being passed around by some of my old cop friends. I have a friend in the FBI who I'll talk to when he gets back in town. She's not running at night anymore, and since she doesn't like to work out inside, instead of going to the gym, I run with her in the mornings. She keeps the door to her studio locked at all times, and I pick her up any night that she's there. She has the number to my cell phone and I bought her one that she promised to carry at all times, though she hates it."

"So Caro finally has a dreaded tracking device. You've done well, Grasshopper."

Brian laughed. "Thank you."

"Well, I see my date looking for me." Tracy said as she stood. "I'd better go. You'll keep me abreast of the situation, won't you?"

Brian stood as well. "Of course. I'll see you later." He bent and kissed her cheek.

"Well, well, well. Not only do you have the lovely Caroline in your grip, but you also command the attention of her friend." A mocking voice came from behind Brian.

Brian turned to see a tall, pale man with red hair smiling derisively at him and said slowly, "Do I know you?"

"Randolph Kittrickson the third, at your service."
The man offered his hand.

Brian took it reluctantly as he stared at the man.
"Brian Keenan." He watched as the man finished off a
Scotch and then grabbed a glass of champagne from a
waiter.

"Oh, I know who you are," Kittrickson slurred his
words before downing the champagne in one gulp and
sitting the empty glass on a table. "Everyone in the
room knows who you are. You're the lucky bastard
who's going to get to go home with Sexy Singleton
tonight."

Brian narrowed his eyes and took a step closer.
"Watch your step, Kittrickson."

The man held his hands up in defense. "Hey pal,
I'm only saying what most of the men here in this
room are thinking. There's no need to get upset. I actually came over here to help you out, friend. You must
be new at this—dating black women, I mean. I've
been watching you and you've been doing it all wrong.
You've been too attentive to her, treating her like she
could actually be your real girlfriend, like she means
something to you. You've got to be careful, or else she's
liable to start getting ideas of permanency and trust
me, you don't want that. You really don't!"

It was lucky for the man that Brian was in a brief
state of surprise at what he was hearing. If he hadn't
been, the man would have been lying on the floor. As
it was, the surprise gave Brian a chance to think before

he acted and he was glad he did. He didn't want to ruin Caroline's event by spilling blood.

Knowing his options in what he could do were limited, Brian stepped even closer to Kittrickson, grabbed his bow tie and gave it a vicious twist. While the other man turned red and struggled to breathe, Brian said through clenched teeth, "I'm not your friend, your pal or anything else. In fact, if I weren't more secure, I'd be ashamed to be only one of a few white men in this room with you. You're drunk and you're a disgrace. Stay away from me and stay away from Caroline and Tracy!"

Brian lightly shoved the man away and walked off as Kittrickson doubled over while taking deep breaths.

Brian caught sight of Caroline on the dance floor and watched as a gray-haired man swirled her into a lavish turn. She smiled and patted the man's cheek. Inspiration struck him while he watched Caroline dance and he made his way to the other side of the ballroom.

"Yes, Mr. Chester, Chicago's Children has had a wonderful year." Caroline tried to say with interest as the older man escorted her off the floor and onto the sidelines. She was exhausted, but she still wanted one last dance with Brian.

"You know my dear," the seventy-something Mr. Chester said and patted her hand. "I'm so pleased that Chicago's Children will dedicate the new playground to my wife. Essie would have been pleased had she lived."

"We're happy to do it, Mr. Chester. After all, you and your late wife have devoted so much to the foundation over the years." Caroline said with an absent smile as she let her eyes wander away from his nutbrown face. Where was Brian?

"Ladies and gentleman," the bandleader said over the microphone. "This next song goes out to Caroline from Brian, with a message. 'Caroline, I couldn't have written it better myself.' Please bear with me ladies and gentleman," the bandleader continued, "as I try to do justice to a beautiful classic. Etta, I hope you'll forgive me." He finished before sliding smoothly into the strains of the song Etta James was best known for, "At Last."

Everything around Caroline ceased to exist for her as she heard what the bandleader said. All conversation, all laughter, all sound—stopped. Turning, she saw Brian standing at the edge of the dance floor with a smile on his face and his hands held out in question. Overwhelmed, she covered her mouth with her hands and shook her head.

At last...

Brian smiled tenderly as he watched her walk over and then into his arms. "You're crazy." She said to him in a tear-clogged voice as she buried her head in his chest. She cried even more when his arms came around her. "This is so sweet."

The bandleader found them through the crowd, smiled at them and sang about love finally coming along.

Chuckling softly and shaking his head in puzzlement at how she could sound happy and still be crying, he closed his eyes and kissed the top of her head, feeling inordinately lucky.

The singer continued to sing about lonely days being over

"Why am I crazy? I'm in love with you and I want everyone to know it. Now seemed as perfect a time as any." He said and looked around the room challengingly. While there was still some lingering resentment, most people were smiling, especially the women.

Caroline nuzzled her head under his chin until he was compelled to kiss the top of her head again. She framed his face with her hands and brought his mouth down for a slow, lingering kiss. "You're wonderful, just wonderful." She said with shining eyes.

"Do that again, and I'll know you really mean it."

Caroline chuckled and complied. "The first kiss will have my mother's phone lines burning up tonight. The second one will have her burning up my phone lines tomorrow to discuss proper behavior. Oh, but I don't care. It's perfect, Brian. You're perfect!

"How did you know I needed something just like this, right here, right now?" She said and wrapped her arms around his neck and swayed to the music.

"I did it mostly for myself. I wanted an excuse to hold you close in my arms and I wanted you to know just how much I love you. Now," he said, pausing as the last strains of the song began to play. "This should bring your mother right to your doorstep."

Caroline smiled at him in puzzlement.

He took her arms from around his neck and kissed each of her hands.

The bandleader uttered words about a spell being cast at the sight of a smile.

Never taking his eyes from hers, Brian swept Caroline into a deep, expansive dip.

As the singer sang the lovely words about being in heaven because he had found the woman he loved, Brian became more in tune with Caroline and the music. He bent over her and sought her mouth with his own hot, open one, kissing her just as the singer said the last two words of the song.

'At last.'

———⟋⟍———

Caroline eyes opened into the early morning sunlight. Stretching, she felt a tingle start in her toes and work its way up to other pulse points. *Last night was wonderful. I feel so deliciously…wanton,* she thought, biting her bottom lip and closing her eyes as she remembered exactly what had transpired between her and Brian the night before when they'd gotten to his loft. Turning her head, she looked at him as he slept on his stomach on the other side of the bed.

She sat up and crawled over rumpled sheets and a discarded pillow to land soft, warm and naked on his bare back. Stretching out so that they touched in every conceivable place, she tunneled her fingers through his hair and pleasured herself by twirling her tongue around his ear. Catching his earlobe between her teeth, she bit it softly and pulled it into her mouth, sucking gently for several seconds.

After releasing his earlobe, she tracked wet, steamy kisses from the nape of his neck to his shoulder blades. She rubbed the palms of her hands slowly and roughly across the span of his back, digging in deep and hard. Making her own toes curl, she slid her hands underneath his chest and fingered his flat nipples, teasing them into hard points.

"You'd better stop, Caroline," Brian said in a raspy voice when he felt her hands stray further south as she pressed her own hardened nipples into his back. He'd been awake since she'd landed on his back, but he didn't want to interrupt her sensual journey. "I can't guarantee what will happen if you don't stop."

"Well," she drew the word out until it had three syllables as she licked his ear again. "I can hazard a guess, but why don't we see anyway?" She breathed into his ear

Brian turned over, flipping her off his back and onto her own. "You want to tease, huh?" He asked as he caught her legs between his and leaned over her. "Someone's in a naughty mood this morning."

She flattened her palms on his chest and ran her fingers up along his skin until they met behind his neck. Gazing up at him through eyes that were at half-mast from desire, she purred knowingly, "You like it."

"Can't resist it," he agreed and bent his head to nuzzle her neck with his chin. The friction from his early morning stubble made her tighten her grip a fraction and using his lips, tongue and teeth, he took a leisurely tour up her neck. He kissed the curve behind her ear, licked it, softly blew on it and had the pleasure of feeling her legs shift restlessly beneath him.

Caroline framed his face and lifted it from her neck. Pulling his head down, she swirled the tip of her tongue around the outer rim of his lips. Unable to close her eyes because she couldn't resist the pull of his, she first nibbled on his top lip, flicked it in apology with her tongue and then gave her attention to his bottom lip. Brian groaned deep in his throat and crushed her mouth with his. She responded eagerly, arching her back as his hands explored the rest of her body.

Using his knee to spread her legs, Brian sank gratefully into her warmth, eliciting groans of relief from the both of them.

"'Nothing is more fine than being in Caroline in the—moor-or-or-nin,'" Brian later ad-libbed the old song as he prepared to leave her body.

Caroline slowly opened eyes filled with lazy amusement to look up at him and just as slowly closed them again. "Fool," she said affectionately.

Falling onto his back next to her, he waited for her to find her usual position on his chest before he said, "If I'd known one song could make you so amorous, I would have played it long ago. Hell, I'd have played it right after I met you."

Caroline laughed and then said seriously, "It wasn't the song, precisely." She lifted her chin to rest it on her hands, as they lay folded on his chest. "It was the idea of the song. Just the idea of it, the idea behind it, made me love you more and made me want to…well, you *know,*" she finished and ducked her head so that it was resting back in its original position.

"Yeah, I know." Brian said, amused at how she could sometimes be so bashful with him, when other times she was downright shameless. Rubbing her back, he said, "I do know what you're talking about because the song made me feel the same way."

"Okay," Caroline said with a hard squeeze. "Now that we've gotten all of the mushy stuff out for the day, I have to shower. I need to go home and wait for my mother's call about last night." She climbed over him and headed for the bathroom.

Brian watched her and stood. "Well as long as she's calling anyway, I may as well keep you here a little longer and give her the subject of staying out all night to talk to you about." He said and followed her into the bathroom.

CHAPTER 16

"I'll be driving back to Chicago, right?" Caroline asked belligerently as Brian took the last curve leading to her family's cottage.She'd already been irritated when he picked her up that morning because the sculpture she'd been working on for days suddenly didn't seem right. Then they'd had an argument because she'd gotten up before dawn to go over to her studio and she hadn't called him to come and go with her.

Brian clenched his hands on the wheel in irritation. The two-hour drive from Chicago to southern Michigan had been one of the longest in his life. The scenery was flat with lots of tall grass and trees to highlight their way. But above all, Caroline in a petulant mood was hard to take, and her mood only worsened his as the drive wore on, making him grit his teeth. He'd been angry since she'd called him from her studio that morning and told him to pick her up from there. The way he saw it, she refused to take the issue of her safety seriously and it didn't make sense. The argument they'd had about it that morning hadn't alleviated any of his anger because she just wouldn't listen to him and it bothered the hell out of him.

He supposed he'd known they were going to have an "eventful" trip when she'd slammed the phone down in his ear that morning after he'd tried to talk to her about being at the studio by herself. He'd had an even bigger clue when it took her a full three minutes to open the door to her studio for him. He'd determined that he'd ignore her sulking though, after she'd refused to go into the little café with him when he'd stopped to pick up bagels and coffee. He'd also been determined to ignore the fact that she refused anything to eat and answered all his questions with monosyllabic answers.

He'd been willing to put up with her switching the radio station every two minutes. He'd even been willing to overlook the fact that she barely spoke during the whole trip. But this question of hers, which seemed to come out of nowhere, he couldn't ignore. This irrelevant question made him ask angrily, "What's your problem Caroline?"

"I don't have a problem," she said peevishly, folding her arms across her chest and throwing her shoulders back onto the seat like a spoiled teenager. "You're the one who won't let me drive your precious car. I'm surprised you let me ride in it." She mumbled the last sentence with a toss of her head.

The hair toss is what did it. It was like waving a red flag in front of an angry bull. Brian jerked the wheel and pulled the car to the side of the road. Taking off his seat belt, he leaned over and put his face in hers. "If you wanted me to play father to your spoiled child in this relationship Caroline, all you had to do was say so. I'll be happy to accommodate you. Would you like for me to ground you now or would you rather wait until we get to the cottage?"

"Oh, how droll," Caroline said with a false smile and in a bored voice. "I hate to tell you this Brian, but you're the only one who thinks you're witty," she said and turned her head away in disgust. "Whatever."

Brian grabbed her chin and forced her head back around. "You are driving me crazy Caroline and you're acting like a spoiled brat. The way I feel right now, I'm amazed I can still look at you without screaming." He said.

"Like I said," she said slowly and succinctly while she looked at him. "WHAT-ever, Brian." Pushing his hand away, she released her own seat belt and got out of the car. "Don't grab me like that again." She said as she slammed the door and walked away.

Brian leaned his head back on his seat and closed his eyes. First he counted to 50, then 100. He didn't know what the problem was, but they needed to fix it before they arrived at her parents', otherwise they'd all be miserable. Sighing, he opened his eyes and got out of the car to follow her.

Caroline slowed her furious pace and leaned against a tree. She knew she was acting like she'd lost her mind, but she couldn't help it. She was so scared. Who am I kidding, she asked herself, I'm terrified. That morning as she'd prepared to go over to her studio, it had hit her. The show she had coming up at the Rutledge would be the most important thing in her career. And if she wasn't successful at the renowned gallery, her career could be ruined. This one show could determine almost everything she did in terms of her art for the rest of her life.

The veracity of that statement and the immense weight it brought with it had staggered her and she'd been struggling to find her footing underneath it ever since the thought had occurred to her. Insecurities about her work that she'd never even known she'd had, had come rushing through her to make themselves known and unaccustomed to having those kinds of feelings about something she'd always been so sure about, she'd taken it out on Brian. She'd acted so crazily and so unpredictably, that she was surprised he hadn't kicked her out of the car.

Hearing his approach, she sniffed and put her sunglasses on to hide the evidence of frustrated tears that she refused to let fall.

"Hi," she said and smiled tremulously when he stepped directly in front of her. "I'm sorry for acting like such a bitch."

"I don't want an apology, Caroline. I want to know the reason why there's a need for an apology." He said as he leaned in to take the sunglasses off her face so he could see her eyes. "What's going on?"

Caroline turned her head to avoid his hand and tried to shrug nonchalantly. "I've just been in a bad mood, that's all." She turned her head even more and stared off into the distance.

Recognizing the move as one of evasion, Brian stretched his arms so that a hand rested on either side of her head, effectively caging her in. As always when she wanted to avoid telling him something, she couldn't keep eye contact, despite the fact that she was wearing dark glasses. "You call that a bad mood? That was more like a furious windstorm that touched down and destroyed everything in its path as a hot-tempered child does someone else's toys. Tell me what's going on here." He said and snatched the sunglasses off her face before she could stop him. "Why have you been crying?" He demanded.

Flustered, Caroline tried to take the glasses back. Feeling foolish as she ineffectually stretched to get them out of his hand, she gave up with a sigh and sent him a narrowed stare.

Everything about her, from her folded arms to her compressed lips said to leave her alone, but Brian simply ignored the signs and deliberately moved in closer as he put his hand holding the sunglasses back on the tree. "What's wrong with you? You've been acting like a two-year old in desperate need of a nap since I picked you up this morning and I want to know why."

Caroline stiffened. "I don't appreciate the way you keep referring to children when you're discussing me. I am not a child to be disciplined. That's completely unacceptable. What's wrong with you?"

Brian looked at her, surprised that she was making such a big deal out of it. He ran his hand over his face while he recalled what he said. "I was just joking. You know, trying to be witty? I'm sorry if it offends you."

"Okay. Still, I am an adult capable of many things, including thinking, making decisions and acting crazy-out-of-my-mind sometimes. Your statement makes me think that you have some sort of patriarchal attitude towards me. If it's going to work between us, you need to make up your mind that I am a fully functioning adult and this is a partnership. I don't need to be handled, taken care of, or disciplined." She realized she was rambling far off the subject, but she couldn't help herself.

Brian thought she was overstating the matter, but said, "Fine. I do view our relationship as a partnership. I do not see you as a child and as I said, I'm sorry if you are offended and if you think I was out of line. I'm also sorry that you're trying to deflect your responsibility by trying to make what I said a bigger deal than it actually was. And now that we've avoided the subject long enough, can we get down to business?"

Caroline was sheepishly apologetic as she looked up at him. "You're right and I'm sorry. And since this is supposed to be an adult relationship, I guess I know I owe you an explanation for how I've been acting." Playing with the tabs of his navy windbreaker, she stalled by saying, "You're going to think I'm being foolish because I think I'm being foolish."

"Let me be the judge of that."

"It's about my show." Finally looking at him, she said, "I'm afraid Brian. No—make that scared to death."

"It's only natural to be scared. After all, it's a big deal." Brian said and pushed some wayward strands of hair out of her eyes.

"It's more than that. I'm petrified! What if it doesn't work? I mean, what if no one likes my stuff?"

Brian lifted her chin to look into her eyes. He was surprised at how upset she was. "Where did this come from? I've never known you to be so unsure of your talent. In fact, sometimes you've been downright arrogant about it, and justifiably so from what I've seen so far. Why the sudden uncertainty?"

Caroline took a deep breath and impatiently blinked back tears again. "I just thought about what this show could mean for me and for my career and the enormity of it all frightened me. What if I blow it? What if my work isn't good enough? What if everything I've done in preparation for the show just doesn't cut it?"

"Hey," Brian said and pulled her into his arms. He'd never seen her this way before. As she snuggled against him, he could feel the tension that had her muscles stretched as tautly as telephone wires. "You shouldn't think in terms of 'what-if'. Doing so in this instance can only drive you crazy, because you'll always be able to find something that will cause you to worry. Caroline, you know you're a talented artist and everything else after that is gravy." He said as he massaged her back.

Caroline let out a startled laugh. "Gravy? What are you talking about?"

"I mean, it will be easy for you. Those art critics and patrons will see what a tremendous gift you have and they'll be salivating in their ascots. Besides, aren't you the one who told me that art is subjective?"

"Yes. So?"

"So, being that by its very nature art is subjective, it only follows that if one person doesn't like it, there's someone out there who will. If you're not a smashing success at the Rutledge—and I have no doubt you will be—you'll be a smashing success somewhere else. It's a no-brainer, as Linda would say."

He makes it seem so simple, Caroline thought and relaxed a bit. "Still, it *is* the Rutledge—"

"Rutledge, Schmutledge. If they're one of the tops in the world, then they know what they're talking about and that's why they offered you a showing. And if things don't work out there, we'll find you another top gallery to which to peddle your wares." He said, chuckling when she pinched him.

Sighing again, Caroline held him tighter. "I guess you're right. I feel like such an idiot for behaving the way I did. I've never done that before. You must have thought I'd gone crazy."

"No, not really. Though I did think that you wanted to drive *me* crazy."

"Well, as I said, I am sorry. I don't even remember cutting up like that as a child. My parents wouldn't have allowed it."

Brian was curious. He always was whenever she spoke of her family. "No? What would they have done if you had?"

"Well, the usual method of discipline in our house was withholding things—television, telephone, a favorite toy. My parents never really spanked us. I've always hated spankings. I don't like the idea of hitting children. What about you?"

"I've never really thought about it because I haven't been around children all that much. My parents never spanked me, though I will give them credit for having some creative punishments." Brian said.

"My dad used to try, but all I had to do was cry and he'd change his mind. He was such a softy, it got so I didn't even have to let the tears fall. All it took was one look at my wet eyes and he'd either be running for the hills, calling my mother or pulling me in his lap to comfort me."

"In other words, he spoiled you and you manipulated him."

"Hey! I plead guilty to being spoiled, but not to manipulation. Just the thought of my father spanking me would make me feel horrible. I was a very good, sweet child."

"I'm sure." Brian said with comical skepticism, as he released her to start walking back to the car. "Girls who grow up to be willful and stubborn are never born that way.

They're just the sweetest things when they're little girls." He said with a loud snort. And under his breath, but just loud enough for her to hear, he mumbled, "Yeah right."

Laughing, Caroline ran after him and jumped on his back. "Hey, is that supposed to be an insult? I'll have you know that those are two qualities I think should be prized in little girls everywhere. Sauciness, cleverness and spunk are the others. Those things however, do not preclude sweetness. And I was very sweet." She said in his ear as she playfully yanked his hair. "Say it! Say 'Caroline was a sweet little girl who never gave her parents a moment's trouble.'"

Brian caught her under her jean-clad legs and hitched her up more securely. "If you really were a sweet little girl, you'd know it's wrong to ask someone to lie for you." In mock regret, he said, "Though, I can't say I'm surprised."

Caroline laughed again and tugged his hair so she could better reach his mouth. "You win." She said after she'd kissed him. "Who wants to be sweet anyway? It's too boring."

Brian smiled to himself, pleased that her mind was on something else besides her show.

"You call this a cottage?" Brian asked as he looked over the two-story house with its elaborate portico and several balconies. "This is more like a small mansion." He said as he parked the car behind several other cars on the winding driveway leading to the house. With red brick everywhere except for the porch and the balconies, which were painted white, the house seemed to fit in perfectly with the lake that ran behind it and the lush greenery in the front of it.

"Isn't it great? My parents and my aunt and uncle bought it right after they signed a contract with one of the chain grocery stores to have Grandmother's sold in all their stores in the Midwest. I've been coming here since I was about five years old." Caroline finished as they carried their bags onto the porch.

"Well it's a beautiful home. You must have had great summers here."

"Yes. Swimming, water skiing, boating; it was always a blast when we came. And the best part about it was Mom and Dad always took us back home just before we started whining about missing our friends and the city. We never stayed long enough to get bored. But my cousins weren't so lucky; they almost always stayed the entire summer. I always felt sorry for them when we would leave." She reached out for the door, but it was opened before she could hoist the knob.

"Aunt Caroline! I was hoping that was your car I heard drive up!" A lanky girl with a mouthful of colorful braces and a head full of French braids said as she threw herself in Caroline's arms for a hard hug. "I'm so glad you're here!"

Caroline returned the hug and stepped back, holding the girl's hands in hers. "Vanessa Helen

Johnston I've known you for your entire life and never in those 12 years have you given me such an enthusiastic greeting." Caroline said and lifting her brow suspiciously, she asked, "What gives?"

"I must warn you," Caroline said with mock severity after the girl remained silent while fidgeting and giving Brian repeated sidelong looks. "The penalty for stalling and or lying is a night in the clink."

Vanessa giggled and rolled her eyes. "It's nothing, really." She said after peeking at Brian again.

"What is it, honey?" Caroline asked.

"I'll have to whisper it. It's kind of personal." She said, embarrassment turning her light brown face an interesting shade of muted red.

"Well let us get inside first and then you can whisper all the embarrassing secrets you want."

"All right then." Caroline said, once she and Brian had sat their bags down and were standing near a spiral staircase. "Spill your guts, kid."

Rolling her eyes again and giggling behind her hand, Vanessa looked at Brian one last time before leaning over to whisper something in Caroline's ear.

As she listened to the girl's excited whispers, Caroline pursed her lips and threw Brian a thoughtful look as she tried to stifle a laugh. Brian raised his brow in question and tried not to squirm as two pairs of considering eyes looked in his direction.

Straightening after the girl had finished whispering Caroline fixed her face in serious lines and said.

"Yes, I would say he has remarkable talent in that area. But that doesn't mean that everyone will because everyone isn't the same. However, I have to say it might be well worth your time to find out about your friend, but only if you want to."

Beaming, Vanessa kissed Caroline on the cheek. "Thanks, Aunt Caroline." Turning to Brian, she offered her narrow hand and said in what she thought was her best mature voice, "Hello. I'm Vanessa Helen Johnston, as you may have already heard Aunt Caroline say. You may call me Van. I'm pleased to meet you."

"Hi Van. I'm Brian and you can call me Bri. I'm pleased to meet you as well." Brian said as he took her hand and gave it a solemn shake, causing her to blush to the roots of her hair and roll her eyes again.

Clearly flustered, Vanessa released his hand and fled, completely ruining her mature act.

"What was that all about?" Brian asked in confusion.

"Oh," Caroline said with her tongue in her cheek. "She just wanted to know if you were a good kisser?"

"What?"

"She asked me if you were a good kisser." Caroline said again as she studied his embarrassed face. "She needed to know 'because you see Aunt Caroline, there's this really cool Caucasian boy in my dance class and he asked me if I would give him his first kiss. Because it will be my first kiss too, I wanted to know if your boyfriend was a good kisser. Since he's

Caucasian too, I thought you could tell me what they kiss like. My friend Regina says that it might be different than kissing an African-American boy. And since I've never kissed absolutely anyone before, I thought you could help me and tell me if I should try it.'" Caroline said in a high pitched voice that by turns hitched and halted in its excitement just the way Vanessa's had.

Brian felt his face turn red. "Don't laugh." He said in warning as he watched Caroline all but choke to death in trying to contain her mirth. "I don't think I like the idea of a 12-year-old girl thinking of me as some sort of lab rat for kissing." He said in male disgust.

"But darling," she said, as she walked over to him with legs left shaky from suppressed laughter. Stopping by his side, she vainly cleared her throat and continued, "It's only natural that she would. After all, you're so…so…babe-a-licious." She said and one look at his face had her grabbing his upper arm with both hands and leaning her head on his shoulder because she was laughing so hard. "I'm sorry, but I couldn't resist. You should see your face!"

Brian's eyes narrowed as he stood there, literally being her straight man. "I'm going to kill Linda the next time I see her." Was all he said and had Caroline looking at him, only to drop her head back on his shoulder as she succumbed to laughter again.

"Oh, God." Caroline said after several minutes of laughing. "I'm sorry, but your face was just so funny."

She said lifting her head and smiling at him. "You're just so adorable when you're embarrassed."

Sighing in disgust, Brian said, "Caroline, no man wants to be considered adorable. Hell, I don't know one guy who didn't start hating the term the minute he turned 10."

"Well, you'll just have to deal with it because you are. If it's any consolation, you're also a great kisser and you're fantastic in…other areas." She said in a low voice.

Pulling her around to stand in front of him, Brian said, "Well that's gratifying to hear. Why don't I come to your room tonight and you can show me just how fantastic you think I am?" She'd already told him to expect to be put in separate rooms.

"I think I'd like that." Caroline said, smiling when she felt his hands cup her bottom. "But you can't. Since Van is here, I'm sure I'll be sharing a room."

Brian pulled her against him and took her lips, teasing her until her mouth became seeking and greedy beneath his.

"Excuse me." A clipped voice said coldly. "I hope we're not interrupting anything."

Brian raised his head to find himself face to face with the two people who could only be Caroline's parents.

CHAPTER 17

"Mom, Dad!" Caroline said excitedly and hurried over to greet them. Brian followed at a slower pace. From the way her father looked at him it seemed he was going to have the same problem with him that he'd had initially with her brother So be it, he thought with a mental shrug. He determined that he wouldn't unpack right away. The older man was huge with a barrel chest, ham-like hands and large frame that was well turned out in khaki slacks and a hunter green shirt.

Patricia gave him a gentle look that said she knew what he was thinking and her wry smile was so knowing that he almost ducked his head sheepishly. Tracy had been right; Caroline had gotten her beauty straight from her mother. From Patricia's thick hair lying on her shoulders to her almost wrinkle-free brown skin to her long, still-slender frame showcased by a floaty, periwinkle sundress, Brian knew he was seeing exactly what Caroline would look like in 20 years. "I'm Brian." He said, offering his hand.

"Patricia. It's lovely to meet you. Finally." She smiled warmly and leaned in to kiss his cheek. "As you may have guessed, it's been a while since my husband has seen his daughter." She said dryly as they watched Charles Singleton pick Caroline up and swing her around.

"Put me down Dad." Caroline said laughingly. "I want you to meet Brian."

Releasing his daughter, Charles wiped the smile from his face and cleared the joy from his piercing black eyes as he turned his attention to Brian. "Hello, I'm Charles, but that's Mr. Singleton to you." He said.

Caroline sucked in a breath and released it again with a quick whoosh. "Dad, I can't believe——"

"It's okay, Caroline." Brian interrupted her without looking at her and stuck out his hand in challenge. "Your father and I understand each other perfectly." Brian said slowly and studied the man's wide, dark face with its strong chin and a nose that had to have been broken at least twice. "Don't we sir?"

"You think so?" Charles asked with a lift of his brow. "If we know each other so well, tell me what I'm thinking now."

"Really," Caroline said in frustration as she looked from one man to the other. "This is ridiculous. You're both acting like dogs fighting over a bone."

"You're thinking that I have some nerve putting my hands on your daughter and that I'd better not be thinking about taking it any further." Pausing to add magnitude to his next statement, Brian gave Charles as challenging a look as he had given him. "I know what you're thinking because Caroline looks exactly like her mother and her father probably thought the same thing when you first came knocking on his door."

"Oh for heaven's sake!" Caroline threw her hands up angrily. "What's that supposed to mean?!"

"He knows." Brian said with a nod towards Charles, not wavering as he met the older man's stare.

"Let's go Caro." Patricia said, taking Caroline by her shoulders and steering her out of the room. "They're men; they will do stupid things that they interpret as machismo, a singularly male trait that they mistakenly believe is an attractive one to have." She finished, clearly disgusted. "Behave Charles." She said over her shoulder.

"This is unbelievable!" Caroline almost yelled as she stalked ahead of her mother. "My own father squaring off with my boyfriend. How…how…how…"

"Infantile?" Patricia suggested as she followed Caroline into the kitchen and sat down at the table.

"Yeah, that's the perfect word for it. Infantile." Caroline opened the refrigerator and pulled out a glass pitcher of lemonade. She held the pitcher up questioningly to her mother and turned to take two glasses from the cabinet. "Why are you so calm about this?" She asked her mother as she brought the glasses over to the table and sat down.

Patricia smiled into her glass as she took a sip. "Experience child. Pure, unadulterated, embarrassing experience."

"Are you saying Dad has done this before?"

"Yes, only he was on the receiving end. Brian was right; my father treated Charles the same way when I first brought him home."

"But why?"

"Don't be modest Caroline. All you have to do is look in the mirror Brian is well aware that your father knows that Brian is having the same wicked thoughts about you that your father had and still has about me." She laughed when Caroline flushed guiltily and avoided her eyes. "Don't be embarrassed, you and I have always been able to talk about sex and I know that healthy people have healthy urges."

Caroline laughed. "You're right about that, but I'm not embarrassed because you know. It's just the thought of Dad even having the slightest idea that Brian and I are intimate that bothers me."

"I hate to break it to you Caroline," Patricia said with a deadpan look. "But your father knows that you have the same urges other adults have. It is this knowledge that is compelling him to act like a complete jackass right now. It's like they say, sometimes a little knowledge can be a dangerous thing in the hands of the wrong people. Caroline," she said with feigned gravity as she covered her hand, "I'm afraid that your father must be considered one of the wrong people."

Caroline laughed. "Well, I just hope dad doesn't act too crazy and say something we'll all regret later"

"There's a strong possibility that he just might do that. You're his daughter and he'll never think any man is good enough for you. I won't either, but I at least know that there's such a thing as almost perfect."

"Thanks, Mom." Caroline said and leaned over and kissed her "Love you."

"As always," Patricia said as she put her hand on Caroline's cheek, "I love you too."

Caroline picked up her lemonade and took a long swallow. "Where is everyone? Lee? Genevieve? The cousins? Grandma? And I know Tracy's here because I ran into Van at the front door. Who, by the way, I didn't know was coming."

Vanessa was Tracy's uncle's child from a second marriage and she'd worshipped her cousin since she could walk. Because Caroline was always with Tracy, Vanessa had included her in her circle of love and had always called both of them aunt.

"I don't think Tracy had originally planned to bring her, but I get the feeling Van wheedled until Tracy had no choice but to call us and see if it was okay to bring her along. Van apparently loves it here as much as the two of you did when you were kids. As for where everyone is, Tracy and Lee went into town to pick up more groceries and they took Genevieve with them. Van's up in that old tree house, your cousins won't be arriving until later this evening and your grandmother is upstairs sleeping."

"She's all right, isn't she? Is anything wrong?" Caroline asked in concern.

"Of course Mother's all right, but she's almost 80-years old and she needs her rest now and again." Patricia said reassuringly.

"Well, I guess it's just you and me kid. At least until the two baboons in the other room decide to come to their senses. If they have any left, that is."

Patricia laughed. "I don't know. That's asking a lot."

Neither Caroline nor Patricia would have been very surprised, and they definitely wouldn't have been pleased, to know that Brian and Charles were still standing exactly where they'd left them. And they were still circling each other like animals protecting their territory.

"So far, I don't like you too much, boy." Charles said, looking closely at Brian to see what his reaction would be.

Brian raised a brow. "Well, I guess since you qualified that statement with 'so far', I can assume your dislike doesn't have anything to do with the fact that I'm white. And since I haven't done much of anything since I arrived except kiss your daughter, shall I also assume that that's the reason you dislike me?" He paused for a moment and then added slowly, "So far?"

Cocky bastard, Charles thought, unaware that his son had thought the same thing when he'd met Brian. "Though I'm not thrilled that you're white, that's none of my business. But I don't have to tell you that. You think you're pretty smart, don't you son?" He asked with cold eyes and an even colder voice.

"Yes." Brian said without hesitation. "Yes, I do. Any man who plans on spending the rest of his life with a woman like Caroline would have to not only think it, but he'd also have to be it."

"So that's the way the wind blows, is it?" Charles asked with a slow nod of his head and then abruptly turned on his heel and walked into an adjoining room. He was arrogant enough to expect Brian to follow.

Brian could only think that Caroline was damned lucky that he loved her, otherwise there would be no way in hell he would put up with such a jerk like her father. Walking slowly, he followed Charles into what appeared to be a small library. He found him standing near the window with a glass of amber liquid in his hand.

"Close the door." Charles said. "Have a brandy?"

Sensing that he was somehow being tested, Brian still said, "No thanks. It's a little early for me."

"Please yourself then," Charles said, and Brian could swear he heard him mumble with ill humor, "It's after 12 for God's sake. Sounds just like the wife."

"Excuse me?" Brian asked in confusion.

"Nothing, never mind." Charles said and walked over to sit on one of the two small sofas in the middle of the room. Gesturing to the other one, he said, "Sit."

"So," Charles said again, once Brian was seated across from him. "You think you can just waltz in here, say you're going to spend the rest of your life with my daughter and everything will be hunky-dory, huh? I'm afraid it doesn't quite work that way."

"That's not up to you, is it? It's strictly Caroline's and my business."

"Not entirely." Charles said with a calculating look. "You see, while Caroline is my daughter and I love her dearly, I'd leave her out of my will without hesitation if I thought it would save her from an opportunist looking for a free ride."

Brian had shot off the sofa to angrily stand over him, long before Charles had finished his sentence. "I'm not after Caroline's money, and you do her a disservice by even suggesting that anyone would be with her for her money. I don't need her money or yours. I have my own. Just be grateful that you're her father, otherwise I'd ask you to step outside."

Charles stood up himself. "If you think you can take me boy, then go ahead, give it your best shot."

Incensed almost beyond reason, Brian took a deliberate step back before he did just that. "I don't think so. For Caroline's sake, I'll keep this conversation between us. You stay out of my way this weekend, and I'll stay out of yours." Brian said before he turned and stalked to the door. It was pushed open just as he laid his hand on the knob. Seeing Patricia, he nodded stiffly before walking past her.

"What have you done now Charles?" Patricia asked as she walked over to him. She saw the gleeful satisfaction shining from his eyes and sighed as she sat down next to him on the sofa. "Don't tell me you used that taking Caroline out of your will bit again?" She asked tiredly.

Charles grabbed her by the shoulders and gave her a hard, smacking kiss. "The boy will do good by our Caro, Patty. He's crazy in love with her and he's perfect. Damned if I'm not starting to like him!" He said with unconcealed delight.

"Well from the look on his face as he stormed past me, I'm afraid he won't be saying the same about you anytime soon. You just better hope he doesn't tell Caroline about your behavior."

"He won't." Charles said confidently. "He thinks he's just found out what a horrible man I am and he doesn't want to disillusion Caroline about her dear old dad. That's how I know the man loves her. He was practically gnashing his teeth when he said, very right-eously I might add, that he wouldn't tell her."

"Yes, that's now, when he doesn't know that you're not really a rotten old codger." Patricia said patiently, with no small amount of satisfaction of her own. "What are you going to do when he realizes that you're not the ass you presented yourself to be, and tells Caroline about this stunt you pulled just to get back at you?"

Charles' smile faltered a bit. "You don't think the boy would actually do that to his soon-to-be father-in-law do you? Surely he knows by now how vicious Caroline can be when she's been crossed. If she finds out she'll…"

"Rip out your tongue and feed it to you for lunch?" Patricia suggested helpfully. "I know that's what I would do."

Charles threw her a sidelong glance of exasperation. "You're not helping things by exaggerating Patty. And besides, it's her mouth I'm worried about. The girl can flay the most experienced swordsman from ten paces with that tongue of hers."

"It's your own fault." Patricia said gently and kissed his cheek. He just looked so miserable, she couldn't resist.

"Yes, well," Charles said as he stood and resolutely squared his shoulders as if he were preparing for battle. "I'd do it again to make sure she was happy."

CHAPTER 18

Caroline lay down on her back on the sofa, using Brian as her pillow as he sat at the end of the sofa with one leg stretched out on the side of her and the other one bent and stretched out to the floor. He was reading a book and she was flipping an art magazine. They were in the solarium. The little room was sparsely furnished with one long sofa and a small dinette set. The walls were kept bare of pictures for fear of fading from the sun.

They'd all eaten a light lunch when Tracy and Lee arrived home from the grocery store. And after a rousing game of basketball on the small court in the back of the house, Caroline had decided she'd needed to take a break. She had been in the room for about an hour before Brian had come looking for her and for thirty minutes, the only sounds heard in the room were the flipping of pages. She closed her eyes in pleasure as he ran his fingers through her hair.

"So Brian, what do you think of my family?" Caroline asked as she turned the last page of the magazine. Placing it on the back of the sofa she turned over on her stomach and rested her chin on his chest while she wrapped her arms around his waist and looked up at him.

"I like them." Brian said absently as he started a new paragraph. "Especially your grandmother She's a real pistol."

"So, how mad are you at my dad?" Caroline asked.

Brian closed his book and looked down the length of her bare legs as she bent her knees so that her legs and bare feet were sticking up in the air. She'd changed into white jean cut-offs and a yellow tank to combat the heat. He'd decided to change out of his jeans as well. He was wearing a pair of khaki shorts and a T-shirt. "I'm sorry, what did you say? I was thinking about something else," he said when she briefly tightened her arms about his waist.

"I asked how mad are you at my dad."

Brian sighed. the last person he wanted to talk about was her father. He still got mad just thinking about the man's insults. "I told you I don't want to talk about my conversation with your dad. I'll only say that the man is different from anybody I've ever met."

"But what happened? What did he say to you?"

"Let's just say we understand each other and that's more than I can say about some of my other relationships with people."

"But what…"

"Teetee 'Wo-line! 'Teetee 'Wo-line!" Where awe you? Teetee 'Woline!" Caroline was interrupted by a childish voice that became progressively louder with each word uttered, and then forlornly but still loudly, "Did you poof-disappeayh?"

Caroline smiled, sat up and swung her legs to the side of the couch. "Teetee's in here, baby!" she called "I'm in the solarium."

"Kay, that's t'wiffic!" They heard the happy reply long before they saw anyone.

" 'T'wiffic'? What is 't'wiffic?' " Brian asked.

"She is trying to say 'terrific'" Caroline said.

"You've got a surprise for me?" Caroline said in exaggerated pleasure to her niece Genevieve, when the three-year old finally came running into the rom. "C'mere you! I missed you!" Caroline said, opening her arms wide so Genevieve could run into them. Whatever the child had behind her back was lost in the folds of her dress.

"You just saw me a few minutes 'go." Genevieve protested with a giggle as she nonetheless snuggled closer into Caroline's arms.

"I still miss you!" Caroline said as she gave her one last squeeze before releasing her to look at her. Her chubby cheeks were stained with something purple and her big, tea-colored, doe eyes shined intelligently from her small face. With her stubborn chin, pert nose, and full mouth she was a hybrid of her parents. Her light brown hair turned into two braids that hung on either side of her head with red ribbons securing the ends as they swirled under her chin. The little red and purple sundress gave her slender arms, legs and knobby knees exposure to the summer sun.

Caroline hadn't seen her brother's child often that summer and she had really missed her. She was used to spending at least a weekend a month with the child but because Genevieve had spent much of her time at her maternal grandparent's place in Wisconsin, weekend visits hadn't taken place often.

Genevieve threw Brian a wide smile. "Hi, Bwian! I'm gonna call you Unca' Bwian, kay? Van says you'we like my unca' 'cause you and Teeteee 'Woline are gonna get maweed one day."

Brian look at Caroline for clarification and when she whispered the explanation in his ear he smiled. Well, just because Caroline and I haven't discussed marriage, that doesn't mean that a 12-year old shouldn't with a three-year old, he thought dryly. Smiling at Genevieve he said, "That's fine Genevieve, you can call me Uncle Brian. You can even call me 'Teetee' Brian if you'd like."

Genevieve giggled. "You'we silly. I can't call you 'Teetee Brian'."

Making a face of confusion Brian said, "Why can't you call me Teetee Brian? You call Caroline Teetee."

Genevieve lost her smile and turned her head to look at Caroline with a lifted brow that seemed to ask "Is he serious?" When Caroline only shrugged her shoulders, Genevieve turned back to Brian and said slowly, "Can't call you 'Teetee Brian' 'cause Teetee is foe ladies and unca' is foe mans." When Brian still looked confused she pointed at Caroline and said "She is a lady and you is—awe—a man."

Brian smiled at her self-correction. the kid was brighter than a newly minted penny. Hitting himself in the forehead with his palm he said, "Oh, you're right! Of course l have to be called Uncle Brian. That makes perfect sense, doesn't it?"

She beamed at him. Very good Unca' Brian; you'we so smawt!" she said, repeating what the adults in her life said to her whenever she did something brilliant.

Chuckling, Caroline said, "Is my surprise what you have behind your back?"

Barely able to contain her excitement, Genevieve nodded her head vigorously and put her left hand behind her back to join the right one.

"Well…," Caroline said when the child remained silent, "Are you going to give it to me?"

"Nuh-uh. You have to guess first! Use you'we 'magination!"

"Okay then. Let's see, uh, its a banana!"

"No!"

"A kitty."

"No!"

"Is it a tricycle?" Caroline asked and when the girl shook her head no she said, "Give me a hint What color is it?"

"It's gween!" Genevieve said excitedly, her voice full of anticipation.

"Green, huh? How about broccoli? Is it broccoli?"

"Yuck! C'mon Teetee 'Woline, supwises awe fun things. Bwoccoli isn't fun!"

Hearing a guttural sound coming from behind Genevieve's back, Caroline tensed suspiciously. "What was that?" she asked, her mouth suddenly dry.

"It's the supwise!" Genevieve said happily.

Brian felt Caroline's hand clench on his thigh and looked at her. Her suddenly ashen face concerned him and he asked, "Are you all right?"

Caroline appeared to ignore him. She didn't look away from Genevieve and with a frozen smile and gritted teeth she said "It's a uh, a uh…frog." She was able to get it out right before her mouth filled with water and her heart sped up like a locomotive. "Sweetheart," she said, trying not to hurt Genevieve's feelings. "I don't need to see it. Just take it out back and I'll visit it later."

"Caroline? What's wrong?" Brian asked as she leaned back against him.

"Vewy good! It is a fwog!" Genevieve said at the same time and whipped the frog from around her back and shoved it towards Caroline.

"Oh God!" Caroline gasped and, giving up the idea of being self-sacrificing, she all but crawled into Brian's lap as she tried to get away from the frog. Turning her head she buried it in his chest and gripped the front of his shirt. "It's a frog Brian!" she whispered hoarsely. "Get it away from me!"

"You don't like the supwise? But it's a lovely fwog," Genevieve protested and Brian saw that her bottom lip was quivering, a sure sign of emerging tears.

Keeping his arm around Caroline, he reached out and passed his hand over Genevieve's hair. "Of course it is, sweetheart, it's beautiful. Your teetee likes it. She would just rather see it when it's in the water. Why don't you take it out back…"

"No, that's okay," Caroline said weakly and looked at Genevieve. "Uh, sweetheart could you put the frog behind your back?" When Genevieve complied Caroline wiped sweat from her brow and said, "Okay listen baby. Do you remember how scared you were when your friend Tommy's puppy got loose and chased you around the playground?"

Pouting, Genevieve nodded her head. "Stupid dog tried to bite me."

"And you were so scared you threw up, right? Well that's how I am with frogs, sweetie. When I was little some frogs scared me and made me sick and now I don't like them. Do you understand?"

"Yes, I'll take it away. You angwy at me?" she asked.

"No, sweetie, never," Caroline said and leaned over for a kiss. When Genevieve raised her arm to hug her, she brought the frog in front again and Caroline jerked back.

"Oops, I'm sowwy. I'll take it out now," the child said and ran from the room.

Closing her eyes again, Caroline leaned over and put her head between the knees. "Don't you dare laugh at me," she warned him.

"Frogs Caroline? You're scared of frogs?"

"No," she said definitively and lifted her head. "I'm terrified of them. and they often give me nightmares and make me puke."

Seeing that her face still had a loss of color, he put his arm around her shoulders and pulled her into his side. "What happened?"

"When I was little, about seven, we had a huge thunder storm here. It was worse than anything I had experienced in Chicago. Anyway once things had calmed down and it was only drizzling, I went outside and down the hill so I could take a look at the lake. Well, it started raining again and it got really windy so that l had to close my eyes against it. The force of the wind made the rain feel like stinging needles against my skin and I started crying and tried to run back to the house.

"But the wind was so strong, it was a struggle and my fear slowed me down even more. Anyway I finally made it up the hill, practically on my hands and knees, and I was making my way to the back door when all of a sudden I seemed to be surrounded by all these frogs. I stepped on one and the squishing sound it made sickened me. So, I'm standing there and there are all of these frogs jumping around my feet and my legs. Well after everything else that had happened that did it for me and I just lost it. I just stood there in the rain and started screaming hysterically. I couldn't move."

"Where were your parents? Lee?"

"I'd sneaked out of the house, you see, and my parents didn't even know I was gone. It wasn't until I started screaming that they knew something was wrong. My father came running out, thinking my life was in danger or something. When he saw that there was nothing really physically wrong, he picked me up and carried me inside, telling me that everything was okay and there were only about five frogs out there, who had probably already found their way back to the pond. Lee teased me about my fear for years after that. But since then I've never been able to look at a frog without breaking out in a sweat and feeling sick to my stomach."

"Well, thank God frog invasions aren't an everyday occurrence in Chicago."

"Ha, ha."

"Hey," Lee said from the doorway and Caroline and Brian looked over to see him holding Genevieve in his arms. "Are we interrupting anything?"

"No, of course not," Brian said and Lee came into the room.

"I wanted to apologize for the frog, Cee Cee. When I saw her with it earlier, it didn't even occur to me that she'd want to share it with you," Lee said and sat down.

"It's all right, Lee. Genevieve had no way of knowing that her teetee was afraid of frogs. Did you, sweetie?" Caroline asked and held out her arms so Genevieve could crawl into her lap.

Lee smiled when Genevieve wrapped her legs around Caroline's waist and her arms around her neck and held on tightly. "Brian can I talk to you for a minute?" he asked and stood.

Surprised, Brian said, "Sure." Standing, he followed Lee to the other side of the room.

"About my dad, Brian…"

"I don't want to talk about your dad, as I might say something we'd both regret."

"You don't have to say anything. I'll do all the talking. All right?"

Brian nodded his head reluctantly.

"First of all my dad told me what he said to you today when you got here, and I just want you to know that he's not usually so insulting. It has nothing to do with you personally. He would have done the same thing to anyone Caroline had brought home with her."

"Is that supposed to excuse his insults?"

"No, but I'm hoping it will make it easier to understand. It was all a test Brian. He was only testing you to see how you'd react."

Brian frowned in disgust. "Oh, and did I pass?"

Well, he was happy with your reaction. He feels better about everything now."

"Why are you telling me all this?"

"Because I've seen the way my sister looks at you and the way you look at her and I know that your relationship is not just some passing fancy on your part."

"And?" Brian said expectantly.

"And, if you are going to become a part of this family I'd rather everyone try to get along. Which reminds me, what are your plans for my sister?"

Brian shrugged as if the answer were obvious. "I'm going to marry her."

Lee raised a brow at the arrogant tone. "What does she have to say about that?"

Brian turned to look at Caroline as she played with Genevieve. When she leaned to whisper something in Genevieve's ear and made the child giggle helplessly and threw her arms around her neck again, he felt something inside him melt and a picture of Caroline pregnant with his child flashed in his head. The image was so vivid, he closed his eyes for a moment to savor it. He turned back to Lee. "I'm sorry, what was the question?"

Lee saw the dazed look in his eyes. "Are you okay?" he asked and looked over to the sofa himself just to be sure nothing was wrong. "You look as if you've seen a ghost."

Sticking his hands in his pockets, Brian rocked back on his heels. "I think maybe I have," he mumbled reflectively. Shaking his head he said, "I appreciate your talking to me, and I guess giving your blessing of my relationship with Caroline. That is what you were doing, wasn't it?" he asked.

Startled, Lee bent his neck and sheepishly ran his hand over his bald head. "Huh, I guess maybe it was.

Not that you need it, and Caroline would kill me if she knew I had the nerve to even offer it."

Brian chuckled. "Yeah, she would."

"Just treat her right Brian. That's all my parents and I want."

Brian looked at Lee and saw genuine love and concern for his sister reflected in his eyes. "I love her and no one is more important to me," he said quietly.

"Good," Lee said happily and slapped him on the back. "Now let's keep this conversation between ourselves, shall we? We wouldn't want to cause Caroline any unnecessary concern. You know how she worries."

Brian gave him a skeptical look "Sure, if you say so."

CHAPTER 19

"So, intrepid one, are you positive this Brian fellow is the one for you?" Caroline's grandmother asked her from across the kitchen as she flipped another blueberry pancake on the griddle. It was early Sunday morning and she and Caroline were the only two up and about.

Looking up from her plate to make absolutely sure her grandmother's back was still turned, Caroline made a face. For as long as she could remember, Lucy Culpepper had called she and her brother by words that she felt described their behavior and or their personality at the time. Caroline had been several adjectives while growing up. When she'd first sassed her mother, she'd been "cheeky one," when she'd graduated tops in her class, she'd been "brilliant one" and when she'd broken her arm while trying to do a wheelie on her bike, for three, very long weeks afterward, she'd been "demented, foolish one". When there wasn't any outlandish behavior to comment on, however, she was just "dear one" or "darling one."

Caroline sighed. So now she was "Intrepid one". She guessed that meant that her grandmother thought she was taking a big chance by being in a relationship with Brian. "Not you too, Nana."

Lucy turned around in surprise. Her chestnut eyes snapped a question at Caroline while her papery brown skin pulled tautly against her cheekbones, belying her displeasure. "What do you mean, 'not you too Nana'? Surely you're not comparing me to the narrow-minded, ignorant one? You wouldn't dare."

"I'm sorry." Caroline hurried to appease her. "I didn't know where the conversation was leading and I jumped to conclusions. I guess I should have known you would never think the way Uncle James does."

"That's right, you should have." Lucy said and turned back to her pancakes. "Your uncle is holding on tightly to some hard and fast rules from the old days that shouldn't have become rules—nor traditions—in the first place."

"But why is he like that and Dad isn't? How can they have such radically different opinions on the same subject? After all, they were raised by the same parents in the same household." Caroline said in frustration.

"I seem to recall hearing a story about your uncle being terrorized as a boy in Mississippi by a group of white boys. They caught him alone once when he was about 16 and they beat him so badly that he had to be hospitalized. He's never forgotten it, but the problem is, he's let it taint things for him."

"I didn't know about that. I suppose that explains some things, but Brian isn't one of the boys who beat him up 40 years ago. Dad's from Mississippi and he doesn't think that way and I'm sure he's experienced the same prejudices. Maybe he never got beat up, but life was hard. Dad was kind of disappointed at first, but it was more because Brian isn't black than it was that he's white. Uncle James is angry because Brian is white."

"Your dad and uncle are two different people. And you're right, your father was never beaten to a pulp like your uncle was, simply because he's black."

"I know, but Uncle James is doing the same thing—he's judging Brian simply on the basis of his skin color. Do you know Uncle James almost left and went back to the city last night?"

"Yes, the man is in a lot of pain. Your uncle is a fine man, a great husband and a good father, but his behavior last night was completely out of line and unnecessary. He should never have called Brian 'honky'—especially in front of the children."

"I don't think he was thinking Nana. I think Uncle James was running on pure emotions."

Lucy turned off the griddle and came over and sat next to Caroline at the table. Patting Caroline's hand reassuringly, she said, "Well, your Brian handled himself well and that's all that counts. Anyone could see that the man loves you."

"Yes." Caroline said. "When Brian told Uncle James that he was making a fool of himself and worse, he was scaring the children and teaching them the wrong thing, I thought Uncle James was going to explode. Thank God he just left the table."

"Yes, well, people are rarely logical when their emotions are involved and are going at full throttle. Now," she said as she settled back in her chair. "My question still stands—are you positive that Brian is the one?"

"Yes, Nana. Absolutely."

"What makes you so sure?"

"I'm positive because I can't even remember what my life was like before he came into it. Nothing or no one who came before or will come after him even matters. When I'm with Brian, I'm the happiest, the most secure and the most comfortable I've ever been." She shrugged. "I guess he's home for me."

"That's wonderful and that's all anyone could ever hope for in a lifetime. I had that with your grandfather and they were the happiest fifty years of my life. I asked you about your feelings for Brian because I know what it's like to have people against you when you're in love. Nobody in my family wanted me to be with your grandfather because he was a laborer without a college education. But I stuck to my guns and eventually they all came around. But I married him before then. I loved Harold and I didn't have time to wait around for them to come to their senses."

"That's how I feel. I don't have time to let other people and their opinions run my life. I love Brian and I'm going to be with him. I wish it could be as simple as that, but I know it isn't. However, I'm ready to face those who would try to make it complicated."

"Good for you, intrepid one." Lucy said with a big smile.

"Morning all." Brian said as he walked into the kitchen. Walking over to the table, he bent down and kissed Lucy on the cheek. "Are those blueberry pancakes I spotted on the counter? if they're the famous ones I've heard so much about, I'll be your vassal for life."

Lucy chuckled. "Yes they are and when do you start?"

"Immediately. Right after I've eaten about 10 or 20 of them." Brian said and walked around the table to kiss Caroline.

She placed her hand on the side of his face. "Mmm, I missed you last night." She whispered softly as he lifted his head. "We were just talking about you." She said louder while she watched him drop nearly half the pancakes off the platter onto his plate.

Snagging the syrup, Brian walked over and sat down next to Lucy. "Yeah? All good I hope."

"Of course," Caroline said with a smile, deciding not to rehash the whole thing. They'd already discussed it the night before, with her apologizing for her uncle and him telling her he was fine. There really was nothing more to say about it.

Brian took a bite of his pancakes and closed his eyes in pleasure. "These are wonderful." He said to Lucy. "Will you marry me?"

"Hey!" Caroline said. "At least wait until I'm out of the room before you proposition my grand-mother."

Brian looked at her spotless plate. "Aren't you having any? Your grandmother's blueberry pancakes were all you talked about for a week straight before we came here."

"I already did, thank you very much. Some of us don't like to laze about in bed."

"But your plate is spotless."

"I never eat Nana's blueberry pancakes with syrup; they're perfect as is. You'll notice I don't have any silverware either. These little babies are all I need to enjoy the Eighth Wonder of the World as we fondly call them around here."

Brian watched her wiggle her fingers in the air and winked. "Well, whatever suits your fancy, I always say."

Lucy laughed. "She always did act like she'd been raised in a barn when it came to eating my pancakes. Genevieve's the same way."

"Speaking of the little angel," Tracy said cheer-fully as she entered the kitchen. "She's upstairs looking for you Caroline—she said something about the beach?"

"We have a date to build sand castles." Caroline said and stood.

"Enjoy," Tracy said, watching Brian take more pancakes. "Hey, don't be a pig!"

Caroline laughed and left the two of them arguing over pancakes.

—⁓—

Brian watched as Charles flipped some burgers over on the grill. It was early evening and since the weather was so beautiful, the family had decided to have a barbecue again. He looked over to see Caroline sitting on the patio swing with her cousin Joshua, talking and laughing. He found Joshua and his brother Jerome to be pretty cool. And Jerome's seven-year old son was an adorable kid.

As Brian thought about his children, James stepped outside and slid the patio doors closed behind him. Brian watched him look around for a conversation to join and when his eyes fell on him, Brian only looked at him. James' hard lips compressed into a thin line and he stalked over to talk to Jerome.

Everyone in the Singleton family had apologized to Brian at one point or another for the man's behavior. Everyone but James. Even Caroline's father had and Brian had been able to tell that they were all frustrated and embarrassed by James' continued insistence on treating him like a pariah. He'd told them all the same thing he'd told Caroline: it didn't matter. He would have liked it if he and James could get along, or at least be civil, but he wasn't going to lose any sleep over it.

He understood that James had had a bad time of it, but he didn't feel that he should have to pay for it. He didn't mind that James shot him dirty looks every five seconds or that he refused to speak to him. What did bother him was how James had cornered Caroline and tried to make her feel guilty about her dating him. Caroline had handled him just fine, telling him basically the same thing she'd told the man in the greasy spoon, but it had pissed Brian off nonetheless.

He'd wanted to take the guy and plant his fist in his gullet, but instead he'd walked away without being noticed. Maybe if James' wife weren't sick and had been able to come, he wouldn't be acting so rudely. That was what Caroline said, but Brian thought that her presence wouldn't have made a difference.

"Hi, Unca Bwian."

Brian looked down into Genevieve's smiling face and felt his heart melt. "Hi sweetheart."

Genevieve climbed up his legs to sit sideways on his lap and grabbed his chin in her chubby hands. "Why are you sitting here all 'lone?"

"Oh, I was just thinking, that's all."

"'Awe' you finished thinking now?"

"Yes." Brian said with a smile and tweaked her nose.

"Good, 'cause you don't look happy when you think. You look mad. But now you look happy."

"That's because I am. Do you know why?" When she shook her head no, he said, "Because you're here. You make me happy."

"I'm glad. Know what?"

"No, I don't. What?"

"I'm going ovah to Teetee Wo-line's house. I'm going to spend the night. And we awe going to go to the zoo and the fawm in the zoo and then we awe goin' to wide in the paddle boats. Wanna come with Teetee Wo-line and me?"

"I would love to sweetie. Do you know when you're going to go over to Auntie Caroline's house?"

Genevieve nodded her head. "Weally, weally soon. Not tomowwow though, when it's time to go back to the city. I'm coming ovah in this many weeks." She finished happily and held up two fingers.

"Two weeks? You're going to spend the night in two weeks? Are you sure about that?" Brian asked. That was the weekend he'd planned to go visit his mom and Frank and he'd forgotten to ask Caroline if she could make it.

"Yes. Teetee Wo-line made 'wangements with Mommy and Daddy. Wanna come?"

"I can't sweetheart because I'll be out of town. But I'll go to the zoo with you another time, okay?"

Genevieve looked disappointed. "Too bad foe you Unca Bwian. It's always fun at Teetee Wo-line's house. Sometimes she lets me sleep with her, but mostly I sleep by myself in the guess' woom."

Brian looked at her forlorn face. "You like sleeping with Auntie Caroline, huh?"

"Yes. It's weally fun sleeping in bed with Teetee Wo-line."

Brian found it hard to keep a straight face. "You said it, kid." He mumbled to himself.

"If you don't go to outta town and pwomise to stay, I betcha Teetee Wo-line will let you sleep with her."

"Do you really think so?"

"Mmm hmm. Let's go ask her!" She said as she jumped off his lap and grabbed his hand.

"Hey baby!" Caroline said when Genevieve came and stood in front of her. "What can I do for you?" She asked her and then looked up at Brian who stood with his hands in his pockets and an expectant look on his face.

"Can Unca Bwian sleep in bed with you if he pwomises not to go to outta town and go to the zoo with us?"

"What?" Caroline exclaimed and looked suspiciously up at Brian, who tried his best to look innocent.

"Unca Bwian will go to the zoo if you let him sleep in bed with you, 'cause it's weally, weally fun to sleep in bed with you." Genevieve explained patiently.

Joshua choked in his glass. "Uh, excuse me," He said as he looked from one adult to the other. "I think I need a refill. Come on Genevieve, you come with me. I'll find us some cookies." He grabbed the child's hand and beat a hasty retreat.

Caroline narrowed her eyes at Brian. "Explain."

Brian held his hands up and shrugged his shoulders. "I swear I had nothing to do with it. It was all her idea."

"Yeah, I'll bet." Caroline said in a voice that dripped skepticism.

"I swear." Brian said again and laughed helplessly. "She was telling me about your planned weekend together and she asked me if I wanted to join you. I told her I couldn't because I had to be out of town, so to sweeten the proposal, so to speak, she offered to let me sleep in bed with you because it's, and I quote, 'weally, weally fun.' And since I can't fault the kid for telling the God's honest truth, I came over here with her to ask you." Taking her hand, he pulled her up from the swing and bent his head to whisper in her ear, "Please Teetee Wo-line, may I sleep in bed with you?"

Caroline closed her eyes against the shiver that ran deliciously through her. She knew what would happen next. "Let me go. Everyone's watching." She whispered.

Brian lifted his head and took a look around. "No one's watching us and even if they were, who cares?"

"I'm not going to make out with you with my whole family here." She said with finality and stepped back out of his arms. "Meet me on the beach in fifteen minutes." Laughing as the frustration on his face turned into anticipation, she walked away.

From across the deck, Patricia smiled as she watched the two of them. "Aren't they lovely together?" She asked her husband.

Charles grunted. "He seems to be a good guy, I'll say that much. A man could wish he'd stop putting his hands on Caroline so much, though."

"Don't be such a hypocritical fuddy-duddy, Charles." Patricia chided gently. "You couldn't keep your hands off me, either. You still can't and I'm grateful for it."

Having no defense, Charles stammered, "Yeah…well…"

"Exactly. They love each other. Anyone looking at them can see that."

"You're right, I know. It's just that she's my baby girl and it's not easy watching her get pawed all the time."

"Now you know how my father felt." Patricia said without sympathy.

"Yes, now I know why your father hated my guts for so long."

"Never that, darling. He just…disliked you. Strongly." She said and hugged him.

Charles took his eyes off the grill to shoot his wife a look. Her laughing eyes eased his heart and spread warmth through his chest. It had always been that way. "I can hardly fault a man for falling for any daughter of yours, can I? As your husband, I understand his feelings perfectly. I love you, Pat."

—m—

Brian ran down a mental checklist as he carried his bag down the spiral staircase. Caroline's bag was already in the car and she was off somewhere saying goodbye to her family. Brian paused at the bottom of the stairwell as James came towards him. He looked like he'd been lying in wait.

Letting his anger and impatience show clearly in his eyes, he stared expectantly at James.

The older man came right to the point. "Why don't you stay with your own kind? Stick with white women. Caroline's one of our best and brightest and I resent you dating her and making her unattainable to black men."

"You can't be serious!" Brian said.

James was indignant. "I most certainly am. Caroline is a good, black woman and what she needs is a good, black man. Not some white boy, usurping what's ours, as white men have been doing for centuries."

"Look Mr. Singleton, I know I can't even begin to imagine your life experiences with white people, but I shouldn't be blamed for what someone else has done to you. I'm sorry for what happened to you, but Caroline and I have a relationship. We are just two people who happened to meet and fall in love. It's as simple as that. I can't help being white."

If possible, James looked angrier. "Listen here, boy, I don't trust—"

"James!" Charles said from across the room "Stop it right now! This has gone far enough. How dare you—"

"No, how dare you! How dare you sit back and watch your only daughter take up with a white man! Where is your sense of unity?"

"Who my children become involved with does not define my loyalty to the black race James. Just like your loyalty to the black race is not defined by your children's personal relationships. It can't be, because we can not tell them what to do. We can not think for them." He said quietly to his brother. Turning to Brian, he said, "Caroline is out back saying goodbye to the children. Despite everything, it was a pleasure meeting you. Don't be a stranger."

Brian shook his hand, picked up his bag and turned to walk to the back of the house. He wanted to stay and give James a piece of his mind, but knew it would be useless. Sighing, he went to get Caroline so they could go home.

CHAPTER 20

"You're sure I won't be cramping your style by coming over on a Friday night Brian?" Linda asked as she followed him into his loft. "I mean, I did wheedle the dinner invitation out of Caroline, but we can do it another time if it's more convenient. I won't mind."

"For the last time Linda, I'm looking forward to having dinner with you." Brian said as he sat his brief-case down. "Now please sit down and be comfortable." He said, taking off his summer-weight jacket and hanging it in the hall closet.

"Okay, if you insist," she said happily as she enthusiastically plopped down on the leather couch. "You've made a lot of changes since I was here last." She said, looking around at the black and white prints on the walls and the plush, black carpeting. "The last time I was here, you only had this magnificent couch, now you've got the matching chair and tables to go with it. I like it." She said as he passed her a pop and sat down on the smaller sofa across from her. "Looks like someone's got a woman in his life." She said teasingly and comically wriggled her brow.

"Actually, I'd decorated this place long before I met Caroline, Ms. Smarty Pants." He said and took a swig of his beer.

"Hey!" Linda said in protest. "Why do you get a beer and I get a can of pop? What's up with that?"

Brian grimaced. "I'm sorry. I can't get the idea that you aren't a kid anymore out of my head."

"Well, I'm not, so how about gettin' me something with a little zip, so I can really take a load off?" She said and held out the pop.

Brian looked at her expectant baby face with its young eyes and deep dimples and shook his head. "Nope. Sorry kid, I just can't. I have visions of your dad pounding me into dust and of your mother wagging her finger in my face and I tremble."

"Oh, for God's sake." Linda said in disgust and stood, her short skirt twirling around her bare legs. "If you're going to be such a wimp about this, I'll get it myself." She walked into the kitchen "Where's Caroline?" She called out.

"She'll be here soon. She had appointments downtown today. She'll come straight here once she's finished."

"So how's everything going between you two?" Linda asked as she took her original place on the sofa. "Have you had any problems?" She continued, and when she saw his face close off, she added hastily, "Of the outside kind, I mean. You know, have you been confronted about the race thing?"

Brian frowned. "Of course." He said in disgust. "This is America, right? What do you expect?"

"That bad, huh?" Linda asked in sympathy.

"Bad enough, but we're handling it. We have no choice."

"No, I guess you don't if you plan to stay together. How did it go when you met her family?"

Thinking back on the past weekend made Brian frown even more. "For the most part, her family is really cool. They're a great bunch of people. With the exception of her uncle, I pretty much liked everyone."

"Her uncle's a jerk, I guess. Do you think he'll be a big problem?"

"He could be, but we're not going to let him."

"Good. Have you told my parents about your relationship yet?"

Brian lifted his brow and gave her a knowing look. "You mean you haven't?"

Linda had the good grace to look sheepish. "Okay, so I told them. But I was just so happy that you'd found such a great person like Caroline, that I couldn't contain myself. I had to tell somebody!" She said in her defense when he continued to give her a bland stare. "It's not exactly a topic one can discuss around the office. Thanks to Ida." She muttered sullenly.

"I wouldn't want details about my personal life bandied about the office even if Ida didn't work there." Brian said.

"What about Ida?" Caroline asked as she walked into the room.

"God, Caroline is there ever a time when you don't look great?" Linda asked with envy as she took in Caroline's sky blue mini-skirted suit with matching pumps and flesh-colored nylons. She had her hair down and curled around her face and shoulders.

Caroline looked at her through her sunglasses and smiled. "Thanks. I think." She said as she walked over to Brian and leaned down to give him a brief kiss.

As she used the sofa as leverage to straighten, he yanked on her arm, toppling her into his lap. She yelped in embarrassment, "Hey! Not now Brian—"

Brian silenced any and all protests by covering her mouth with his. Pulling her sunglasses off and tangling his hands in her hair, he held her face in place and devoured her mouth until she was wrapping her arms around him and helplessly responding. Linda was right. The woman always looked beautiful and damned sexy, he added to himself. How was he supposed to keep his hands off?

Finally lifting his head, he smiled. "Now that's a proper greeting."

In wonder, he watched as her eyes went from being blinded by arousal to clear, narrow slits. "Ouch!" He yelled as he felt her take the sensitive skin on the underside of his upper arm and twist it.

"That's what you get." She whispered as she struggled off of his lap. "We do have company." She said and felt heat rush to her cheeks as she looked over to find Linda looking at them in amused fascination. Grimacing, she went over and sat next to her on the sofa. "How are you Linda? It's good to see you." She said, giving her a hug.

"I'm fine. It's good to see you too." Linda said, returning the hug. She looked over Caroline's shoulder to see Brian still rubbing his arm, but with a big smile on his face.

"Now what's this about Ida?" Caroline asked as she unbuttoned her jacket and settled back.

Just like the first day they'd met, Brian couldn't take his eyes off the little shell of a blouse revealed beneath the jacket, and wasn't really paying attention to Linda's answer to Caroline's question. When what she was saying started to sink in, it was too late to intervene.

"Brian was just telling me that Ida working at Inclusion doesn't make a difference on whether or not he wants your relationship gossiped about. Of course, he doesn't want people talking about his business. But I was just about to tell him that after that dressing down he gave Ida, I wouldn't be surprised if she left soon."

Caroline looked at Brian. "What dressing down?"

Brian sighed and sent Linda a glare. "Thanks a lot, kid." Ignoring the clueless look she gave him, he looked at Caroline. "A few weeks ago, I gave Ida a warning. I told her that if I ever heard that she'd deliberately tried to sabotage someone else's work, she'd be fired." He waited for the argument.

"Sabotage?" Linda said in confusion. "What sabotage?"

Both Brian and Caroline ignored her. "Good. I'd say she needed a warning, maybe more than that." Caroline said and seeing the surprised look on his face, she explained. "I never expected you to ignore the incident with the fax forever Brian, just while I was there. After all, you can't take the chance that she'd think she could get away with her behavior a second time."

"What behavior?" Linda asked in frustration.

"I'm going upstairs to change." Caroline said and stood. "I'll be right back."

"But, but…" Linda said to her departing back. Sighing, she turned her head to look at Brian. "What is she talking about?"

"You're the one who brought up the disciplinarian action I brought against Ida, so you should know."

"But I don't. I only know that she got into trouble, not what it was all about. Won't you tell me?"

Brian smiled happily. "Nope."

Linda knew he would take pleasure in her begging, so she closed her mouth and pretended disinterest. When Caroline came back downstairs in cotton shorts and a T-shirt, the television was on and they were watching the evening news. "What's for dinner?" She asked Brian as she sat down next to him.

"Shhh." He said as he watched. "They're talking about an elderly couple who was found dead in their home this morning. When they flashed their picture, I thought they looked familiar."

"Oh my God," Caroline said slowly when a picture of the couple appeared on the screen again. "That's the old couple playing chess...the one from the park. I took their pictures, remember?" Clutching Brian's arm, Caroline leaned forward to hear more details.

"I knew I recognized them." Brian said.

"Did they say how they were killed?" Caroline asked as the segment went off.

"They were shot. They think it may have been a robbery attempt because the house was torn apart." Linda said.

Caroline felt suddenly weary and sad. "I —I've never known anyone whose been killed before. I don't think I've even known anyone who has known someone whose been killed."

Linda picked up the remote and turned off the television. "It's so sad. God, they were in their eighties at least. When you make it that far, you're supposed to at least be able to die non-violently."

"Yeah." Brian said, massaging his bent neck and getting up to go into the kitchen to toss his beer bottle into the trash.

The sudden pall over the room made Caroline edgy and she jumped up from the sofa. "I say we go out to dinner. I need to get out. How about Ethiopian or Mexican food? Do you mind Linda?"

"No, not at all." Linda said, Caroline's mood affecting her.

"Good. I'll just go get changed again." Caroline said.

"Let's just go." Brian said, also wanting to get out. "You look fine."

—⁓—

Pete took his time as he drove to Brickman's house. He hadn't meant to kill the old couple; it had been the absolute last thing he'd wanted to do, but it had been unavoidable. He'd killed before and it hadn't bothered him, but this time it had been hard. His reasons for not wanting to kill them were his own. No one needed to know that they reminded him of his grandparents. So if he didn't produce results with his usual swiftness or as quickly as Brickman wanted them, then that was Pete's problem and he'd been prepared to face the consequences.

He knew Brickman had expected him to kill the old couple long ago, and he'd been fast running out of excuses as to why he hadn't. Yesterday, he'd run out of excuses, and they'd run out of time. None of it would have had to happen if Brickman weren't so damned arrogant, Pete thought angrily as he gripped the steering wheel tightly. Pete had offered to go get the ice coffees himself that Sunday, but Brickman had insisted upon going out that day. And now two innocent, old people were dead because of it.

Killing those two had been the hardest thing he'd ever had to do for the sake of his career. He'd been sitting in his car watching their building all morning. His legs were cramped and his stomach was growling, so he'd been thrilled when he'd seen them walk out the building. He'd waited fifteen minutes to be sure they were gone and then he went to work. It had been easy getting in past the doorman, and once he found their apartment, it had taken a simple lock pick to get in. Thanks to the old man always looking out the window, he'd known that they lived on the third floor and had the fifth apartment from the right.

He'd hoped he'd be able to get in and out; he didn't want to be in any longer than fifteen minutes, thirty tops. He'd stood outside their door and put the silencer on his gun on the off chance that someone else lived with them or they had visitors that he had no way of knowing about. Pulling over to the side of the road, Pete closed his eyes as he recalled the terrified looks on the couple's faces when they came home and found him in their apartment. Maybe they'd forgotten something. Who knew? At any rate, he'd heard them come in and was ducking into the kitchen when they turned the corner and saw him.

For a few frozen seconds that seemed to go on forever, everyone was motionless and then the old lady opened her mouth as if she were going to scream, and he'd been forced to do it. He'd had to shoot her. Her husband came next. There'd been no alternative. He couldn't take the chance that they wouldn't call the police after he was gone. Never mind that he hadn't come there intending to rob or hurt them, because both of those things are what happened in the end. Because he killed them, he had to make it look like a botched robbery attempt. When he'd left, by way of the stairs and the back door, he'd taken some jewelry, silver and a painting with him.

After he'd shot them, he'd just stood there, unable to move for a few minutes. And then something had clicked in his brain and he'd started looking for the photographer's card. He'd searched everywhere—in purses, junk drawers, pockets, desk drawers—everywhere. Pete started the car again and pulled back into traffic. Sighing, he thought about how discontented he'd felt lately. He didn't like his work anymore and he hated Brickman and the control he had over him. He especially hated his contempt for the basic humanness of other people. As for the photographer, he was glad he hadn't found her card. It kept her away from Brickman a little longer.

—⁓—

Alex Brickman stared out his window at his pool and landscaped backyard. Located in a remote area outside the city limits, the house was one of his many hideaways. He'd been there a week now to escape the crowds that would be pouring into the city to take advantage of the last weeks of warm weather.

He could see the spires and towers of the city's downtown skyscrapers even now, from thirty miles away. He'd learned to wear layers to keep from freezing in what seemed to be unfairly long winters and when he wanted fresh-water seafood, all he had to do was pick up the phone and it would be delivered on his doorstep within hours. So yes, he'd adjusted to this new city. And he'd be damned if he'd be forced to leave it now and go somewhere else.

That damned Kovlovsky had screwed things up with his infernal bumbling. If he didn't need him so badly, he'd have killed him just like he'd done his friend. As it was, he needed as many people as possible on this job and he was starting to think that maybe it had been a mistake to kill Stan. When he'd seen the news story about the dead old couple on the news, he'd smiled in satisfaction and finished eating.

He'd even had a smile for Kovlovsky when he'd walked into his study thirty minutes ago. Finally, he'd thought, I'll get the film and the girl. But of course, that was not to be. As Kovlovsky had stood there explaining what had happened, he'd begun to realize that he was more upset that he wouldn't be getting the girl than he was about the lack of film. He meant to have her, no matter what the cost.

Kovlovsky had thought to appease him with a few trinkets and baubles and he'd taken them, even though they were a poor substitute for what he really wanted. Even so, the jewelry and the painting would fetch a nice piece of change in the nefarious underworld in which he had done his best networking.

He'd been somewhat placated by the idea Kovlovsky had to make their search easier than it had been thus far. The plan was remarkably simple and so obvious that he was amazed they hadn't thought of it before.

Brickman turned away from the window, walked out of the study and up the stairs to his bedroom. He looked at the woman lying on the bed. She saw where he was looking and craftily stretched so that the sheet fell, exposing her bare breasts. She really is beautiful, he thought. She just wasn't the one he really wanted.

Ida smiled. She'd crept down the stairs in just enough time to hear Brickman discussing the murder of two old people. Hearing him calmly discuss murder scared her, but in a strange way, she was also turned on and excited by his lethal ruthlessness. On one level, she was scared of Brickman, but on another one—one closer to the surface—she couldn't get enough of him. His wealth, his power and his generosity were like drugs to her system sometimes.

That didn't mean that her loyalties were split, however. Her first loyalty was always to herself. Because of that, there was no way she would tell Brickman who Caroline was. Ida knew that once Brickman found Caroline, she herself would be kicked out. She didn't like Caroline and she wanted her out of her way, but she wasn't going to sign her own eviction notice just to help Brickman get what he wanted. She had to make sure she had Brian back first and after that, she'd tell Brickman everything he wanted to know. In the meantime, she needed to scare Caroline into leaving Brian and once she was gone and no longer clouding his senses, Brian would realize that they shouldn't have broken up two years before. She'd just make herself available until he did.

She planned to step up her plan to scare Caroline when Brian left town the following week. It wouldn't be difficult. She knew exactly what to do. She smiled and began to help Brickman unbutton his shirt. Caroline may have money and fancy homes and cars, but she wouldn't have Brian for much longer.

CHAPTER 21

Brian let himself into Caroline's condo and quietly closed the door behind him. It was early Sunday morning and if she and Genevieve were still sleeping, he didn't want to wake them. He'd been in Detroit since Wednesday visiting his parents and had gotten up early that morning to make the five-hour drive back to Chicago. He thought if Caroline hadn't already taken Genevieve to the zoo, the three of them could go that morning.

As he walked down the hallway, he thought he heard crying. Following the sounds, he rounded the corner and walked down a shorter hail to the guest bedroom. Genevieve was standing on the side of the bed in a tiny blue gown with some sort of cartoon character on it, rubbing her eyes and crying. Not wanting to scare her, Brian knocked softly on the door.

Genevieve looked up at him with tear-drenched eyes. "Hi Unca Bwian." She hiccupped before burying her face in her hands and crying harder.

Brian went down on his knees in front of her. "Hey, hey. What's all this?" He asked gently as he took her hands away from her face.

Genevieve's lower lip poked out and she avoided his eyes, looking everywhere but at him. "Come on, kiddo. Tell Uncle Brian what's wrong and I'll help you fix it."

Finally looking at him, she whispered so softly that he had to bend down even more to hear her, "Had an 'axedent'." She said miserably with a touch of anger.

"Axedent?" Brian repeated in confusion and kept saying it until it made sense. "Oh, you had an accident. Oh honey, did you wet the bed?" He said when it dawned on him what could have a child so upset so early in the morning. "It's okay."

"Not okay. I'm a big girl; not 'sposed to wet the bed."

"But it is okay sweetheart. Auntie Caroline won't be angry with you. She'll know it was just an accident."

"I know Teetee 'Wo-line won't be mad." The child said in exasperation as she pulled back out of his arms. "Cause I didn't mean to do it. Just dweamed about goin' to the potty and went potty in the bed. I hate dweams and hate to potty in the bed!" She finished and crossed her arms angrily.

This time Brian couldn't prevent a smile from blooming on his face. He hugged her so she wouldn't see it. "You know what we're going to do? We're going to get you all cleaned up. How about I run you a bath? You'll feel much better when you're dry, won't you?" He said holding her by her arms and looking in her face.

Genevieve nodded reluctantly. "All wight. Use Teetee Wo-line's pwetty blue bubble bath?"

"Of course! You can't have a bath without pretty, blue bubbles, now can you?!" He asked as he poked her in her stomach.

The child finally smiled. "You'we silly Unca Bwian. The bubbles won't be blue; only blue befoe you put them in the waddah. Not aftah. They turn white when you put them in the waddah, but they awe still pwetty."

"You bet." Brian said, ready to pick her up.

"No!" Genevieve said anxiously. "Don't pick me up! I'm wet! Yuck!"

"Oh, yeah. That's right." Brian said, properly chastised. Taking her hand, he walked with her into the guest bathroom.

Caroline stretched awake and turned over so that she was lying on her side. Yawning hugely, she rubbed her tired eyes and thought about getting out of bed to fix breakfast. I'm just so tired, she thought as she continued to rub her eyes.

"Good morning." Brian said from the doorway.

Caroline lowered her hands. "You're back." She said with a pleased smile and held her arms out.

Brian came over and sat on the bed for a hug. "I missed you." He said into her hair.

"Me too. You didn't tell me you'd be back so early when I talked to you last night." She said. "Why not?"

"It was a last minute decision. I thought it would be cool to spend the day with you and Genevieve.

Speaking of the little general, she must have worn you out yesterday. I've never known you to sleep so late."

"Late? What time is it?" Caroline asked, pulling out of his arms.

"It's ten minutes to eleven."

"Oh my God! Where's Genevieve? She should have been in here hours ago. She's usually in here by eight at least."

"Calm down," Brian said, holding her in place as she moved to get out of bed. "She's fine. In fact, she's already had her bath and she's getting dressed in the guest room."

"You gave her a bath? That wasn't necessary; she had one before bed last night."

"Oh, it was necessary all right. She had a little accident while she was dreaming." He said distractedly, taking in her tousled sexiness.

"Oh, poor baby." Caroline said with a small smile. "She's always so humiliated when she wets the bed."

"More than humiliated. I'd say she was angry, but a bunch of your blue bubble bath and a certain rubber ducky helped her to release all the negative energy."

"My bubble bath," Caroline said in consternation. "How much did you use? That stuff is not cheap, you know."

"What can I say? The kid has expensive tastes." Brian said as he leaned over her, trapping her against the headboard. "Just like someone else I know." He finished just before taking her mouth with his own.

Name of God, he'd missed the taste of her. He found it almost impossible not to devour.

Struggling to catch her breath and to keep up, Caroline wrapped her arms around him and opened her mouth to his questing tongue.

"Unca Bwian! I got my clothes on! Did you wake Teetee Wo-line?" Genevieve called as she ran down the hail.

Brian broke off the kiss and rested his forehead on Caroline's. "Your niece has lousy timing."

Chuckling, Caroline ran her finger down his cheek. "She'll be leaving this evening and then we'll see just what kind of timing you have."

"Hi Teetee Wo-line!" Genevieve said as she dashed into the room in blue shorts and a blue and yellow patterned shirt. Seeing Brian on the bed, she climbed onto his lap and asked, "Fun in Teetee Wo-line's bed, isn't it? You goin' to spend the night now?"

"Uh, uh…" At a loss for words, Brian looked over at Caroline, who only smiled and lifted a brow expectantly.

His eyes promising revenge, Brian turned away from Caroline and stood, making Genevieve shriek with laughter as he turned her upside down. "How about a trip to the zoo today?"

"Went alweady with Teetee Wo-line." Genevieve shrieked around her giggles.

"Yes," Brian said, lifting her up so that her legs were wrapped around his waist and she was looking at his face. "But that was with Auntie Caroline. You've never been with me and I'm the best kid-taker to the zoo there is! You don't know what fun at the zoo is until you've gone with me!"

Genevieve looked skeptical. Turning to Caroline, she said, "Weally?"

Caroline shrugged her shoulders. "I don't know, baby—"

"Teetee. Wo-line." Genevieve said with soft disappointment and a pleading look. "You pwomised. I told you. I'm not a baby; I'm just the baby of the fam'ly."

Caroline gamely swallowed a chuckle and fixed her face in repentant lines. "That's right, I'm sorry. I promise I won't forget again. But how about we go to zoo with Brian just to see if he really is as fun as he says he is?"

"Okay!" Genevieve said excitedly.

"You go take the sheets off your bed and I'll go shower and Uncle Brian will make us breakfast." She finished with a sly look at Brian as he put Genevieve down.

"Okay!" Genevieve said again and ran from the room

"What am I supposed to make for breakfast? What does she like?" Brian asked, watching as Caroline gathered clean underwear from a drawer.

"Relax." She said over her shoulder as she walked into the bathroom. "There are some frozen waffles in the freezer. All you have to do is pop two in the toaster."

"So, what made you sleep so late today? What exactly did Genevieve have you doing?" Brian asked Caroline as they sat across the table from each other eating breakfast. Genevieve was already finished and was in the living room playing with toys.

"No, it wasn't Genevieve." Caroline said after swallowing a bite of waffle. "I kept getting these calls."

Brian looked at her. "Again? I thought they'd stopped."

"They had, but now they've started up again. I guess it started at about ten and went on at least once every hour until at least four in the morning. It was weird. I had to answer because it could have been an emergency. The first couple of times, I even thought it might be you calling me again."

"I hope you're not thinking that it was someone calling the wrong number or kids playing pranks like you did before." Brian said.

Caroline looked up. "It could have been. I just know it was annoying and kept me up most of the night."

Brian sighed in irritation. "Caroline, you've got to take this more seriously. A normal person would not dial a wrong number more than twice. And from what you've just said, someone called you at least seven times during the night and hung up every time. Did they say anything this time?"

Caroline shrugged uncomfortably. She hated keeping secrets from him, but if he acted this way over phone calls, he'd go crazy if he found out about the note. "Only a couple of times. The last few times, the voice said, 'give it to me' and then they called me a whore. Maybe it really was some kids playing on the phone."

"Could you tell if the voice was male or female?" When she said no, he asked,

"Did you activate Caller ID like I suggested?"

"No. I haven't had the time."

"Did the calls just start up again last night?"

"No, they started on Thursday, I guess. What?" She mumbled defensively when he just looked at her. "I thought they were kids playing around!"

Brian shook his head and went to the bedroom. "Let's see if we can find out who our mystery caller is. You haven't gotten anymore calls since that last one, have you?"

"No." Caroline said and watched as he pressed three buttons on the phone.

"Damn." Brian said, hanging up the phone. "The call can't be traced.

"Don't worry about it Bri. I'll get Caller ID tomorrow. I'll even buy another phone with the display window. I'll put that one in the kitchen."

"I guess I'll have to settle for that for now."

"Please do." Caroline said sarcastically. "I've done everything else you've wanted, haven't I? I don't even jog at night anymore and I haven't been through the park in ages. And you'll be happy to know that I've signed up for self-defense classes again and I always carry my pepper spray."

Brian looked surprised. "Maybe I owe you an apology. Maybe you are taking this seriously."

Caroline walked away on the pretense of getting her purse so she could hide her guilt from him. She told herself that keeping the secret was necessary. If he found out that the note she'd found on her car when she'd left her studio on Thursday had warned her specifically to stay away from him, he'd do something ridiculous and possibly put himself in danger. She had to take care of it herself. She'd just be more careful.

"Hi Cat," Caroline said later that day when her sister-in-law opened the door to her South Side home. She smiled when Genevieve happily threw herself at her mother.

"You haven't met Brian," Caroline said.

Catherine Langley-Singleton straightened with her daughter in her arms and turned to greet Brian with a smile. "No, I haven't met you yet, but I feel like I know you, as much as Sweet Gee here has brought your name up since Labor Day." She kissed the top of Genevieve's head and offered Brian her hand. "How are you 'Unca Bwian'?"

Brian smiled at the attractive dark-skinned woman. "I hope you don't mind that she calls me that. She told me that she was going to, and as you know, your daughter is hard to resist."

"Trust me," Cat said with another smile, as she turned to walk deeper into the house. "Nobody knows that better than I. Can I offer you guys something to drink?" She asked as they followed her into the large, airy kitchen.

"Anything cold would be good for me." Caroline said and Brian agreed.

Cat bent to put Genevieve down and smiled into her daughter's eyes. "I have a surprise for you. Guess who's here? Daddy's in the backyard!"

"Goody!" Genevieve said and was around the center island and out the door before her mother could get to the refrigerator to take out a pitcher of iced tea.

"Lee's here?" Caroline asked as Cat handed her and Brian glasses of tea.

Hearing the expectant and happy surprise in her voice, Cat said cautiously, "He's just here to finish that playhouse that Genevieve's been wanting forever. Nothing else." She said firmly and reached out to pat Caroline's hand when she saw her shoulders droop slightly in disappointment.

Looking away from her, Cat turned to Brian with a friendly smile. "Brian, I'm sure Lee could use a hand out there. Are you comfortable with a hammer?"

Recognizing the not-so-subtle hint to make himself scarce, Brian answered in the affirmative, grabbed his iced tea and strode through the back door.

"He seems like a nice guy." Cat said to Caroline as she walked over to the breakfast table on the other side of the kitchen.

"He is, so tell me why you just gave him the bum's rush." Caroline said as she sat across from her.

"I just wanted to talk to you. It's been a while since we've had one of our heart-to-hearts."

Caroline studied her sister-in-law. She was a pretty woman with her sleek, shining cap of black hair that hugged her skull lovingly and stopped right before her ears. The pert little nose, strong chin, classic cheekbones and deep brown eyes had served her well in her job as a news anchor, a position that almost demanded good looks. "I hope you're not going to warn me about the perils of dating Brian. I've already gotten an earful of that from dad, Lee, Uncle James and even perfect strangers."

"No, I wasn't going to do that. Though, Lee did share some of his concerns with me. But after spending some time with Brian, your brother seems to like him well enough. I actually wanted to talk to you about Lee and me. How are you doing with our separation?"

Caroline looked at her in surprise. "You're asking me how I'm doing? The better question is how you're doing. You and Lee have been married for ten years and now it's all but over. I'm not the biggest concern here."

"I know you're not, but I'm worried about you nonetheless. Lee told me how you reacted to the news, and though I am only a few years older than you are, I've always thought of you as my little sister. I'm quite protective of you, you know."

"I know yon are, and I have always thought of you as my big sister. But as for you being protective of me, you don't need to be. I'm not the one you should worry about when it comes to your separation from Lee. Your biggest concerns should be Genevieve and yourself."

"Trust me, they are." Cat said and then hesitantly, "But, I'm not so much concerned with how you're coping, I guess, as I am with how you feel about me now. I don't want to lose your friendship or that closeness that we've always shared. Does that sound selfish?"

"No, of course not." Caroline said and wanting to banish the uncertainty she saw in Cat's eyes, she got up to hug her. "I don't want our relationship to suffer either. And I'm flattered that you would even think about our relationship while you're going through such a difficult time."

"Why wouldn't I?" Cat released her. "Our relationship is very important to me."

"Me too. Mom and Dad still love you, you know. They're saddened by what's happened, of course, but they know that you're not to blame for it."

"Actually, no one is really to blame. It just happened. We grew apart. But I still consider Lee to be one of my closest friends and I'll always love your family." She smiled. "Will you and Brian be staying for dinner? I'm baking a turkey breast and Lee's made his famous Key Lime pie for dessert."

Caroline slanted her a look and flushed a bit as she walked their empty glasses over to the sink. "Well, that all sounds delicious, but I can't. I'm sorry."

Puzzled over Caroline's sudden nervousness, Cat asked, "Why not?"

Caroline turned from the sink. "Well, I don't know if you knew this, but until today, Brian's been out of town since Wednesday."

"I remember you mentioning it to Genevieve when she asked about him Friday night, yes."

"Even before then, I hadn't seen him all week because he worked so late every night to get things finished before he went out of town." Caroline looked at her expectantly. "And I really missed him."

"Oh, I see." Cat said with a small smile.

Caroline grinned. "Yep, I think you do!"

BOOK THREE

CHAPTER 22

"Brian Keenan, you old dog! It's good to see you. How the hell have you been?"

Brian returned the hug of his old friend and partner Jack Winthrop. Smiling as they broke apart, he said, "Not me, you. Captain tells me you've been hot-dogging it in Philly while the rest of the peons stay here in chi-town. How'd it go?" Brian located a booth and sat down.

When Jack had called and asked to meet for lunch Brian had gladly accepted. He studied his friend. Because they had the same build, were virtually the same height and had the same black-as-night hair, people had often thought they were brothers. But coloring was where the similarities ended. Jack had an outrageously beautiful face. His eyes were almost turquoise with unusual double lashes whose length were the envy of every woman he'd ever met. Angled cheekbones, a sculpted chin, a high, wide forehead, full lips and a straight nose had made more than one scout approach him about modeling.

Seeing Jack's brow suddenly mar with a frown and his eyes deepen with disappointment, Brian asked, "The trip was that bad, huh?"

"Let's just say I didn't get what I was looking for. I went out there because I thought the Philly police would be of some help to the bureau in looking for this scum, but all I did was end up spinning my wheels for two months in the city of brotherly love."

"Who are you feds looking for?"

Jack gave him a warning look. "How many times in the last five years have I told you not to call me that? It's FBI to all you local yokels, remember? But you're not even a cop any more so it's sir to you, pal."

Whatever. So tell me about the creep."

Jack studied his old partner for a moment, knowing he could trust him with his life. "It's Brickman."

Brian looked surprised. "Alex Brickman? The Alex Brickman who supposedly got himself blown up in a bust in Boston harbor a few years back? That Alex Brickman?"

"He's the one all right. No one ever believed the little bastard was dead because we had no proof. No bodies were ever found, so we couldn't even compare dental records. It was just all too suspicious and convenient, you know? At any rate, we've always believed he's still alive somewhere in a little rat hole, and a couple of months ago we got a lead that he may be in Philadelphia. Of course, he wasn't and I told them he wasn't. I told them that he was too smart to stay anywhere near the East Coast."

"You sound like you know where he's hiding."

"I don't know it for sure, but my gut and a couple of feelers I put out are telling me that he's in the Midwest. Here in Chicago. It only makes sense. He wouldn't have gone to the left coast because he would know that that would be the second place to look for him after the East Coast and he'd need another huge city for his base of operations." He shrugged, "Logically, he'd have to be here."

"He could use Detroit or Cleveland. And what about St. Louis?"

Jack shook his head. "No, it's not any of those places. It's Chicago. I just know it. Chicago's the only logical place. If you'll remember, Brickman is more than just a drug dealer, he's into culture and he has expensive tastes. Museums, theater, opera, galleries, expensive shops, high-class restaurants. There's no better place in the Midwest to get those things than Chicago. The city's only downfall is its cold-ass winters."

"Well you've always had good hunches. So why aren't they listening to you?"

"I haven't given them enough proof, but I'll find it, and soon. So, you're not the only one who talks to the captain. He tells me you're dating a real beauty."

"Captain always was a gossip, wasn't he? Just like his daughter. Her name is Caroline Singleton and I met her when she came into Inclusion for an interview."

"Singleton, huh? You don't mean Caroline Singleton of the Singletons who make Staggeringly Strawberry and Viciously Vanilla ice cream?"

"That's her. She's one of four lucky scions, in fact. Her parents and aunt and uncle run things. You know them? I thought your families might run in the same circles."

"Yes. I actually met Caroline at one of those debutante balls that my mother managed to guilt me into taking my cousin Gail to years ago, but I'd seen her around before then at different events and parties. I know her brother Lee a bit better. We competed in sports constantly in high school. He's a damned fine lacrosse player." Jack finished and winking mischievously, added, "So you're dating the Ice Cream Princess, huh? She's gorgeous! What's she see in a big lug like you?"

"Don't know. Must be my handsome good looks and devastating charm."

"Oh, I didn't know." Jack said in mock surprise. "I haven't seen Caroline in years, but I hadn't heard that she'd gone blind! She'd have to be to think of you that way."

Brian chuckled. "You're right. All the good looks in the free world went into your pretty mug." He said and knowing how uncomfortable his friend was about his ridiculously handsome face, he continued, "How did Sheila the dispatcher put it? Oh yeah, I remember. Your face is so beautiful, you should be put in the

Louvre or some other elite art museum with the rest of the beautiful masterpieces of the world."

Jack grimaced. "All right; enough already. Tell me more about Caroline. Does she have any interesting friends or cousins who might want to date a G-man with a French mama and WASP papa?"

"Are you serious?" Brian asked in surprise because he knew his friend was never at a loss for female companionship. He was also a love 'em and leave 'em kind of guy.

"No…I don't know." Jack said, knowing exactly what Brian was thinking. "I was just kidding."

"Well let me know when you figure it out. I think I know someone who would be perfect for you. She's smart, bitingly witty, independent, candid and loyal." Brian said, thinking of Tracy and how she was probably the one woman who could slow Jack down.

"What is this? Are you so gone over that lady of yours that you now think everyone has to be in love to find happiness?" Jack asked.

"I'm usually the last one to even think about setting someone up with someone else, but just hear me out. I'm not saying you should fall in love with her, but I am saying you two would hit it off."

"No way. You're going at this a little too hard for my comfort. She must be a real dog. What is it? Does she need plastic surgery?"

Brian thought about Tracy again and chuckled lightly. "No, far from it, but you'd be in need of some if she ever heard you say that."

"Well then, she must be a harpy who can't keep her mouth shut."

Brian held his hands up in surrender. "Look Jack, if you're not interested, you're not interested. Changing the subject now." He said deliberately. "How's your mom doing and when do you think she'll invite me over for another delicious French meal?"

Jack snorted. "You're welcome anytime, just don't expect me to tag along. I'm never in the mood for speeches on how it's my duty as the lone offspring to give them *beaucoup des petits-enfants* or as my father would say, a boatload of grandchildren."

Chuckling in earnest now, Brian raised his hand to signal the waiter. "I understand. My mother did the same thing when I went to see her a couple of weeks ago."

"How is your mom? Has she met Caroline?"

"Mom and Frank are doing well. They haven't met Caroline yet, but she's going to Detroit with me for Thanksgiving."

"I'm sure she'll love them. Who wouldn't?"

"Oh, I'm not worried about that. I'm not worried about them liking Caroline, either."

"Then what are you worried about? The fact that you're telling me what you're not worried about tells me that there's something you are worried about." Jack explained when Brian gave him a questioning look.

Brian placed his order and waited for Jack to place his before saying, "I did want to tell you something and see if you had any ideas that I hadn't thought of." He told him about the things that had been happening to Caroline.

"It does sound like something's going on. I'd keep doing the same things you're doing if I were you. Sounds like she may have a stalker, especially with the phone calls she's started getting. Any ex-boyfriends?"

"I asked her that, but before me, she hadn't really dated anyone seriously for a couple of years and the last relationship she was in ended amicably."

"You know a stalker doesn't have to be someone she knows. It could be anyone who saw her somewhere and started obsessing. Has she gotten more phone calls since the time you were out of town?"

"Yeah, almost every night. I bought her a phone with a display window and she called the phone company to get Caller ID, but the only thing that shows up on the display when the person calls is the word 'private.' This weekend, I think we'll go to an animal shelter and pick up a dog. It would just make me feel better when I'm out of town or when I can't go over to her place for some reason."

"Good idea. Get something that you know will make a lot of noise and will attack when necessary. I know I'm being alarming, but you can't be too careful. In the meantime, why don't I take a look at the sketch she drew? Maybe I'll recognize the jerk from the park."

"I'll drop it by your office tomorrow."

"Sounds good. I have meetings, but just leave it with the receptionist if I'm not around."

"All right." Brian said. When his cell phone let out a shrill ring, he pulled it from his shirt pocket. "Hello."

"Hi darling, it's me." Caroline said.

"Hey beautiful. What's wrong?" He asked, detecting nerves in her voice.

"Nothing. Why do you assume that there is?"

"Well, for one, you never call me on my cell phone and two, your voice just sounds weird."

"Well, I'm okay and I called your cell phone because you weren't in your office. I just wanted to tell you not to come by to pick me up at the studio after work today. I won't be there."

"Why not?"

"I'm just not getting anything done today, so I came home. I'm going to have some lunch and maybe watch a little television."

"How'd you get home?"

Caroline sighed impatiently. "I'm a big girl Brian. I can walk, but you'll be happy to know that I took a taxi this time. I'm just tired and didn't feel like walking."

"All right." Brian said suspiciously, far from being placated. "I'll see you around 6:30 then. Should I stop and pick up dinner? How about Thai?"

"Sounds good. Talk to you later."

"Bye, sweetheart." Brian said and broke the connection.

"I take it that was the little woman?" Jack asked with a smirk. "Boy has she got you whipped and trained."

Brian merely smiled before tucking back into his lunch. "You only wish you had it so good, my friend."

"Oh, no." Jack said definitively as he took a sip from his glass of water. "I have a feeling that your and my definitions of 'so good' are completely different when it comes to women."

"If you say so, pal. If you say so."

"I do say so. But hey, don't let me stop you from taking your trip of insanity. It's like that old saying goes, 'to each his own.'" Jack said with an unconcerned shrug.

"You said it." Brian said happily.

Caroline sat pensively on the couch and stared at nothing. The noise of the television was all but forgotten. She knew she shouldn't have lied to Brian, but she'd felt she'd had no choice. The last thing she wanted was for him to rush over in the middle of the day just because she was whining. But God, she really was scared witless. She picked up the note she'd found peeking under her studio door and read it again. Shuddering, she tossed it back onto the table.

It was the fourth note she'd received in as many days and they all said almost exactly the same thing. This one was slightly different, but none of them were like the one she'd received the week before. They didn't even mention Brian's name. The first note had been lying in the hallway outside her studio door. Until she'd read it, she'd thought it was a lost slip of paper. She'd read it, found it creepy and had thrown it out at the first opportunity. The second, third and fourth ones had actually been pushed under the studio door. The fourth one was the only one she'd kept. She'd realized that she was in over her head and couldn't possibly handle it alone, nor could she pretend like nothing was happening. She had to show the note to Brian.

She realized now how stupid it had been to ignore the notes, but she hadn't wanted to believe that someone disliked her enough to actually threaten her. Telling Brian only would have made the threat more real and she hadn't wanted to deal with it.

Well, the fifth note makes it essential that I tell him, she thought. About *all* of the notes—I have no choice. She knew that he would be angry and she was prepared to deal with it. When she heard his key turn in the lock, Caroline jumped up and used the remote to turn off the television. Spotting the note, she snatched it up and stuffed it in the pocket of her khakis just as he appeared.

"Hi." She said, her voice unnaturally high as she nervously wiped her hands on her pants. "What are you doing home so early? It's only 2:30."

Brian eyed her, wondering what was bothering her. Giving her a brief kiss, he said, "I couldn't stop thinking about the way you sounded on the phone, so after lunch I went back to the office, grabbed my things and came home. I'm glad I did." He said as he felt how tense she was. "What's going on?"

Caroline moved away from him, and deciding it was best to just get it over with, she told him about the notes.

Brian was incredulous and furious. Thinking he needed to get away from her to clear his thoughts, he stalked angrily into the kitchen. Pulling the pitcher of water out of the refrigerator, he poured himself a glass and finished it off in two swallows. He heard her call his name from the living room, but he was too angry to answer. Unbelievable, he thought, wondering what else he needed to do to get through to her that she was in danger.

He felt as if he were just a waste of space in her life. If she didn't trust him enough to tell him—her boyfriend *and* a former cop—about the notes, what else hadn't she told him? Feeling that he'd been made powerless by her lack of trust, he took several deep breaths and tried to calm down.

"Brian we have to talk about this." Caroline said quietly from the doorway.

"Not right now, Caroline."

"We have to talk about this." She said again and took his arm. When he broke away with a shrug, she felt as if she'd been slapped.

"You want to talk? Fine. We'll talk." Brian said angrily and trying to ignore the stunned look of hurt on her face, he strode back into the living room.

"I can't believe you didn't tell me about the notes." He began, once she followed him. "Although, considering that you've never taken anything I've ever said about your safety seriously, I don't know why I find it so hard to believe."

Caroline shook her head. "That's not true." She said quietly. "I told you why I didn't tell you initially. And besides, I'm telling you now."

"Sure, you're telling me now, now that you're terrified. In the meantime, while you decided whether or not you could trust me, this nut case has probably been watching you all along."

"It had nothing to do with trusting you Brian. It had to do with me and how scared I was. I didn't want to believe it, so I ignored it, but in the back of my mind, I knew all along that what you were saying was true. I just didn't want it to be."

"You can't just ignore things and expect them to go away. Life doesn't quite work that way."

Sighing at his sarcasm, Caroline said, "I know that. It was just an attempt on my part to feel safe. I can't help but face reality now and I'm sorry if I hurt you while taking so long to do so."

Far from being appeased and bordering on livid, Brian said, "If you're not going to take the issue of your safety seriously Caroline, and trust me as well, then it would just be stupid of me to hang around like this." He turned on his heel. "I can't take this. I'm leaving."

Thinking she had blown everything, Caroline panicked. She ran to catch up with him and grabbed his coat. "Don't walk away Brian. Just talk to me."

Not trusting himself to speak, Brian loosed her hand and turned to face her. He said nothing as he watched her face.

Desperate to make him see her point of view, Caroline said, "I really didn't mean to hurt you. I just wasn't thinking. My actions had absolutely nothing to do with my not trusting you. It was because I knew I could trust you and that you'd make me face things that I didn't tell you. Don't you see? How could I have told you when I was determined to believe that nothing was wrong? I'm sorry, I really am." She said, completely dry-eyed, but with her heart in her throat and stark fear in her eyes.

"Let me see the note," was all he said. And proving to have no willpower against her wide-eyed fear and determination not to cry, when she took the note out of her pocket and stretched her arm to give it to him, he pulled her into his arms. "From now on, tell me about anything suspicious or scary that happens. All right?" He asked.

Unable to speak because of the unadulterated relief blocking her vocal chords, Caroline only nodded and held on tightly.

Brian opened the note and read it aloud. " *You will be made to face the consequences of your actions. The payment extracted will be painful. Give me what I want and you won't suffer. Let things remain as they are and*

*you will regret it. Leave town now and you will live. Stay
and you will die.'* Hmm. Pretty dramatic way to say,
'you'll get yours.' You're sure that the other three said
the same thing?" He asked as he folded the computer-
generated note and put it in his pocket.

"No, it was almost the exact same thing. The first
ones didn't actually say that I would die if I didn't
leave town, but they did warn me to leave town."

"And the one that came when I was out of town
was completely different than the ones that came this
week?"

"Yes, it warned me to stay away from you 'or else.'
It was also made up differently. It wasn't printed in
black and white. It was on bright yellow paper and the
letters were cut out from magazines. I don't know who
would be sending me these notes and I don't know
what the writer is talking about."

"You have no idea at all what the writer means
when he says you'll suffer the consequences of your
behavior or when he says to give him what he wants?"

"No." Caroline said in frustration, and unable to
keep still, she moved out of his arms to pace. "I've
thought about it over and over again and I don't know
what the person could possibly be talking about. I
haven't done anything to anyone!"

Brian took her shoulders to keep her still. "It's all
right," he said, massaging her neck to alleviate some
of the tension there. "We'll figure it out. Now I need
you to promise me that you'll let me, a *former cop*, try

to keep you safe. You have to promise that you'll listen to me."

Caroline nodded. "All right. I'll listen, but that doesn't mean that I'm just going to fall in line like a good soldier if I don't agree with everything."

"It goes back to trust Caroline. You need to trust me if I'm going to help."

She blew out a breath. "You're right, of course. It's just that I'm so used to being independent and doing things on my own, it's hard for me to believe that someone else might know what's best for me. In any situation."

"The first thing we have to do is contact the police and let them know what's going on. There may not be a whole lot they can do, especially since you and I have both touched the note, but they'll at least be aware of what's going on."

Caroline nodded. "I knew you'd want to call the police. What else?"

"I was going to save this until the weekend, but in light of what's been going on, I think we should go today. We're going to the animal shelter to get you a dog who won't be afraid to attack." Brian finished, despite the fact that she'd starting shaking her head no as soon as he'd said 'animal shelter'.

"Brian, I'm not a dog person. I'm not even an animal person."

"You don't like dogs? Everyone likes dogs."

"It's not that I don't like them. It's just that I've never wanted one. I stay away from them. I'm not afraid of dogs, it's only that they're always everywhere and they get into things. And I don't want one living here in my teeny-weenie, little condo taking up all my space, shedding its hair, slobbering over everything. Just the thought of one living here…with me…and having to clean up after it on walks…" She shuddered with distaste. "Nasty."

Brian looked down into her face and kept his hands on her arms. He smiled at the combination of disgruntlement and true disgust showing on her face. "Teeny-weenie? This place could fit a family of four, with room to spare. Easily. Besides, we'll get one that won't be so big, just big enough to make a difference." He said persuasively.

"No." She said decisively. "I don't want a dog."

"You need someone here with you when I'm not and a dog will make a great noisemaker in case someone tries to get in here or if you're ever approached when you're out by yourself. You need protection."

"I told you that I'm brushing up on my self-defense skills. I hadn't taken a course in about seven years, but it hasn't been hard getting started again. I'd rather know how to protect myself than wait around for some one to save me."

"I know, but in the meantime, a dog will still be helpful."

"You're not going to budge on this, are you?" She asked and when he shook his head no, she capitulated.

"All right, but I don't want a dog that's already set in its ways and difficult to train."

He kissed her pouting lips and took her hand. "I don't care, so long as it makes enough noise to wake up the entire neighborhood and or scare the bravest criminal. Now let's go pay a visit to our local Officer Friendly."

She nodded again and then turned pensive.

"What is it?" Brian asked.

"Were you really ready to walk out on me?"

He hugged her again. "I wasn't going to leave permanently, just until I'd cooled down. You can't get rid of me that easily." He said into the top of her head. "Ouch! Hey!" He said in protest and jumped back away from her.

"Making me think you wanted things to be over between us was a horrible thing to do." She said, watching him rub the spot under his arm where she'd pinched him. "Don't you ever scare me like that again." She said and moved back into his arms.

"I didn't mean for you to think that, but I'm glad that you did." He said while rubbing her back. "Not that I like the idea of you being scared, but now you know how it feels to think that you may be on the verge of losing the most important person in your life. It's how I've felt lately, especially when you refused to take precautions."

"Point taken." Caroline said quietly.

CHAPTER 23

October brought a gust of cold air to Chicago with its arrival, causing the temperature to hover in the high forties for the first part of the month. Bright colored leaves fell from trees and swept down the city's corridors, spurred on by the strong winds that seemed to get more forceful by the day.

It was on one of these blustery days that Pete Kovlovsky once again found himself standing in front of Alex Brickman's big desk trying to gather his thoughts to come up with a plausible explanation for another unforgivable failure. His gut told him that there would be nothing he could say to Brickman that wouldn't send the man over the edge. Brickman's anger was palpable as he stared at him.

As Pete watched, Brickman tamed his back and pulled himself together with a seemingly negligible amount of effort. And when he turned back to face Pete, it was as if the lowly knave of seconds before had never even existed. Pinning him in place with his pale eyes, Brickman said in his cultured voice that was never hurried and was always unconcerned, "So Mr. Kovlovsky. What excuse have you for me this time? Hmm?

What reason will you present to me for not having what belongs to me with you—right here, right now?"

Pete did not make the mistake of thinking that Brickman was only referring to the film. He cleared his throat. Keep it clean and simple, he told himself. Stick as close to the truth as possible. "I apologize sir, but my original plan did not pan out. In the past weeks, my team and I have gone through every female photographer listed in the phone book, and we didn't find her listed there."

"Every female photographer—North Side, South Side and West Side?"

"Yes sir. We were quite thorough."

"And now that we've discovered that you've wasted a colossal amount of time that we couldn't afford in the first place, what do you think you and your team should do now Mr. Kovlovsky?"

"Well, sir, might I suggest that we may be worrying for no reason at all? After all, it's been a couple of months since your picture was taken and surely we'd have heard on the news by now if the photographer had recognized you. Maybe you were too far in the background to be more than anything but a blur."

Brickman's nose flared as he fought to control the anger that the suggestion aroused. "What makes you think we'd have heard anything? I've got two governments looking for me and the last thing any one of them would do is alert the media if they were hot on my trail. So the woman may not have recognized me and so I may not even be distinguishable in any photos, but I'm not willing to take that chance. And Mr. Kovlovsky, I'll be sorely disappointed if you tell me that you're willing to take risks with my life. Surely, you're not that daring." He finished, and then almost as if it were an afterthought, "Are you Mr. Kovlovsky?"

"No, of course not sir. I wasn't thinking and I apologize."

Brickman's only hint that he'd heard him was an almost imperceptible nod of his head. "So glad we're on the same page, Mr. Kovlovsky. Now, I believe I have a much better plan than your oh-so brilliant one to just give up on finding her. I've had Antonio make a sketch of the woman as I described her. He is quite the multifaceted one, our cook is. You and a few others will take the copies of this sketch and canvas Lincoln Park with it. Start at the point where we last saw her and spread out. Ask anyone and everyone who frequents that park.

"I don't care how you get the information I need Mr. Kovlovsky, just get it. If you have to act like a grieving husband, do it. If you must play the role of a police officer, do it. Just get it done. Do not hand out the sketch, just show it around and be discreet while you do it. Have we an understanding, Mr. Kovlovsky?"

"Yes sir."

"Lovely. Mia will give you what you need on your way out." He said by way of dismissal.

Pete left, wondering how they could possibly be discreet while asking 'anyone and everyone'. His hatred for Brickman was getting stronger every day that he was on the photographer case.

—ᴍ—

Ida hurried as she made her way through the reception area of the office. She had faxes to make and orders to place. The company's growth was only making more work for her. She didn't mind it, however. She relished being in control of who got what and what went where. As office manager, she had power and she knew that she intimidated many of the employees, especially the younger ones. Just because she didn't have a fancy, muckity-muck title didn't mean that she didn't know her worth. And she made sure that everyone else knew it as well.

She turned her head distractedly as she heard the elevator doors open. Well, well, the slut is back, she thought as she turned fully around and watched Caroline step off the elevator. Almost choking on her envy, she took in Caroline's outfit. The slim skirt of chocolate-brown suede covered her hips smoothly, while the short-waisted matching jacket worked in conjunction with a cream colored turtleneck to high-light her brown skin. She'd topped the outfit off with gold hoop earrings and chocolate, knee-high, leather boots that looked soft as butter to the touch. So did the large leather bag.

A silk scarf in varying shades of brown held her hair back in a curly ponytail at the nape of her neck. Ida estimated that with the expensive sunglasses perched on Caroline's nose, the cost of the complete ensemble would have been between twelve and fifteen hundred dollars. I wonder what Brian made her do to get that outfit, Ida thought nastily. Or maybe mommy and daddy's megabucks paid for it. Either way, it was unfair that Caroline should be able to get something for nothing.

As she studied her, Ida looked for signs of nervousness or fear in Caroline. When she didn't see signs of either emotion, she became even angrier. "So, checking up on Brian, huh? I guess he doesn't feel he needs to tell you *everything*. He's not here." Ida said, greedy satisfaction coming through in every syllable she uttered.

Caroline turned away from the receptionist. "Oh, hello Ida. I didn't see you there." She said, her falsely jovial smile and hard eyes telling Ida that the exact opposite was true. "Now what was that you were saying?" She asked Ida, fixing a pretended look of anticipation on her face.

"I said—"

Caroline held up a hand. "Wait, hold that thought." She said and turned back to the receptionist. "Okay, as I was saying, Brian asked me to wait in his office until he returns from his meeting." She returned the receptionist's knowing smile and turned back to Ida. "I'm sorry. You were saying?" She asked with a questioning lift of her brow.

Arrogant bitch, Ida thought sourly, her anger making her eyes spark and her skin flush. "You think you're so—"

Suddenly fed up with the other woman's irrational dislike and weary of playing games with her, Caroline interrupted Ida before she could get a full head of steam. "This is not the place for this Ida. In fact, there's never a right place for this sort of thing. You don't like me and I don't like you. Please, let's just leave it at that." She looked at the receptionist. "When Brian arrives, please tell him that I'm here. Thanks." She started down the hall to the back of the office space, bypassing Ida on her way.

What a trial that woman is, Caroline thought as she walked into Brian's office. After putting her sunglasses back in their case and into her bag, she placed the bag in one of the chairs that faced the desk. She turned around to shut the door and a gusty sigh of frustration escaped her when she saw Ida standing there. "What now, Ida?"

Ida stepped into Brian's office and shut the door. "What are you doing here, Caroline?"

Caroline folded her arms and lifted a brow at the impudent question. "Not that it's any of your business, but I should think that the answer to that question is remarkably obvious."

"You don't mind taking potshots at me and getting me in trouble when you're alone with Brian, but when you're alone with me, you want to take the high road. Well look around you, Caroline. This is my turf. Let's see how tough you are now."

"You're crazy, Ida and I have no idea what you're talking about." Caroline said, confusion clear in her voice.

"I'll get Brian back, you know." Ida said slyly, wanting to hurt Caroline and put doubt in her mind. "It's only a matter of time. I know the signs. He's already coming on to me and pretty soon, he'll be asking me to come back to his bed. He always did have a ravenous appetite when it came to me. He wants me and soon, he'll have me."

Unbelievable, Caroline thought and snorted out a laugh. "If that were true Ida, you'd be welcome to him. I'd be the first one to tell him to go."

"You say that now, but when it happens, we'll see what you say—"

"Oh, please!" Caroline said impatiently. "You're so insulting—to me and to yourself! I don't have time for these kinds of tactics that even the most immature, insecure high school girl would think long and hard about before she used them. Look, what you had with Brian was over a long time ago. Why are you still struggling to get it back? Never mind, I don't even want to know the answer. Forget I asked that. Just go away Ida. Please."

"I don't need to struggle to get anything back, especially when it's well on its way home already—"

"For God's sake, Ida! Don't you get it? I'm not going to lower myself to humor your lies. And even if everything you're saying is true; I don't fight over men. Period. So just give up and go away Ida. Because either way you look at it, you're wasting your time. I'm not going to satisfy any of your twisted needs today."

"Whore." Ida said, wishing vehemently that she'd told Brickman what she knew.

"That's very good. Feel better now?"

"Don't play with me, Caroline. You'll regret it if you do because you can't win."

Caroline sighed. "Okay, I won't. *Now* will you go away?"

"Oh, you're so high and mighty with your expensive clothes and fancy attitude, but I know the truth about you. I know what kind of person you really are. You're a slut, Caroline. You're the kind of woman who sleeps with a man to get what she wants or for a promotion. I know that's what you did with Brian. Why else would you be hired to be the Art Director at your age?"

Caroline became alarmed. The situation was rapidly starting to remind her of the last confrontation she'd had with Ida, where the other woman seemed to just go off on tangents and had almost worked herself into a frenzy. As she looked at Ida's face, Caroline took a step back. The other woman's face was so red, it was almost purple and her eyes were starting to turn glassy, while her hands were clenched into tight fists.

"Take it easy Ida." Caroline said slowly.

"You take it easy, you no-talented *puta!*" Ida said calmly and quietly. "Only really talented people get positions like you had when they're so young. And you had no talent. That's how I know you slept with Brian to get the job and that's why I don't believe people when they say you're doing an art show at the Rutledge. If you are, you must have slept with someone there too. You may have everyone else fooled, but not me. It's like I said, you're a whore. That's the only way to explain all the things you're getting." She finished and shrugged.

Caroline was speechless with shock for a moment. "How dare you?!" She finally exploded. "What kind of a person are you to say those kinds of things when you know nothing about me?" Turning on her heel, she paced to the other side of the room. "You've got problems Ida, and I don't know what they are. In fact, I don't even care what they are. I don't know why you've fixated on blaming me for whatever it is you're unhappy about or whatever it is you didn't get, but want. I don't care what it is—a man, a job, whatever! Don't blame me for your unhappiness. I don't believe this!" And completely at a loss now, Caroline threw her hands up in defeat. She'd never dealt with anyone as irrational and nasty as Ida before and so was truly out of her depth.

"The only thing you have that I want is Brian, and you barely have that. But that's okay, you can think what you like. It will just make things that much sweeter for me when you finally get your comeuppance. You'll realize then that it's not what you have that's at issue here—it's what you don't have. I have what Brian wants and you don't. It's as simple as that."

The frown of confusion that had graced Caroline's face for the past ten minutes only created deeper grooves as she tried to make sense of what she was hearing. This woman is certifiable, she thought. "I know I'm going to be sorry for asking this, but if it will get you to leave, I'll do it. What exactly is it that you think you have that Brian wants?"

Ida laughed. "Are you blind? Look at me!" She said, spreading her arms wide. "I've got the kind of figure men die for; fight each other for. While you, on the other hand, are all skin and bones with no curves anywhere to turn on even the horniest man."

"Mm hmm." Caroline mumbled, nodding gravely. "So in other words, you're the stuff men dream of and I'm…for lack of a better word…not. Okay." She said perkily. "That clears up a lot of things for me, so thanks. Are we done now?"

Furious that Caroline appeared to be making fun of her, Ida said, "Not by a long shot, you skinny…"

"What the hell's going on here?" Brian demanded as he walked into the office. Walking past Ida, he went over to Caroline. "I heard you all the way in the hall."

"Nothing's going on." Caroline said, accepting his brief kiss. "Just a little girl talk. Ida was just leaving. Weren't you Ida?" She said, shooting her a pointed look.

Ida looked from Brian to Caroline, still seeing the shared kiss and taking in his protective stance. "Fine." Was all she said over her shoulder as she strode angrily from the room.

Brian turned to face Caroline. "What was that all about?"

"Oh, Ida was just ranting again. It's nothing serious." Caroline said, stalling for time and distance before she told him. She hoped to talk him out of making a big deal out of the situation. "I'll tell you later."

"What happened Caroline?" He demanded, feeling the tension in her shoulders.

"I'll tell you later," she said again as she went around him to scoop up her bag. "I promise. Now I'm hungry. Where are you taking me for lunch?"

Not nearly satisfied with her answer, Brian followed as she left his office.

Ida stalked to her desk and slammed down into her chair. She picked up the telephone receiver and angrily began to punch in Brickman's number. I'll teach Caroline not to mess with me, she thought as her finger prepared to hit the last number. Just then, Brian walked out of his office and began talking to Carl. She couldn't do it. She hung up the phone and rubbed her forehead in agitation.

Her life was beginning to take its toll on her. She was constantly broke and every penny she made from her side work for Brickman went into the coffers of a gambling boat. She hadn't won any money in weeks. To add to her worries, Brickman had started making dissatisfied sounds about her gambling. She was afraid if she didn't stop the gambling, he would kick her out of his bed and out of the condo in which he'd set her up. She wasn't ready for that. She wanted Brian back in her life before she let go of anything.

Her gambling was the reason she'd taken a two-week vacation to visit her parents in Florida. Because Brickman would consider going to Gamblers' Anonymous a weakness, she'd wanted to see if she could quit cold turkey. So far the vacation had helped her in that respect—she'd been gambling-free for 16 days—but she hadn't been able to completely forget her life in Chicago. Every day that she was in Florida, she'd noticed a man watching her parents' house. She'd recognized him as one of Brickman's men and she'd known that she had to bring the situation to a head sooner rather than later.

CHAPTER 24

"All right, Caroline. You've put me off long enough." Brian said from across the table from her They d decided to have lunch at Bandera, a popular restaurant located on the city's famed Michigan Avenue. "What was going on between you and Ida when I came into my office? And why are you trying so hard to avoid telling me?"

"It's not my fault that we were held up by Maria and Carl. What was I supposed to do? Ignore them? I haven't seen either of them in months and we had a little catching up to do. All right," she said with a sigh when he just looked at her. With as little fanfare as possible, she told him about her confrontation with Ida.

Brian sat back in his chair contemplatively, his cop's mind suddenly suspicious.

"I didn't want to tell you right away because I didn't want you to do something stupidly macho and fire her or something." Caroline said after he'd been silent for more than a few minutes. "As I've told you before, I can handle Ida."

Brian looked at her. "I'm sorry. What did you say?"

"What are you thinking Brian?"

"I'm thinking that our friend Ida is your stalker."

Caroline was speechless for a moment. "Ida? No. I admit she acts crazy sometimes, but…

"Exactly." Brian said when she trailed off into silence. "Think about it Caroline. You said yourself that she seemed to be blaming you for something during your argument, right? She basically said that you didn't get what you have from merit, but from sleeping around. Well, the notes said that you would be made to face the consequences of your actions—"

"Yes, but—"

"Just hear me out Caroline. If she really thinks that you've accomplished the things you've accomplished on your back, then in her mind, you should be punished. Ida's the one sending the notes and making the phone calls, all right. And her saying that you prostitute yourself for your career is just an excuse on her part to come after you. It's her way of justifying her anger and dislike because you and I are together."

"But why would she start harassing me just recently? You and I have been together for months."

"I've been thinking about that and I think it was probably Linda who set her off."

"Linda! Why would she—"

"I'm not saying that she deliberately did it. Remember how she came over for dinner at the loft that Friday in September? Well, all she kept asking us about was our trip to your family's cottage. I'm sure she was just full of information when she went back to work. You know how she loves to talk about things that she thinks are interesting. The calls started coming the next week, didn't they? I think Linda's stories about us and how she thinks we make a great couple probably got Ida going."

"I don't know Brian." Caroline said and sat back in her chair. "I got calls before then, remember? And besides, it's all just so creepy. Ida?"

"It doesn't matter who it is, it would still be creepy. But if what I've said isn't enough to convince you, how about the fact that Ida was out of town on vacation all last week and the week before that? She didn't get back into the office until today. You haven't gotten a call in two weeks and you haven't gotten a note since then, either."

"But I have gotten a note. I received one about eleven days ago. Remember?"

"That's right, you did." Brian thought for a moment. "I don't know how she did it, but I still feel Ida's responsible. She could easily have found you. Both your home and studio addresses and phone numbers are still on Inclusion's employee phone list."

"Okay, I'll give you that, but what about the guy from the park? You said you thought that he was after me for purposes other than raping and mugging. If Ida's the one whose been stalking me, where does he come in? Surely, I can't have two people wanting to hurt me at the same time."

"I never said that he was the one stalking you. That may have been a completely isolated incident.

But trust me Caroline, Ida's the one whose been stalking you."

"I believe you." She said quietly. "But do you know how it makes me feel to know that someone who barely knows me could dislike me so much? It really pisses me off." She said as she shoved her chair back and stood up. "The little, vindictive witch has been terrorizing me! And for what? Because she wants you back? God you're just a man, you're not worth going to jail over!"

"Stop. You're embarrassing me with all this affection." Brian said wryly before grabbing her wrist. "Where are you going?"

"Back to your office, of course. Where else would I be going? I'm not going to let her get away with this."

"Sit down Caroline." He said, adding a little pressure to her wrist. "You can't confront Ida."

Caroline looked at him as if he'd lost his mind and slowly sat down. "Of course I can. Why wouldn't I? She needs to know that she can't get away with this."

"You can't because if you do, she'll know that we know and she'll find some other way to get back at you. We need to go to the police with what we suspect. Don't misunderstand the circumstances. Just because you know who the stalker is, doesn't mean she's harmless. You can't just go in and accuse her and expect her to leave you alone. I think she's capable of causing you serious harm. Those notes and phone calls may not have been meant just to scare you. They could be a precursor to something worse."

"But if we just go to the police, they'll just say the same thing they said before: they need more and that I should get my number changed."

"Which is something we're going to do as soon as possible. I let you convince me that you shouldn't before because you said you didn't want to worry your family by telling them what's going on."

"I'm still not going to do it, for that and other reasons, which I've already explained to you. Besides, it hardly matters that she knows my phone number, since she also knows where I live and where my studio is and I'm not going to let her make me feel like I've done something wrong. Why should I have the inconvenience of a changed number? She'll just do something else. She may even start calling you."

"She might." Brian said with an unconcerned shrug. "If she does, then I'll deal with it."

"Exactly. I'll deal with it too. Maybe if we tell her we know, that will push her into revealing her hand."

"I just don't think it's a good idea. It could also make things escalate, make her do something even worse."

"Which I would personally welcome. Don't look at me like that," she protested when Brian shot her a hard look. "I just mean that if she does something other than make phone calls and send notes, it would be a worse offense. As it is, what she's done would probably just get her a slap on the wrist. If she poses a danger to me, I want something that will send her away."

"Stalking is a Class 4 felony Caroline. I would hardly call spending two or more years in prison a slap on the wrist."

"But the police officer said the notes aren't enough to constitute stalking. She said that I would have had to have been followed on at least two occasions. We have no proof that she did that."

"Well if she's not guilty of stalking, she's guilty of harassment at least."

"Sure, if we can catch her."

"She'll slip up."

Caroline sighed and stood up again. "We haven't ordered yet and I'm not hungry anymore. Do you mind if we just go to the police station now?"

"My thought exactly. Let's go."

Brian turned away from the loft window when he heard Caroline murmur something in her sleep. After she'd settled down once again, he looked back out the window. He'd been standing in his pajama pants looking out at nothing for at least two hours. The Ida situation had had Caroline restless since they'd arrived at his loft earlier that evening. She'd still been furious after they'd left the police station, so he'd taken the rest of the day off to be with her. He'd wanted to keep her from going to see Ida herself.

The police had gone to question Ida, promising to let them know the status of things. Of course, Ida had denied everything, which was no less than they'd expected. The police visit was really just a warning to Ida that they suspected her of harassing Caroline and to let her know that the next time something occurred, she'd be the first person they questioned. It hadn't been nearly enough for Caroline or him, but there was nothing more they could do.

"Hey, Motley." Brian looked down at the six-month old collie-shepherd mix as she pressed her cold nose to his leg. He kneeled and gave her a vigorous rub. Caroline had given the dog the last name of her favorite artist, Archibald Motley. She'd also thought the name fit the mismatched dog of black, tan and marigold perfectly.

"Brian?" Caroline whispered from the bed. "Where are you?" She asked as she sat up and pushed the too-large sleeves of his pajama top up on her wrists.

Brian straightened and went over to the bed.

"What time is it?" Caroline asked and lifted the blanket and sheet back for him as he climbed back into bed.

"A little after three." He said as he made himself comfortable.

"I guess I don't have to ask what's got you up so late. Now that we've gone to the police, what do you think will happen next?"

"Knowing Ida, I'd say that the visit from the police has worried her and she'll retreat. I just don't know if it will be a permanent retreat or if it will be just long enough for her to regroup. I don't know how crazy she is."

"What you mean is, you don't know how much she has invested in getting you back. She actually believes that if I were out of the way, you'd come back to her."

"I know that, which is why I'm going to have a talk with her and make it plain that the wind does not blow in that direction."

Caroline lifted her head. "When do you plan on doing this, and where? You can't do it at work. That would be completely inappropriate."

"I thought I'd pay her a visit Saturday. Or maybe I could accidentally-on-purpose bump into her somewhere. She's a creature of habit. On Sundays she likes to go to this little coffee shop near her apartment after mass."

"I think it would be best to bump into her somewhere. I don't think you should go over to her place because she could try to turn that around on you somehow."

"Right. What I really want to do is fire her, but I can't because she could sue the company. With the exception of her hiding your fax, her work performance has been exemplary. And if I were going to fire her for the fax, I should have done it then. So as far as her work is concerned, I have no reason to fire her."

"I know, I know. Do you really think she'll back off now?"

"Yeah, I think she will. Ida is pretty smart and above all else, she's selfish. She'll want to protect herself because the last thing she'll want to do is go to jail."

"Well, I feel safer now, anyway. Since we were able to put a face to the faceless, I don't feel like I'm fighting blindly now. At least I know where the danger could possibly come from and I can be better prepared to protect myself. At first I was jumping at every strange face I saw, wondering if this person or that person was the one sending me the notes and making the phone calls."

"Don't let your guard down too soon Caroline. Ida could still pose a threat. And we still don't know who the guy in the park was or what he wanted."

"But you said it was probably just an isolated incident."

"I meant isolated from Ida, not out of the blue and not to happen again. The more I think about it, the more I think the guy planned it."

"Why would you think that? It doesn't make any sense."

"Well, I told you that Zamboni's was closed and has been for months. Why would he ask you about that bar?"

"Maybe he didn't know it was closed."

"Yes, but why would he say he had to meet a friend there? Like I said, the place is closed."

"Maybe his friend didn't know it either."

"What are the odds of that? No, I think he just picked Zamboni's out of the air as an excuse to get close to you."

"Okay, but even if he did, that still doesn't prove that he had planned to approach me. You make it seem like he was actually looking for me. Maybe he saw me that night and then decided to…to…you know…whatever he was planning to do."

Brian tightened his arms around her. "No. My gut tells me that it was more. My gut and the way you described how he looked at you and approached you."

"Well what am I supposed to do? I'm not going to let myself become a prisoner and stay inside all the time."

"I'm not suggesting you do. As soon as Jack gets in town from whatever secret mission he's on, I'll ask him if he recognizes the guy. In the meantime, I'm just telling you to be careful and take the dog and your mace with you at all times. And of course you'll take a taxi or drive to arty place you have to go where you can't take the dog."

"Yes, yes. I know the drill, Brian." Caroline said around a yawn and drifted off to sleep.

—⁂—

"Be quiet Motley!" Brian heard Caroline say loudly to the dog over her noisy barks. He'd decided to work from home that morning and now he left his office.

When he saw Caroline limping toward the stairs with blood seemingly pouring out of her leg, he hurried over to her. "What the hell happened?" He asked as he helped her up the stairs.

Her face pinched in pain and her stomach roiling with nausea, Caroline said, "Motley, the stupid beast, got all excited over a squirrel and decided to chase it. The only problem was the squirrel decided to run between my legs and Motley followed it, wrapping her leash around my ankle. So when the squirrel took off and Motley chased it, I fell, quite hard, I might add. The stupid mutt didn't stop running right away, so I was dragged for a bit. I hadn't even had my run yet."

They finally reached his bedroom and Brian helped her over and then onto the edge of the bed. "That's no way to talk about our first born Caroline. I'm sure she didn't mean it. She's just a little spirited." He teased.

"Whatever." Caroline said. "The only thing that concerns me right now is the pain in my leg. I'll deal with that little pain in my rear later." She threw the dog an exasperated look as she scampered into the room.

"Take your pants off so I can have a look." Brian said, already pulling at the elastic waist of her jogging pants as he kneeled in front of her.

"Careful Brian, the material's stuck to the sore and it hurts." Caroline said as he slid her pants over her hips and down her knees. Once she'd taken her shoes off and slipped the pants over her feet, she was left in socks, panties and his Northwestern University sweat-shirt that hung inches past her hips.

"It's okay." Brian murmured absently. He looked at the injury that marred her smooth, brown flesh. All the blood had made him think that a trip to the hospital may be necessary, but though the wound was rather large in circumference, it wasn't too deep. "I guess we can forego stitches." He said as he looked up at her. Her eyes were tightly closed, and her bottom lip was caught between her teeth.

"Hey, what's all this?" Brian asked, rubbing her bottom lip until she released it.

Caroline opened her eyes. "You don't know this, but I hate the sight of blood, especially my own. And I'm worse when it comes to pain, even the tiniest bit. I'm embarrassed to say this, but the slightest cut turns me into the biggest wimp. It's been that way since I was a kid."

"Well, just keep your eyes closed and I'll take care of it. I just need a bandage and some antiseptic." Brian said and prepared to stand.

"No!" Caroline said and grabbed his shoulders. "Uhhh…I think a bandage will do just fine. I don't think I need any antiseptic."

Brian took his hands up and down her bare legs to cup the back of her knees and massage the insides with his thumbs. "The antiseptic will ward off any infection."

"But it's going to burn." She said, unable to keep the whine from her voice. "Just use some water to clean it."

"That won't be enough." He said and stood up.

"If you want to torture me, fine." She said to his departing back. "But don't expect me to forget it anytime soon."

"Awww." Brian worked quickly, blowing on her knee when she sucked in a breath at the burning sensation the antiseptic made. "Did mean old Brian hurt poor baby Caroline?" He asked in a teasing voice and leaned down to kiss the bandage.

"Yes and stop teasing me or I'll tell." She said with a fake pout. Tunneling her fingers through his hair, she leaned down to kiss him. He drew her tongue into his mouth, taking the kiss from chaste to amorous in seconds.

He slid his hands underneath the large sweatshirt, over her bottom and up her torso to cup her breasts. Raising himself up, he parted her legs with his knee and lay between them. "You're wearing too many clothes." Caroline breathed, pulling his shirt over his head and roping her legs around him. The feel of heavy denim against the thin silk of her panties created an almost unbearable friction and she moaned.

"So are you." Brian said and took her sweatshirt off. Just as he was unhooking her bra, the doorbell rang. "Oh please God, not now." He said, dropping his forehead to hers.

"Don't answer it." Caroline suggested and sunk her teeth into his chin.

"I have to." He said as the bell pealed again. "It's probably the messenger. I called the office and had Justin send me over some files I need today." He stood and put his shirt back on.

Caroline completed what he'd started with her bra. "I'll be waiting." She said and got under the covers. "But don't take too long or I might fall asleep."

Brian rushed down the stairs and pulled the front door open. His mind was busy imagining all the things he was going to do to Caroline, and as a consequence it took him a moment to realize that it was Ida standing on his doorstep and not a messenger.

Her presence had the same effect that a bucket of cold water thrown on him would have had. His mind wiped clean of all passionate thoughts, he said, "What are you doing here Ida?"

"Hello Brian." She said through clenched teeth. "Carl said you needed these files and I volunteered to drop them off." She deliberately stepped inside.

Brian had his own agenda and he stepped back to let her in as he accepted the files. "Thanks. I have something to say to you Ida—"

"I have something to say to you too. I want to know why you would go to the police and tell them those lies about me. How could you?"

"I simply told the police what I suspected. I think you're the one whose been harassing Caroline and I wanted them to know about it. It's as simple as that."

"You have no proof of that—" Ida began angrily.

"I many not have the proof now, but if you keep it up, I'll have it eventually and you'll find yourself thrown in jail. For two years at least."

"Well keep dreaming, because I'll never…"

"Never what, Ida? Never what?" Brian demanded furiously, grabbing her shoulders when she abruptly cut herself off. He wanted to shake the truth out of her.

"You won't make me say it lover," Ida purred slyly, "so you may as well stop trying. But you can hold me all you want. That I don't mind."

Brian released her in disgust. "I don't want you Ida. Get it through your head: you and I were over a long time ago."

"You're just saying that. The slut must be here and you're saying it for her benefit. Where is she?" She demanded, her eyes darting around.

"If you mean Caroline, she's not here Ida." Brian said, struggling to ignore the name-calling and praying that Caroline would stay upstairs so that Ida would be forced to believe what he was saying. "She could be in China and I would still be saying the same thing. It's over and it has been for a long time."

"You wouldn't feel that way if you weren't involved with her." Ida said.

"Yes I would. If I were absolutely alone and didn't have any dating prospects, I would tell you the same thing. It didn't work for us two years ago Ida and it won't work now. I'm not interested. I wasn't interested before I met Caroline and I'm not interested now."

"But what we had was so good. It only ended because…because…"

"It ended because it was a lousy relationship Ida." Brian said after she'd trailed off in confusion. "I don't want to be cruel, but it was never really all that good to begin with."

"Then why'd it last so long?" She asked defensively.

"Six months is not a long time Ida, but if you must know, I stayed in it that long because I felt sorry for you and I didn't know how to break it off at first. Again, I don't want to be cruel, but your refusal to believe it's over is forcing me to." Brian said, knowing he could be far crueler as he thought about how she'd terrorized Caroline.

"You bastard!" Ida said. "After everything I've done and it was all for you—for us!" She raised her hand to slap him.

Brian caught her wrist inches before her hand connected. "Don't Ida." He said in a soft, dangerous voice. "I promise you, you won't like what I do in retaliation. As for what you supposedly did for me, I don't know what you're talking about. What did you do? Whatever it was, it wasn't for me and it couldn't have been for 'us'. There never has been an 'us' between you and me and there never will be!"

As Brian watched, Ida seemed to wilt before him and she pulled her wrist from his grip. "I suppose you're going to fire me now, right?" She asked in dull tones.

"I'd like to Ida, but I don't have the grounds." He paused deliberately, "Yet."

"You're an idiot, Brian." She said in the same dull tone, as she gathered her dignity around her like a shredded cloak. "If you actually would prefer that skinny bag of bones over me, then you obviously have questionable tastes and you didn't know a good thing when you had it." She said and walked out. Feeling defeated and humiliated, she closed the door with a soft click.

"Well, well." Brian turned at the sound of Caroline's voice. She was sitting at the top of the stairs wearing just his sweatshirt. "I'm glad I stayed awake for the show."

He walked up the stairs and sat down next to her. "How long have you been here?"

"Well, I left the bed so I could hear better around the time she said you had no proof. And I arrived right around that corner there," she said and indicated the corner, "just as you were telling her how the relationship was never very good to begin with. Ouch." She grimaced, rubbed her heart and then tskd. "Brutal."

"I'm glad you didn't come down. Your presence could have blown my game; she'd have never believed I wasn't saying what I said to please you."

"You think I would have come down looking like this?" Caroline asked, spreading her arms wide. "I hadn't planned on coming down because I didn't want it to turn into one of those clichéd 'women fighting over man' things. And besides that, Ida seems to lose all sense of reason when she sees me, so I thought it best if I stayed hidden. I didn't want her to become irrational."

"Well whatever your reasons, I'm glad you didn't show that ugly mug of yours."

"Do you really think she believes you and she'll leave us alone now?"

"I don't know for sure, but I think she will. Time will tell, I guess."

"Yes, I guess so." And determined not to let Ida cast a pall, she smiled. "How about some lunch?"

Ida walked away from Brian's loft, feeling hollow inside. Brian really didn't love her. She knew that now. She supposed she'd known it all along. She just hadn't wanted to believe it. When he'd been holding her wrist, she'd looked into his eyes and seen what looked like hate lurking there and it had hit her full force. He didn't love her—not at all. The worst part about all of it was she'd taken beatings for him and even knowing that she could never have him, she'd do it again because she loved him that much.

Brickman will have to do, she decided right there on the spot. She didn't love him, but she needed him. She hated not having and she would not be homeless again. She still had a problem in Caroline, though. She needed her to stay out of his reach.

CHAPTER 25

Caroline kept her hands over her mother's eyes as they walked into her studio. "Careful Mom, we're almost there," she said as she maneuvered Patricia so that she was standing in the middle of the room.

"Okay. You can open your eyes now." Caroline said, removing her hands. She held her breath as she watched her mother spin around, trying to take in everything at once. She'd finally finished her pieces in preparation for her upcoming show at the Rutledge. The Ida situation, as she and Brian had come to call it, had slowed her down and she hadn't finished as quickly as she'd planned. But it was still only mid-November, and she'd completed everything with time to spare for the January exhibit.

"Well," she said nervously as she wiped her hands down her slacks. "What do you think Mom?"

Patricia looked at her from the other side of the room. "Give me a minute honey, I just started looking."

Forty minutes passed while Patricia took her time going around the room. To Caroline, she appeared to study each piece slowly and thoroughly. Caroline had never been so nervous when it came to showing off her work. She knew she was talented and didn't believe in displaying false modesty. But this was for the brass ring and she wanted everything to be perfect. She watched a slow smile spread across Patricia's face as she took her fingers over a sculpture. The bronze was about two feet tall and captured a chubby-cheeked child in mid-dance as she bent her knees, twisted her feet to one side and held her arms bent in front of her while her fingers snapped out a beat. The child's pure pleasure was evident as one looked at her closed eyes and happy smile. The piece made Patricia smile and was simply titled *Lahddy Dahddy De*.

"Oh!" Patricia said softly with delighted surprise. "It's Genevieve! You've captured her beautifully. I can almost hear the music and feel the motion." She said as she fingered the headphones perched over the child's head. The skirt of the child's dress flew out from her knees and showed off a frilly slip and a bandaged knee. "Promise me you'll hold it for me. Don't sell it to anyone else."

"Oh, Mom. Do you really like it that much?"

"Of course. It's beautiful. I just love the little tennis shoes on her feet and the ribbons and barrettes in her hair. It's perfect. It's almost like she's here in the room. You just make sure you don't try to gouge your mother on the price."

"I'm going to take you for all you've got." Caroline said jokingly.

Patricia chuckled and continued her walk around the studio and after another fifteen minutes, she turned to Caroline. "You are so talented, baby. I'm so proud of you. Everything is so detailed, so expressive and so...so...oh, I can't think of another adjective to describe how amazing they are!" She said laughing as she hugged Caroline.

"Thanks, Mom. Do you have any favorites?"

"Besides that statue of Genevieve, I'd have to say the painting of the two teenagers kissing against the tree takes my fancy and I love the one of the man flying a remote control airplane. I'd also have to say the sculpture of the couple is one that catches my attention. I love the way she's sitting on his back with her legs stretched out. And the look of surprise on his face as he tries to hold her up makes it look like you caught them just at that moment when she'd jumped aboard. I also like—forget it Caroline, I love them all. They're fabulous. Just promise me you won't forget me once you hit it big."

Patricia was laughing, but Caroline took it seriously. "I could never do that, Mom. You're one of the major reasons I'm painting and sculpting at all. You were always so encouraging and supportive. Not that Dad wasn't, but it was different with him. It was like he was indulging his baby girl's whim, while you knew it was just in me to be an artist. You knew it was a part of me, as important to me as eating or breathing. And though I know that I could never say or do enough to show you my appreciation, I do want to say thank you and this is one way. I wanted you to be the first to see what I've done for the show. Thank you for believing in me Mom. I love you for it."

"Oh, baby." Patricia said through tears. Hugging Caroline tightly, she said, "I would support you in whatever you wanted to do and no thanks are ever necessary. Ever. I do it because I love you."

"I know and thank you for that too." Caroline said as they broke from the hug.

"As I said, baby, no thanks are necessary."

"I know, but I just feel that I should say it anyway." Caroline said and pressed a hand to her nervous stomach. "I was so nervous to show you everything, but now I feel great!"

"No need for nerves. I have always loved your work, as a mother and as an art lover. But if there was something that I didn't quite get or didn't particularly care for, I would tell you that too."

"I know." Caroline laughed, "And that's what I was afraid of. Anyway, looking at everything, can you guess what the theme is?"

Patricia took another quiet spin around the room. "Hmm," she murmured thoughtfully. "Is it happiness?"

"Close. I decided to call the show *Love and Happiness.* Some of the pieces show people with their objects of love, some are just of objects that may make people happy or that signifies love and others just show people doing what makes them happy. You don't think it's too sappy, do you? I mean so much art today is what they call 'edgy' and my stuff could hardly be described as that."

"No, it couldn't." Patricia said matter-of-factly. "But it never could be and the Rutledge obviously doesn't want edgy or else they wouldn't have offered you the opportunity for a show. They want you for your particular style, Caroline."

"I'm glad you said that. I really needed to hear it."

"Happy to be of service. Now, how about I take you out to lunch to celebrate the completion of these master-pieces? What would you say to the Walnut Room at Field's?"

"I'd say that sounds great. Just let me go home and change, okay?"

"Of course." Patricia said as she watched Caroline start to tidy up her space. "I guess you plan to show Brian everything this evening, huh? Once he gets home from work."

"Yeah. He's been bugging me for weeks now to let him see everything."

"Are you still planning to go away to celebrate the completion? Can Brian get away?"

"No." Caroline shook her head. "It's too close to the holidays now and he needs to be at work as much as possible since he will be taking time off then. Speaking of which," she said turning to look at her mother, "I hope you and Dad aren't too upset that we won't be joining you for Thanksgiving. Brian really wants me to meet his mother and apparently, she really wants to meet me. I talked to Dad and he didn't sound too happy about me not being there."

"Don't worry about your father." Patricia said with a dismissive wave of her hand. "It's all bluster. He couldn't be happier that Brian is taking you home to meet his mother. To his way of thinking, this will just put him one step closer to you getting married and giving us grand-children."

"You've got to be kidding me. I mean, I want children and I want to marry Brian. But, though I'm sure that both will eventually happen, I'm not sure when. We haven't even really discussed it."

"Well when you do, let me know. I'm anxious for some more grandchildren myself."

"I'm sure Brian has heard similar things from his parents as well. But we're just taking our time, there's no hurry."

"I know, dear." Patricia said, figuring it was best to close the subject. She'd found out everything that she'd wanted and needed to know. "Now shall we go?"

More than a dozen blocks away, Alex Brickman sat behind his desk with his elbows resting on his blotter and his index fingers held together against his mouth. He studied Kovlovsky as the man stood in front of him and looked off at some spot over his shoulder. Brickman did not want to hear that Kovlovsky and his cohorts had failed him again. And he was sure if that were the case, Kovlovsky was even more reluctant to tell it than he was to hear it.

I'm getting terribly sick of this dance, he thought to himself. Yet, here I am reluctant to hear any bad news, and not simply because I want the film. It is because I want the girl more than anything I've ever wanted in my life. This woman has become an obsession and an obsession by its very definition can be dangerous. Nevertheless, I want this girl. I want her so much that in the night, I can actually feel her beside me, over me, beneath me.

When she is finally mine, I will give her the best of everything—cars, homes, jewels, clothing—anything she desires. Ah, my lovely giant, he thought, my riches will be your riches. And your everything will be mine. Only mine.

Brickman pulled himself from his fantasy and looked at Kovlovsky again. "Well Mr. Kovlovsky. It had better be good news you're bringing me this time."

"Sir, we have not been as successful as we had hoped. We have not located the girl, nor have we been able to find out what her name is. We have, however, talked to several people who have seen her often running a specific path through the park. It seems she prefers to do this in the morning."

"Well?" Brickman demanded impatiently when it appeared that that was all Kovlovsky was going to say.

"For the past week, I have had men posted along the path from five a.m. to eleven," and it's been bloody cold, Pete wanted to add. "She has not appeared, sir. We believe it is due to the cold snap that we're experiencing. From the information we have gathered, I have deduced that she is an avid runner and those types never seem to mind the cold, really. I am confident that she will start her morning exercise program again soon, sir And that is why I still have my men on the lookout."

"Not good enough, Mr. Kovlovsky." Brickman said softly and coldly and hurled a Faberge egg against the wall where it smashed into bits and pieces. "I want your men out there 24 hours a day, in shifts. Did it occur to you that she might have switched her schedule? Even creatures of habit like a little variety sometimes. It is purported to be the spice of life, after all."

"Yes sir. Done sir." Kovlovsky said. "My men and I will start right away. We'll find the girl, sir. We'll find her soon."

"'Soon' is not soon enough for me, but it will have to do. But understand this Mr. Kovlovsky, this is the last time I will merely 'make do.' "

"Yes sir. I feel I will be able to bring you good news very soo…uh…very shortly sir. Count on it."

"You have until the end of this month Mr. Kovlovsky, no longer. I expect to see what belongs to me and what will belong to me here in this office within the next two weeks."

"I understand your urgency, sir, but that may not be possible—"

"You will make it possible, Mr. Kovlovsky. That's what you're here for. Again, are we understood?"

"Yes, sir. I'll do my best, sir." He struggled to suppress the rage at Brickman's impossible expectations.

"Very good, Mr. Kovlovsky. You are dismissed."

Kovlovsky left the room wondering how in the hell he was going to "quit" his job with Brickman without getting killed for it. So far, neither luck nor the Lord's blessing had been his close friends during this job. And that my friend, he thought, is a sign.

Brickman pressed the button on his intercom. "Please tell Ms. Martinez I'd like to see her. Immediately." He steepled his fingers together under his chin and closed his eyes in thought. It was time for Ida to tell him everything. He was tired of waiting.

Ida stood on the threshold of his office. She wore a trench coat, heels and nothing else. She was prepared to take another beating if necessary, but she would not tell him who Caroline was. All I have to do is convince Brickman that he doesn't need Caroline, she thought as she closed the door behind herself and started unbuttoning the trench coat.

— ɯ —

"This is so romantic Brian." Caroline said as she looked around the restaurant. Brian had called her from work earlier that day and told her to dress up because he was taking her out to celebrate her having completed the preparation for her art show. The trip to Geja's Café— dubbed the most romantic restaurant in the city—had come as more than a surprise to Caroline, as they'd gone out to celebrate the night before after she had shown him her work. "I love it," she said as she glanced around their booth, which had curtains for privacy and was lit by candlelight. "But you didn't have to do it."

"Of course I did and besides that, I wanted to. We're not only celebrating the fact that you now have some free time on your hands, but we're also celebrating the absence of Ida's presence in your life."

"If it really is absent." Caroline said cautiously. "I know we haven't heard from her in a while, but I can't believe she'd just give up and go away."

"I think she did. I've heard through the grapevine at work that she has a new boyfriend and she may be bringing him to the company holiday party."

"A new boyfriend doesn't necessarily mean that she's given up on you."

"No, it doesn't. But I'm betting she has. Apparently this guy is filthy rich and just showers her with expensive things. He's even bought her a condo. And besides that, she's turned in her resignation." Brian said and watched Caroline's mouth drop open in surprise. He dipped some bread in the fondue appetizer the restaurant was famous for and popped it into her mouth. "Wouldn't want any flies to get in there." He said as she closed her mouth and chewed.

"Why didn't you tell me?!" Caroline demanded. "When did you find out?"

"She gave it to Carl today. It's effective at the top of next year. She won't be back after Christmas. I didn't tell you right away, because I thought it would be a nice surprise."

"Oh, it's a wonderful surprise. But it seems so sudden, doesn't it?"

"Six weeks' notice is sudden?"

"I don't mean in that way, I mean as far as her timing in bringing it to you guys goes. You don't find it suspicious?"

"I guess I would if I didn't know that she hasn't bothered you in some time. Maybe this guy she's seeing has a positive influence. Maybe since he's so wealthy, they decided that she didn't have to work anymore. I just don't know and frankly, I really don't care." Brian said with a shrug.

"Well, what is she going to do?"

"I don't know really, and again, I don't care. But I think Linda did say something about her going back to school or something."

"Great. I hope all of this is true and Ida isn't pulling one over on us just until she can think of some other way she can terrorize me."

"Caroline, when Ida was in full swing, you didn't want to take this seriously. But now that I tell you that you don't have to worry about her anymore, all you want to do is worry. It's a little backwards, don't you think?"

"I did take it seriously, but I didn't want to believe it. There is a difference, you know." She paused and laughed. "And that's a lot of baloney. I just want to be sure, that's all."

"I know and that's good, but I firmly believe that in Ida's mind, I don't rate a comparison to some guy with deep pockets and a propensity to spend his money on her."

Caroline thought about what he said., "You're right, of course. If there's one thing I know about Ida is that she's mercilessly materialistic and she likes the finer things in life. I guess that's two things. Anyway, enough of all this depressing talk. Let's eat, enjoy this fabulous live guitar and get drunk. Let's get drunk on each other tonight."

"Sounds like a wonderful plan to me." Brian said and opened his menu.

She ordered the chicken breast while he ordered a dish called The International, which offered a mix of beef tenderloin, jumbo shrimp and chicken breast.

"That's really good." Caroline said some time later, closing her eyes and savoring yet another bite of shrimp from Brian's plate.

"I wouldn't really know." Brian said dryly. "I've hardly had any."

"I'm sorry. You can have some of mine."

"I've already got chicken. What I don't have now—after you've had 'just one little piece'—is more shrimp and beef."

Laughing at him, Caroline lifted the bottle of wine to replenish her glass. "I'm sorry." She repeated. "It's just that yours is so very, very delicious and mine is just plain delicious." She giggled, puckered her lips and blew him a kiss.

Brian studied her, taking in her half-closed eyes that she appeared to be struggling to keep open and her languid posture. She was on her way to becoming drunk. She'd told him once before that she really had no head for liquor, but he didn't expect that one glass of wine was all it took to make her tipsy. He chuckled to himself as she looked over at him and winked lasciviously. Not that she wasn't adorable when she was halfway drunk, but the last thing he wanted was an inebriated Caroline on his hands. And knowing how much she hated losing control, he didn't doubt that she'd be angry with herself for getting sloshed.

"How about some bread, Caroline?" He asked and passed it over. "You're just a little tipsy."

She straightened indignantly and then like water, became boneless again. "I am not." She said, but took some bread anyway. "It is good, isn't it?" She asked and took a healthy bite. "Oh, I just love it here Brian. We should come here more often." She chattered. "I just love it. Next time it will be my treat, 'kay?"

"It's a deal." He said and watched her attempt for the third time to dip bread into the fondue. "Did I tell you how proud I am of you and your talent?" He asked and took hold of her hand to guide it himself.

Caroline looked at him and smiled. "Yes, but I'll never get tired of hearing it. Thank you."

"I mean it, your talent just takes my breath away. You know which piece I decided I wanted?" He asked and watched her frown in surprise.

"So you want to own something, then? I didn't think…"

"Of course I want some of your work. The only reason I haven't said anything before now is because they're all so wonderful and I couldn't decide."

"Oh." She said, the wine still slowing her faculties a bit. "Which one would you like?"

"I've decided that I want the painting called 'Peace'. You know, the one of that runner's path that snakes through the park. I love how you incorporated all the colors. I especially like that burning blue of the sky and the grayish-green of the lagoon. It's perfect."

"Thank you." She said, needing to hear appreciation for her work like any artist.

"You just make sure it doesn't get sold to someone else at your show."

"By the time my family goes through them, I won't have any pieces available to sell. Maybe I'll keep everything under wraps from now on. I wouldn't want every piece in the show to have a sign saying 'sold' on it."

"Oh, there's plenty to go around. Did you remember to reserve some tickets for my mom and Frank? My mom's really excited about seeing the show."

Caroline was slowly nodding her head. "Yes, I remembered. I just can't believe she'll be coming in for it. She hasn't even met me. She doesn't know if she'll like me."

"Yes she does. She knows that if I'm bringing you home to meet her and my stepdad, then you're special to me and in her mind, if you're special to me, then you must be perfect. And, I've already told her how much I love you."

"Well, that's crazy logic if I ever heard it."

"No it's not. It's a mother's logic. So, are you ready to meet her and my stepdad?"

"Sure. I can't wait. Especially since there's absolutely *no* pressure." She said in her driest tone. "We're leaving Tuesday at noon, right? Just don't forget I have that interview and photo shoot with *The Daily News* that day, so we may have to leave a little later than planned. We wouldn't have to worry about time if they didn't insist on taking the photo themselves. I don't know why they just won't use any of the pictures I already have." She said in frustration.

Brian didn't want her taking pictures either, but for a completely different reason. "*The Daily News* prefers to use its own photos. Justin tells me that they've always been that way." He shrugged. "I guess he should know since he has a contact at just about every media outlet in the city. Are you sure you want to do this?" He asked with a frown. "I know that the experience you had when you were 18 still bothers you."

"No, I can do it. I really don't want to do it, but if it will get people to come out to the Rutledge in January, I'll forget my nerves and fears and make nice and smile pretty."

"There are other ways to publicize this, you know. Your picture doesn't have to be plastered everywhere."

"My picture won't be plastered everywhere. Only in one paper. There's no better way to get people to come out, unless it's an interview on television and I really, really don't want to do that. I want the publicity, but being on television would just be too much for me to deal with. So, I'll just stick with the newspaper."

"All right, then." Brian sighed. "They're coming to your studio, right?"

"Yeah. Something about getting shots of 'the artist at work.' It's just nonsense."

"I don't know why you're so embarrassed about it. Do it and be done with it."

"I'm not embarrassed. I just don't like having my picture taken and I like my privacy."

"So when is the article coming out?"

"It's supposed to run Sunday after next. And she says they may run a smaller piece closer to show date."

"I don't like this Caroline, but you already know that."

Caroline sighed. "Will you stop worrying about that guy in the park, please? I think it was a one-time thing and he missed his shot. Period. You're acting like he's some guy whose sitting around pining for me or he's searching high and low for me and he's just looking for his chance to get me. Besides, none of your cop friends recognized him. That should make you stop worrying."

Secretly, Caroline thought if Brian were right about the man, then taking the picture would be the best thing for her to do. If the man saw the picture, it could draw him out. And if that happened, she wouldn't have to spend the rest of her life wondering if he truly was after her and when he was going to appear again.

"None of my cop friends, no. But I still haven't been able get in contact with Jack. This guy may be familiar to the FBI."

"Well don't you think Jack would have called you by now if there was cause for concern? He wouldn't just leave you waiting."

"The problem is that Jack has been out of town since the day after I saw him, so I don't even know if he's seen the picture. He's been incommunicado."

Caroline covered his hand with hers. "Stop worrying so much, Brian. I'm sure everything is fine. When Jack gets back from wherever it is he went, he'll tell you that nobody in the entire FBI has ever even seen the guy. You'll see."

Brian smiled. "The entire FBI, huh?" He joked, consciously shaking off his mood. He lifted her hand to his mouth and reached over and pulled the curtain closed. "Why don't you join me over here on my side of the booth, Ms. Singleton."

"Why Mr. Keenan, your brazenness surprises me." Caroline said and slid over so that she was practically in his lap. "I feel so decadent." She said into his ear as she leaned into him and flattened her hand on his chest.

"Why?" Brian asked and tried to contain himself when her teeth sank into his ear and gently pulled.

"Because we're about to make out in a public place. A very public place. I haven't done this since I was a teenager." She said and opened her mouth over his. When they came up for air, she'd made it into his lap and his hands were buried in her hair, hair he'd freed of all its pins.

"How about dessert?" He asked her breathlessly as she moved off his lap.

Caroline's head jerked up and her eyes clouded in confusion. "Dessert?"

"Yes, dessert." Brian said with a smile. "But we'll have it at your place."

Her eyes lit up. "Pay the check, darling." She said with an intimate smile.

CHAPTER 26

Janice Bunch flicked her long blonde hair over her shoulder and prepared to leave Caroline's studio 'Thanks again Ms. Singleton for agreeing to have the interview here in your studio. It's always nice to kill two birds with one stone and I think we've gotten some great photos."

"Call me Caroline." Caroline said with a distracted smile as she watched the photographer pack up her gear. She just wanted it to be over. She didn't really mind the interview, but being posed like a mannequin for an hour or more just was not her cup of tea.

Janice smiled as she watched Caroline frown at Tabitha's equipment. The lady did not like to be photographed; that much was obvious. It was also refreshing. Rarely did she meet an interview subject who didn't love having her picture taken, especially when that subject was as attractive as Caroline.

From beneath her lashes, Janice looked over the wool pantsuit Caroline had chosen to wear for the interview. Despite the fact that they'd told her they'd wanted to set a scene of the artist at work, she'd worn the expensive black suit with its thin pin stripes, black pumps and a white blouse. The collar of the blouse was spread over the collar of the jacket and the long sleeves of the blouse reached past the end of the jacket and were folded over neatly. Diamond cuff links warred with the shine of the diamonds twinkling in her ears. Stunning and aware of it, Janice surmised, but not concerned with it.

"Don't forget that the article will be out this upcoming Sunday." Janice said, gaining Caroline's attention again. "I can have a couple of copies sent to you if you'd like."

"That would be lovely, thanks." Caroline said. "Could you possibly have a couple sent to Joseph Talmadge at the Rutledge? He'd like some for publicity."

"It's all been arranged." Janice said as she and Tabitha followed Caroline to the door. "Joseph called me yesterday."

"Wonderful." Caroline said with a smile and turned to open the door. "Hi, darling." She said with pleasure when she saw Brian. "You're early."

Interesting, Janice thought as she watched the gorgeous hunk of man greet Caroline with a kiss. Sensing tension, she turned her head to see that Tabitha's fair complexion was mottled with red and her wide forehead was creased with distaste. Interesting, Janice thought again. Tabitha was new to the paper and this was only their second time working together, so Janice had no idea of the other woman's…politics.

Tabitha blanched as she watched Brian kiss Caroline. *How disgusting,* she thought, her old-fashioned Southern sensibilities more than a little offended by the sight. *I'll work with them. I'll even eat with them. But kiss one of them? Out of the question.*

"This is Brian." Caroline said, holding his hand. "Brian this is Janice Bunch and Tabitha—I'm sorry, I didn't get your last name."

"Madison." Tabitha said through stiff lips. Caroline frowned, sensing that there was suddenly a problem.

"Hello." Brian said, holding the door so they could walk out. Ignoring the photographer's animosity he swept his eyes over Caroline, loving the sexy contrast of the man-like suit with the purely feminine curled hair falling around her shoulders.

"That was annoying." Caroline said when Brian shut the door. "That photographer was much friendlier before you got here."

"She's just another bigoted idiot who should mind her own business." Brian said with finality. "I'm beat, let's sit." He said, taking her hand again and moving across the room to an old chair, the only thing to sit on in the whole place. Settling her so that she was sitting sideways on his lap, he folded his arms around her. "How was it?"

"It was okay, I guess." She said with a shrug. "I just hated taking so many pictures. When she finished with me, she kept taking pictures of my studio and my work." She shuddered. "I couldn't wait for them to leave."

"Well, it's over now." Brian said massaging her shoulders as she let her head find its favorite place underneath his chin. "How was the interview itself?"

"I suppose it was fine. She asked questions about Grandmother's Ice Cream and what it was like growing up in 'such a wealthy family', even though the paper promised to keep my family out of it. So I just didn't talk about it. She also wanted to know weird things like why I had Lauryn Hill, Macy Gray and Janet Jackson all playing on the CD changer. She said it was just to get a better picture, but I still found it annoying. I wanted it over with."

Brian decided to try a little levity. "Janet Jackson, huh? I love the look of her."

Caroline snorted and said warningly, "Watch yourself, bud. Besides, she's more than looks. You might be surprised to find that she actually has talent."

"You're the only one for me." He said, but couldn't resist teasing, "I'm just saying I can appreciate a woman like Janet Jackson's talent and looks."

"This is ridiculous. Why are we even talking about it?" She asked.

"You said you were listening to Macy Gray, Lauryn Hill and the lovely Ms. Jackson." He said playfully and tugged on one of her curls.

"That's an interesting mix of artists. One is funky soul, one is evolved hip/hop with some soul thrown in and the other one is pop slash R&B. Maybe the reporter was just curious. It shouldn't be such a big deal." He finished.

"It's not. It's just one example of the many things that made the interview irritating." She lifted her hand to rub her neck. "Like I said, I'm just glad it's over."

Brian's eyes couldn't miss the flash and fire. "Hey. Are those my cuff links?" He asked in surprise and grabbed her wrist to see for himself.

"Hmm?" Distracted, Caroline looked at her wrist. "Oh, yes. Yes they are. Don't you just love the way they go so perfectly with my suit and earrings?" She stretched out her arm accommodatingly.

"Some might say that they would go even better with a tuxedo." He said wryly. She was always rifling through his closet and more than once he'd gone to get something to wear, only to find that she was already wearing it.

Caroline pursed her lips, trying not to smile as she studied her outstretched arm. "Yes." She stretched the word out, as if she were seriously considering his statement. "Yes, I suppose they might. If they were the staid, traditional type." She said and loosened his tie.

"I object." Brian said softly, slipping his hands under her jacket to pull her blouse out of her pants. "Are you calling me staid?"

"I'm just saying if the cufflinks don't fit, don't try to force them." She unbuttoned the first two buttons of his shirt and placed an opened mouth kiss in the hollow of his neck.

Brian moaned as her lips lingered and she used her tongue. "Just what are you doing, Ms. Singleton?"

"Having my way with you, of course. I've had a low-level hankering for you all day. It became full-blown the minute I opened the door and saw you in this fabulous shirt. I just love it when you wear it because it matches your eyes perfectly." She said and greedily took his mouth with her own, taking him over so quickly, he could barely think straight.

"Well I aim to please." Brian said when he was able to catch his breath.

Caroline closed her eyes when his hands came up to cup her breasts. Her still-buttoned blouse and camisole restricted his movement and the pressure of it made her moan and stretch her back. "Mmm…what if…" she paused to lick her lips when he began flicking her nipples with his thumbs. "What if I wanted…" With a wicked smile, she bent to whisper something in his ear and then rose and sat back down astride his lap.

Brian swallowed with difficulty and cleared his throat. "Uh, I think that can be arranged." He watched her arch her neck and leaned over and nipped it with his teeth. "Unbutton your blouse."

Caroline opened her eyes and looked into his as she undid each button of her blouse. She watched his brow arch inquiringly when he noticed exactly what she was wearing underneath.

"Is that what I think it is?"

She smiled seductively. "It might be. I suppose I could have been wearing this when I described my clothes to you on the phone that day."

"Dare I dream that you're wearing the blue butterfly?" He asked with desperate hope.

She gave a wicked chuckle. "You'll have to wait and see. I will say that I wanted to surprise you. I was hoping we'd have time for this before we got on the road to Michigan, especially since I conked out on you the other night after dinner."

"Well baby, I wasn't looking for a rain check, but this more than makes up for the other night." Brian said before leaning in to kiss the skin above the camisole.

Caroline undid the cuff links and shimmied her shoulders so that the jacket and blouse dropped behind her. She wrapped her arms around his head and tunneled her fingers through his hair as he fastened his mouth on her nipple and began to suckle it through the satin. Resisting her efforts to lift his head, he gave the other breast the same treatment. That apparently wasn't enough for him and he briefly lifted his mouth before he dragged the camisole up until it was bunched underneath her arms.

Reclaiming her nipple, he pushed it hard against the roof of his mouth, and did the same to the other one. His fingers gripped her bare back and held her in place until she squirmed wildly on his lap, her hands flexing in his hair to hold his head in place. "Brian," she said urgently. It was a demand and a plea.

He lifted his head and gazed at her. She ducked and pressed a hard kiss to his mouth. "Take your clothes off." She whispered huskily as she finished unbuttoning his shirt and slipped it off his shoulders. She then pulled his T-shirt over his head. "Your chest is wonderful." She said as she ran her fingers over it as if she were trying to leave imprints. She bent her neck and rained kisses all over it.

After ridding her of her camisole, Brian once again covered her breasts with his hands. "I love to see my hands against your skin—the contrasts of dark to light, soft to hard, small to big—always get me going." Caroline looked down and the sight of his hands on her, combined with his words sent a convulsive shiver through her. She covered his mouth with hers, pulling his tongue into her mouth and sucking for all she was worth.

As she twined her arms around his neck, he took care of her pants, unbuttoning them and pulling the zipper down. He slipped his hand inside, making her gasp and break off the kiss. "Time for your treat," she said and moved off his lap.

Standing in front of him and never letting her eyes leave his face lest she miss his reaction, she kicked off her shoes and stepped out of her pants. She smiled triumphantly when she saw his reaction to what she was wearing.

Brian narrowed his eyes against the increased intensity of the heat that was already rushing through him as he stared at her and wondered what he'd done to be so lucky. She was wearing a white garter belt, which clipped onto sheer, thigh-high white stockings that stretched and enticingly hugged her from the middle of her thighs to the bottom of her feet. Nestled within was the white underwear he'd never forgotten about. He groaned aloud as he caught a glimpse of the famous blue butterfly. "Come here." He said roughly.

Caroline stayed where she was and lifted her right leg so that it bent while her foot rested on his knee. Taking her time, she undid the two hooks holding the stocking in place and slowly rolled the nylon down her leg. She repeated her actions on her other leg and then removed the garter belt.

Brian swallowed audibly as he watched her and felt himself break out in a sweat. She wore nothing but diamonds and panties. Gripping her waist, he moved her in front of him and bent his head to place his open mouth on the butterfly. Her knees weakened and he pulled her underwear down. "Step out of them." He mumbled hoarsely. When she complied, he lifted her astride his lap again. "All aboard, sweetheart." Barely moving her, he toed off his shoes and got his pants down.

Caroline hummed in the back of her throat as she felt him begin to enter her. Slowly. Deeply. Oh God, she thought, this is torture. Exquisite torture. That was her last thought before she went over, screaming his name. Brian soon followed.

A short time later, she folded her arms between their bodies, snuggled closer and buried her chilled nose in his neck. "Cold." She mumbled with her eyes closed.

Brian rubbed his hands over her back in an effort to chase away the slight chill. "We have to get up soon. Not only is this chair really hard on the nether regions, but if we don't leave within the hour, we'll never make it to my mother's in time for dinner."

Caroline's head popped up and she looked at him in embarrassed dismay. "Oh my God, Brian! I can't believe we did it in a chair. You're such a bad influence. My mother has sat in this chair!"

Brian laughed. "You're the one who started it. Besides, I'm sure the chair is happy to finally have seen some action. Ecstatic, even."

"It's not funny." She said and slapped him lightly on his chest. "I'll have to replace it now, since it's the only thing I have for people to sit on when they visit."

"Fine. Buy another one and I'll take this one to my place." He said as he stood with her in his arms, adjusting her so her legs were hanging over his arm. "And every time I look at it, I'll smile. Very happily, I might add."

Caroline finally realized how ridiculous she sounded and laughed with him as he walked them into the small bathroom. She curled into him and whispered in his ear. "How is the essential part of your nether regions holding out?"

Six hours later, Brian pulled into the driveway of a modest A-frame house with a large front yard.

"Are you sure you can't tell it's there?" Caroline asked almost frantically as she adjusted the rearview mirror so that she could look into it with worried eyes.

Brian laughed and took hold of her hands so she'd stop fiddling with the turtleneck of her sweater. She'd made him stop at her house on the way out of town so she could replace the white blouse. "Caroline, will you stop? You're almost as covered up as a nun would be. My mother is not going to notice. And even if she did, she wouldn't care."

"You can laugh Brian, but it's all your fault. You shouldn't have done it. Your mother is going to think I'm a...a...a tramp or a slut or...or something worse."

"Okay, now you're being ridiculous. First of all, the hickey is on your chest, not your neck and unless she has X-ray vision, there's no way in hell my mother can see it. Secondly, like I said, even if she did see it, she wouldn't care! What's gotten into you? She's my mother, not some sort of monster and she's really looking forward to meeting you. In fact, I'm sure that's her peeking out the window now, wondering if I'm letting you have your trampy, sluttish way with me in the back seat."

Caroline gasped in dismay and quickly turned her head. Brian laughed again. "I'm just joking. You need to relax," he said, tightening his grip so she couldn't hit or pinch him, as she was wont to do when he teased her.

Caroline sighed and closed her eyes. "You're right. I'm just a little nervous, I guess. I don't know why, because she'll either like me or she won't. It's as simple as that."

"True, but she'll love you because I love you and she knows that I would never have even made the effort to bring you here if you weren't so obviously wonderful in all respects." He watched her press her hand to her stomach and take a deep breath.

"Thanks. I needed that," she said with a shaky smile. "Okay, let's go."

"Well, praise be to God; they're finally getting out of the car." Fiona said as she watched Brian open his door and climb out. She was looking through a small break in the drapes so that she could see outside without being seen. She silently thanked the city for placing a street lamp right in front of the house.

"You shouldn't be spying on them Fi." Frank said admonishingly from the comfort of his easy chair. He briefly lifted his eyes. "Come away from there now." He said absently and went back to watching the football game.

Ignoring him, Fiona continued to watch as Brian walked around the car and opened the door on the passenger side. "Oh, isn't she lovely." She said softly with a smile as Caroline laughed at something Brian said and raised her mouth for a brief kiss. As she watched Brian tuck a lock of hair behind Caroline's ear and kiss her forehead, she unaccountably felt her eyes fill with tears and turned away from the window, slightly embarrassed for having seen such a tender moment. Grateful that Brian had his own key, she went into the kitchen to check on her dinner and compose herself.

"Ready?" Brian asked Caroline as he slipped his key in the lock.

"As ready as I'll ever be." She said with an attempt at a smile and walked in ahead of him.

She walked straight into a pair of enveloping arms. Holding tightly to her overnight bag so she wouldn't drop it, she looked into the laughing green eyes of Frank Applegate. "How do you do, young lady?"

He asked, still holding her. "I hope you don't mind the hug, but after Brian's last visit, I feel like I already know you."

Caroline smiled in relief at being so warmly welcomed. "No I don't," she said and kissed his cheek. "So long as you don't mind that."

Brian stepped up behind her to put his arm around her shoulders. "Hey, old man," he said to Frank. "You tryin' to make time with my woman?"

Frank laughed and pulled him in for a hug. "Course not. I've got enough on my plate with your mother?' They were standing right by a staircase and Caroline leaned on the newel post to get out of their way.

"I heard that." Fiona said as she walked through the dining room to stand on the threshold of the living room.

Caroline looked over to find a trim, attractive woman dressed in navy slacks and a white blouse. She had Brian's eyes and they were smiling. Thank God. She smiled herself and walked over to meet Brian's mother. "I wondered where he'd gotten such glorious black hair." She said as she let herself be enveloped in another hug. "It's so good to finally meet you." She hugged back.

"You too, lass. I'm glad you could come." Fiona said. "Ah, here's my boy." She said and broke away from Caroline to greet Brian. She laughed as he picked her up and spun her around. "Put me down, boy. You're making your poor old mother dizzy, you are."

"I'm sorry we're late, Mrs. Applegate." Caroline said when Brian had put Fiona back on her feet. "I hope we didn't ruin dinner."

"Don't worry about it dear. You're only a little late, so we didn't suffer overmuch."

"Good." Brian said. "Where is Caroline sleeping?"

Fiona looked at him and raised a suspicious brow.

Brian laughed. "You've got a dirty mind Mom and you're embarrassing Caroline. I only ask because I need to know where to put her bag. Is she upstairs or down?" The house had four bedrooms; two were upstairs and two were down.

"She'll be upstairs. Right across the hail from Frank and me." She tacked on for good measure. "You'll be downstairs in your usual room."

"Yes ma'am." Brian saluted and picked up Caroline's bag to walk it upstairs.

Caroline smiled at his retreating back and turned to look at Fiona. "I love the way you've decorated your home, Mrs. Applegate." She said, taking in the dusky pink sofa and armchair and the cherry entertainment center. The wails were covered in dusky pink and cream striped wallpaper, while the floor boasted plush cream carpeting.

"It's Fiona or Fi and thank you. Frank didn't like it at first, but so long as he's got a comfortable place to park his backside, he doesn't complain overmuch. Do you, Frank?"

"What?" Frank asked in distraction. He'd already parked said backside again and was watching the game.

Caroline chuckled when Fiona tskd and rolled her eyes. "Do you mind if I freshen up before dinner? I'm feeling a little gritty from our trip."

"Of course I don't mind. Just head up the stairs; your room is on the right and the guest bathroom connects to it. Dinner will be ready in another twenty minutes."

"Thanks." Caroline said. "If you'll give me a minute, I'd love to come down and help."

"There's no need lass, but thank you. Everything's baking and simmering already. I hope you like corn beef and cabbage."

"I do." Caroline affirmed. "I'll be down to help you set your table, okay?"

"That would be lovely." Fiona said.

"It's a deal then. Don't start without me." Caroline turned to go up the stairs.

"Be sure to remind that son of mine of how old and creaky this house is, especially the stairs. So Frank and I will hear every move he makes. Every. Single. One." She called after Caroline.

With her foot on the first step, Caroline turned with laughing eyes. "Yes ma'am." She gravely repeated Brian's words and rushed up the stairs.

Caroline turned off the light in the bathroom and padded over to the bed in her stockinged feet and knee-length gown. She felt as if she were in the middle of a weird, psychedelic forest. The comforter had a yellow background with flowers, birds and other animals in different colors all over it. The curtains, slip covers on the chair and even the wallpaper matched the comforter. Trying hard not to feel nauseated by so much flora and fauna, she climbed into bed, turned off the bedside light and closed her eyes.

Minutes later, her eyes popped open in alarm as she felt a hand cover her mouth and a heavy weight on top of her. Immediately, she began to scream and struggle, ineffectually pulling at the wide wrist of the hand over her mouth.

"Hey, calm down. It's only me." Brian whispered urgently in her ear and removed his hand. Knowing her propensity to hit first and ask questions later, he closed his mouth over hers, kissing her until her body became pliant and her arms curved around his neck. Lifting his head, he whispered, "I'm sorry I scared you. I just wanted to say a proper good night, but I didn't want you to say anything that my mom would hear."

"Get off me." She whispered indignantly and pinched him. "You must weigh a ton." When he'd lifted his chest off of hers so she could breath easier, she asked, "What do you mean a 'proper good night'? And how'd you get up here without anyone hearing you, anyway? Those have got to be some of the noisiest stairs I've ever climbed."

"It's easy, if you know which stairs are noisy and which aren't and I do." As he was talking, he was pulling the covers down.

"What are you doing?" She whispered and grabbed hold of the comforter.

"I told you, I want to say a proper good night." He said and pulled the covers away with one hard yank. There was just enough light coming from the street for him to get a good look at her. "What's that you're wearing?" He asked in true shock.

Caroline's lips twitched. "It's a flannel nightgown, you idiot. It is November in Michigan, you know."

"But you don't own anything like that. I mean, I've never seen you wear anything remotely similar to it." He said with dismay and distaste in his voice, as he looked down at the high-necked, long-sleeved garment that he imagined could be the scourge of men everywhere.

This time Caroline's laugh did bubble out. "I don't have to wear it at home because you're always in bed with me. I knew you wouldn't be—at least you're not supposed to be—while we're here, so I brought this along to stay warm."

"Well, take it off." Brian said and began the task himself.

Caroline slapped at his hands as his fingers fiddled with the buttons. "Stop it. I will not." She whispered, still trying not to laugh fully.

"Come on sweetheart. Be a sport." He said and pushed her hands aside.

"Brian." She said firmly. "Stop it. We can't." That was said with less certainty as he brushed her breasts with the back of his fingers.

Brian heard the weakness and exploited it. Bending his head, he took her mouth again, letting his tongue take over. When he felt her arms around his neck again, he began pressing kisses to the corners of her mouth.

"We can't," She repeated, but it was more like a question as she tried to capture his mouth with hers. "Your mother will hear us."

"Not if you don't make those wonderful, little, operatic sounds I love so much." He whispered and kissed her fully.

"Don't tease." She hummed and opened her legs when she felt his hand slide underneath her gown and grasp her thigh. "I'm not the only one who makes sounds."

"I'll be quiet too. She won't hear a thing, I promise."

"But what about the bed? Won't it…" She trailed off, unable to complete her thought as his hand slid up her thigh and slipped beneath the leg of her underwear.

"It's brand new. They just bought it the last time I was here." He said softly. "I'm sure it hasn't been used, so it won't make a sound."

Caroline bit her lip to keep one of those operatic sounds he was so fond of from escaping and tightened her arms around his neck. "If…if you're…sure." She said.

"If I wasn't, it would be too late to stop now." Brian said and helped rid her of her gown.

"I've got to go." He said a short time later and kissed her. Caroline's only indication that she heard him was a tightening of her arms around his neck.

"Caroline, I really have to go." He said insistently. "Look," he said when she still didn't release him. "You know I have to go before morning comes."

"Just stay a little longer." She whispered and finally opened her eyes.

"I may not wake up in time to leave. My mother is an early riser." He said, knowing it was a lost cause. He knew that holding him and being held by him after making love were two of her favorite habits. They were habits he'd become accustomed to before he realized it.

"Just stay a little longer." She repeated, kissing his chin and gently bumping it with her nose. "Please."

He sighed and kissed her forehead, knowing he was defeated. "All right." He said, rolling to his side so she was lying on his chest. "But you'd better wake me in time."

—⁓—

Across the hall, Fiona made herself comfortable on Frank's chest. "Fancies himself a clever boy, our Brian does." She said wryly. "The big sneak."

Frank chuckled sleepily. "You have to admit, he was damned quiet coming up the stairs. I never even heard him."

"Well as to that, neither did I. He was not so lucky when it came to the bed, however. Even if it is new." She said with a sniff before closing her eyes.

Frank was silent a moment before saying, "You know, I hope the two of them know what they're doing."

Fiona lifted her head from his chest. "You mean their relationship?" After Frank's affirmative, she said, "I've thought about that myself. You know for all its melting pot philosophy, America is not a very tolerant place. And I have to admit that I'm concerned about how they will be treated."

"So am I. Is it worth it, I wonder?"

"Why Frank Applegate, of course it's worth it. True love is worth everything!"

CHAPTER 27

"She's a lovely girl, Brian." Fiona said Friday morning as he installed new software on her computer. "She's very bright. Her parents must be extremely proud to have such a daughter." Leaning over his shoulder, she looked out the window to see Caroline across the street taking pictures of children playing football in the park.

"Mm hm." Brian commented absently, his face frowning in concentration.

"Why, I bet they look forward to the day when they can have a grandchild as smart and as beautiful as Caroline to bounce on their knee." She said with studied indifference as she realigned a perfectly straight picture on the desk.

"Mm hm—wait. What did you say?" Brian finally turned to look at his mother.

"I said that I'm sure that Caroline's parents are anxious for grandchildren, just as Frank and I are." Fiona said with an innocent smile.

"That's what I thought you said. Look, Mom, I love Caroline. In fact, I can't picture myself spending my life with anyone else but her. However—"

"Oh, that's lovely. Just lovely." Fiona said with a clasp of her hands and misty eyes.

"However," Brian repeated emphatically, "I don't think we'll be having children soon. Traditionally, marriage comes first." He said and turned back to his work.

"Don't be smart." She said mildly and tugged on the hair hanging over his collar. "Since you brought the subject up, when are you getting married? You can't wait too long with a beautiful woman like Caroline. Some other man might propose to her and snatch her right out from under your nose. Be careful, me boy."

Brian laughed. "It's not like that, Mom. Caroline is not the kind of woman who stays with someone simply because she wants to get married. Now," he said as he finished installing her software. "I'm sure it's going to happen, and when it does, you'll be one of the first to know. All done." He punched a couple of keys and swiveled around to face his mother.

"But when do you—"

"Please, Mom." He interrupted. "Caroline and I haven't even discussed it yet, so I don't have an answer for you."

"Well don't drag your feet too long. I'm not getting any younger, you know."

Brian stood up. "I'll keep that in mind." He said and bent to kiss her cheek. "Now, I'm off to find the smart, beautiful woman you're so fond of."

"Um, excuse me lady." Caroline lowered her camera and turned to see a pudgy boy of about 12 with dark, sparkling, inquisitive eyes staring at her. He was carrying a football. What a little cutie, she thought.

She smiled. "Hi. What's your name?"

"Jamal, but people call me David."

"Why do people call you David if your name is Jamal?"

"Cause that's the way it is." He said with a shrug. "Also, my middle name is David." He laughed at his own joke, showing off a mouth full of colored metal.

"Hey, those are *some* braces you got there. They're pretty cool."

He frowned. "Yeah, some people may think so. I don't."

Caroline smiled. "Well, what can I do for you David?"

"I wanted to tell you that instead of standing there like a spectator, you should join in the fun. We could use another player out there." He said with a wide smile and gestured over his shoulder.

Caroline looked over to see about a dozen other boys standing and watching. She looked down at her blue jeans and leather jacket. "I don't know." She said doubtfully. "I don't think I'm quite dressed for football."

"Aw, come on. You're wearing sneaks, aren't you? All you have to do is braid your hair or something and

take off your jacket. You're wearing a sweater, so you'll
be warm enough." He said, looking at the red wool.

Caroline bit her lip, thinking. She hadn't played
football in years. It might be fun to get out there.

"Come on, lady." David said impatiently. "You
gonna be a spectator your whole life?"

"Okay. I'll do it, but only if you call me Caroline.
Just let me put my camera back in its bag and I'll be
right over."

"Great, thanks. I'll just go tell the guys."

Caroline bent to put her camera away and then
straightened. Just as she started braiding her hair, she
heard a loud, raucous outcry of "Yes!" come from the
other side of the park. She looked over to see the boys
high-fiving each other and patting David on the back.
She smiled, glad to be of help.

"Caroline."

She turned to see Brian and waved. "Hi, Bri." She
said when he reached her.

"Hey. What have you been up to all this time?" He
asked, taking her hand.

"Burr." He said. "Your hand is ice-cold. What have
you been doing?"

"I've been snapping pictures of those kids over
there, so I needed to take my gloves off." She stretched
to press a kiss on his mouth.

Just as he began to deepen the kiss, Brian heard
spontaneous exclamations of dismay. Curious, he
turned his head to see the group of boys staring and

looking disappointed, yet hopeful at the same time. "What's up with them, I wonder."

"You know how boys that age are, they're probably completely disgusted by kissing." Caroline said. "I suppose I've lost their respect, since I'm acting 'girlie.' They probably won't want me to join their football game now."

"Let me get this straight. You're going to play tackle football with that group of boys over there?"

"Yeah. So?"

"Whose idea was it? Yours or theirs?"

"It was theirs. One of the kids said they needed another player. Why?"

"Sneaky little bastards." Brian said almost admiringly. "First of all, those boys aren't disgusted by our kiss. In fact, they wouldn't mind getting their hands on you themselves. That's why they asked you to join their game."

"What?" Caroline was baffled.

"Those boys want you to join the game so they'll have a chance to tackle you. In short, they probably want to cop a few feels."

"No way." She said incredulously and looked over at the boys.

"Trust me, Caroline. I used to be an adolescent boy myself and there wouldn't have been anything I liked better than having a nice looking girl join the game. Let me guess," he said, taking a longer look at the boys. "They sent the little, chubby one with the big, brown eyes over, right? He's the cute one and was more likely to tug on your heartstrings."

"But that's...that's..."

"Exactly how boys think." Brian said calmly.

"You mean they were going to...to..." Again, shock made her unable to complete her sentence.

"Tackle you as many times as possible? Yes," Brian said with a slow nod, "yes they were."

"The little perverts—I don't think that's funny at all." She said, looking over at them and narrowing her eyes.

"It's not and I'm sure they think they're clever, but they don't think they're doing anything wrong." Brian said, holding her by her arms. He could practically feel her vibrating beneath his hands.

"Well, they're about to find out how wrong they were." Caroline said and moved to walk to the other side of the park.

"Wait. I have an idea. Just follow my lead."

"Hello, boys." Brian said, making sure to look each of them in the eye. He received a mumbled chorus of nervous hellos in reply.

"I'm Brian. My mother lives in that black and white house across the street there. You all know Caroline here, as she's been taking pictures all morning. She tells me you guys want her to join the game. The thing is, she's my lady and I get real protective." He ignored the disgusted snort Caroline made from behind him and continued, "And since I'm a cop, I sometimes bring my work home with me. So if

I thought that you guys had asked her to play football with you for any other reason than the fact that you needed another player, I'd have to think long and hard about not reporting you for sexual harassment or something." He stopped to make sure they were taking it all in.

What followed next could only be described as stunned silence. David finally broke the quiet, speaking rapidly and nervously, "Oh God, Officer, Sergeant, Sir. We're sorry. It's just that she's such a babe, you know?"

"Yeah and plus, she's a girl!" This came squeakily from a tall, blonde boy with pimples and frightened blue eyes.

"Okay, okay." Brian held up his hand to stem the sudden tide of apologies and explanations they were all trying to get out at once. "I'll let you slide this time. Just don't let it happen again."

"Whatever you say, mister."

"Sure. No harm, no foul."

"You're wrong." Caroline said, stepping in front of Brian with her arms folded. "There could have been a lot of harm done and your idea certainly was *foul*, devious and disgusting. You might have thought you were being clever, but I would not have thought—and don't think—that your idea was the least bit amusing. And I'm sure no girl, or her parents, would find it amusing either."

The boys looked sheepish and again, they all tried to apologize at once.

"Like I said, just don't let it happen again." Brian said sternly as he put his arm around Caroline's shoulders. "To anyone."

"Liar." Caroline said to him as they walked across the park. "When was the last time you wore a badge, uh, Officer-Sergeant-Sir?" She finished in a gruff voice.

"Hey, it was inspired and you know it. It got their attention, didn't it?"

"I guess it did."

"And to show your appreciation for all my work, I thought you might play a little one-on-one with me later."

"Dream on, pal. I can't take another one of your mom's suspicious looks."

He laughed and took her hand. The look in his eyes made her stop. "What is it?" She asked.

"I've been thinking. How would you like to stay here a couple of extra days? Say, until Monday or Tuesday?"

Caroline's brow wrinkled in curiosity. "Why? I thought you had to get back for work."

"I do, but I thought that you might want to stay."

Caroline started shaking her head no before he finished his sentence. "No. I'm not going to stay here, especially if you're going back. I know what you're up to Brian and it won't work."

"If you know what I'm up to, then you should realize I'm only suggesting you stay because I want you to be safe. Your picture and your name will be in the paper in two days and whoever has been looking for you will more than likely see it."

"Exactly…You can't keep me here forever, so if they find out where I live my staying here won't matter, will it? They'll just keep coming back until they catch me at home. Besides, I'm safe where you are and if there really is someone out there looking for me, I'd rather get it over with instead of looking over my shoulder all the time."

"I knew you were banking on the stalker seeing you in the paper when you agreed to take that picture."

"Well, yeah." She said with a guilty shrug. "I mean, why else would I have agreed? I want it this way because I'm sick of being scared all the time. Don't you get it? Whoever it is, or may be, already has too much control over my life. I don't want him to keep having it indefinitely. And remember Brian, you're basing all of this on how scared I was when you caught up with me in the park that night. I mean, it could still just have been a fluke. This way, if it isn't and the guy comes after me, at least I'll know."

Brian gave her a look of complete disbelief. "I know it isn't a fluke; my gut tells me it isn't. And it's not a matter of if, but when. When this guys comes after you, I want you to be safe and that won't happen at your condo."

"I've been brushing up on my self-defense and it's all coming back to me. I'll be fine and you'll be there with me and so will Motley since we're picking her up from Tracy's on the way into town tomorrow." She was determined that one way or the other, it would all be over soon.

Brian sighed. "You may as well know that I've arranged for a couple of my police friends to stake out your condo, just in case the guy does come."

"What! And you didn't tell me? After the big lecture you gave me on not keeping secrets, you keep something like that from me. Well I like that." She said huffily and sucked her teeth.

"I'm telling you now. Forgive me if I wanted to give you a couple of days where you didn't have to think about someone coming after you or where you could sleep through the night without jerking awake." He said in sarcastic disgust. "I was hoping to make you see reason before I told you, but obviously that's not going to happen." He finished.

"So, I guess you're saying I'm being unreasonable!" She said, completely ignoring his second statement. "Well, I beg to differ. I want to go home. I don't want to stay here. I don't think that's being unreasonable. I think your wanting me to stay here is. That's what I think." She said and turned to leave.

"Wait a minute!" Brian said and took her arm. "How am I being unreasonable because I want you to be safe? You're so stubborn and spoiled that things have to be your way all the time. All I'm asking is that you stay here where you'll be safe and let me take care of things in. Chicago."

"No." She said stiffly, taking hold of his hand and trying to push it away.

Refusing to release her, Brian asked. "Is that all you're going to say?"

"What else is there to say? I don't want to stay and the guy, if there is one, may not even try to make a move without my being there and everything will have been a complete waste of time. I want it over in one fell swoop. Period. I don't want to have to leave my home over and over again. I think there will be a better chance of catching Mr. Mysterious if I'm there. I just want to get it done! I'm sick of rearranging my life because of some would-be/could-be psycho!"

Brian looked at the stubborn set of her chin and clinched his jaw to keep from saying something he knew he'd regret later. He released her arm and held up his hands. "Fine. If that's the way you want it, that's the way it will be."

"It is and you're an ass for not telling me your plans—especially when they concern me." Caroline said and stalked angrily across the street without him.

"Well, dear. Have you enjoyed your visit here to Detroit?" Fiona asked Caroline later that day as they sat in the kitchen having tea and cookies. The kitchen with its bright yellow curtains and walls brought sunshine to mind, despite the slate gray sky.

"Oh, immensely. I was so excited to meet you because Brian is crazy about you and he can't say enough good things about you. I was also nervous to meet you—because Brian is crazy about you and he can't say enough good things about you." She finished wryly.

Fiona laughed. "Well, it's good to know when a boy is proud of his old mum. One can never get enough of that. Now that you're here, are you still nervous?"

"No, of course not." Caroline hurried to say. "You've been wonderful and extremely welcoming. I just wanted to make a good impression on you, that's all. It's never mattered so much to me before."

"Why was it so important for you to make a good impression on me?"

Caroline gave her a sidelong look. "You're joking, right? Surely you know how much Brian means to me and so, of course it's important that you like me." Though now, she mused, the mean thoughts I'm having about your son would probably shock you.

"Oh, you needn't have worried, lass. I've liked you for months now, since the summer as a matter of fact. That was the first time Brian ever mentioned you, you see. And every time he's spoken of you since, there has been such quiet happiness in his voice that I want to do cartwheels. I was always worried that he'd never find the right woman to settle down with. He's always been so picky, Brian has. So when he said he'd be bringing you here for the holiday...well I ask you, why wouldn't I like you? You make him happy and I trust his judgment. That's all."

"Thank you." Caroline said hesitantly.

Fiona laughed again. "You're thinking that you'd rather be liked for yourself and not because of someone else's feelings about you. I don't blame you. That's a good way to be, that, and you're a better person for it. I like you for you, Caroline."

"Again, I'm unsure as to whether or not I should say thank you or…or…"

"Go to hell?" Fiona suggested helpfully. "I wouldn't hold it against you if you did. After all, who am I to be sitting in judgment like this? I assure you, Caroline, I don't mean to offend. I'm just pleased that you and I get along and like each other. It just makes things easier. Wouldn't you agree?"

"Yes." Caroline said with a smile. "Did the fact that I'm black ever concern you?"

"It didn't. I'm sure it bothers some and that worries me because people can certainly behave like idiots. However, it's not my place to tell Brian whom he should fall in love with. I figure finding true love is hard enough as it is and putting restrictions on it based on skin color just makes it doubly so. Again, wouldn't you agree?"

"Yes I would. I wish more people thought that way. It's hard not to notice the looks people give us. I try not to let it bother me and I'm successful most of the time. But sometimes, I just want to scream or confront them. Of course I don't and the feeling passes rather quickly. Brian on the other hand, has the ability to just ignore it as if it means absolutely nothing."

"That sounds like Brian. He's like his father in that way. If it's not threatening him or his loved ones in some way, then it doesn't exist. It has no impact. And when you think about it, it makes sense. After all, a perfect stranger walking down the street is going to have no more impact on your life than a single raindrop falling into the ocean will have on the ocean. It just isn't meaningful."

"Yes, but raindrop after raindrop after raindrop falling will make a difference eventually."

"Which is why you've got to take it one raindrop—or hostile stranger—at a time and not worry about the next one that might come along. And even if you pass a thousand more hostile strangers, you've got to know that you can't change what they're feeling and by the same token, they can't change what you're feeling. No impact. Unless you allow it."

Caroline smiled. "I like you Fiona."

"Ah," She said, feigning astonishment, "that's good to know." She chuckled with Caroline. Well, I guess the girl's not going to talk about the trouble between her and Brian, she thought as she noticed that the strain around Caroline's mouth and the unhappiness in her eyes hadn't abated any since she'd come inside. And Brian, the lovesick boy had been gnashing his teeth all afternoon and they were both avoiding each other. I guess they'll work it out on their own, she thought with a mental shrug.

Fiona smiled again. "Brian tells me you're quite the talented artist. Fancy doing a portrait of Frank and me? Frank has a birthday coming up in February and I think that would make a lovely gift. I'd pay you your usual fee, of course."

"I don't have a usual fee and even if I did, I wouldn't charge you. I'd love to paint your portrait. I'll use one of the pictures I took on Thanksgiving; you were both dressed up then."

"Lovely. It's all settled then. Do you think it will be ready when we come for your show in January?"

"Of course it will be."

"Good." She said and put her teacup back in its saucer with a snap. "Now that we've gotten through the pleasantries, I'd like to get down to serious business." She said with a frown and took a deep breath. "Since we're practically family, how large of a discount can I expect to get on your family's marvelous ice cream?"

For the first time in hours, Caroline laughed with genuine amusement. "I'll see what I can do."

Brian walked forcefully up the stairs, uncaring of the noise he was making. Caroline had ignored him all through dinner and had only given monosyllabic answers when he'd addressed her directly while everyone was sitting around watching television. Well, he was tired of her giving him the cold shoulder and he was determined that they were going to clear the air.

Caroline deliberately turned on her side so that her back was facing the door when she heard it start to creak open. "Go away Brian." She said over her shoulder.

He ignored her and shut the door. "Listen to me, Caroline." He said and sat on the bed near her hip.

"There's nothing more to say. I'm going back to Chicago and you don't want me to. You asked cops to stake out my condo and didn't even tell me. What else is there?" By this time she was on her back and leaning back on her elbows.

"I've already explained my reasons for those things." Brian said. "I'd do it again to keep you safe and I won't apologize."

"How can you not apologize Brian?" She asked and frustrated, she hit him in his chest with the flat of her hand. "You're the one who's so big on being open and honest with one another and I agreed with you. You should have told me about the police officers and you know it. If I'd done something like that without telling you, you'd be angry."

"You're right, but I'm still not sorry that you had a few days without worry."

Caroline studied him thoughtfully as she thought about what he'd said in the park about his reasons for not telling her. "I'm not some delicate piece of china that you need to protect Brian. I need to know these things. While I appreciate your thoughtfulness, it's still aggravating that you want to treat me like I'm helpless. You wouldn't want me doing the same thing to you."

"I don't treat you like you're helpless. And it wouldn't be the same if I were in your situation."

"You do and of course it would be the same!" She whispered fiercely and hit him again. "Stop being a chauvinist! You can't withhold information from me for any reason if you don't want me doing the same thing under the same circumstances. It doesn't make sense."

"We're not going to agree on this. I'd do it again if I had the option."

Caroline sighed. "Fine, so long as you know I'd do the same."

"Are we finished fighting now?" Brian wanted to know.

"I don't know. Are we?"

"If it's up to me, then we are." He lowered himself into the bed. "I missed you."

"We can't." Caroline repeated her resistance of the other night as she kept her mouth out of reach of his. "Your mother—" her voice trailed off as his mouth closed over her breast. She held onto the sides of his head as her eyes fell shut. "Just promise to be quiet."

"Mmm hmm. I'll be just as quiet as you will be."

CHAPTER 28

"So tell me about the cops who are coming over." Caroline said Saturday night as she dropped her bag in the living room of her condo and bent to pet Motley, who was snuggling against her legs.

"They're just a couple of friends from another life." Brian said tiredly as he dropped down on the couch. "But I know I can trust them. They're doing it because they know how serious this is." He finished with a meaningful look at her.

Caroline sighed and sat next to him. "Okay, I get it. I know it's serious. All of that stuff I said the other day about not knowing if there was a stalker was said out of anger. I trust your instincts and if you say that there's a need to worry, then there is."

"I'm glad to hear it, but I still don't like how you're making yourself bait."

"I know and I'm sorry that you're worried. I'm worried too, but I'm more ready for this to be over than I am scared." She said and leaned her head on his shoulder.

"I know, I know. I've called Jack a couple of times and I still haven't heard anything back from him. My friends will be here early tomorrow, but you won't see them. I can count on Motley to do her part and bark like crazy. Now all I need for you to do is promise me you'll do what I say."

She kissed his cheek in amends because she knew how much it bothered him to have her there. "I promise. I just want everything to be over. Just think, this time tomorrow, I could be living my life the way I want to and not the way the actions of a psycho dictate."

"It may not happen tomorrow, Caroline." He cautioned. "He may not even see the picture."

"Don't say that. This may sound odd, but we need to think positively."

Brian's laugh was mirthless. "God, you're insane. Do you know that?"

"But you love me anyway," she said.

—⁂—

Brickman picked up the early morning edition of *The Daily News.* "Well, well, well." He said with a pleased smile as his quarry stared up at him from the paper. "Caroline Singleton, is it? You should be easy enough to find."

He couldn't have been more pleased. He picked up his telephone and called Kovlovsky. "Mr. Kovlovsky. Her name is Caroline Singleton. Find her and bring her to me." He hung up the phone with a satisfied snap.

He'd begun to think that he wouldn't find her. His men were having no luck and Ida still insisted that she didn't know who she was. Well, he didn't need Ida now.

Though she was fantastic in bed and increased his bottom line, he wanted her gone as soon as possible.

He turned to look at her as she lay sleeping next to him in bed. It was a pity he'd had to mar that pretty, brown face. He gently stroked his hand through her hair, and reaching the ends, gave it a hard yank. "Wake up Ida."

Ida opened her eyes and smiled sleepily up at him. "Good morning."

"Good morning my dear." Brickman said placidly. "Sleep well?"

"You know I always do when I'm with you." She said.

"Well, time to get up now." He said cavalierly and slapped her backside.

Ida frowned at his retreating form as he walked into the connecting bathroom. Pushing up on her elbows, she reached over for the newspaper. "Oh, damn." She whispered as she looked at Caroline's smiling face. He knew who Caroline was and now it would take a matter of minutes to find out where she lived. "Damn, I should have kept the pressure on her to leave!" She mumbled as she struggled out of bed.

"Think Ida, think." She told herself as she found the clothes she'd been wearing the day before lying across a chair. She hurriedly dressed as she shot nervous glances towards the bathroom door. As long as she heard the shower running, she'd be fine.

She slid her feet into her shoes and rushed to snatch her coat from the closet. "You bastard." She whispered furiously to the absent Brickman. She'd thought she'd been making headway in making him forget Caroline. She'd even decided to quit her job in order to spend more time with him.

When she'd approached him about quitting her job, he'd insisted she stay until January, so he could reap the benefits of the drug sales she made at her office building a little longer. But other than that, he'd said nothing else about it, so she'd thought that she'd been making progress. Obviously, she'd been mistaken. Now she'd lose everything if she didn't get to Caroline before his henchmen did.

Ida took a deep breath and started to think. She realized that even if she reached Caroline first, it would still be over for her because Brickman would kill her. He'd be so angry at not finding Caroline that he'd lash out at her. Ida also knew that he'd kill her once he found Caroline. He'd have to after he kidnapped Caroline because she knew too much. Either way she was a dead woman, but she could still save Brian. She had to let him know what was going on. She dialed Caroline's number on her cell phone as she raced down the stairs to the front door. It rang several times before her voicemail picked up. Ida angrily clicked off and ran out the door.

She dialed Brian's number. Again, no answer. She ran down the stairs of Brickman's brownstone and hailed a cab. Maybe she wouldn't find Caroline and Brian at Caroline's condo, but that was the best place to go. If they weren't there, at least she'd know they were safe at Brian's. There was no way they'd be at Caroline's studio so early in the morning—at least she didn't think they would.

Brian woke up reaching for Caroline. He opened his eyes when he felt nothing but empty space where she was supposed to be laying. Hearing the television, he got out of bed and padded softly to the living room. She was curled up in a corner of the couch with a mug in her hand. Sniffing the air, he realized she was drinking herbal tea—flower-flavored by the smell of it. The baggy sweats, thick socks and wool blanket gave him a hint as to what was wrong. He made a sound of sympathy. "Poor baby," he said as he sat at her hip. "You've got your period. It's a bad one, huh?"

"Yeah." Her voice was clogged. "I didn't want to wake you, so I came out here."

"God, you sound terrible. Have you got a cold, too?"

"Yes. In fact, I've taken the last of my cold medication. I'm sure I'll need more later. Will you go pick some up for me at the drug store?"

Brian frowned a little. "I don't know about that. Have you taken anything for your period?"

"The last pill I had, which obviously wasn't enough because I still feel like I'm dying. I'll need you to pick some medicine up for that too. I left my supply at your house two months ago. The hot water bottle is helping, but not fast enough."

He looked at her droopy eyes. "You look like you're about to pass out."

"The cold medicine is supposed to cause drowsiness and I think mixing it with the other medicine makes it even worse. Are you going to go pick that stuff up for me? You could go to the 24 hour right on the corner."

"I don't know. I don't want to leave you, not with your picture coming out."

"But your friends are here and it will only take you about ten minutes to go and come back."

"My friends aren't due here until seven and it's only about 6:30 now."

"Please." She said around a yawn and then grimaced in pain. "Motley's here and the pain is really killing me. Plus, the cold medicine I took was for stuffiness and congestion, not a sore throat and fever." She finished and sneezed in rapid succession six times.

Brian put his hand to her head. The heat emanating from her skin convinced him. "All right," he said, rising. "I'll be right back." He was dressed and out the door within five minutes.

Caroline put her mug down and wrapped the blanket tighter around her. Curling herself into a ball, she stopped fighting her drowsiness and fell asleep with Motley at the other end of the couch where Brian had deposited her on his way out.

Pete tiredly removed the lock pick from its casing. Brickman had gotten him out of bed at an obscenely early hour that morning. Yawning, he dropped the pick, causing Tony to make a sound of disgust from behind him. At Brickman's insistence, Tony was along for back up. Ignoring the other man, Pete bent to pick the tool up and straightened. He felt sorry for Caroline Singleton and angry with himself for blowing it. But since Tony was with him, he had no choice, he had to go in and get her. He glanced at his watch. It was 6:52.

"Yeah." Brian's answer to his cell phone was short and clipped as he stood in line at the drug store waiting to pay for his items. It was 6:50 and he wanted to get back to Caroline's.

"Listen, Brian." Jack said urgently. "I know your guy. He's one of Alex Brickman's henchmen. You said he followed Caroline in the park?"

"What? Brickman?!" Brian said and looked around in a daze. His eyes fell on the newspaper rack and he saw Caroline's face smiling up at him from the front page. They'd placed her picture in the preview column that showed what the different sections offered. "God, he knows where she is now. Her picture is in today's paper."

"Calm down and listen to me." Jack said. "If this guy did follow your lady, she's in big trouble and she needs protection. Where are you? You didn't answer your phone at home."

"I'm on my way back to Caroline's." Brian said as he dropped his items and rushed out the door.

"Tell me where she lives. I'll meet you there." Jack said. "Okay," he said catching the address between Brian's hurried puffs. "That's just a few blocks away. I'll be right there."

Caroline awoke to Motley's barking. She heard the phone ring one time before it fell silent. She must have just missed the call. Befuddled, she lifted her head to see the dog standing on the couch and barking towards the hall. Her brain was fuzzy from the medicine and she said,

"Be quiet Motley! I'm trying to sleep." She dropped her head back down and closed her eyes.

Motley jumped down and ran into the hall, barking insanely. Caroline's muddled brain finally realized what was going on and she jerked up in alarm, only to drop her head between her knees as dizziness took over. She heard the door slowly creak open and she heard Motley's barking cut off abruptly as she uttered a sharp cry of pain.

Moving as fast as she could, Caroline ran down the hail towards her bedroom, pausing briefly to shut the door to the guest bedroom. She shut and locked her bedroom door. "Oh God, Oh God, Oh God, Oh God," She mumbled in litany as she ran to the bedside phone and punched in 911. "Please help me. Someone's breaking into my house and I think they've killed my dog." Giving them her address, she knew she needed to get off the phone and protect herself, so she placed the receiver on the bed to ensure an open line so the operator could trace the call.

She ran into the bathroom and just as she shut that door, she heard the door to the guest bedroom being kicked in. She kept telling herself to stop and think calmly, but she couldn't quite manage it. Stifling a sneeze and her fear, she tried to be quiet as she looked under the sink and grabbed an aerosol can of foam bathtub cleaner. As she stood, she heard a kick at the door. "Damn it!" She heard a deep voice say. "It won't give!"

"Then shoot it. Just shoot the lock off Pete. You've got a silencer." Another voice said impatiently.

In a panic, Caroline looked around for a place to hide. She was too high up to climb out the window. Seeing no other choice, she opened the bathroom door to throw them off and she climbed into the tub. If she stood behind the door, she was liable to be knocked out with it as they pushed their way inside. There were two of them. Maybe she wouldn't be able to get both of them, but one of them would have blind eyes and a burning nose to remember her by.

"What are you doing here?" Brian asked the two uniformed cops over his shoulder as he hurried to the front door of Caroline's building.

"Out of the way, sir." One of them said in dismissal. "We have reports of a break-in in progress and gunfire in this building."

Brian snatched the outer door open, only to find his arm grabbed from behind. He turned around, swinging. "Whoa, Brian." His friend Curt said and held up his hands. "Why don't you let me and Jeff and these uniforms go in first. We have the guns." He knew that there was no way he was going to be able to keep Brian outside.

"All right." Brian said. "Just hurry up!"

"I'm coming too." Jack said as he hurried up behind them and displayed his identification.

"Brian!" Ida shouted as she slammed the door to the taxi and rushed to the sidewalk. "I need to talk to you!"

"Get out of here Ida!" Brian said angrily. He ran into the building.

"Ma'am, I'm going to have to ask you to stay back."
One of the police officers said and grabbed Ida's arm as
she tried to enter the building.

They were getting closer to the bathroom. Caroline
could hear them searching for her—under the bed, in
the closet. She kept her eye on the bathroom mirror,
which she could see through a break in the shower
curtains. With no warning, a man with dark hair and
eyes rushed into the bathroom, startling her into gasping
and giving away her position. He yanked the curtains
aside and she raised the can, pushed it in his face and
pressed the nozzle.

Angry, but still afraid, she lifted her foot and kicked
him square in his chest with enough force to send him
careening backward. Screaming and digging at his eyes,
the man fell over and hit his head on the edge of the sink
and was silent.

Caroline hurried out of the tub and was bending over
to pick up the man's gun. "I wouldn't do that if I were
you little lady." She looked over to find the man from the
park standing on the threshold and pointing a gun at her.

"It is you." She said dazedly.

"Jesus. Look what you did to Tony." He said, taking
a good look at the other man. "All right lady. Stand up
slowly and walk over here." He motioned with the gun.
"Why couldn't you have done what I told you to in the
notes? I told you to get out of town. I didn't want him to
find you. I had it all figured out after I saw you at the
store a few weeks ago. It was easy enough to follow you.
The notes were supposed to scare you, but you didn't

listen. Now I have to take you to Brickman and it's your own fault. So first you're just gonna give me the film and then we're gonna get the hell out of here."

Caroline stood slowly, trying hard not to let what he was saying confuse her. He'd been the one sending the notes? Surprising them both, she kicked the door shut in his face. And knowing she had no time, she picked up the other man's gun, hating the unfamiliar feel of it, but knowing she needed it. She shakily pointed it at the door.

"Police! Drop the gun!" She heard a female voice say.

"You drop your gun, you cop bitch!" She heard the man say. And that was the last word she heard before the shooting started. She screamed and dropping the gun, she climbed into the bathtub again, her mind frozen in terror.

Well, ain't this a bitch, Pete thought to himself when he heard the cop tell him to drop the gun. Here I am chasing down a woman for Brickman and some other woman catches me. I might as well die now, because Brickman is going to make my life a living hell, whether I'm in the joint or not. I've been in prison before and there's no way in hell I'm going back. He turned and raised his gun. "You drop your gun, you cop bitch!"

Brian kicked the bathroom door open and hurried in. He paused less than a second when he saw the man on the floor and panicked for a moment when Caroline was nowhere in sight. He pushed the shower curtains aside and his heart clenched in his chest when he saw her. She had her legs bent with her knees in her chest and her face buried between them. Her arms were protectively covering her head. Kneeling, he gingerly touched her head, afraid she was hurt in some way. "Caroline." That was all he said before she turned and buried her face in his chest, locking her arms around him.

"Are you hurt?" He asked urgently, his arms gripping her to him tightly.

She frantically shook her head no, still not speaking. Her tears were soaking his shirtfront and she trembled uncontrollably.

"It's all right, sweetheart." He said softly. "It's all right." He continued to mumble in comfort as he shakily stood with her in his arms and carried her out of the bathroom, his hand pressing her head into his chest. He carried her into the living room and sat with her in his lap.

They sat that way for a long time before they were disturbed. "I'm sorry to bother you Brian." Jack said. "But I wanted to let you know what was going on. Tony Anders, that's the guy in the bathroom, is knocked out cold. We've called an ambulance for him. Pete Kovlovsky, the guy from the park, is dead."

Caroline shuddered, whimpered in fear and tightened her arms around Brian's waist. He rubbed her back and bent his head to whisper, "Shh, sweetheart. I've got you. He can't hurt you."

"Don't leave." She mumbled. "Please, don't leave."

"I won't, baby. I won't." He said soothingly. He looked up at Jack again. "What's next?"

"Well, as soon as our guy on the bathroom floor is better, we'll start questioning him."

"What about Brickman? Do you think he has anything to do with this? Or was the guy acting alone?" Brian asked.

"I would say so, yes. They both work for Brickman and—"

"He was going to take me to Brickman." Caroline said in a croaky voice and lifted her head.

"What?" Brian's arms tightened around her.

"The guy from the park…he said that he'd been sending me the notes all along. He told me he followed me from the store weeks ago and that he hadn't wanted Brickman to find me, so he sent the notes to scare me enough to leave town."

"Did he say anything else?" Jack asked urgently.

Caroline narrowed her eyes in thought. "He said something about film—that I was going to give him the film and we were going to go."

"What film?"

"I don't know." She said and tears filled her eyes again. "I think they killed Motley, Brian. I couldn't see, but I think they killed her."

"No they didn't." He said reassuringly. "They probably kicked her, but she's all right. We just need to take her to the vet."

"Are you sure he didn't say anything else, Caroline?" Jack asked. "I'm sorry to badger you, but it's important."

Caroline looked at him. "He didn't say anything else, I'm sure of it."

"And you have no idea what film he's talking about?"

"No, I'm sorry but I don't. I can't really think right now." She turned back to Brian. "I want to leave Brian. Can we get Motley and go to your place? I want to leave." She said again, more desperately and her hands clenched in his shirt. Just the thought of what had taken place in her home made her want to curl up and hide.

"Yes, of course we can." Brian said calmingly and rubbed her back.

"One last thing, Brian." Jack said. "We'll still be going after Brickman, but now there's one more charge to add to the list. Attempted kidnapping. At least now I know for sure that he is in the Chicago area. I'm hoping Anders will give him up to save his own ass and I'm praying Brickman doesn't disappear before we can tighten the net. The locals are cleaning up in there and we should be out of your hair soon."

"Thanks Jack." Brian shook his hand.

"I'm just sorry I couldn't have prevented this, but the bureau had me off chasing phantoms and incommunicado. I'm sorry about everything Caroline, but it's good to see you again—even under these circumstances. I'll get Brickman for you. Count on it."

—∾—

Brickman looked out of the window of his private jet and curled his fingers around his glass of wine until the delicate crystal snapped. His companion who sat beside him gasped and hurriedly began to clean up the mess. "Oh sir, look what you've done to yourself."

Brickman spared the man a glance and then looked out the window again. The fussbudget Crinkle was another mistake to lay at someone's door. He hadn't wanted to bring only him, but he'd had little choice. Crinkle had been with him for years and was quite loyal, but he wasn't competent in the ways he needed him to be. Crinkle was competent with numbers and organization, but he was good for little else.

Brickman didn't know for certain who was behind him having to leave town so quickly, but he'd find out and quickly. Just as with Boston, he'd had to pack up and leave Chicago with his tail tucked between his legs.

He'd known fairly early that Kovlovsky and Anders had gotten themselves caught. He'd known just as surely as if someone had whispered it in his ear. His first clue was when he'd come from the shower and found Ida and the newspaper gone. He was pretty sure the bitch had gone and tipped the photographer off. His only other hint that everything had gone wrong was his gut and he hadn't gotten where he was by ignoring it.

He'd hurriedly began making electronic transfers of his U.S. holdings, sending most of his money to an offshore account. He'd also taken care of having most of his valuable artwork boxed and shipped. Those things would follow him to his next destination. He looked down with a modicum of regret at Chicago. It was anger that he had a lot of. Whoever had blown his operation would pay and they would pay dearly. First he'd find Ida and take care of her, and then he'd find whoever else was responsible for him losing his Chicago operation.

EPILOGUE

The Rutledge Gallery was filled with art lovers. Caroline looked around at the glitzy crowd and smiled nervously. Less than two months before, she was being attacked in her own home and now here she was amongst the glitterati of Chicago. Life was funny sometimes. She and Brian had pinpointed the month when she'd first seen Kovlovsky and she developed all the pictures she'd taken around that time in search of a clue.

They'd finally found it. Brickman, Kovlovsky and a few other men were standing in the background of the picture she'd taken of the elderly couple. They were surprised to see Ida in the picture as well. Though Ida said she'd been in a relationship with Brickman, they suspected that there was more that she wasn't telling. She'd admitted to sending Caroline the first note only, but had refused to admit that she'd made the phone calls. Brian was convinced that she had. Caroline chose not to pursue it. She knew that Ida had only come to warn them so Brian wouldn't get hurt, but she was still grateful.

They didn't know if Brickman was responsible for the death of the couple, but Brian and Jack suspected he was. Ida denied any knowledge of that as well and had left town. No one knew where she'd gone. They'd lost her trail in Miami.

Just as Jack had feared, Brickman had pulled up stakes and there was no trace of him in the city. The police felt that if it hadn't taken Anders over four hours to give him up, they would have had Brickman in custody. By the time they'd thought to talk to Ida, it had been too late. As it was, the story of Caroline's ordeal had been on every news channel and they figured Brickman had been forewarned. Jack had told her repeatedly that Brickman was definitely on the run and wouldn't take the chance of coming back for her, but she still had nightmares.

Brian came up beside her and took her hand. He knew she had nightmares because they always woke him up. He also knew they were coming less frequently now. He wouldn't be satisfied until they stopped haunting her altogether. The first time she'd awakened with a scream in her throat, it had severely shaken him. It was still doing so.

She'd gotten back her appetite and some of the weight that she could ill afford to lose, but he could still feel the unusual thinness when he held her in his arms. Thank God she'd listened to the police officer and was getting counseling. "Don't look so nervous." He said with a smile. "You're a smash—in the art world and in that dress."

She looked down at the new, black, velvet, knee-length dress with its scooped collar and long sleeves.

"This old thing," she said, tongue in cheek. "It's a rag."

"That's better." Brian said. "Your work is selling like crazy. Everyone loves you! They'd buy more if there was anymore available."

"I know." She said, pressing a nervous hand to her stomach. "That's what scares me. What are they going to expect next time?"

"Whatever it is, I'm sure you'll exceed it. Now, let's talk about something else. Our parents are getting along wonderfully, don't you think?"

Caroline looked over at the group that also included Lee, Tracy, Catherine and Genevieve. She smiled as Genevieve laughed. "Yes, and I'm so relieved."

"Me too, but even if they weren't it wouldn't stop me from doing this." He said and kneeled.

"What are you doing?" She looked around to see if anyone was watching them.

"Get up Brian!"

Brian ignored her grasping hands and pulled a small, velvet box from the pocket of his tuxedo. "Caroline Singleton—talented artist, toast of the art world, beautiful woman, and most importantly, love of my life—will you marry me?"

Caroline smiled with tears in her eyes, not at all surprised. "Of course I will. Now, will you get up from there?" She let him place the ring on her finger and closed her hand in a fist so that it wouldn't slide off. As he stood, she pulled him close, looped her arms around his neck and looked into his eyes. "I love you Brian."

"I love you. Is your mom watching?" He asked with a devilish light in his eye.

Caroline peeked over his shoulder to see both their families staring in avid interest. "Yes. Why?"

"Because now she won't have to wait to call you in the morning after I do this." He said just before he covered her mouth with his and kissed her until they were both breathless.

POSTLUDE

Ida closed her eyes to block out the newspaper picture of Brian laughing with a smiling Caroline in his arms. So they were getting married. Not only did she have a successful career, but Caroline got the guy as well. So all the pundits were wrong. It was possible to have it all. Ida crumpled the paper and threw it across the room. God, she hated her—hated her even more now than she did before. It was because of her that she was in her current predicament. She'd lost everything and was in hiding.

2008 Reprint Mass Market Titles

January

Cautious Heart
Cheris F. Hodges
ISBN-13: 978-1-58571-301-1
ISBN-10: 1-58571-301-5
$6.99

Suddenly You
Crystal Hubbard
ISBN-13: 978-1-58571-302-8
ISBN-10: 1-58571-302-3
$6.99

February

Passion
T. T. Henderson
ISBN-13: 978-1-58571-303-5
ISBN-10: 1-58571-303-1
$6.99

Whispers in the Sand
LaFlorya Gauthier
ISBN-13: 978-1-58571-304-2
ISBN-10: 1-58571-304-x
$6.99

March

Life Is Never As It Seems
J. J. Michael
ISBN-13: 978-1-58571-305-9
ISBN-10: 1-58571-305-8
$6.99

Beyond the Rapture
Beverly Clark
ISBN-13: 978-1-58571-306-6
ISBN-10: 1-58571-306-6
$6.99

April

A Heart's Awakening
Veronica Parker
ISBN-13: 978-1-58571-307-3
ISBN-10: 1-58571-307-4
$6.99

Breeze
Robin Lynette Hampton
ISBN-13: 978-1-58571-308-0
ISBN-10: 1-58571-308-2
$6.99

May

I'll Be Your Shelter
Giselle Carmichael
ISBN-13: 978-1-58571-309-7
ISBN-10: 1-58571-309-0
$6.99

Careless Whispers
Rochelle Alers
ISBN-13: 978-1-58571-310-3
ISBN-10: 1-58571-310-4
$6.99

June

Sin
Crystal Rhodes
ISBN-13: 978-1-58571-311-0
ISBN-10: 1-58571-311-2
$6.99

Dark Storm Rising
Chinelu Moore
ISBN-13: 978-1-58571-312-7
ISBN-10: 1-58571-312-0
$6.99

2008 Reprint Mass Market Titles (continued)

July

Object of His Desire
A.C. Arthur
ISBN-13: 978-1-58571-313-4
ISBN-10: 1-58571-313-9
$6.99

Angel's Paradise
Janice Angelique
ISBN-13: 978-1-58571-314-1
ISBN-10: 1-58571-314-7
$6.99

August

Unbreak My Heart
Dar Tomlinson
ISBN-13: 978-1-58571-315-8
ISBN-10: 1-58571-315-5
$6.99

All I Ask
Barbara Keaton
ISBN-13: 978-1-58571-316-5
ISBN-10: 1-58571-316-3
$6.99

September

Icie
Pamela Leigh Starr
ISBN-13: 978-1-58571-275-5
ISBN-10: 1-58571-275-2
$6.99

At Last
Lisa Riley
ISBN-13: 978-1-58571-276-2
ISBN-10: 1-58571-276-0
$6.99

October

Everlastin' Love
Gay G. Gunn
ISBN-13: 978-1-58571-277-9
ISBN-10: 1-58571-277-9
$6.99

Three Wishes
Seressia Glass
ISBN-13: 978-1-58571-278-6
ISBN-10: 1-58571-278-7
$6.99

November

Yesterday Is Gone
Beverly Clark
ISBN-13: 978-1-58571-279-3
ISBN-10: 1-58571-279-5
$6.99

Again My Love
Kayla Perrin
ISBN-13: 978-1-58571-280-9
ISBN-10: 1-58571-280-9
$6.99

December

Office Policy
A.C. Arthur
ISBN-13: 978-1-58571-281-6
ISBN-10: 1-58571-281-7
$6.99

Rendezvous With Fate
Jeanne Sumerix
ISBN-13: 978-1-58571-283-3
ISBN-10: 1-58571-283-3
$6.99

2008 New Mass Market Titles

January

Where I Want To Be
Maryam Diaab
ISBN-13: 978-1-58571-268-7
ISBN-10: 1-58571-268-X
$6.99

Never Say Never
Michele Cameron
ISBN-13: 978-1-58571-269-4
ISBN-10: 1-58571-269-8
$6.99

February

Stolen Memories
Michele Sudler
ISBN-13: 978-1-58571-270-0
ISBN-10: 1-58571-270-1
$6.99

Dawn's Harbor
Kymberly Hunt
ISBN-13: 978-1-58571-271-7
ISBN-10: 1-58571-271-X
$6.99

March

Undying Love
Renee Alexis
ISBN-13: 978-1-58571-272-4
ISBN-10: 1-58571-272-8
$6.99

Blame It On Paradise
Crystal Hubbard
ISBN-13: 978-1-58571-273-1
ISBN-10: 1-58571-273-6
$6.99

April

When A Man Loves A Woman
La Connie Taylor-Jones
ISBN-13: 978-1-58571-274-8
ISBN-10: 1-58571-274-4
$6.99

Choices
Tammy Williams
ISBN-13: 978-1-58571-300-4
ISBN-10: 1-58571-300-7
$6.99

May

Dream Runner
Gail McFarland
ISBN-13: 978-1-58571-317-2
ISBN-10: 1-58571-317-1
$6.99

Southern Fried Standards
S.R. Maddox
ISBN-13: 978-1-58571-318-9
ISBN-10: 1-58571-318-X
$6.99

June

Looking for Lily
Africa Fine
ISBN-13: 978-1-58571-319-6
ISBN-10: 1-58571-319-8
$6.99

Bliss, Inc.
Chamein Canton
ISBN-13: 978-1-58571-325-7
ISBN-10: 1-58571-325-2
$6.99

2008 New Mass Market Titles (continued)

July

Love's Secrets
Yolanda McVey
ISBN-13: 978-1-58571-321-9
ISBN-10: 1-58571-321-X
$6.99

Things Forbidden
Maryam Diaab
ISBN-13: 978-1-58571-327-1
ISBN-10: 1-58571-327-9
$6.99

August

Storm
Pamela Leigh Starr
ISBN-13: 978-1-58571-323-3
ISBN-10: 1-58571-323-6
$6.99

Passion's Furies
AlTonya Washington
ISBN-13: 978-1-58571-324-0
ISBN-10: 1-58571-324-4
$6.99

September

Three Doors Down
Michele Sudler
ISBN-13: 978-1-58571-332-5
ISBN-10: 1-58571-332-5
$6.99

Mr Fix-It
Crystal Hubbard
ISBN-13: 978-1-58571-326-4
ISBN-10: 1-58571-326-0
$6.99

October

Moments of Clarity
Michele Cameron
ISBN-13: 978-1-58571-330-1
ISBN-10: 1-58571-330-9
$6.99

Lady Preacher
K.T. Richey
ISBN-13: 978-1-58571-333-2
ISBN-10: 1-58571-333-3
$6.99

November

This Life Isn't Perfect Holla
Sandra Foy
ISBN: 978-1-58571-331-8
ISBN-10: 1-58571-331-7
$6.99

Promises Made
Bernice Layton
ISBN-13: 978-1-58571-334-9
ISBN-10: 1-58571-334-1
$6.99

December

A Voice Behind Thunder
Carrie Elizabeth Greene
ISBN-13: 978-1-58571-329-5
ISBN-10: 1-58571-329-5
$6.99

The More Things Change
Chamein Canton
ISBN-13: 978-1-58571-328-8
ISBN-10: 1-58571-328-7
$6.99

Other Genesis Press, Inc. Titles

A Dangerous Deception	J.M. Jeffries	$8.95
A Dangerous Love	J.M. Jeffries	$8.95
A Dangerous Obsession	J.M. Jeffries	$8.95
A Drummer's Beat to Mend	Kei Swanson	$9.95
A Happy Life	Charlotte Harris	$9.95
A Heart's Awakening	Veronica Parker	$9.95
A Lark on the Wing	Phyliss Hamilton	$9.95
A Love of Her Own	Cheris F. Hodges	$9.95
A Love to Cherish	Beverly Clark	$8.95
A Risk of Rain	Dar Tomlinson	$8.95
A Taste of Temptation	Reneé Alexis	$9.95
A Twist of Fate	Beverly Clark	$8.95
A Will to Love	Angie Daniels	$9.95
Acquisitions	Kimberley White	$8.95
Across	Carol Payne	$12.95
After the Vows	Leslie Esdaile	$10.95
(Summer Anthology)	T.T. Henderson	
	Jacqueline Thomas	
Again My Love	Kayla Perrin	$10.95
Against the Wind	Gwynne Forster	$8.95
All I Ask	Barbara Keaton	$8.95
Always You	Crystal Hubbard	$6.99
Ambrosia	T.T. Henderson	$8.95
An Unfinished Love Affair	Barbara Keaton	$8.95
And Then Came You	Dorothy Elizabeth Love	$8.95
Angel's Paradise	Janice Angelique	$9.95
At Last	Lisa G. Riley	$8.95
Best of Friends	Natalie Dunbar	$8.95
Beyond the Rapture	Beverly Clark	$9.95
Blaze	Barbara Keaton	$9.95
Blood Lust	J. M. Jeffries	$9.95
Blood Seduction	J.M. Jeffries	$9.95

Other Genesis Press, Inc. Titles (continued)

Bodyguard	Andrea Jackson	$9.95
Boss of Me	Diana Nyad	$8.95
Bound by Love	Beverly Clark	$8.95
Breeze	Robin Hampton Allen	$10.95
Broken	Dar Tomlinson	$24.95
By Design	Barbara Keaton	$8.95
Cajun Heat	Charlene Berry	$8.95
Careless Whispers	Rochelle Alers	$8.95
Cats & Other Tales	Marilyn Wagner	$8.95
Caught in a Trap	Andre Michelle	$8.95
Caught Up In the Rapture	Lisa G. Riley	$9.95
Cautious Heart	Cheris F Hodges	$8.95
Chances	Pamela Leigh Starr	$8.95
Cherish the Flame	Beverly Clark	$8.95
Class Reunion	Irma Jenkins/ John Brown	$12.95
Code Name: Diva	J.M. Jeffries	$9.95
Conquering Dr. Wexler's Heart	Kimberley White	$9.95
Corporate Seduction	A.C. Arthur	$9.95
Crossing Paths, Tempting Memories	Dorothy Elizabeth Love	$9.95
Crush	Crystal Hubbard	$9.95
Cypress Whisperings	Phyllis Hamilton	$8.95
Dark Embrace	Crystal Wilson Harris	$8.95
Dark Storm Rising	Chinelu Moore	$10.95
Daughter of the Wind	Joan Xian	$8.95
Deadly Sacrifice	Jack Kean	$22.95
Designer Passion	Dar Tomlinson Diana Richeaux	$8.95
Do Over	Celya Bowers	$9.95
Dreamtective	Liz Swados	$5.95

Other Genesis Press, Inc. Titles (continued)

Other Genesis Press, Inc. Titles (continued)

I Married a Reclining Chair	Lisa M. Fuhs	$8.95
I'll Be Your Shelter	Giselle Carmichael	$8.95
I'll Paint a Sun	A.J. Garrotto	$9.95
Icie	Pamela Leigh Starr	$8.95
Illusions	Pamela Leigh Starr	$8.95
Indigo After Dark Vol. I	Nia Dixon/Angelique	$10.95
Indigo After Dark Vol. II	Dolores Bundy/ Cole Riley	$10.95
Indigo After Dark Vol. III	Montana Blue/ Coco Morena	$10.95
Indigo After Dark Vol. IV	Cassandra Colt/	$14.95
Indigo After Dark Vol. V	Delilah Dawson	$14.95
Indiscretions	Donna Hill	$8.95
Intentional Mistakes	Michele Sudler	$9.95
Interlude	Donna Hill	$8.95
Intimate Intentions	Angie Daniels	$8.95
It's Not Over Yet	J.J. Michael	$9.95
Jolie's Surrender	Edwina Martin-Arnold	$8.95
Kiss or Keep	Debra Phillips	$8.95
Lace	Giselle Carmichael	$9.95
Last Train to Memphis	Elsa Cook	$12.95
Lasting Valor	Ken Olsen	$24.95
Let Us Prey	Hunter Lundy	$25.95
Lies Too Long	Pamela Ridley	$13.95
Life Is Never As It Seems	J.J. Michael	$12.95
Lighter Shade of Brown	Vicki Andrews	$8.95
Love Always	Mildred E. Riley	$10.95
Love Doesn't Come Easy	Charlyne Dickerson	$8.95
Love Unveiled	Gloria Greene	$10.95
Love's Deception	Charlene Berry	$10.95
Love's Destiny	M. Loui Quezada	$8.95
Mae's Promise	Melody Walcott	$8.95

Other Genesis Press, Inc. Titles (continued)

Other Genesis Press, Inc. Titles (continued)

Path of Fire	T.T. Henderson	$8.95
Path of Thorns	Annetta P. Lee	$9.95
Peace Be Still	Colette Haywood	$12.95
Picture Perfect	Reon Carter	$8.95
Playing for Keeps	Stephanie Salinas	$8.95
Pride & Joi	Gay G. Gunn	$8.95
Promises to Keep	Alicia Wiggins	$8.95
Quiet Storm	Donna Hill	$10.95
Reckless Surrender	Rochelle Alers	$6.95
Red Polka Dot in a World of Plaid	Varian Johnson	$12.95
Reluctant Captive	Joyce Jackson	$8.95
Rendezvous with Fate	Jeanne Sumerix	$8.95
Revelations	Cheris F. Hodges	$8.95
Rivers of the Soul	Leslie Esdaile	$8.95
Rocky Mountain Romance	Kathleen Suzanne	$8.95
Rooms of the Heart	Donna Hill	$8.95
Rough on Rats and Tough on Cats	Chris Parker	$12.95
Secret Library Vol. 1	Nina Sheridan	$18.95
Secret Library Vol. 2	Cassandra Colt	$8.95
Secret Thunder	Annetta P. Lee	$9.95
Shades of Brown	Denise Becker	$8.95
Shades of Desire	Monica White	$8.95
Shadows in the Moonlight	Jeanne Sumerix	$8.95
Sin	Crystal Rhodes	$8.95
Small Whispers	Annetta P. Lee	$6.99
So Amazing	Sinclair LeBeau	$8.95
Somebody's Someone	Sinclair LeBeau	$8.95
Someone to Love	Alicia Wiggins	$8.95
Song in the Park	Martin Brant	$15.95
Soul Eyes	Wayne L. Wilson	$12.95

Other Genesis Press, Inc. Titles (continued)

Soul to Soul	Donna Hill	$8.95
Southern Comfort	J.M. Jeffries	$8.95
Still the Storm	Sharon Robinson	$8.95
Still Waters Run Deep	Leslie Esdaile	$8.95
Stolen Kisses	Dominiqua Douglas	$9.95
Stories to Excite You	Anna Forrest/Divine	$14.95
Subtle Secrets	Wanda Y. Thomas	$8.95
Suddenly You	Crystal Hubbard	$9.95
Sweet Repercussions	Kimberley White	$9.95
Sweet Sensations	Gwendolyn Bolton	$9.95
Sweet Tomorrows	Kimberly White	$8.95
Taken by You	Dorothy Elizabeth Love	$9.95
Tattooed Tears	T. T. Henderson	$8.95
The Color Line	Lizzette Grayson Carter	$9.95
The Color of Trouble	Dyanne Davis	$8.95
The Disappearance of Allison Jones	Kayla Perrin	$5.95
The Fires Within	Beverly Clark	$9.95
The Foursome	Celya Bowers	$6.99
The Honey Dipper's Legacy	Pannell-Allen	$14.95
The Joker's Love Tune	Sidney Rickman	$15.95
The Little Pretender	Barbara Cartland	$10.95
The Love We Had	Natalie Dunbar	$8.95
The Man Who Could Fly	Bob & Milana Beamon	$18.95
The Missing Link	Charlyne Dickerson	$8.95
The Mission	Pamela Leigh Starr	$6.99
The Perfect Frame	Beverly Clark	$9.95
The Price of Love	Sinclair LeBeau	$8.95
The Smoking Life	Ilene Barth	$29.95
The Words of the Pitcher	Kei Swanson	$8.95
Three Wishes	Seressia Glass	$8.95
Ties That Bind	Kathleen Suzanne	$8.95

Other Genesis Press, Inc. Titles (continued)

Tiger Woods	Libby Hughes	$5.95
Time is of the Essence	Angie Daniels	$9.95
Timeless Devotion	Bella McFarland	$9.95
Tomorrow's Promise	Leslie Esdaile	$8.95
Truly Inseparable	Wanda Y. Thomas	$8.95
Two Sides to Every Story	Dyanne Davis	$9.95
Unbreak My Heart	Dar Tomlinson	$8.95
Uncommon Prayer	Kenneth Swanson	$9.95
Unconditional Love	Alicia Wiggins	$8.95
Unconditional	A.C. Arthur	$9.95
Until Death Do Us Part	Susan Paul	$8.95
Vows of Passion	Bella McFarland	$9.95
Wedding Gown	Dyanne Davis	$8.95
What's Under Benjamin's Bed	Sandra Schaffer	$8.95
When Dreams Float	Dorothy Elizabeth Love	$8.95
When I'm With You	LaConnie Taylor-Jones	$6.99
Whispers in the Night	Dorothy Elizabeth Love	$8.95
Whispers in the Sand	LaFlorya Gauthier	$10.95
Who's That Lady?	Andrea Jackson	$9.95
Wild Ravens	Altonya Washington	$9.95
Yesterday Is Gone	Beverly Clark	$10.95
Yesterday's Dreams, Tomorrow's Promises	Reon Laudat	$8.95
Your Precious Love	Sinclair LeBeau	$8.95

Dull, Drab, Love Life?

Passion Going Nowhere?

Tired Of Being Alone?

Does Every Direction You Look For Love

Lead You Astray?

Genesis Press presents
The launching of our new website.

RecaptureTheRomance.Co

Ignite
The Flame!

ESCAPE WITH INDIGO !!!!

Join Indigo Book Club©
It's simple, easy and secure.

Sign up and receive the new
releases
every month + Free shipping
and
20% off the cover price.

Go online to www.genesis-
press.com and click on Bookclub
or
call 1-888-INDIGO-1

Order Form

Mail to: Genesis Press, Inc.
P.O. Box 101
Columbus, MS 39703

Name _____
Address _____
City/State _____ Zip _____
Telephone _____

Ship to (if different from above)
Name _____
Address _____
City/State _____ Zip _____
Telephone _____

Credit Card Information
Credit Card # _____ ☐ Visa ☐ Mastercard
Expiration Date (mm/yy) _____ ☐ AmEx ☐ Discover

Qty.	Author	Title	Price	Total

Use this order
form, or call
1-888-INDIGO-1

Total for books _____
Shipping and handling:
  $5 first two books,
  $1 each additional book _____
Total S & H _____
Total amount enclosed _____

Mississippi residents add 7% sales tax